Glimpserama

∞

Major Roxbrough

Rev. date: 07/25/2017

To order additional copies of this book, contact:
Xlibris
800-056-3182
www.Xlibrispublishing.co.uk
Orders@Xlibrispublishing.co.uk
764717

Glimpserama

With thanks for your friendship and support
For John and Lillian

best wishes

Major Roseborough.

Dedicated to Clare;
for her support and constant source of inspiration.

Contents

ORANG-U-CAN

ONE

WHEN EDGAR ANTONY Castle entered the room, exhaustion tugging at every fibre of his body he knew at once that the old bastard had finally slipped away, when no one else was there. So like him to hang on till three in the morning. The various tubes and monitors that were attached to his old husk were being gently withdrawn by one of the nurses. E. A. Castle noticed almost absently what a trim piece of ass she had. His subliminal command to his contacts had dimmed them to fifty percent, his nose filters had similarly been commanded to filter at maximum.

'*Good job I'm wearing black*', he thought to himself. Although in truth three quarter length Edwardian frock coats were back in fashion and black and royal blue were the colours of the season.

Suddenly sensing his presence, the medical young woman turned and her face held an expression of sympathy,

"I'm sorry mister Castle, but he's gone".

'*Sorry*', Castle thought, '*I'm ruddy ecstatic. No more endless bullying and accusations of incompetence, but now, I might just be out of a job*'!

He mumbled his thanks to her and slowly strode out of the hospital room in order to allow her to get on with her job of tidying up the corpse. He had an urgent netvid to send now, to the firm's solicitor, Stubbsinge. The most pressing matter would be the reading of the will, who would be named successor to the Trentavoria Corporation? So massive was it, so wealthy that on all the planets it was known simply as Corporation.

Magnus Quintilius Trentavoria had been married several times during his lengthy and successful business lifetime. His only issue from all those unions had been a single daughter, who had perished in a flitter accident some years past. The only relative Magnus Quintilius Trentavoria then recognised, was his drug addled granddaughter, Clare.

E. A. Castle thought about her for the merest of seconds, surely the old goat would not let Corporation crumble in her incompetent hands, she could not even manage a good crap. No; he was the obvious candidate for the post, though other eager executives would also consider themselves equally adept. The two who stood a chance in Castle's eyes were Erasmus Speakman, head of advertising and Villutyre Milinkovic head of distribution. Sure there were others, but those two were the only sensible contenders.

"He's gone", was all Castle said when he had finally roused Stubbsinge from his bed. The image on the screen stared back at him on his own tiny screen, his hair unkempt, bleary eyed.

'I aught to ping him more often at this time of night', Castle thought to himself, *'It's fun'.*

Stubbsinge nodded, "I'll get things moving at this end", he promised, "For the good of Corporation of course and erm, there are some rather strange arrangements to make regarding disposal of the body".

E. A. Castle felt instantly annoyed, he knew nothing about that, to which the solicitor, referred and he did not like being on the outside of any conclave, for all was holy when it concerned the late, great, Magnus Quintilius Trentavoria.

He did resist the urge to ask however, no way was he going to give Stubbsinge the satisfaction of telling him to wait and see.

Moments later he was outside the strange, sanitary smell of the hospital, it's interminable neon glare, the muted mutterings of patients and nurses alike. He lit a medcig with his thumb, it's safe self combusting tip flaring momentarily to life. He let the safe tobacco go deep into his lungs; enjoying the crisp night air, cool without being cold. Then, before hailing a flitter to take him back to his apartment he ground the stub of the medcig under the foot of his hand made loafers. A vehicle slid beside him when he least expected it, the sensors must have caught the upward motion of his arm, it's passenger door hissed open and allowing him access to the dim but fresh interior.

"Minerva Villas", he instructed the mechaman driver absently, whilst at the same time dialling his nasal filter to zero, his contacts to fully clear. He settled back into the plush pseudo leather upholstery for the short ride from the Santo y Real hospital, down to the harbour area of Cartagena. He should netvid Speakman and Milinkovic, but right at that moment he could not be bothered and anyway he had little to tell them. Instead his mind went out to what he knew about Clare Trentavoria.

She had been a spoiled little rich kid, doted on by her wealthy and powerful grandfather ever since the day she was born. In trouble the instant she attended vidclasses, then in further bother with the law, finally the descent into Snufz dependency.

Ironic when Snufz was the one narcotic that the old man had spent all his life trying to distance himself from. Only two things had ever come from the three Mars expeditions, one was Dodoprots and the other was Snufz. The very fact that Dodoprot creation and production had made Trentavoria much of his wealth, had always indirectly (or directly) linked him with the other; Snufz.

Castle's mind went back to the day when the third expedition to Mars had made exciting vids on the netcasts. Captain Couplander had discovered the underground caverns of the red planet. Not only that, but mere hours later the net had broadcast the even more exciting proclamation that on some of the rock in the caverns, fed by water seeping from the polar caps, lichen was growing!

The only trouble was, that once it was brought back to Earth it promptly turned into brown, arid dust. It could not survive in Earth's rich oxygen and gravity. Until, that was, Professor Baadareina Hoyle took some of it's DNA and spliced it with DNA from simple yeast. The result was a bizarre hybrid Mars/Earth plant that thrived like a weed. Once harvested and dried it made a narcotic that made tobacco and alcohol tame by comparison. Hoyle had taken the result straight to Trentavoria and the old bastard had secretly began a manufacturing production that would make him wealthy beyond all imagining. It made no difference that it soon became an illegal substance. By that time Corporation was beyond the powers of the law, beyond even the powers of most world powers.

The dried plant once processed correctly was called Snufz; Snufz once snorted like the stuff it had been innocently named after was a mind bending and deeply addictive narcotic. Before anyone realised just how insidious it was, thousands and then millions were addicted. None even wanted it stopped as a result, even if such had been possible. Only the incredibly strong minded or those flukishly free of it's addictive qualities were safe from it

Meanwhile, Baadareina Hoyle, innocent of what he had created, went on to create a second and even more profound DNA splice. This time, bizarrely, with DNA from a Dodo! The semi-alien creature that was born from such a fantastic experiment became known as the Dodoprot. It was a bird, flightless, incredibly nutritious and obviously chicken tasting. That was when 'the' business man of Corporation commissioned his own rocket to Mars and with a team of appropriate people, set up a breeding farm for the Dodoprot; on Mars! Dodo, the name of the bird, prot taken from the beginning of the word protein.

The bird was the answer to Earth's teaming starving in the third world and even beyond. In the process it made Trentavoria, with his keen business acumen and organisation skills in transportation, the richest man in the solar system. It did not do any damage to Hoyle's bank account either!

Castle's mind was brought back to the present, as the flitter cruised to a sighing halt. The vessel was back at his apartment. Climbing out the back couch he dropped more than enough shilling notes into the mechaman's slot and headed for his block, as the flitter sighed back up into the night sky. Castle noted with some appreciation, that the sky had changed from deepest azure to the violet of a promised dawn. Fingers of startling roseate clawed into the cupola. He took out his packet of medcig's and thumbed one to life. The tobacco, devoid of all it's tar, but with nicotine a plenty made him even more soporific. Not so chilled that his instincts were not absent however. The subtle breeze that wafted in from the sea brought also the faintest tinge of after shave.

Castle knew in that split second that he was not alone. As the needle phutted from the muzzle, he dived to the concrete, rolling with athletic prowess. Just in time it seemed, to almost feel it flick above his head. It had come from a needle gun, a silent assassin's favoured weapon of choice, for though silent it's poisoned tip would kill in mere seconds. Castle rolled over twice as quickly as his trained muscles could enable him, with his free arm he pulled out of his three quarter coat his own laser and fired in the direction the needle had issued. He was rewarded with a grunt of pain, the low shot had burned through the ankle of the figure dressed from head to foot in black. The would be killer toppled onto the ground as Castle leaped to his feet, his laser aimed all the while at the dark clad outline.

"So", he began quietly, "The bid for power of Corporation begins almost at once. Trentavoria isn't even cold yet and intrigue is with me".

The assassin made to lift the needle gun, but Castle barked,

"Do that and I'll burn your hand off"!

The other dropped the weapon at once,

"Now push it away", Castle commanded, "We need to have a little talk".

"Save your breath", was the spat response, "I'm not giving you any names, nor the merest scrap of information".

"Oh! I already know it", Castle lied, "It's Speakman".

Yet, though he watched the other's eyes, there was no flicker of emotion, or recognition of any sort.

"Perhaps, I meant Milinkovic".

Same lack of result. Castle bent down, his laser trained on the killer all the while,

"I can see it is going to take a little persuasion to get the result I need".

"Go to Hades", the other fumed and then, "Ladybird"!

Even as the would be killer grunted it, Castle knew it was his 'S' word. Sure enough the villain gripped his chest, gasped a couple of times and then fell back;

quite dead. Obviously the suicide micro-pile had exploded in the chambers of his heart and killed him almost instantly.

Castle left the corpse, in deep thought, it was the second he had seen inside an hour. He hastened up to his apartment. Though he crept in as quietly as he could however, the minute he was in the entrance, the light went on in the bedroom and Dawn joined him, dressed in her robe.

"Sorry. I didn't mean to wake you".

"I wasn't really asleep", she admitted, pecking him on the cheek and going toward the kitchen, "I'm guessing he's gone, being as you're in so early"?

"Yeah the king is dead, long live the king, who ever he turns out to be. Make enough for three babe, Ibbopargia will be joining us".

"Hades teeth E. A, what have you gone and done now"? Castle's girlfriend demanded.

"Is it alright if we wait until the detective sergeant gets here"? he asked resignedly, "I don't want to have to go through it all twice"?

Thirty minutes later he, Dawn and Ibbopargia were seated around the dining table munching toast and drinking breakfast tea.

"The men will have dealt with the body by now", Ibbopargia told Castle. "Do you think you can manage to keep out of trouble for the next twenty four hours or so E. A."?

"Haven't you been listening Ricardo"? Dawn demanded, "Someone tried to kill him! That's right 'kill' him. Not a beating, not a warning, but doing to death! Aren't you going to offer police protection or something".

"There's no need for that babe", Castle told her, "I'll get myself a bodyguard privately. It seems that now Trentavoria's dead things are going to get pretty interesting around here".

"You and I are old friends E. A.", Ibbopargia began then, "But there are only so many favours I can do for you, don't start a private war, no matter how provoked. I'll go and have a word with your two heads of department, try and calm things down".

"It doesn't sound like you have much hope of finding out which of them hired someone to bump me off"?

Ibbopargia spread his arms, with fingers of his hands extended, "It could be neither".

"Who else wants to kill my Edgar"? Dawn sounded even more worried then.

"I'm not ruling out the shady mister Stubbsinge", the detective noted, "Nor even the granddaughter, what was her name".

"The last I heard Clare Trentavoria was in rehab, in a private facility on the moon", Castle told him.

"The last you heard", Ibbopargia, raised an eyebrow and then rose slowly from his seat, "Be careful E. A. and keep in touch. See you both later, thanks for the breakfast Dawn".

He let himself out. Castle looked at the wall clock, the mist still floating from the kettle, the pleasant rosy light beginning to spill through the french windows.

"Four thirty a.m. I think I'll go and grab a couple of hours before I have to go into the office".

Dawn pressed into his arms, "Mind if I join you"? she wanted to know.

TWO

CASTLE'S SECRETARY, THE ever efficient and equally decorative Geraldine looked surprised at her bosses appearance, causing him to remark,

"I'm still alive Geraldine".

"It's been on the local net site", Geraldine gasped somewhat superfluously. If Castle farted in a restaurant it would be on the local site. Brushing back a strand of deep brunette hair with an absent minded hand, she informed him,

"Stubbsinge is in your office already". This surprised Castle. Was the solicitor ready to read the will? What other business could he be calling about and so early? He could think of nothing off hand.

He merely nodded and strode into his own place of study. It was a clean fresh place with oaken floors and rubber wood panelling on all the shelf heavy walls. Stubbsinge was seated in the visitors chair, a straight backed affair of plush blue psuedovelvet.

"E. A.", the tonsure headed man began rising, offering his hand. Castle shook it, finding it limp and lacking real conviction and vigour. Could this be the hand of one who had set a murderer upon him? He then rounded the computerised desk to take his own chair.

"With Corporation this size, speed is essential", Stubbsinge began somewhat superfluously, "Who do you want present E. A."?

Before Castle could respond the intercom sounded, Geraldine Orwenoot told him,

"There's a gentleman to see you sir, a mister Violet".

As Stubbsinge's eyebrows rose, Castle replied,

"Have him come right in please Geraldine".

"Mister Violet" the solicitor echoed, "I don't believe I know of such an associate"?

The door opened and in strode a bulk of a man who looked like he had been chiseled from solid granite. His blonde hair was buzz cut and his face as was usual was clean shaven, with cold grey eyes he demanded,

"Vhich von of you iz Castle", the baritone rumble fit his persona perfectly, added to which, was a thick German accent.

"I am he" Castle said, "Did the 'organisation' send you"?

Violet nodded and then instructed, "Get away from za vindow and opaque it if it does zat".

Obediently Castle did as advised, while Stubbsinge demanded,

"Organisation? What sort of organisation have you contacts with E. A. I have not been informed about these details. As solicitor to Corporation I demand to know what in Tartarus is going on"?

"Mister Violet here is my bodyguard". Castle was enjoying the other's confusion. After a certain dramatic pause he continued, This morning an attempt was made on my life, do you know anything about that Stubbsinge"?

"Don't be preposterous", the solicitor exploded, "Why would I wish to do such a thing? Why would anyone? Have you been making some dangerous enemies Castle? You haven't been dealing in the darker side of our affairs have you"?

"The darker side", Castle echoed with a voice laden with irony, "I think perhaps all of us have done that all of our working lives at Corporation. You more than most. In fact let me be quite plain, perhaps you have had a sneaky peep at the will and perhaps it names me new director of Corporation and perhaps it makes you my deputy".

He had risen from his own seat and was standing looming over the short solicitor, his weight resting on his hands,

"You'll take that back Castle", Stubbsinge demanded darkly, "I would never do such a criminal thing".

In answer Violet actually growled and placed himself between Castle and the diminutive solicitor, whom he towered over.

"Well; forget it", Stubbsinge decided, "All of us have been guilty of an, shall we say, business indiscretion from time to time, I'm going to put such a nonsensical suggestion down to upsetment. I would never betray my oaths as a member of the law council and I think you damn well know it".

"Anyway", Castle began placatingly, "Surely the reading of the will comes after the funeral"?

"You've not seen the vidnews"?

Castle sighed, "I've been kinda busy trying to stay alive; what news are you talking about"?

Stubbsinge raised himself to his full one hundred and sixty two centimetres and informed, "Trentavoria's body went missing, ten minutes after you left the hospital".

"Someone stole the corpse"?!

"Well it didn't get up and walk out of the place did it"?

"But why"? Castle was astounded, "What possible reason would they have for doing such a thing"?

"Maybe we should be looking for a deranged taxidermist"?

Then Castle remembered that the old man had made some sort of strange post morte arrangement With a sect called, *'The Following of the Stolen Heart'* and he suggested as much to Stubbsinge. The solicitor was not party to such an arrangement however. Whilst the two of them lapsed into momentary reflective silence, the intercom broke into life once more,

"The head of advertising is here to see you sir".

"Have him come right in", Castle sighed, the vultures were circling it seemed.

The rather distinguished looking Erasmus Speakman breezed into the office. He boasted a shock of well coiffured silver hair, keen glinting eyes and stood some one hundred and ninety one centimetres.

"Who's this"? he demanded of Violet. The bodyguard glowered but remained tacit.

"Good morning to you too Erasmus", Castle returned sardonically. "This is my bodyguard. The attempt on my life this morning was not successful, thanks for asking".

"I'm not surprised there was one", Speakman returned, "I told you not to do that deal with the Mars Cartel".

"He thinks one of us was behind it", Stubbsinge interjected, "A pre-emptive strike for control of Corporation".

Speakman grinned icily, "If I was at the back of it, the attempt would not have been bungled, I'd have hired the best".

Once more Violet glowered, but remained silent. Speakman went on,

"Perhaps the old fox's body was taken by members of that silly sect he was a member of and got you to join? I see you aren't wearing that silly necklace today"?

Actually the talisman of rhodium was beneath Castle's shirt. On a silver chain was the symbol of the Illuminati-Masons A pyramid transected by the sun containing the moon and the eye of all knowledge. Speakman seemed to be enjoying the floor and went on,

"Maybe they think to bring him back to life, like that Jewish prophet, what was his name"?

"Jesus"! Stubbsinge cursed. "Don't we have better things to occupy our time? Like maybe the reading of the will"?

"Milinkovic should be here", Castle observed, "And Trentavoria's granddaughter".

He waved an arm of affirmation at Speakman, who was himself raising his eyebrows near the drinks cabinet. The head of advertising poured himself a double synthvodka and asked the solicitor what he wanted. Stubbsinge had the same, Castle went for a sweet sherry, as expected Violet merely shook his head.

Speakman laughed, "That criminal Snufzhead. Even the old man wouldn't be cracked enough to name her his heir".

"Put jam on it won't you", the solicitor cursed, as was the current vernacular, "If we get Milinkovic, there is no further need for delay, Corporation needs a Director and fast, otherwise our competitors will pounce, while we tarry".

"That's a laugh", Speakman chided, "We don't have any competitors, Trentavoria saw to that over the years".

"Well some will spring up if we hang about", the solicitor warned.

"You seem awfully keen to read it out, Stubbsinge", Castle noted.

"Don't start up on that again", Stubbsinge requested politely, one eye on Violet. "Let's just get Villutyre in here and get on with it".

Castle pressed his intercom, "Geraldine, can you ping mister Milinkovic and ask him to come to my office post haste please"

"Yes sir".

Castle strode over to the drinks cabinet, "Who'd like another drink while we wait for him"? he asked.

"It's a bit early", noted Stubbsinge, "But as it's a momentous day, I'll have another synthvodka".

Speakman asked for another with a little more grace and Castle poured himself a second sherry, not a synthetic neither, but the real thing, one of his only vices along with med smoking. He thumbed a medcig into life, while Stubbsinge stoked his pipe with medicobacc. For his part Speakman had neither, he had once been a heavy smoker but had given it up some years previously.

Mister Violet had nothing of any sort and would not even accept a seat, but placed himself at Castle's shoulder. The deputy felt like he was seated next to a tall stone column. After several moments of awkward silence, Geraldine's voice came over the com and informed them that Villutyre Milinkovic was no where to be found.

"Probably with the old man's body", Speakman suggested, "Trying desperately to reanimate it ha ha ha".

Castle did not think that funny, instead he offered,

"If I know Villutyre he'll be on a shuttle".

"You mean..." Speakman let the sentence hang.

"I mean on his way to the moon".

"Well he's always been a great one for pussy", Speakman suggested as the solicitor winced at the crudity. Castle grinned finding both amusing.

"In which case it becomes more urgent that we get this will read and see where everyone stands", Stubbsinge finally insisted.

They all looked at the deputy director,

"Very well", Castle conceded, "With several key personnel missing and Trentavoria's body stolen, read the damn thing, Stubbsinge".

The solicitor eagerly tore open the envelope, which hither-to had resided in his briefcase. How quaint to actually commit it to paper. He began to read the pertinent document aloud. Once he was past all the legal preamble, he went on, ".....I bequeath fifty one percent of the stocks of Corporation and also the post of managing director to my dear granddaughter Clare Trentavoria. The posts of deputy director, head of distribution and advertising to remain unchanged until said Clare Trentavoria deems it necessary to make any changes she feels her induction into Corporation merit. Finally, once the legalities of these changes are complete I instruct the deputy director to cease Corporation's association with Stubbsinge, Batesso and Aitkendoss solicitors".

Stubbsinge continued to conclude the reading until it's end without any show of emotion. Once it had all been actioned he and his firm were out in the cold.

Speakman was the first to fill the gap in silence,

"The girl gets the plum post! That's just ridiculous, she's no business woman. She's not even compos mentis half of the time".

Castle observed dryly, "When it all comes down to it, blood's thicker than water. The old goat could not really have been expected to leave his vast fortune to anyone outside of his family".

"But we are his family", the head of advertising pointed out morosely, "Or have been for the past twenty years".

"There will obviously be a transition", Castle mused, "But we must work toward making it as smooth as possible. The first thing Clare Trentavoria will need is a law firm".

"On which note I take my leave of you gentlemen", Stubbsinge remarked bleakly and rising, he left them, still musing over the changes the will was going to make.

"Do you think we should follow Milinkovic to the moon? If, indeed that's where he's gone"? Speakman asked then.

"As deputy director, running the firm until Clare Trentavoria takes over, I think it essential I should go", Castle said, "I'm leaving you in charge of the good ship while I'm gone".

"Not so fast", the head of advertising taunted half in jest, "If she's fit, you want first crack at her".

"You forget Erasmus, I have a girlfriend", Castle tried to retain his dignity, but in Speakman's company it was not always possible.

"You're going to get her off the Snufz and then you're going to shag what's left of her brains out aren't you"? Speakman was in full flow. "Dawn will be back here on Earth while you cosy up to the new boss".

"We have not seen images of her since she was a child", Castle smiled still trying to remain reasonable.

"Well I've seen pixers of her mother and she was well worth one".

"Erasmus, I am going for the good of Corporation".

"I don't know"? Speakman rubbed his chin thoughtfully, "After all there's nothing quite like the feeling of having your dick in a pretty girl's pretty mouth. I think perhaps I should come with you, you know, to keep you out of trouble".

"And leave Corporation in the hands of whom exactly"?

"Very well", Speakman mused, "Have a good trip then E. A.".

THREE

CASTLE WAS NOT a good traveller, he had been in space only half a dozen times in twice as many years. With the bulky Violet at his side he was even more nervous. Damn Clare Trentavoria, why could she not have gone into rehab in Spain, it would have been so much easier? He glanced past Violet's inordinately large chest to the circular window and saw the moon so large, it filled the entire view. The sleek silver sides of the module rose up forbiddingly in what became the ceiling, even the floor on certain occasions. Such observations were bound to give one vertigo even before considering velocity. Faster than a bullet leaving a pistol the advertisements said and everyone knew advertisements never lied! Castle closed his eyes for the moment and pretended he was still in bed in Spain.

What surprised him most was the lack of noise in space. Obviously the engines had roared to escape Earth's gravity. Then they had cut out and were only noisy once again when the craft was braking to land on the moon.

With the advent of cool-fusion it had taken the trip duration down to fifteen hours, most of which was spent speeding up and then slowing down. Castle could feel the vibration of the mighty shuttle's rocket's even though the soundproofed cabin cut out it's entire cacophonous blast. He was suddenly glad Speakman had insisted he go first class, second and third would be in a noise so loud that conversation was impossible. Not only that but the hostesses would not have been as glamorous, nor pneumatic. The brunette who had served he and his bodyguard had boasted at least an 'e' cup. Castle thought that when he returned to Earth he might persuade Dawn to go up a couple of cup sizes.

She would probably agree if in return he agreed to contract and not just for the three years neither. She would want a five year stint for going under the knife. Then their would be a bit of improvement to her ass.

The shuttle suddenly lurched and Castle swallowed, was it supposed to do that. The busty brunette was at his side then,

"We've landed gentlemen, I trust you both had a pleasant flight"? In order to persuade Castle, she had her left breast pressed against his arm, it was not an unpleasant experience. Added to that tiny thrill was the heady perfume she bought, which she had tried to sell them during the flight, after the freeze dried Dodoprot served up with a generous portion of microwave-fries.

"Oh! We're down", he noted somewhat obtusely, musing that he would like her to do that to him. "Yes it was excellent thank you".

"Before we disembark can I get you anything else sir", she asked looking innocently into Castle's eyes. He bit back the enquiry that a blowjob in the lounge, was probably out of the question.

"No we're fine thanks, we've both filled in our questionnaires; five stars".

"Thank you sir, please remain in your seats until the captain instructs you to go to the for'ard air lock".

Castle assured that they would, during the entire intercourse Violet had remained silent.

"Is this your first time on the moon"? Castle asked him.

"I'm not at liberty to discuss that matter", the tacit bodyguard informed not for the first time. "Don't worry, your life will be safe, my presence insures that".

They disembarked, Castle gripping the stewardess' hand long enough to indicate his attraction toward her. She smiled broadly showing ruby lip gloss and straightened bleached teeth. She hoped he would fly Horizon again in the near future where it would be her pleasure to serve him.

Castle presented a far from usual appearance being bearded and with long blonde hair which he kept swept back into a pony tail. Women noticed him. Some obviously did not like what they saw, but more, did and he was never short of female companionship.

Within an hour the strange duo had left the shuttle through the airlock to the domed shuttle port. Their bags were brought to them by hand (first class only) and a runaround took them to the Excelsior. On route was a glittering array of neon lit shops. They presented various wares and services and the brothel, was as usual, lit with a tasteful amber glow and no heading. They were in Copernicus, not surprisingly the rehab centre was situated in Mare Tranquillitatis region. It was 23:15hours G.M.T.

A bus boy showed them to their suite and Castle pressed a fifty shillin piece into his palm. As the boy was about to thank him, he followed it with two further fifty shillin coins,

"For the maids", Castle explained, "Make sure they get it please and if we don't get clean linen and scrupulously cleaned suite every day for the duration of our stay, I'll know the reason why".

The youth nodded, slipped the money into his frock coat and was gone.

Castle surveyed their surroundings. Blue walls, pale blue bedding, all tastefully lit with light emitting diodes of various depths of blue. Violet had in the mean time inspected the bathroom and his grunt of satisfaction was enough for Castle.

"I'll just check in with various party's and then let's unpack later and go and get some supper", he said to his bodyguard, "We'll go and see the new Managing Director of the Bennesia Rest Home for the Firmly Established tomorrow morning".

Violet neither expressed fatigue nor preference, he was almost as unfeeling as the new C5 androids.

"Strange coincidence though don't you think", Castle mused almost to himself, "Being placed in suite twenty three. My seat on the shuttle was twenty three too".

He flipped on his netpad and hit the icon for Dawn. almost at once her beauteous features filled the screen, the delay was only a couple of seconds.

"Hi precious other", she beamed at him, "Have you found her then, what's she like she's not prettier than me is she"?

Castle chuckled, "We've only just disembarked and gotten to our suite precious other. I just wanted you to know that the journey went without incident".

"Oh, alright; only my mother net vid and...........".

Castle let her go on for several moments managing to feign interest all the while. He could do that whilst thinking of other things when back on Earth. Finally she paused for breath and he made his farewells and cut the connection. The next icon he tried was Milinkovic', he let it submit for several seconds before closing it down. The head of distribution was still unavailable it seemed! Speakman was next on his list,

"I just tried Villutyre on the link Erasmus and he's still not answering, have you heard from him"?

"No, but I've put in a call to Detective Ibbopargia", the head of advertising informed, "Discretely of course. I guess you are pinging me to let me know the flight was trouble free"?

"Exactly, sorry if it's late, we're on G.M.T. here so I thought you might still be up"?

"I was, the vultures are beginning to circle....".

"Let me guess", Castle cut in, "Alovar Hornrunner, Drorb Makers-Guild and Piotr Tiptingle junior".

"The very same unholy trio who tried to take on Corporation three years ago", Speakman agreed, "Even adding their vast wealth together they haven't the clout to take us on".

"Are they cozying up to the bulls on the market".

Speakman nodded, "Just as I have some of our own boys doing likewise, it'll soon peter out".

"Great stuff Erasmus, I'll keep in touch, night".

"Good night E. A." Speakman cut the link and Castle folded away his pad.

Suddenly and abruptly the lights went out and the pseudo-grav went off, at exactly the same moment. Castle moved; in the weak actual gravity of the moon he floated into the air, banging his leg on the cabinet of storage drawers, beside his bed. The lights flickered once, twice and then the gravity returned and the illumination of the suit flickered back to permanent life. Violet seemed to be in exactly the same place as before. On the intercom a calm voice assured,

"Ladies and gentlemen, guests of this hotel, there was a momentary power failure, rest assured our technicians are investigating it, the phenomenon should not recur".

Castle rubbed his leg where the impact had taken place,

"Wonder what that was about"?

Violet seemed unmoved, "No one threatened you mister Castle your security is not compromised".

"Come on then let's find a restaurant".

The two of them were still observing the time as G.M.T. certain facilities were available around the clock, on the moon and food was one of them.

The bizarre duo found a restaurant called the Blue Parrot. Castle led the way through the gentle blue illumination and took a seat at a table without any consideration. Almost at once an A5 android was beside them asking them what they would like, the menu was on the psuedoplast surface of the table. Castle ordered

Chilli con carne, while Violet went for steak. The android complemented both of them on their choice and went to fetch the order, only then did Castle notice the number of the table, it was twenty three!

"What are the chances of that"? Castle asked his bodyguard, but the hulk gave no response.

He gazed after the mecha-man of psuedo-skin, nylo-planyon muscles and electro-nervous system. Originally the androids had been created to perform only the dangerous jobs that humans were not willing to risk themselves pursuing. The mines on Mars being the first of those. As time went by however, the androids began to be refined, became more humanoid in appearance and filtered down into menial work that humans were not willing to lower themselves doing. The waiter that had just taken the duo's order was a perfect example of that. Obviously a C5; although his skin was smooth and unblemished, gone was the days of rigid mouths and red electric sensors for eyes, the limbs moved without sound and freely and in a dark alleyway the waiter could have passed for human.

It returned with their order, there was actually a smile upon it's face. Castle laughed, the day would come when Speakman or Milinkovic would pick up a woman, intent upon horizontal activities, only to discover they had nearly shagged a machine. Then his grin turned wry, realising it might happen, in fact, to him!

They ate for a while in silence until Castle, who was taking a sip of his Aspro Clear, asked,

"Do you realise how big the company is that makes this stuff, Violet"? When the bodyguard simply grunted Castle went on determinedly, "It's almost as big as Corporation, they make drinking water for most of the Earth, also for Mars; here and even the tracking station on Venus".

"I prefer Orang-U-Can", Violet said in response, with a passion Castle had thought the bulky giant incapable.

"That pop", he laughed, "It's just a recycled idea from the twenty second century, originally called Orangrape".

"I like it", Violet grinned. He was not a individual with a face that suited smiling. Castle let it drop.

FOUR

THE FOLLOWING MORNING they took the tube to Mare Tranquillitatis, another novel experience for them both, though to look at Violet, one would not have believed it. It ended swiftly however, for the distance betwixt the two regions was not excessive. The facility was called rather clumsily "Bennesia Rest Home for the Firmly Established". Castle thought even Speakman could have done better than that. In truth Speakman was a superb sales director, but the rivalry between the two men meant that the deputy director would never have admitted it.

From the appropriate stop to the doors was a short walk, the strange bouncing hop, that was the only way to walk on the satellite. Psuedo gravity would not return until inside the sanatorium. Thankfully there was recycled air however, so they did not have the clumsy and time consuming bother of climbing into suits. Castle wore a frock coat of royal blue with a white roll collar shirt and concealed buttons, the height of fashion in fact. Violet continued to be clad in all deep purple and Castle wondered if he had only one outfit.

They had heard on the radio-net that morning that the power failure of the night before had been caused by a solar flare. Then promptly forgot the information. All of Castle's thoughts were now directed toward his imminent meeting with Clare Trentavoria.

They entered by a huge oval throughway and felt the psuedo gravity abruptly grip their limbs, wandering over to the rather obvious reception desk. It was manned by an A5. This one was fashioned into a redheaded female and the original sculpture had been of a very attractive woman. Despite knowing the mechanoid was not human, Castle afforded it his most winning smile and informed the rather good looking machine who he was. Behind the rather life-like green eyes, photo-electric cells scanned the deputy directors features, also identifying Castle by his oh so human retinal record.

"Please go to the waiting area gentlemen", the electronic voice requested in assuring deep contralto, "Doctor Bennesia is expecting you and will join you directly".

Castle was not sure he liked the sound of that, fearing they would be in for a long wait, while the administrator proved to them how busy he was. He was almost instantly filled with ennui and began to casually scan the hideous modern art on the otherwise tasteful blue walls. then he entertained himself by trying to see if the android had nice legs,

'*Stop it you sick bastard*', he thought to himself and then, '*I wonder if they've given her auburn pubic hair to match the hue on her head*'?

No sooner had that thought amused him than a distinguished individual with a shock of white hair, dressed in a short white smock, came to greet them.

"Mister Castle", Bennesia said holding out a slim hand, his shake was slack and limp wristed.

"You know why I am here doctor", Castle said, knowing Orwenoot had sent him a message before he had left for the moon.

"Yes, erm... yes I do", Bennesia sounded nervous and distant.

"Is everything alright? Miss Trentavoria is well is she"? the deputy director wished to know.

"Oh yes; she's fine, fine", Bennesia murmured, but Castle did not think he sounded sure.

"Excellent", Castle pretended to enthuse, "Well doctor! Can we see her then, this is mister Violet, he is my personal security. Where I go, he goes"

"Mister Violet", Bennesia gave the giant a stiff bow of his head. Yet he did not move.

"What is it doctor"? Castle asked then growing a tad concerned and slightly agitated, "What is wrong".

"Nothing, nothing", Bennesia tried to assure, "Only........".

"Only what"? Castle pressed, beginning to lose his temper with the man's dithering.

"It's just that I wish to ask you....", Bennesia stammered and then finally, "If you would reconsider and not bother miss Trentavoria at all".

"Not bother her"! Castle was amazed and irritated in equal measure, "Not bother her doctor? Do you realise that I must see her, on a matter of high financial business"?

"But she is not a well person", Bennesia began lamely. Castle never let him finish.

"Doctor, you assured me she was well, now I must insist that you take us to her and right now"!

Bennesia was nothing if not obdurate, "I think perhaps I have not made myself fully clear to you Mister Castle and I apologise for that. What I mean to tell you, to convey to you with utmost sincerity, is that seeing Clare Trentavoria would be dangerous".

"Doctor", Castle began carefully, "I appreciate your concern, truly I do. However I must insist on seeing her, the future of Corporation lies in her hands".

"I think perhaps you don't fully understand", the doctor still persisted, "I didn't mean dangerous to her, I meant dangerous to you"!

"Vat's iz zis"? Violet demanded in his thick German accent, "Dangerous how, is she armed"?

"Oh no, nothing like that", Bennesia held up his hands palms forward, "I meant dangerous by association".

"I've had enough of this Doctor", Castle fumed shouldering past the medic, "Which room is she in"?

Violet hurried to be at his shoulder as they hurried down a corridor behind the medic.

"Room twenty three; but.....".

He tailed off as Castle and his bodyguard strode from his range of speech.

The deputy director of Corporation thought to himself, *'Twenty three! Again! Is this some sort of screwy conspiracy? Are the norns set against me or something'?*

Yet he never broke stride to the room and rapped upon it with his knuckles. It yawed open almost at once and Castle was not prepared for the young lady that appeared before him.

Clare Trentavoria was quite tall for a woman, some one hundred and seventy five centimetres, she was slim, but had a superb bust which Castle judged to be an 'e' cup. Her bosom was pert and even in the warmth of the clinic the nipples were thrusting against the cotton fabric of her vest. When Castle raised his eyes from them he saw a beautiful face framed by hair, the colour of butterscotch. Her most striking feature of all however were her deep blue eyes; before which, were tiny panes of glass on a slim bracket that was anchored on her ears and nose. Castle seemed to recall the antique device was indeed called 'glasses'. Why anyone should resort to such a contrivance however, when laser surgery was so common was quite beyond him.

"Yes"? she asked and her voice was a smooth and deeply sensuous sound.

Castle coughed to regain his composure, then informed her,

"I'm E. A. Castle, your grandfather's deputy at Corporation, may I come in Miss Trentavoria? I have some news for you"?

"Who's that"? she demanded sharply of Violet and Castle explained.

"You may enter then", she agreed, "Alone".

"He said danger", Violet protested, but Castle replied,

"I think I'll be fine", as he drank in the girl's unexpected pulchritude, "Wait out here please, that's an order".

The beautiful girl held open the door and Castle entered.

At that moment he was making the biggest mistake of his life!

FIVE

CLARE TRENTAVORIA CLOSED the door with a certain awkward ferocity and leaned her back on it, telling him at once,

"I know he's dead, we're allowed netvids in here".

"Magnus Quintilius Trentavoria has indeed passed", Castle began carefully, "And our Corporation solicitor has already read the will. I'm afraid your grandfather's body has been ah, currently misplaced".

"Nonsense", the girl astonished him in return, "It was placed aboard Trentavoria Twenty Three *'The Following of the Stolen Heart'* fired it toward Venus".

"Trentavoria Twenty Three"? Castle echoed, ignoring for the moment the number appearing yet again. He was beginning to feel the conversation was already slipping away from him, the initiative, with the girl.

"A high powered rocket he had built some time ago", Clare Trentavoria disturbed Castle with her superior knowledge, "In order that his body could be disposed of in precisely the correct fashion".

"That fashion! Dissolved in the acid of the second planet"?

"Oh no", she smiled enigmatically, "A fusion with the very buildining stuff of our solar system, the return to the great parent molecules and atoms, so that from such fussion, can come rest".

"Do you then know the result of the reading of the will"? Castle asked, ignoring the bizarre means of corpse disposal. The girl shook her head, asking instead,

"Would you like some Snufz mister Castle"?

"Aah, no, thank you", he was deeply startled by that, "And call me Ed please"?

"I assure you it's premo grade Ed", the girl went on, seemingly oblivious of his emotions, "And in it's purest form it's not addictive".

"No thank you. Can we get back to the business of.....".

"A drink then and some tobacco"? She cut him off. There seemed no way that Clare Trentavoria could be rushed into a conversation of his choosing.

Castle was thrown into confusion. He did not want to annoy her however, so he conceded,

"I'll take a small sherry then, thank you and a medcig".

"A small sherry", the girl laughed, which sounded fine to Castle's ears, "Don't be such a frinky, have a whisky or a vodka and a real cigarette".

Castle did not know what a 'frinky' was, but he did not think it was anything impressive and he needed to impress Clare Trentavoria. Keep his well paid job, worth thousand of shillin's per annum. So he conceded,

"Very well, a vodka thank you and a cigarette".

"I'll give you an Alpine then".

"An Alpine"?

"An Alpine cigarette. You've never smoked unless you've had an Alpine; that smooth creamy taste that never burns your tongue or leaves your mouth with anything other than that fresh alpine taste".

He let her go on for the while thinking Speakman would certainly make something of her taste in tobacco. While she was pouring the drinks, one for each of them, he finally had the chance to tell her,

"Miss Trentavoria, your grandfather left you fifty one percent of the stocks of Corporation and the post of managing director, I was hoping that you would allow me to.........".

"Don't you mean Orang-U-Can", she cut in. Castle was confused, could the girl really truly believe that her grandfathers empire was the soft drinks firm?

"No I don't mean Orang-U-Can, erm miss Trentavoria......".

"Your drink; Ed. Do sit down, here's your Alpine, I'll get you a light, these do not have the self igniting tip".

Castle took both and seated himself on a black leather couch, the room was quite spacious and fully self contained it seemed. He was finding talking to miss Trentavoria the most confusing conversation in his life. She magiced a lighter from somewhere and leaned over to light his cigarette; her breasts jiggled magnificently causing Castle to wonder if they were actually natural.

Then she seated herself beside him, despite the fact there was also a vacant chair in the room. Her thigh was warm and firmly pressed against his own. He could smell her perfume, like every physical aspect of her, it was divine.

"Now then", she began, inhaling deeply on her own cigarette, "What is it you want to tell me"?

Castle took a drag of his own cigarette, feeling the nicotine hit his brain almost immediately.

"You're the director of Corporation miss Trentavoria", he said simply, he took a sip of the vodka, his head was suddenly swimming.

"Call me Clare"? she asked and then, "And it's Orang-U-Can you know. Tell me what post do you hold at Orang-U-Can".

Thinking her possibly deranged he took another drag of the cigarette another swig of the vodka, the room was growing fuzzy and comforting, he was unused to strong alcohol and nicotine,

"I'm deputy director; erm, Clare and I hope you'll keep me on in the post. At least until you've found your feet in the corp....., erm company".

The room was beginning to spin then, what the hell was in the cigarette? The drink? Had the beautiful girl actually slipped him a mickey finn?

"Well that depends upon how good you are", the girl was saying.

"I assure you I have all the relevant diplomas and can show you my track record for....."

"No silly", she laughed, "How good you are in bed"!

Castle did not think the girl could shock him any more than she already had, but she had managed it.

"I beg your pardon, ah a joke; yes very funny".

"Let me freshen your drink", she rose, leaving a delightful trail of heady scent in her wake, "And no, I'm not kidding Ed".

"You honestly mean to say......."!

"That I'm not employing you unless you're a decent piece of ass! Here get this down you Ed, you need to unwind a bit".

In a total daze, Castle took the drink and took a lengthy pull on it, in his hands the cigarette was trembling, he felt slightly nauseous and very very dizzy. He took another deep drag on the cigarette and began,

"Eye sea you in a turn, a you turn", he began dizzily before getting a grip upon himself. "Now see here young lady I am a loyal employee of Corporation and I have a girlf......."

"Orang-U-Can", she finished for him, "And a handsome sexy man Ed, come on have another cigarette and then we'll have rampant sex, because that's basically what I'm after"!

"I don't feel quite myself miss Trentavoria", Castle confessed.

She was handing him another cigarette and the room was turning a delightful deep blue of hue. He took it almost distractedly and she lit if for him.

"That's alright Ed", she said soothingly, "Because you can feel me instead, do you find it hot in here"? Because I do".

With which she promptly removed her shirt and seated herself before him in only her brassiere. Her bosom was magnificent, but Castle kept his eyes closed for the moment, hoping when he opened them, the room and he, would return to some semblance of normality. Then her mouth was on his and she kissed him frenziedly and in the style made poplar originally by the French.

"Miss Trentavoria", he gasped, but found he could not get to his feet.

"If you're going to tup me, you'll have to stop calling me that", she warned and she promptly took off her brassiere.

SIX

CASTLE ROSE UP on an elbow and tried to remember what had happened. He was in bed with Clare Trentavoria. The room was typically feminine, pink walls, white bedclothes and plenty of pillows and throws cushions, before he could see more he realised both of them were naked. He gazed down at the girls body as she lay sleeping, she was certainly a knock out and that is what she had done to him! Her eyes opened and she smiled,

"Yes, I'll keep you on", she told him, "Well done Ed you're still deputy director of Orang-U-Can. You'll need to show me the ropes. Both in business and some more of those moves you just demonstrated in bed".

Castle was racked with guilt, thinking of Dawn, he rose and tugged on his boxers, searching around for the rest of his clothes, they were strewn across the floor, a trail of guilt and betrayal,

"Clare", he began, the name sounding enigmatic on his tongue, "Corporation, I am deputy director of Corporation".

In answer she smiled mysteriously and asked, "Tell me how did you find the Snufz? I prefer to snort it, but it certainly has some interesting effects smoked too".

"You drugged me"! Castle gasped, hurrying into the rest of his hastily gathered clothing and remembering the warning given and unheeded, by doctor Bennesia. "That is beyond.......".

"You go and pack", she cut in, "I'll do the same and we can return to Earth together".

Castle's leg suddenly ached, he pulled up his breeks and examined a huge blue bruise, where he had banged it on the furniture the night before; only the bruise looked more than a few hours old! Everything suddenly seemed slightly unreal, more like a vivid dream than reality,

"How long have we been in here"? he demanded

"Well, let's see, I had to have more than one test of your romantic prowess", she chuckled. "Don't worry about Green, I sacked him for you".

"Green? Who by Satan's teeth is Green".

"That lump you left outside your door, you don't need him any more, if anyone tries to hurt you you'll have my protection".

'You're absolutely out of your tree', Castle thought and without another word strode from the bedroom, on into the living quarter to the outer door and threw it open. Violet was obviously not there. He hesitated but for a second before proceeding down the corridor and a man he knew very well met him at the end of it,

"Villutyre! Thank the swaddling clothes of sweet baby Jesus, what are you doing here? What's with the white coat? Playing doctor are you ha ha ha"?

He could hear his own voice raised an octave in pitch, on the edge of hysteria. In answer Milinkovic raised an eyebrow and asked calmly,

"Will miss Trentavoria be requiring anything now you are leaving now, mister Castle, are you to become the new director of Corporation, or has the heady responsibility fallen on the shoulders of another"?

"What are you talking about"? Castle began to lose his feeling of reason, "And take off that ridiculous coat, you'd better come with me and the girl, back to Earth".

"Mister Castle", Milinkovic smiled sadly, "I am the administrator of this facility and have a medical degree to boot".

Castle suddenly smiled, "Oh I get it, you and Speakman cooked up this little practical joke. Okay you got me, very funny ha ha hah. Now; let's go home eh"?

"I did warn you about seeing miss Trentavoria", Milinkovic responded calmly, "But you were most insistent upon it".

"Give it a rest Villutyre. Either take off the coat and come with me, or to Hades with you, I'll go back to Earth with her and leave you here".

Milinkovic smiled sadly but remained silent, leaving Castle nothing to do but stride away in hopeless temper. His mind in turmoil, he got back on the tube almost on automatic pilot. Afterward remembering nothing of the journey. Jumping off before it had fully come to a halt, he strode back to the Excelsior in the pseudograv of the moon station, once again he was back at Copernicus. Then picking up his tablet he pinged the object of his ire. Her attractive features swam into instant focus on the HD monitor and he asked her,

"It's me, are you packed, are you ready to return to Earth"?

"Excuse me, but before we go any further do you know who 'I am', and who the blazes are you, how did you get my number".

Blinking he demanded, "What are you talking about Clare"? I've not that many minutes ago left your bed; are you having a psychotic episode or something. Can you put doctor Bennesia on"?

"Psychotic episode", the girl echoed, looking totally bemused, her previous ire evaporated in just so many seconds. "No I don't believe I'm tripping.... but.... it's not always easy to tell".

"Can you put doctor...erm, the doctor on please Clare"? Castle wondered how much Snufz he had taken, if he had experienced an episode of his own whilst at the rehab facility? He sincerely hoped it would be Bennesia's features that swam into view next. Whilst he waited however, he was disconcerted to find that of Violet's former presence in the suite, there was not the scantiest sign. He had packed and gone, before Castle could catch him and press him back into service. When a man's features filled the tablet screen, he had no idea who it was the doctor was yet another individual who, he was not expecting to see.

"Voleskip", the man introduced. Uncertainly Castle began,

"Doctor I am E. A. Castle of Corporation".

"Collendine Voleskip M.D... What can I do for you mister Castle".

"I wish to have Clare Trentavoria signed over to me, to take her back to Corporation. She has just inherited fifty one percent of stocks in the firm and the post of Managing Director. May I ask by the by if you are one of Doctor Bennesia's colleagues"?

Voleskip's brow furrowed in consternation, "Corporation you say. I thought miss Trentavoria heiress to the Orang-U-Can empire"?

"No, that's part of her illusion", Castle persisted a trifle uncertainly. "I believe her dependency on Snufz in the past has left her a little bit confused. That will all be cleared up once we get her back to Earth".

"I don't know who you are really mister Castle", Voleskip began, "But I am aware of Orang-U-Can, I drink it regularly. I have of course heard Corporation, to my mind it is owned by the business genius Alovar Hornrunner, he made his fortunes by investing in Dodoprot, that sir is common knowledge".

"Doctor", Castle asked with far more patience than he had erstwhile believed himself capable, "Do you visit miss Trentavoria regularly"?

"Of course", Voleskip admitted, "She's my patient, now good day sir, do not use this address again". With that he promptly cut the connection.

Castle seated himself on his bed and daydreamed for several moments, was everyone involved in some bizarre conspiracy against only he? Or, worse, was he actually losing his grip on reality?

He pinged Dawn, but the number toned off, obviously she was out somewhere without her tablet. He hesitated over trying Speakman, if he were behind all this then speaking to him would only serve to deepen his confusion. Then glumly he realised there was no one else he could trust. Unbidden Ibbopargia suddenly occurred to him and he pinged the appropriate number. The detective's dark features appeared on the screen.

"Richard", he began, "Have you had any progress finding out who tried to kill me"? It suddenly seemed like an age past.

"Detective Ibbopargia", came the gruff response, "To whom am I communicating"?

"To me Richard", Castle returned in confusion, "It's E. A. we spoke only hours ago, we've known each other for years".

"I am sorry sir", began the police detective carefully, "But I do not know who you are".

"Sorry to have troubled you officer", Castle sighed resignedly and cut the connection.

Only Speakman or Milinkovic, backed by the enormous power of Corporation could have enough sway to get his old friend to behave in the way he had.

Finally, determinedly, he pinged Speakman and the head of advertising came into view on his pad,

"Just checking in again", he began, then, "Shit Edgar you look terrible, what the damnation happened to you"?

"I've had a bit of a rough time of it", Castle admitted, "I'll tell you all about it when I get back to Earth".

"Someone didn't try to kill you again did they"?

Castle was instantly suspicious, "No Erasmus, I have had a bodyguard with me at all times".

"Well why don't you get some sleep and then finish with the contract tomorrow"?

"Suddenly the floor seemed to give way beneath Castle's feet and he asked hollowly, "Contract"?

Speakman nodded, "Yes the contract you insisted on going to conclude despite all my efforts. You've not frenged it up have you, the old man will be furious if you have"?

"Old man"?

"Edgar, what the hell is going on up there, I got the moon conglomerate to agree to the installation of all our machines moon-wide, all you had to do was get them to sign on the dotted line, you have brought the contract in haven't you"?

Castle giggled feeling something nibble at the edge of his sanity, "What is the name of the firm we work for Erasmus".

"Shite in a bucket Edgar, what the frenge are you talking about. Is Villutyre there, let me talk to him".

"Villutyre Milinkovic is now in charge of the insane asylum up here on the moon".

"What! It's no good Edgar, I'm going to have to report this to the old man".

"Who the frenge is the old man anyway", Castle laughed, a rancorous sound without humour.

"You know full well we work for Drorb Makers-Guild, the genius behind Aspro-clear".

"You aught to be on the stage Erasmus", Castle chortled, "Acting is one of your hidden talents".

He cut the connection and shrugged. They were all in on it then? No matter, for he would show them all, he would get Clare Trentavoria and he would take her back to Earth. Before that however he would indeed take a little nap and he fell back on the bed and instantly fell into a deep sleep.

SEVEN

WHEN HE AWOKE but three hours later he felt much better. His head felt clear and he went for a hot shower, turning the water to cold for as long as he could stand it at the end. He dressed in a frock coat of navy checks and a plain sky high collared shirt, his britches were the popular three quarter length which stopped at the knee and his sock were up to them. He placed patent psuedo-leather, buckled shoes of black on his feet and then carefully packed all his other belongings.

Thoughtfully he pinged a certain number and a voice said over a blank screen,

"Ja"?

"I need the services of a discrete bodyguard. Might that be mister Violet I have contacted"?

"Ver are you"?

"Copernicus, Moon, Excelsior hotel room twenty three, my name is......"

"Ve know your name Herr Burg".

"How long before someone can be here"? Castle wished to know, of course they knew who he was, he had hired Violet and others before him over the years.

"Twenty five minutes, stay in your room". The connection was cut.

"Right then", Castle murmured, "If Voleskip won't release Trentavoria, I'll bust her out"!

Twenty five minutes seemed like a long time when one was just waiting, but inevitably it passed and later his door pinged and he allowed a suitably hulking brute access into his room. The newcomer did not identify himself, so Castle asked,

"What's your name"?

"I haf nein name, androids do not need zem, my designation iz E23", the answer, though synthetic, came once more in a thick German accent.

"Why did the engineer who created you give you a German accent"? Castle was amused.

"Herr Baumeister vas a great man", the hulking android began, "He had much sense of humour ja"?

"Ja", Castle agreed, "I'll call you Gastgeber, that will have to do for now, and there is no way I'm going to call you 23. We are going to get a young woman out of the rehab facility at Mare Tranquillitatis, are you armed"?

The android pulled his three quarter length coat to one side, to reveal the largest snout nosed blaster Castle had ever seen. The strange duo left a few moments later. Castle had already had his luggage taken to the shuttle bay.

With mixed emotions he climbed from the tube and strode toward the rehab facility. The impressive android in his wake. Surely by now he would meet the elusive Doctor Bennesia? The impressive red headed android was once again at reception. Her electrode eyes recognised Castle and she glanced hesitantly at Gastgeber, then pressed her intercom and after only the merest of delays, Collendine Voleskip M.D. slowly came to greet them. Castle was mildly dismayed, just how long was the effects of Snufz supposed to last?

"I will not beat about the bush doctor", he began, his tone more confident than he felt, "Sign Clare Trentavoria into my care. There will be no debate, no prevarication, I want her and she is coming with us".

"Miss Trentavoria was well enough to sign herself in mister Castle and the only way she will leave is by signing herself out".

"Get me Bennesia", Castle demanded.

"You mentioned that individual earlier sir", Voleskip observed frostily, "Neither doctor Milinkovic nor I have ever heard of him".

"Alright then, I'll talk to Milinkovic", Castle agreed desperately, his head beginning to buzz.

"I'm afraid he's not at the facility at present", Voleskip resentfully remarked, "I am currently in charge here".

"Milinkovic is never present is he"? Castle ground out resentfully before realising that the sentence was possibly non sensible. In impotent annoyance he finally barked, "Gastgeber, get me past this man"!

What Castle was not expecting by issuing such a demand, was the method the huge android employed however. The Germanic bodyguard promptly drew his blaster and fired at the doctor from point blank range. Voleskip's head exploded in a spatter of seared flesh and bone.

"Hades Teeth"! Castle cursed, feeling like he might lose consciousness at any moment, "You've killed him, that was down right unreasoning murder, why did you do it"?

"You asked me to get past him", the murderer murmured, "Und see, ve can now go past the late doctor".

A siren began to wail, the alarm of the facility. Gastgeber turned toward the android receptionist.

"No"! Castle wailed, "Leave it be, what did you expect it to do? Come on we must act swiftly". As they ran to room twenty three, Castle thought to himself,

'How are we going to get off the moon now? The constables will be all over this and at the shuttle bay'.

Yet still he hurried, not knowing what else to do. He was vaguely aware of the fantastic realism of the android's locomotion.

Without knocking, he threw open the door and burst into Clare Trentavoria's quarters.

"Miss Trentavoria", he called, "We have to leave and quickly, are you ready to go"?

From out of the bedroom the dark blonde sauntered, she was in the process of snorting Snufz, a cigarette hanging casually from the corner of her mouth.

"Fringe"! Castle cursed, "Not now for goodness sake, what were you thinking"?

"Hey Ed baby; chill", the girl murmured, "Haven't you heard the news"?

"We have to go, tell me on the way to the bay", Castle urged desperately.

To his deep agitation she seated herself on the sofa, "Grandfather has sent a signal to the tracking station on Venus".

Clearly she was insane.

"Your grandfather died". In resigned defeat he flopped down onto the sofa beside her.

"Have some of this it's primo, you won't get hooked".

In a daze Castle took a pinch of the narcotic and sniffed strongly. Within seconds his agitation vanished, a tremendous sense of well being flushed through his brain. So Voleskip was dead, big deal, he could easily explain it, he had not killed him. He glanced over to the still open door, of Gastgeber, there was no sign, obviously he had taken to his heels. The constables of Moon Constabulary would be there very soon. The room's blueness seemed the most beautiful hue he had ever witnessed. He smelled the girl's perfume, it was the most divine odour he that had ever drifted into his nostrils.

Almost absently she asked him,

"How is your thigh now, where they had to inject you? Have a cigarette"?

"No, that can't be right," his speech was slurred, indistinct, "The needle in my thigh was when Speakman tried to kill me, or was it Milinkovic, or maybe even Stubbsinge"?

As she handed him a cigarette, and her lighter she told him, "The message was twenty three".

"I saw your grandfather die", he told her lighting the cigarette and drawing the smoke deeply into his lungs.

"I believe you", she replied simply, "The trip to Venus made him one with the cosmos, revitalised him, the very stuff of our being gives life to many things".

"Okay so what does twenty three mean then"? Castle asked wishing the walls had not suddenly started dripping some sort of fluid.

"As deputy director of Orang-U-Can I thought you'd know"?!

Before the stoned Castle could respond to that, two figures hesitantly entered the room, dressed in long grey smock coats, they were obviously moon constables.

"Which of you stole the stuff", one of them sort of barked, his features were slightly canine, Castle thought, he giggled.

His amusement did little to deter the constable,

"What's your name and what are you both doing in this room together, these quarters are for sole occupation".

"Well what's yours"? Castle tittered, the girl laughed too.

"I am Inspector Spagliatelli", the constable who had done all the talking said carefully exaggerating every word, "Eduardo Spagliatelli and this is Inspector Archie Normanton. Now you tell me your name"?

"Castle, inspector, deputy director of Corporation".

"Corporation"? Normanton echoed, speaking for the first time, "Do you mean Corporation that belongs to, Alovar Hornrunner"?

Castle watched in fascination as the heads of the two constables changed to those of black dogs.

"He doesn't know what he means", Spagliatelli grumbled, "He's obviously delusional, or he wouldn't be in here. Alright fellow, let's see some I. D. that's if they let you keep it in here".

Castle laughed, "I'm not a patient in here, I was visiting miss Trentavoria".

Spagliatelli turned to Normanton, "Go get the doctor we ain't gonna get any sense out of this screwball".

"You'll have a job on there inspector", Castle could not stop laughing, "He's dead".

Just give me some I. D. if you have any fellow", Spagliatelli demanded, his red tongue ran along the length of his canine muzzle. Castle dove into the inside pocket of his three quarter length coat and pulled out his passport and identity card,

"There you go", he said amiably, finally managing to stop laughing at the constable.

Spagliatelli flipped it open, "Right mister Hossvars which room should you be in"?

Before Castle could register his disbelief a voice came from the doorway,

"This is his room inspector, it's the young lady who is keeping an eye on him for the moment".

Castle's jaw dropped, the figure who had spoken was doctor, Collendine Voleskip.

"People don't stay dead anymore", Castle muttered to himself, "Can I see that passport please inspector"?

Spagliatelli shrugged and handed it over, beneath Castle's own pixilated image was the name Siggy Hossvars.

"Speakman and Milinkovic have done this to me", Castle realised aloud, finally realising how insidious their entire plan had been, then to Spagliatelli, "Vidnet Corporation please inspector and ask to speak to the head of the advertising department. This is all an elaborate confidence trick. Once he realises how illegal it's become, he'll explain everything. I am Edgar Antony Castle. This identity card and passport are forgeries, or, they belong to mister Hossvars with my image superimposed over them".

"Don't you realise how paranoid that sounds Siggy"?, Voleskip asked. "And what's this about the dead? Are you seriously asking the inspector to bother a member of Alovar Hornrunner's team with this, this puerile fabrication"?

"You're in on it", Castle smiled, still feeling euphoric, thanks to the Snufz, "Obviously it was an android replica of you that Gastgeber blasted. Sorry about this Clare, I'll have this all sorted out and then we can go to Earth together".

"You can leave him now nurse", Voleskip said to her, "His spasm is over. What did he do this time inspector".

As Spagliatelli was saying "Bust the glass frontage of the tobacconists and took a shelf full of the filthy stuff", Clare was rising from her position on the sofa, Castle grabbed her by the wrist,

"What are you doing Clare? Tell them you're not a nurse, tell them about Corporation, or Speakman and Milinkovic will have me out and then they'll start on you"!

Everyone in the room seamed to hesitate, waiting for the beautiful girl to say something one way or the other. Finally she smiled,

"It's a sad case gentlemen, he really believes every word he is speaking, Snufz dependency does that to the mind after long term use. Miss Trentavoria is in a similar state in another room of this very facility".

"What"! Castle blinked, wishing the Snufz had not dulled his senses to such a degree, "But you're Clare Trentavoria".

By was of tacit answer the beautiful woman turned a plastic I. D. disc to the two members of the Moon Constabulary.

Spagliatelli read aloud, "Christine Lattenuma, Senior Carer".

Lattenuma told the two of them "He thinks he is going to take me to Earth, not unusual for a patient to grow an attachment to his carer though".

"You frenging bitch", Castle cursed, euphoria dissolving, "They're all in it together inspector, Speakman, Milinkovic, her and the so called doctor here. It's all been a clever ruse to out me from the company".

"What company would that be mister Hossvars", Spagliatelli asked sympathetically. Castle thought for perhaps twenty seconds before replying,

"Orang-U-Can".

MEN'S WORK

ONE

A COLD WIND gusted across the rubescent landscape of Mars. The atmosphere was thin, the tree planting programme was still in it's infancy. Mankind was forced to live beneath vast interconnected bubbles of special reinforced plastic. Despite this seeming restriction however, those who had known little or nothing else carried on their lives with all the weaknesses and foibles that they had demonstrated since their coming into being, six and a half thousand years hence.

Into this strange mix then came a new intelligence. An artificial intellect born of man himself, the machine. These were no shining automaton with electronically harsh voices however. They were the androids and the latest range could pass themselves off as human, so adept was their creation. They were the next rung on the ladder of evolution and mankind had yet to realise that one day they would inherit the solar system.

Menschlich strode into the bosses' office with casual ease, the interior was dusty, stank of stale tobacco and the light came only from a slim port high above their heads. The quality of the illumination was rose coloured, the light of Mars. He never complained about the local pollution, for most of those who lived on Mars sought to ease they daily stresses with med-cigs.

"You pinged me chief", Menschlich observed somewhat superfluously.

"Next job", his boss growled in ill humour. The boss was never in a good state of mien. A pudgy fist turned the pad toward Menschlich. Upon the screen was an address in one of the opulent southern domes. Even on Mars a class system had developed, the rich had their own sectors and most of them lay in the south.

"Go to it, do what the lady says", came the gruff and tacit order.

Turning smoothly on his heels Menschlich left the office gratefully, the smoke had began to sting his solenoid synthetic eyes; he was an android! More than that however he was an E23 and if one did not know, he was created from steel, nyloplanyon and pseudo-skin, then he could easily pass for human. He was stronger and faster than any human that had ever lived however and that made him eminently suited to his current occupation.

Leaving Medusa dome by tube, he took the long ride to Erigone. The minute he exited at the southern dome, he observed the difference, that those who had could afford compared to the workers in the north.

All the painted surfaces were freshly done, those that were not painted were of chromium, stainless steel or plastoglass. The journey itself had been above the surface of the red planet, the tube, transparently walled. The scenery had been magnificent, but Menschlich had been created upon the moon and so was used to strange vistas. The rusty horizon and pink sky had left him unimpressed, the startling quality of the sun in the super thin atmosphere. He had the ability to look directly at it without damage, but lacked the desire.

Erigone was quite a different story. Man-made and super futuristic in design and construction it impressed a futuristically designed automaton. For several moments Menschlich did not move, but merely surveyed the magnificence of his surroundings.

"Trouble buddy"? an American voice asked him in a Texan twang.

Not zat I am aware of", Menschlich returned in the heavy German accent of all Professor Herr Baumeister's creations. Obviously the American was a tourist but he did not recognise Menschlich as an android, simply because of that.

"Say you're from Germany ain't you"? came the next question. Menschlich nodded.

"Well this is my first time on Mars", the American told him, "Maybe you could tell me all the hot spots to visit, waddya say"?

Menschlich was not certain why the man had suddenly developed a twitch, his eye seemed to be bothering him, it kept opening and closing quite rapidly.

"Unfortunately", Menschlich began, "I am myself a visitor, I am from Medusa, not Erigone".

"I get that buddy, it's as though I just asked a Texan for recommendations to the juicy parts of Berlin".

Menschlich accessed his memory banks and then returned diplomatically, "It would be similar", he agreed, "Now if you will excuse me sir, I have business to attend to here".

The American wished him well and Menschlich accessed his memory for the address of the job. All he knew, was he was to do what the lady said. The boss had sent him on several jobs of discretion before and he concluded that it was of the same sort.

Within the dome was a spider network of corridors and passages, all sealed from the icy, oxygen light atmosphere of the planet. Some were connected by escalators, some by moving walkways which were like flat escalators and there was the opportunity to stride beside either if one so desired, in order to engage in simple walking. The address he had been given fit into the latter, near to the 'hub' of the web.

Menschlich rather liked the simple aspect of locomotion and began to stride the distance to the apartment. Walking parallel to the flat moving walkways, swifter also. He passed blazing neon signs advertising the interior's wares. Occasionally music drifted out from them and sometimes it was the ancient music of the Earthman, Vangelis, which he found very soothing. The 'Newmar' movement of electronic vibes was based upon the ancient tunes, but most of it was now of course produced by machines. Even Menschlich felt he could detect more emotion in the ancient variety, which he preferred.

At one doorway that was a dull puce in colour, a girl dressed only in a scanty lycra bikini, approached him, glanced him up and down appreciatively and asked,

"Hey handsome, wanna date, straight stuff only fifteen shillins"?

Menschlich had never thought of himself as handsome, in fact the android had never done much self analysis of any sort. Not only did he not know why he had been referred to as handsome, but he did not know what 'straight stuff' was.

"Is zat a fair price"? he asked in total naivety.

"Oh Phobos", the girl cursed, "You're after something kinky aren't you? Listen, I don't do three some's and I don't do S & M, so what did you have in mind"?

"Vould it be alright if I left it for ze time being"? Menschlich wanted to know.

"Huh, another fag eh"? She walked away disconsolately, obviously business was slack, as was she!

He walked on and after half an hour, was it the western rim of the network of tubes that lay on Mars red surface. He easily located a portal marked Erigone Estate number 41218. For in the synthetic environment all was clearly signed and labelled. This was the destination that he was required to present himself at. Menschlich rapped on the pseudo-plas door and waited, it opened after several moments and a tall blonde man with noticeably rigid posture answered, raising an eyebrow at his presence,

"What ever it is you are selling; we don't want any", he began, his tone high pitched and haughty. "Now, if you'll leave the portal to these apartments, I for one, would be most grateful".

Undeterred, Menschlich accessed his data base and asked, "Are you mister Comuszepse"?

"I am not", the tall blonde offered, "I am Withers; Miss Comuszepse's butler".

"It eez with Miss Comuszepse that I have some business".

"Indeed"! the butler sounded sceptical, "What is the nature of this so called business"?

"Zhat sir, is confidential".

From behind the elongated servant, a voice sounded, "That's alright Withers, let the young man in".

With a sniff of disdain, Withers hesitantly stood to one side and Menschlich squeezed past. The young woman that awaited him beyond was tall, elegant and strikingly beautiful. Golden hair cascaded down her slim shoulders and her red frock barely hid the magnificent swell of her breasts. Menschlich had never encountered such a stunning human female before, not in his entire existence.

"Please come in", she asked him, "I am Esterzoke Comuszepse".

She offered Menschlich her slim hand immaculately manicured as it was and he shook it gently,

"Please have a seat mister...."?

"Menschlich", he offered, he did not give her his first name, he did not have one.

"That will be all Withers", the young woman told her butler. Despite the instruction though the latter hesitated,

"Had I best not stay, just in case"? Withers wanted to know.

It caused the android to wonder in case of what, but he made no comment, merely smiled politely and waited to see what would happen next.

"I'm sure I will be quite safe", this, with a delightful smile toward the android, "I'll call you if I need anything".

She waited until the butler had left the elaborately furnished and voluminous lounge. Menschlich gazed about him. Some of the contents of the room were actually worth 'silver' shillins. There was a Martian sculpture in one corner, taken from the caverns, discovered by Couplander, on the third expedition to the planet they now resided upon. Unfortunately it had no discernable shape, no clue as to the form of it's creator. On one wall was a genuine original Roxbrough canvas and on another, some of the ancient African art was probably priceless. Comuszepse was not without fabulous wealth it seemed.

"A drink mister Menschlich"? the elegant blonde asked, having drifted over to the cabinet. Within lay superb cut glass crystal tumblers and the various options were also in decanters, not the ugly bottles the suppliers originally poured them into.

"Danke", the android accepted politely, for though he ran on a cool fusion micro-pile, he also possessed the ability to take nutrients from organic material and possessed an alimentary canal like any other biped. "I vould like a vodka".

"Ice"?

"Please, Ja".

She poured two vodkas over ice and conveyed one to Menschlich, "I saw you admiring the Roxbrough, my favourite of his work; Café en una Calle Mojada, one of his colour period".

"It is soothing", the android remarked, hoping he had conveyed the correct emotive response.

Esterzoke Comuszepse gazed at it, then breathed, "You are quite right".

"Vhat is the reason for hiring me dame"? Menschlich felt it was time to go to business.

"A simple task really", she began, "Yet not one without some small element of jeopardy. That is why I pinged the service".

"Quite right dame, you did ze correct thing", Menschlich reeled out the correct patter.

Esterzoke please, call me Esterzoke and what may I call you"?

Menschlich thought for a second and then lied, "My first name is Vahrheit".

"That means truth does it not Wahrheit"?

Menschlich nodded, "Hopefully an omen".

She looked thoughtful, took a sip of her drink and then placed it carefully on a place mat so as not to mark the Lloyd Thompson coffee table, a magnificent piece in green marble and highly polished walnut.

"Yes of course", she agreed and glided to her feet. Her every movement was graceful and also provided him with a whiff of 'Pink Touch'. She left the room, no doubt to get something pertinent to the case. Menschlich hoped so at any rate, despite the woman's friendly demeanour he was not totally at ease in her presence. Returning after but an instant, she held a slim parcel in one of her elegant hands. Bending down she passed it to him and he saw the magnificent décolletage of her bare shoulders neck and generous mound of her bosom.

The parcel was actually wrapped in brown paper!!

Menschlich felt the texture of it, he had never seen nor felt paper before,

"Ze contents of this wrapping must be very valuable to wrap it so", he remarked, to which, she replied earnestly,

"It's vitally important that the contents reaches it's destination Wahrheit, I am going to ask you under no circumstances what so ever to open the parcel, do you give me your solemn promise"?

"It is none of my business, so if zhat is your instruction, I so give you my vord".

The beauty smiled and he bathed in her approval,

"Get that item to an address I will give you and you will earn my sincere gratitude, along with the payment of course, shall we say a silver shillin"?

It was a fantastic sum well beyond what he had been expecting he had thought she would merely offer a promissory thumb, but to his continued surprise she took a bullion piece and pressed it into his hand. A genuine silver shillin 100% argent. Esterzoke held his hand a moment longer than was necessary and looked directly into Menschlich's deep green eyes,

"My sincere gratitude Wahrheit and I can be 'very' grateful"!

As if to underline this she licked her lips very slowly. Menschlich had the appropriate equipment even though he had never used it and he felt a momentarily disconcerting tightness in his groin. He rose awkwardly,

"I go to zhe address as soon as you give it to me, just tell me vhere it is and I vill memorise it"?

"Dryas - Kalidonisto Estate number 91315", she murmured eyeing him to see his reaction.

The far north, it could not possibly have been further away from Erigone. Not only that it seemed incongruous that such a fine and wealthy woman would deal with anyone in the more modest quarters of Mars. It could not have been more of a contrast, Dryas it particular was where the less fortunate people resided!

TWO

MENSCHLICH ACCESSED THE distance in his internal memory banks, he could not do the journey in one Martian day. Though he did not need sleep, he frequently took the opportunity to rest, helping increase the life expectancy of his capacitors, batteries and other vital components. So he planned to travel to Lucus and there take a room resting for several hours before continuing on to his destination. He hailed a cart hiring it to take him back to the tube, not wishing to take the additional time by walking. It was driven by a human, as opposed to a mecha-man, this was the sort of eccentricity Erigone was famous for.

Despite his promise to Esterzoke Comuszepse, he decided to open the innocuous brown paper parcel; after all, for all he knew, he might be carrying a needle bomb about his person. The fact that is was wrapped in the pulped material taken from an Earth tree also disconcerted him slightly. With a thumb nail as sharp as any razor, he sliced the top of the parcel and gazed inside.

His concentration was such that he did not notice the carty was watching him through the wing mirror of the low slung electric vehicle. The contents took Menschlich by surprise, it would have taken his breath away, if he did in fact, breathe. Bonds! Hundreds of them judging by the thickness of the wad. Orang-U-Can bonds.

Menschlich knew that stock of such a company would be worth a good thousand or two shillins, even if the stock was only worth a few sestertius each. (one hundred sestertius equalled a shillin, one hundred shillin equalled a silver shillin). He was thrown suddenly forward in his seat as the Carty (as that was what Menschlich had chosen to call him) slammed on the brakes and before he could recover his balance the other was around the side of the cart and pointing a snub nosed blaster at the android.

"Out", he commanded, calmly. This was obviously not the first time the vagabond had performed such an act.

Menschlich climbed out of the back of the cart making no sudden movements. Though a blaster would not kill him, it would disable him for some time, throw his gyro's out of kilter for one thing.

"You do not vish to do zhis", he tried. In answer the carty grinned showing yellowed crooked teeth,

"You know what I'm going to say to that don't you Kraut"?

"Zhat you indeed do, ja"?

The carty nodded, "Now Kraut, start walking and don't turn around, Go back the way we came, I wouldn't want to run you over".

The thought was farcical, though probably lighter than the vehicle, Menschlich was certainly constructed of much more resilient material, but of course the larcenous carty had no idea that such was the case.

"May ve not come to some sort of agreement"? the android asked.

"Yeah we can do that mister, I ask you to start walking, like I did and you start walking, that's an agreement right"?

Carefully Menschlich did as bidden, the cart began to move away. He calmly watched it disappear around a bend in the tube and then began to run. He could run faster than any cart, but kept his speed to that just a little less velocity intensive. The element of surprise would be at it's best when carty had reached his destination and was least expecting the android's appearance.

North of Erigone was the area called Scandia and the most southern bubble in Scandia was the town of Swedeway. No doubt the carty would have to pass through it, even if he didn't stop there and so that was where Menschlich jogged.

It involved passing once more through the heart of Erigone on a series of moving walkways that ran parallel to the cart tracks. Despite the urgency of his task, Menschlich was once again entranced by the opulence and ostentation of Erigone. Then he picked up the northern tubes and took the headings for Swedeway. He judged himself forty minutes behind Carty; perfect!

Jogging once more through a two lane tube that showed the vista of Mars through it's transparent sides, he was offered a lift more than once, but did not want to catch the villain just quite yet. The two operators who kindly stopped must have thought him mad for refusing aid, for neither of them seemed to guess or deduce his real actuality. He could have jogged at such a pace for forty nine hours or so, or two Martian days. Out side it was summer and the temperature was a balmy fifteen degrees centigrade, however once nightfall fell it would drop to minus fifty degrees and the tubes had to be heated to avoid massive condensation. Menschlich found that he was actually enjoying being on a mission, in which he made all the decisions, maybe after all this was over he would go freelance?

The mechanical construction that passed for a man reached the outskirts of Swedeway, his internal cooling system quite active, were he human he would have been sweating. The huge single dome of the comparatively tiny town could not have been a greater contrast to Erigone. It was not a poor place, but everything was scaled down and of lesser proclamation, some would have found it tasteful, the android saw it as comparatively less exciting. The first building he chanced upon was a restaurant, or perhaps a canteen, he was not entirely certain. He went inside.

Several individuals were seated around pseudo-plast tables drinking various beverages. Some were eating flat-bread wraps, others bowls of hot food. The walls were adorned with cheap posters and the skirting was grimy even though the pseudo-plas was easy enough to clean. In all it represented a place in which the proprietor was less than proud of his establishment. Menschlich went up to the serving counter, a stout bearded Martian came up to greet him,

"What will it be"?

"I am looking for someone who drives carts, one driver in particular, for a special journey, he vas recommended to me".

"Well, German, we only give out information to customers", the man said with a mirthless smile, "Are you a customer, German"?

Menschlich understood the inference only too well, "A cup of Terran tea then please my gut man", he requested.

"We don't serve Terran tea here, German, look at the board for frenge's sake".

His sales technique could do with some polish.

Behind the man's head was a huge white board, upon which was inscribed in dry marker the fare that the establishment offered. The font was done by hand, unusual in itself, it was also a barely readable scrawl.

"In zat case a cup of Gyndesian tea if you please".

"Sure German, take a seat, I'll bring it to you".

"And ze information"?

"Ifin 'I' seat myself at your table that's extra. Don't fret someone will fetch your drink. That's if you are appreciative of the service"?

Menschlich placed a full shillin on the counter,

"Vill zat suffice"?

The proprietor performed an act of legerdemain, of which, any magician would have been proud and his smile informed Menschlich that no change would be forthcoming.

Taking a seat near the visage of the canteen the android waited patiently. Presently a young woman dressed in a stained white apron sauntered over to him and placing his tea before him seated her self opposite. She was around one hundred and sixty eight centimetres in height, only perhaps forty six kilogramme's. Her hair was brown, fine and quite lank. Yet was not unattractive, in an elfin sort of way.

"I don't sit without drinking, German", she told him almost apologetically, obviously a house rule she did not fully agree with. When she used the nationality it was not as though to insult him, simply to recognise his beginnings.

"Of course", he responded politely, "Vhat vould you like my dear"?

"A gin, fifty sestertius".

Menschlich handed over a second shillin coin, "Keep ze rest for yourself my dear, for service rendered so to speak".

"Thanks mister", her mood brightened somewhat, she waved to the man behind the counter and he promptly brought a glass of gin. It was the cruder and cheaper Martian variety and a dull ochre in colour.

"Now then", the girl began, trying to sound confident, but Menschlich could see that she anything but, "Where do you wish to conduct our conversation, down here, or upstairs"?

She nodded toward an escalator that was not working, a second floor to the bubble.

"Down here is fine is it not"? Menschlich was puzzled, "Vat is there on the first floor zhat is not down here"?

"My schlafzimmer of course", she told him, one of the few words she knew in German perhaps.

"Vhat is in your bedroom zhat is not down here"? in some areas, Menschlich was still very much a naive automaton.

"My bed", the girl tried to smile, but the conversation clearly did not sit well with her.

"You may fall asleep", Menschlich observed, "And I am wishing to know where is the Carty I seek".

The girl shrugged her shoulders, evidently assuming that Menschlich had no interest in her in that way.

"I understand it is a particular driver you are looking for"?

"Ja, he is one hundred and seventy eight centimetres in height, weighing eighty three kilogramme's. He is today varing a black cap, red nylon shirt and grey slacks, his shoes are pseudo leather and brown also".

"So you know him well, or your powers of observation are quite acute"?

Menschlich said nothing to this and she went on,

"It is Justaka Ajhbenta that you seek, he sometimes works out of the Blue Butterfly down on the plaza".

"Danke", he said simply and rose fluidly to leave.

"You have not drunk your tea", she noted almost alarmed.

"You have it Frau, I am not thirsty", he told her honestly enough. He left the canteen swiftly and took a right toward the broader and taller visage in the bubble. It was not long before his swift stride had eaten up the distance to the Blue Butterfly, which proclaimed itself a restaurant, hotel and house of drinking.

Menschlich entered the open doorway of the place and scanned the bodies present in the room, quicker than any man could have. At the very same instant he recognised Justaka Ajhbenta, the villainous carty saw him looking both startled and understandably surprised. He was leaning on the reception desk frontage, talking to a young man behind it. Without the slightest hesitation, he broke into a run, heading for what was presumably a back entrance or exit to the place. Behind the frontage of various establishments in the bubbles there was usually an alleyway, used in the main by delivery vehicles and waste disposal, just as in any big city on Earth.

Ajhbenta obviously sought to escape Menschlich by such a route. The android snapped into a hasty pursuit and from the folds of his frock coat, he pulled a needle gun, just in case matters took a more hostile turn. Sure enough beyond the kitchens was a rear doorway and Menschlich burst through it but seconds behind his prey.

"Stop, or I 'vill' fire", the android barked.

Ajhbenta brought himself to an abrupt halt and fumbled in the folds of his own clothing.

"Do not do zat", Menschlich warned, "Zhis is a needle gun in my hand und it is loaded vith neuronic needles".

Ajhbenta froze, obviously he had heard what a neuronic needle could do. It entered the body by means of the needle of course, but then the neuro-toxin attacked the central nervous system and rendered instant paralysis. The result was also known to be excruciatingly painful, by those who had endured the misfortune of having experienced it. In fact so much so, that some individuals promptly died of either shock or cardiac arrest. It was said to be less deadly than a blaster, but few could have boasted of comparing the two by virtue of having compared the experience.

The carty smiled, "I don't have them any more", he told the android.

"Zhis I doubt", Menschlich reasoned, "For insufficient time has elapsed for you to have effected an illegal trade. I sink you vas in the process of doing so vhen I entered the Blue Butterfly, I sink zhe bonds are still about your person".

"Come and search me if you want Kraut", the carty spat then, "You'll find nothing".

"If zhat proves zhe case vhen I vill be vanting zhe name of he, to whom, you have sold zhem", Menschlich replied and went forward to effect a search.

Two things then happened in the same split second. The first was that Ajhbenta suddenly kicked out, his foot sending the android's needle gun spinning from his hand. The second was that his chest exploded in a shower of burst flesh and seared gore. Menschlich span around to see the youth who had been behind the reception counter, in his fist was a snout nosed blaster and from it came the slim line of smoke proclaiming that it had just been fired.

"They are still on his body", the youth told Menschlich, "I had just finished telling him I wasn't interested, would have given the Butterfly a bad name if word had gotten out".

"There vas no need to kill him"?Menschlich observed.

"He would have killed you, once he had raised his own gun", came the reply.

Menschlich went over to the charred smoking flesh, that was the remains of the dead carty. Without a thought, he searched the body and located the parcel, though stained with blood, it was otherwise undamaged.

"Danke. If you are hoping for some reward......."

"I'm not", the youth cut him short, "But do me a small favour though will you"?

"Unbedingt, erm absolutely".

"Get the Hades out of here before the constable's arrive, it will be easier to lie about the entire episode if there are no witnesses".

THREE

MENSCHLICH PROCEEDED WITH his journey heading for the tube station and caught one heading north. He had lost half a day and by the time it stopped at Acheron, he judged it the destination to take some rest and let his cells regenerate. The very first hotel he encountered in Acheron was the Hotel Doskonaly, run by Poles obviously. He went to the reception desk and booked a single room for the night.

The hotel was strangely old fashioned in both appearance and furnishing, but immaculately clean and with the usual facilities.

"Will you be wanting evening meal"? the young woman at the desk wished to know, he informed her that he did not. Going to the room allotted him by the girl, he was just about to lie down and go into sleep mode, when there was a knock on the door. How bizarre? No one could know of his presence in the town. Puzzled he opened it he observed silently by a young woman waiting without,

"Vhat can I do for you"? he asked.

"It's what I can do for you sir", she smiled, "I'm clean and disease free and my rates are very reasonable, what would you like"?

"Zhere is nothing I need", he told her puzzled.

""Really", she confidently pushed past him into the room, leaving an invisible trail of soft perfume in her wake,

"Are you going to offer me a drink first, there is a mini bar over in the corner".

"Who are you"? Menschlich wanted to know, "Und vhy have you come to zhis room"?

"I'm Szczesliwy Voleclimber, originally from Poland and I'm here to keep you company this evening. Among other things of course, that is up to you as long as it does not involve my suffering any pain".

"I am sorry dear dame, but I vas about to go to bed, I vill certainly let you have a drink and vhen you will leave ja"?

"Bed is where I'm the most fun honey", she told him with a smile.

"Aah" Menschlich finally understood, striding over to the small drinks cabinet, "You are a whore ja, vhat vill you have"?

Szczesliwy Voleclimber's mouth twisted in distaste and she told him, "I prefer the term comfort girl and I'll have a vodka, Earth, not that awful Martian filth".

Menschlich poured two vodkas and told her, "I have never been with a woman in zhat vay Fräulein Voleclimber".

An hour later Menschlich said to her, as she strived to catch her breath,

"Let us try another position"?

"No honey please, be a treasure, there's only so many orgasms a girl wants in one night, let me get some rest please"?

"I am just glad everything vorks alright", he told her.

"Honey, don't worry about that, everything works a real treat".

The instant she stopped talking, her breathing became deeper and she began to softly snore. Menschlich, a smile upon his face, went into sleep mode beside her.

When he reactivated hours later, she was gone and so was the shillin he had left her on the unit at the bed's side. He arose and took a shower, something that was rarely necessary, but his private parts were crusty and had a strange aroma to them. Dressing quickly, he left the hotel as smoothly as he could and returned to the tube station. Once aboard, he took the opportunity to look at his pad.

War had been declared by Germany against Poland over the mining rights on the newly acquired moon Callisto. The moon was rich in minerals and organic compounds and with the advent of cool fusion, a trip out to it, took only forty five hours. The Germans had been first to it, Poland second and both had made immediate claims of sole mining rights to the Earth Council of Planets. The E. C. P. had promptly decided that mining rights should be shared. The German's being confined mostly to the north, the Poles to the south. It was the worst possible decision they could have made.

Disputes began almost at once and after sixteen months of wrangling, a German mining bubble had exploded, the atmosphere being lost, killing the seven hundred and fifty workers that had been inside it. Despite the fact that it was highly probable that it had been merely an accident, Germany had immediately accused Poland of sabotage. Two days later war was the result. Menschlich read the bulletins with a curious sensation running through his circuits, one of ire. He felt annoyed by the Poles, not questioning the validity of Germany's claims in the slightest. He read on, two war fleets had left Frankfurt and Katowice the previous evening and the writer of the bulletin little doubted that once they reached their destinations, the future of Callisto would be war torn.

He had to concentrate upon matters more immediate however, for the tube was rapidly approaching the area of Dryas and the bubble city of Kalidonisto. The tube ground to a halt and Menschlich almost skipped off.

Finally!!!

He was in the destination town, in which he was to hand over the bonds. He exited the tube station hardly noticing the busy throng of the other commuters. Beyond were the inevitable arcades and he passed through, what now becoming a familiar site. The visages of light and coloured neon proclaimed a variety of wares and services. His only desire at that moment however, was to find Kalidonisto Estate number 91315 and to conclude the mission. Instead of taking a cart Menschlich chose to ride the moving walkways; slower, but with zero risk of being robbed again. Such was unlikely however, for the brown paper parcel was this time kept well out of sight, in his inside Velcro closing pocket.

The city was just like Erigone, being a spiders web of tubes, a series of inter-connected circular wheels, shunting in many places by spokes. It did not take him long to navigate through the spider's maze though, for he possessed eidetic memory and thusly never went down the same spoke nor ring twice. Thus after three quarters of an hour he was outside the door of the apposite apartment. Outside dusk had rapidly given way to darkness and the tubes were illuminated by elongated strings of light emitting diodes. It lent the tubes of Mars a forbidding quality that was almost macabre. Menschlich ignored such suggestion.

The door opened in answer to his knocking. In the jamb back-lit by lamps, was a slim, short figure of a man. Menschlich had not been told who to deliver the parcel to, merely given the address, so he said to the man,

"I haf zhe package".

"Package"? the diminutive occupant of apartment 91315 echoed, "I'm sorry I don't understand, should I know what you're talking about"? His face held innocent confusion, while the eery light of the planet glinted off the perspiration on his bald pate.

"I am from Fräulein Esterzoke Comuszepse", Menschlich went on to explain, "Are you not expecting me"?

Before the little man could answer, a woman's voice behind him asked,

"Who is it Chododit, what do they want"?

The man turned and his tone became suddenly much more obsequious, "A German gentleman, my love, says he has a package for this address, from a .....", he turned back to the android, "Who did you say had sent you sir"?

Before the android could respond, the woman did so on his behalf,

"It's alright Chododit, I know all about it", her voice commanded, "Please show him in"?

Chododit looked surprised but stood promptly to one side, to allow Menschlich entrance. The android stepped into a furnished apartment. Upon a deep couch of oxblood pseudo-leather an attractive woman was hastily tapping an ipad. At his appearance, she glanced up at Menschlich and asked,

"You've been sent by Esterzoke Comuszepse haven't you"?

Menschlich nodded not sure if he liked the situation, the woman seeing his mien rose and asked,

"Excuse my manners and the confusion, I am Blízkosi Stromu, my husband knows nothing of my arrangement with miss Comuszepse. Will you have a drink or do you have to be going".

As they shook hands Menschlich noticed the expensive rings on her fingers and the gold bracelet about her wrist. Yet her husband did not look like he could commend such a salary to be affording such ostentation. Unable to decide what she would have preferred him to do, he relied,

"Zhat is gracious of you Fräulein, vhat do you have to offer me"?

He saw then that she would have preferred him to leave, but she told him, "Martian rum, brandy, vodka or whiskey, plus Martian tea or coffee".

"Surely we can do better than that my dear"? Chododit interjected, having closed the door with the maximum of care. He rounded the android so as to address him directly,

"We have Earth rum or vodka too, Herr Menschlich".

The android decided he did not like the woman, but her husband had attempted to use a German address to put him at his ease, so he smiled to him and accepted a glass of vodka; from Earth.

Blízkosi Stromu poured the drink and pressed it into Menschlich's hand, as her husband, suddenly curious asked,

"Tell me have you travelled far Herr Menschlich".

"Please don't bother our guest, Chododit, he looks tired and would probably prefer to drink the vodka and be on his way".

Before Menschlich could reply that such was not, in fact, the case, the door burst open and a tall heavily bearded man wearing a black hat and black mask over his eyes, rushed unannounced into the apartment! In a thin nasal bark he snapped,

"No one move, or I'll use this gun".

His voice was highly pitched, probably with nervous fear and Menschlich did not doubt that the threat was very real indeed, yet he could not reach his own weapon, before he thought the intruder would fire. So, instead, he remained motionless and let the tableau play itself for the moment.

"We have few valuables", Chododit responded, obviously aware that his wife probably wore most of them, "Take what you wish but please don't harm anyone".

By way of answer the tall straight figure strode toward the short husband and clubbed him to the floor with the weapon. Menschlich was curiously watching to see his wife's reaction, as he had suspected she seemed unmoved by it. The only fear in her eyes was for herself it appeared.

The masked intruder waved the weapon in Menschlich's direction and the android was doubly curious, he had never seen the like of such a hand gun before. Yet his knowledge and training in the use of almost every possible one available on Mars, was extensive.

"Okay pal", whined the intruder, "Hand over the package".

"Package? Vhat is zhis about package"? Menschlich lied.

"Right you want to do it the hard way do you", the would be thief snapped and promptly pulled the trigger on the unusually configured gun.

FOUR

WHEN MENSCHLICH BEGAN to feel his circuits return to something approaching normal function once more, he realised the weapon had been an E. M. Pulse Pistol. They were rare indeed and obviously something the android could never employ himself. The electro-magnetic wave had knocked out his circuits for an indeterminate period. Fortunately the android's self diagnostic and self replicating circuits had effects repairs almost instantly and he rose slowly and with great care, to a sitting position.

Of Blízkosi Stromu there was no sign!

Her diminutive husband on the other hand was still sprawled on a rather nice Gambian rug, totally unconscious, a huge livid bruise starting to swell on his forehead. Menschlich rose, checked to make certain he was fully functional and then went in search of the kitchen. Returning moments later with a cloth dripping with cold water, he carefully applied it to Chododit Stromu's battered skull. The patient instantly opened his eyes,

"Lie still meine Herr", the android instructed, "I vill ping an ambula-cart".

"My wife", Stromu gasped, "Is she alright, where is she now"?

Calmly Menschlich told him the truth, "I haf no idea Herr Stromu, she vhas gone vhen I too regained consciousness, she may haf gone for help, or perhaps the assailant took her vith him".

Stromu tried to rise at this revelation, but fell back gasping in pain, "She's so beautiful, the blackguard will be sure to rape her, my poor poor Blízkosi, what are we to do? Are you uninjured yourself sir? What the devil was in that package that it should cause such a disaster"?

Menschlich felt like telling the battered little man that he thought rape unlikely, but instead he decided aloud,

"Ve haf to get you to a hospital. Forget zhe package, I never opened it to find out vhat it contained. Now please lie still vhile I ping for aid"?

By the time the ambula-cart arrived, Menschlich's circuits had resumed acceptable parameters. He discretely slipped away before the constabulary were to arrive and had no other course of action but to let Esterzoke Comuszepse know exactly what had happened at number 91315 Kalidonisto Estate. He did not have her email let alone her Skype so he had the unenviable task of getting it from his boss. It was only then that he realised his pad was gone. When he searched his pockets he discovered all his money was gone too, including that which the boss would require a hefty percentage of, for taking the assignment.

Some minutes later he found a cyber-cafe and got the proprietor to agree to one quick ping before he had to pay for access to the net. The Boss take not take the news well,

"Frenge! You failed a client and now you're asking me for credit to get back to Erigone, why in Hades do you want to go back if you frenged the whole scene up"?

The android would have liked to tell the boss just what he thought to his profane questions, but instead he merely replied,

"Because the assignment is not completed yet sir", Menschlich liked to remind the boss of the company slogan on just such occasions as these, 'Ve never quit until zhe job is done'!

"Do you even know what the assignment 'is' or would have been if you hadn't frenged up"?

"Not yet, nein", Menschlich admitted, "But I intend to find out"!

Finally after yet another burst of profane expletives, reluctantly extended him a loan on future assignments. The direct bank transfer was accomplished at once and the proprietor of the cyber-cafe paid enough for net use of thirty minutes. Menschlich used the thumb pad to get some shillin notes, then he pinged Esterzoke Comuszepse, on the Skype identity that the boss had reluctantly provided.

Her beautiful features swam into view knotted with concern, Menschlich went straight to the point.

"I failed Fräulein Comuszepse", he began, simply and directly, it was always the best way in such rare circumstances. "I got to zhe correct address und vas about to deliver zhe bonds, vhen a masked assailant burst in upon us und stole zhem".

"Bonds, Wahrheit"? she sounded shocked and disappointed in equal measure, "You opened the package, when I expressly asked you not to"?

"For all I knew it could haf contained somezhing illegal, harmful, or both, I had to, it vas zhe only responsible sing to do".

She suddenly sagged on the screen, "Well forget about the whole thing then Wahrheit, thank you for at least getting as far as you did".

"Vhat do you mean forget zhe whole sing, zhe bonds are gone, vhat vill you do"?

"I don't know, but I wont involve you anymore, please forget I ever did"?

"Zhis is not so easy for me", he observed, "Und not only zhat I sink I know some sings zhat I did not know before, I am on my vay back to you Fräulein Comuszepse".

She visibly brightened despite the dissatisfaction with the state of affairs, "And nothing I can do, can make you change your mind"?

"Nothing".

"Then I ask but one favour in the mean time"?

"Name it"?

"That when we meet you stop calling me Fräulein Comuszepse, I will be waiting for you, though what you can do to help me I don't know".

"Ve shall see about zhat", he suggested and cut the connection.

He was back in business. All he needed now was a weapon and then he could make the lengthy return journey to Erigone.

FIVE

THE FRONTAGE OF the store that sold various weapons was not lit up by neon, as was it's neighbour's either side. Rather it was a simple painted sign of Georgia fonted letters painted onto a brown field.

'Authorised weapon seller'

it read.

Menschlich went inside. As he entered the port to the shop itself a small siren proclaimed his arrival. Quick as a flash a stout C5 android appeared behind the strengthened glass counter. The walls of the store were of reinforced glass, behind which was a variety of weapons, both personal and some used military. The illumination in the cases was of low voltage, rendering a creepy atmosphere to the entire interior.

"Good morning sir, how can I be of assistance", the androids mechanical tones wished to know.

"Do you sell E. M. Pulse Pistols"? Menschlich asked simply and directly. He was talking to another machine there was no need to begin with superfluous pleasantries.

"Of course the finest currently available on the market sir".

"I vonder did you recently sell such a veapon to a tall bearded man vearing a black hat? If so I vould like a look at the receipt if you please"?

"Sir, I cannot............", the android began, but a five shillin note stopped him, it was whisked away with a speed that was not possible by a human.

The android began to tap the ipad before him and then twisted it around for Menschlich to scan, it was very bright in contrast to the dimly lit shop, the perpetrator of the robbery had given his name as one, Räubdieb Thewirs of Cebrenia. Menschlich doubted Thewirs had ever been anywhere near Cebrenia which lay to the east.

"I vould now like to buy a needle gun", he told the delighted android.

"Certainly sir which model would you like to see, we stock the V7, X12 and Needle Supreme; of course the latter has the added facility of loading with a greater variety of ammunition".

"I'll take zhe Supreme und a full pack of neuronic needles if you so please".

"Certainly sir, may I just point out that the neuronic needles are not always deadly sometimes the target survives, now the cardio-fatal needles on the other hand........"

"Zhe neuronic needles vill be fine, danke".

The transaction was made without the proprietor ever even suspecting it was serving one of it's own kind.

Though it was usually very bad news for an android to hurt or maim a human being, Menschlich felt much more comfortable with the gun in a brand new shoulder holster, beneath his frock coat. Thus emboldened he strode to the tube station and boarded one to Biblis F. The Lucus line would not be open for several hours and Menschlich felt a growing urgency within him. The longer he was away from Esterzoke Comuszepse, the more he feared events would unravel that were beyond his control. He had a suspicion of what was happening. Even a suspicion that he knew who was behind it all! However, he could not test his theories until back in Erigone!

So he took his seat on the Biblis F tube and tried to relax. It was not easy, try as he might to close down his circuits, they kept turning themselves back on. Agitation and frustration were relatively new experiences for the android and he did not enjoy the experience of either. The minutes ticked by, he did not even need to check any form of chronometer, his internal clock functioned even if he tried a full shut down. It was not something he would have done in a public place at any rate. So he waited while the minutes dragged into hours and the journey passed.

At Biblis F. he transferred to a tube bound for Erigone, having to endure the entire procedure yet again. The beauty of time was that it never went backwards however and sure enough the tube finally crawled into Erigone as the brilliant star that was Mars' sun was cresting the horizon. The view beyond the transparent tube walls was magnificent in it's rubescent splendour. The brown hills of the planet nestling beneath the faintly pink sky. Menschlich was in no mood to enjoy the visual feast however, he was on a mission and hoping it was nearing it's conclusion. A conclusion that would be to his design and liking.

He ran from the station, his progress causing many to turn their heads and gaze in surprise, but he did not care. He ran up the escalators, ran along the moving walkways and finally reached Erigone Estate number 41218 without breaking sweat nor losing his breath, for he did neither.

The tall blonde Withers, his posture as straight as ever, answered the door.

"Yes"? he asked as though he had never seen Menschlich before.

"Get out of Zhe vay", the android snapped and literally pushed past the butler. Behind him he heard a gasp of outrage, but before anything could be said Esterzoke Comuszepse entered the room and smiled grimly,

"It's alright Withers, Herr Menschlich is here by invitation. That will be all thank you".

The butler left without a word, but his scowl at Menschlich spoke more than several sentences.

"Drink Wahrheit"? the beautiful client asked.

"Nein, I do not vant a drink Esterzoke! I vant zhe truth"?

"Truth", she echoed, shocked at the anger in his voice, "What truth are you talking about"?

"Zhe true reason vhy you are being blackmailed for Orang-U-Can bonds by Blízkosi Stromu".

"Blackmailed"! Comuszepse tried to laugh, but the exclamation had a hard edge to it, "Where did you get that outrageous notion"?

In answer Menschlich strode across the room and grabbed her shoulders in a vice like grip, she tried to squirm free, but had not reckoned with his immense strength,

"You're hurting me"! she complained and he loosened his hold on her, but not enough as to allow her to get free.

"Do you vant my help und sink before you answer, because if you say no, I vill be out of zhat door und you vill never see me again"?

She suddenly sagged, her eyes grew wet and as tears ran in saline rivulets through her make up. Then, in a small voice the beautiful Esterzoke Comuszepse admitted,

"Hades yes, I do want your help Wahrheit".

"Right zhen sit und tell me vhat has happened, start at zhe beginning".

SIX

"IT WAS AT the party", she began, "A party held by the Stromu's. Not in their apartment of course, no it was too big for that, too grand. They hired the ruddy Opera house at Castorius L can you believe that? Well any way, I did not really want to go, I have not been out much since my husband died..........".

"Your husband being Drorb Makers-Guild"?

"Why yes! How did you know that? Oh, the bonds, of course. I never took my husbands name, even when we were married, it sounded, I don't know, sort of like a pseudonym. Anyway it was Withers strangely enough, who finally talked me into going. He told me it would get me out of the apartment and maybe cheer me up a little. In all truth I had missed Drorb fearfully and thought perhaps he might be right. So I went. The first time I met Blízkosi she pressed a glass into my hands and after she had drifted off I took a sip. It was Lichen Rum".

"Martian lichen".

Esterzoke nodded, "I'm afraid so, the very same lichen that Snufz is made from. I'd heard it had hardly the same effects when fermented with yeast and molasses and made into alcohol and of course I wanted to be one of the party so I took a few careful sips and began mixing with the crowd. The effects took me suddenly and all I got was a very warm glow and tremendous feeling of well being. So when Blízkosi appeared again and offered me a 1in2 I took it and let her light it for me".

"You accepted a 1in2"? Menschlich was shocked, "You do know vhy the cigarettes are called zhat"?

"Well yes. Half of the cigarette is tobacco and the other half is Snufz; but I was having a good time, I felt relaxed and happy and didn't think one cigarette would do anything to me".

"But it did, did it not"?

"Well yes, I was half way down it when the room began to melt and I tripped out, that's the phrase isn't it"?

"Ja zhat's zhe phrase".

"The rest seemed like some sort of crazy dream. I need another drink".

She interrupted her narrative to go to the cabinet and pour herself a healthy quantity of Earth Rum,

"Do you want one"?

The android shook his head.

He waited patiently while she got herself comfortable again and finally went on,

"I don't remember much of what happened Wahrheit, not while I was under the effects of the 1in2 anyway. After though, after I shall never forget, not as long as I live".

She paused and took a good swallow of her drink, then went on, emboldened by the liquor,

"I came too on a bed, I was naked and so was he, we were both covered in blood".

"He? To whom are you referring"?

"I never knew his name, he was one of the waiters. I remember noticing him whilst I was still only drinking the Lichen Rum, he was sort of Spanish looking and very handsome. He saw me looking at him and smiled and then, nothing, nothing until I awoke covered in his blood"!

Unmoved Menschlich asked, "Und of course the veapon vhas still in your hand"?

"Why yes, a carving knife, from one of the serving trays in the ball room"?!

"Und it vhas Blízkosi Stromu who found you soon after you regained consciousness"?

"Yes she offered to dispose of the body while I went for a shower. She said the waiter was of no account and wouldn't be missed and that I was an idiot if I went to the Constabulary".

"A point of view upon vhich you both concurred"?

"Wahrheit I was too confused to argue with her, I had no idea what had happened, I only had her supposed account of events and was in no position to argue".

"Vhat vas her account"?

Esterzoke blushed before admitting, "We had gone in the bedroom for sex and when Blízkosi found us she assumed that afterward, we had argued when he had demanded payment for his, ah services".

"Vhen not under zhe influence of 1in2 you vould not have had sex with him"?

"Of course not. Even if I 'had', I would have paid rather than stabbing him".

"So you returned to your apartment here und some time later you received a ping from Blízkosi Stromu".

Esterzoke nodded, "She told me she would keep silent about the murder, if I sent her bonds from Drorb's company". She seemed to sag then and Menschlich instructed her,

"Do as I say und this vill all go away".

"But......."

"Vill you trust me"?

"Yes of course, yes I do Wahrheit, but what can be done"?

"Firstly you must send Vithers on an errand. One zhat vill take him an hour to perform, can you do zhat"?

"Yes, but......".

"Zhen do so; now"!

Menschlich seated himself and waited in the background, while Esterzoke Comuszepse did just as he had directed. He overheard her send him on a fictitious errand. One that ensured he would be missing from the apartment for at least an hour. Once the butler was out of the way Menschlich told the beautiful woman of his suspicions,

"I believe no von is dead Esterzoke. Zherfore you need fear no von of blackmail. Zhe so called murder was set up und I can tell you by whom".

"Who"? she was too puzzled to contradict him at that moment.

"By none other than he whom you just sent upon an errand by your absent butler. Vithers, I am guessing is having an illicit affair vith none other than Blízkosi Stromu. Together zhey fabricated the murder so as to blackmail you for bonds from your late husbands company. The motive for zhis deceit was von of zhe oldest of zhem all, money".

"Do you have any proof to back up your suspicions Wahrheit"? Comuszepse finally found her voice.

"Not yet, but if I am right I vill have shortly. Vhat I do have is some deductions".

"Very well I'm listening, go on"?

"I vas ambushed in Kalidonisto. Ambushed by an assailant who knew the exact details regarding zhe package and it's contents. Knew it vas I who vas conveying it and even vhen I vould arrive at zhe Stromu's apartment. Tell me Esterzoke how many knew of my mission? Vhat I carried"?

"Why just you and I and........".

"Und Vithers who could easily have heard your instructions to me before I left here on zhe way to my journey. Vhen I got to zhe other end Blízkosi Stromu instructed her husband to let me in because she knew my reason for being zhere. She zhen promptly disappeared, leaving her injured husband und me who she thought dead. Remind me who's party vas it"?

"Why it was hers, as I've just told you"?

"Und who urged you to attend the party"?

Realisation dawned on Esterzoke's features then, "Withers, he thought it would get me out of myself".

"Zhe assailant who attacked me vas tall und spoke vith a light timbre, he vore a hat und a thick beard. Tell me Esterzoke, vhere has Vithers been these last few days"?

"He's just returned from a visit to an aged aunt who was ill, she lives in a northern bubble. Well that was what he said. I had no reason to doubt it, but now....".

"Und my final bit of evidence is zhis. Who recommended the use of my agency to take the money to herrin Stromu"?

"Well Withers advised me because......".

"Because he knew he could incapacitate an android with an E. M. Pulse Pistol. The electro-magnetic wave could knock out its circuits for an indeterminate period, but von long enough to be away vith zhe bonds and zhen back here even if it chose to return to you".

"I don't understand that, what android are you talking about........"?

Realisation then crossed her beautiful countenance, "Wahrheit! you're an.........".

"Ja herrin Comuszepse, I am Professor Herr Baumeister's greatest creation to date. Zhe E23, outwardly identical to a flesh und blood man. I can do anything a man can do, but in most cases better, for I am stronger, faster and need less energy".

"You tricked me, you let me think you was a man"!

Amazingly she was angry with him.

"Not actually true", he observed, "At nein time did you ask me if I vas human".

"But I flirted with you, I practically offered......".

"Rest assured I am functional in every way Esterzoke, I have been programmed with a variety of techniques.....".

"I'm not sure I want to know", she responded coldly.

"Vell zhen back to business. I must prove my theories once and for all und I believe I can".

"How? What if Withers simply denies everything"?

"I do not believe he has had zhe time to hide zhe missing bonds in a different location to zhis one, vith your permission I vould like to search his quarters".

A smile returned to her face then, "With one proviso"?

"Vhich is"?

"That I assist you, it could be fun mister android".

It seemed her anger had faded quickly, no doubt partly due to the relief she felt at not being a murderer

"Lead on zhen dear lady".

The apartment was quite spacious and the unlikely duo spend a goodly part of the allotted time searching drawers, cupboards and then the less accessible places such as beneath items, where a package could be strapped with duct. After forty five minutes Esterzoke cried in exasperation,

"It's no good Wahrheit, though I agree with your deductions, the bonds aren't here and that means we have no proof against Withers".

"I still believe he vould have kept zhem close by", Menschlich persisted. "I have not given up hope of finding zhen just yet".

"But we have searched everywhere", the beautiful woman objected flopping into a chair, "Where else is there to look".

"If zhey are not 'in' zhe room, zhen perhaps it is zhe room itself vhich is concealing zhem"?

"I don't understand".

Menschlich looked carefully at the walls of the apartment. As with all walls in the Mars bubbles all over the red planet, they were slightly curved. As with all such walls they were held together with tiny metal rivets. For these were not the outer walls of the bubble, merely those residing inside the much stronger skin of the airtight construction.

Unknown to the woman, the android scanned the walls with electronic receptors that were infinitely more sensitive than human eyes. Within seconds his receptors had detected two such studs that had slightly flattened circumferences. Going over to them he easily removed them, with a fingernail that was tougher than steel. He employed it like a screwdriver once he had cut a countersink into them. A section of the wall came away, a sloping panel of plexi-plas. On the floor behind the panel was a small brown paper parcel.

Gasping in delighted astonishment Esterzoke picked it up and looked inside.

"You've done it Wahrheit, these are the bonds, obviously Withers is the one who is steeling from me what ever the other details".

"I am reasonably confident zhat zhe other details are correct", Menschlich responded, "I sink it is time to ping zhe local constabulary. Vith luck zhey vill arrive at roughly zhe same time as Vithers".

"Will it will mean telling them about the party"?

"Ja it vill, but you must trust me Esterzoke, no one is dead, you vill see".

"Alright Wahrheit, I will trust you", she agreed and hurried to make the net connection that would bring the constables to her apartment.

They had barely had the time to pour and drink a vodka (Earth), than the door chimed. Comuszepse answered it and ushered in two constables, one man and one woman.

"Constable Claudius Maximálistor", the man introduced himself, "And this is Constable Megwinda Meggins. You have a serious crime to report and someone to hand over to us according to your net-vid, miss ah Comuszepse".

"Please come in officers"? Comuszepse asked them, "And allow me to introduce Wahrheit Menschlich, who can explain the details much clearer than I. Will you sit down"?

The officers took seats and carefully listened to Menschlich account of events, when he was finished

Meggins noted,

"But there does not appear to be any sign of this Withers does there"?

"No", Maximálistor chuckled, "Withers does not appear to be 'with' us'"!

Smiling politely Menschlich offered, "He must have determined zhat ve vere onto him vhen Fräulein Comuszepse sent him out on an errand shortly after my arrival here".

"Well at the least, he's guilty of theft", Maximálistor noted, "Probably blackmail too. Right, we'll put out an urgent search for him and we'll investigate the events at Blízkosi Stromu's party. I tend to concur with your hypothesis Herr Menschlich, the fact that you was expected at Kalidonisto all points to Withers. Okay that's it for now and one more thing Miss Comuszepse....".

"Yes constable"?

"Steer clear of Snufz in the future and that includes 1in2 as well".

"Have no fear constable, I will never be tempted ever again".

The two representatives of the law on Mars left the two of them once more alone.

"Vell", Menschlich said rising to his feet, "Zhat seems to be it Esterzoke".

"You're forgetting something", she caught up with him and hung her arms around his neck.

"Und vhat vould zhat be"? he smiled.

"I promised to be very very grateful and I've never been with an android before"!

ARE YOU A PATRIOT?

ONE

WHEN OSOBA WALKED into the Boss's office he was not prepared for two things. He did not know the Boss (Plug) would not be alone and he did not expect the dialogue that his commander began. Peering through the dark smoke of too many med-cig's Plug asked him,

"Are you a patriot Osoba, are you willing to undertake a dangerous mission to make fast the security of your country".

The other man, an aged looking individual who actually maintained facial hair and long wispy hair on his wrinkled pate had a look of the intellectual about him. He added,

"That is the question you must be prepared to answer in the affirmative, if we are to proceed and consider you our man".

"Let me introduce you to Professor Król", Plug offered. "He would be going with you, if you decide to accept the mission.

Osoba turned up his vision to more easily discern Król through the smoke and dim illumination. The fact that the walls were dark stained wood did not make matters any easier. They had began life as shiny mahogany, now years of nicotine had dulled their sheen and darkened their hue.

The professor looked neither strong enough, nor brave enough for the remit, in Osoba's judgment. His rheumy eyes contained a steely glint within them that belied all other visual evidence however. Perhaps he was one of those aged soldiers that never knew when to quit. Outside the bubble that the office was enclosed in, the sun sank beneath the horizon and Osoba heard the dull sigh of the heating fans as the elements began to glow a rich magenta.

Osoba did not like the position Plug had suddenly placed him in. His superior should have conducted this initial offer of mission in private. He obviously had reasoned that Król's presence would be an extra bargaining tool. When the pay was good and Osoba was a diligent employee, such manoeuvring was totally superfluous in his opinion. He thought that the two of them knew each other better than his supervisor obviously judged.

Yet he did not feel intimidated in the slightest. The agency would never send anyone out on an assignment that they had not the heart for.

"May I ask where this mission is going to take place sir"? Osoba enquired. He already had his suspicions regarding the answer.

"I don't see why not, even if you have the knowledge and don't choose to go, you have the security clearance to keep it to yourself", noted the boss.

"It's on Callisto. As you'll already be aware, the German's have declared war on our miners there, not to mention our government on Earth. Till now we've steered clear of the dispute, here on Mars, but it's time for some of our operatives to lend our brave miners a hand".

Strictly speaking Osoba, who was an advanced android, was not Polish. He was the creation of Professor Beltraynial Malinowscy; who was though. Plug, who was a Pole himself, always referred to the agent as being one of his own race.

"What's the job then, sir"? Osoba (who's name meant Person in Polish) tried.

"We can't tell you that unless you agree to be a part of it", Plug responded just as expected. Osoba wondered if Plug had told Król that the agent that may be going with him, would not be human. The Professor continued to scrutinise him with those glinting flint-like eyes. Finally Osoba nodded,

"Alright, I will do the best job I can as usual sir".

"Excellent", Król actually clapped his hands. "Now I can tell you that I've been on Callisto before Pan Osoba, that I will be your guide once we get there".

"In what capacity Professor"?

"Why as Professor of Geomorphology", Król told him.

"And in my field of speciality we will reap havoc on the cursed Germans. You will pose as my nephew, that will be your cover. While your actual mission will be to plant enough explosives beneath certain bulkheads at the head of mines on the moon, bulkheads where the Germans are mining, so as to completely wreck their operations and thus make the continuation of hostilities meaningless".

"So I plant some bombs at the site of German mines. Why do I need you Professor".

"What do you know about the evolution of topographic and bathymetric features created by physical, chemical or biological processes operating at or below the surface of Callisto"? Came the question by way of an answer.

"Right", Osoba agreed, "The actual positioning of the explosives is crucial so you're in the team. I expect part of my remit is to protect you too, is it"?

"Yes", Król beamed, "And you have one other vital talent that I do not possess according to Plug here".

"That being"?

"That in addition to Polish, you speak excellent and unaccented German".

Osoba could have added that he spoke twenty different Earth languages, not one with any hint of an accent to he, who's mother tongue it was. He was yet to learn whether the old man knew he was a construct though. Then in the Professor's next question, he had his answer,

"So I am to be Uncle Bede from now on, agent, what pray is your first name"?

Plug gave him a glare that told him not to reveal his true nature, so Osoba had to think quickly, for androids only ever had one name,

"It's Izydor".

"Excellent", Król enthused, "And what Uncle would not shorten it to Nephew Izzy"?

"What uncle indeed", Osoba observed sardonically.

"I suggest you take a week before leaving", Plug ordered.

"The first mining vessel from here to Callisto doesn't leave till then anyway. It will give you a chance to teach the Professor a few basic skills in self defence and weapon use, just to be on the safe side".

Osoba nodded, "I have a farewell to make too Boss, just in case".

"Which will you do first then Izzy"? the Professor wanted to know.

"Some basic training for you I think"", Osoba reasoned.

"Then while I see to the personal matter, you get to allow your sore muscles to recover. Please get your effects together and then come with me, as of now you are a member of the training barracks here".

"I have seen no barracks", the older man remarked as the duo left Plug's office together following a quick farewell.

"That is because they are beneath the lowest level", Osoba explained "Sub-Martian to be exact".

TWO

F IVE DAYS LATER Osoba was alone, travelling from Dryas, southerly to Caralis F, where certain secret laboratories resided. He reflected upon how well Król had done for a man of his advanced years. He had proved a crack shot with a hand weapon, not quite so good with anything heavier and when it came to unarmed combat, just about average, which was in itself, remarkable. Where he had truly excelled however was in the construction of explosives from the most innocuous of materials, he was after all, a man who had lived by the power of his intellect.

The tube ground to a hissing halt and Osoba jumped from it onto the thick pelxi-plas platform. From there it was but a short walk to a certain apartment; beneath which was his destination. He was on his way to see his kindly aging creator and friend, Professor Beltraynial Malinowscy. He halted at the door to the apartment, having been oblivious to his surroundings, his mind was focused solely on his visit and beyond, the mission to Callisto.

It was said that the sun would look like an amazingly bright star from the mines surface. A circle one fifth the size of the moon as seen from Earth. Yet still bright enough to create night and day, day being a landscape that looked to be in dusk. Of course all of this meant little to Osoba. He who had been created on Mars and never left it before. He was in fact, a Martian-Pole. Callisto /kʔ'lʔstoʔ/ (Jupiter IV) was the second-largest moon of Jupiter, after Ganymede. It was the third-largest moon in the Solar System. The length of it's day, simultaneously its orbital period, was approximately 16.7 Earth days and thus the night is logically of the same duration.

The miners who endured such bizarre conditions were burrowing into the moon's surface for magnesium and iron-bearing hydrated silicates; carbon dioxide, sulphur dioxide, and possibly ammonia and various organic compounds which were by products. A salty ocean one hundred and fifty to two hundred kilometres deep, lay beneath the crust, leading physicists and biologists to theorise upon the nature of possible life, however none had as yet been discovered by any of the mining teams though.

Small ponds of pure water ice with an albedo as high as eighty percent were found on the surface of Callisto, surrounded by much darker materials. The bright patches of land were discovered to be predominately located on elevated surface features: crater rims, scarps, ridges and knobs. They were coated by thin water frost deposits. Darker land areas lay in the lowland surroundings and mantling bright features had proved to be smooth. They formed patches up to five kilometres across within the crater floors and in the inter-crater depressions.

This was mainly where mining had commenced. The advantages of the base on Callisto were low radiation (due to its distance from Jupiter) and geological stability. Such a base was promised to facilitate remote exploration, possibly beyond the solar system in the future. The advantage of working on the moon was it's gravity, which was only an eighth of the Earth's. Of course Osoba was used to Martian gravity which was two thirds of that on Earth, so he would feel less benefit than a native of the solar system's planet of origin.

The door opened and the android saw the kindly features of Malinowscy,

"Osoba! Come in, come in", the professor enthused. "It's an unexpected pleasure to see you, are you travelling and thought you would drop in"?

"No Professor, I came to see you specifically".

"Can I offer you any protein, or lubrication"?

"Thank you, no, I currently need neither. I would like to go down to the laboratory though, see the place again"?

"That is no problem my dear Osoba, come down this very minute"?

The creator of the construct lead the way to a facsimile wall and lightly pressing three pressure pads that were flush to it's surface, caused it to silently slide into the right hand side panelling. It moved easily on servos that were a marvel of engineering in themselves. Down steps the duo trod, the passage lit by faint amber illumination, L.E.D.'s of very low power, just sufficient to the task. They culminated in a cave-like sub-Martian laboratory lined on every centimetre of wall space by electronic equipment. Malinowscy seated himself at a bench, upon a high stool and asked his creation,

"I get the sense that this may be your final visit to the place where you were 'born'. Something it troubling you isn't it"?

With considerable care and accuracy Osoba told the professor about the mission, confidently knowing the knowledge of it would never leave the lab.

"It does sound fraught with danger", Malinowscy agreed when the android was done, "So you came to see the 'old man' thinking it might be the last time. I am moved Osoba. I may be able to help somewhat obliquely too".

"Oh"! his creation began, "How is that Professor"?

"With a few little items I have been working on down here". There was a twinkle in the grey haired man's eyes,

"Some recently, some that have lain in a cupboard for some time, ever since the day I finally perfected them".

Osoba was naturally greatly intrigued, "What sort of items Professor"?

In answer, the little man jumped down from the stool and began to rummage around in a cupboard, which had lain concealed behind a steel sliding door.

Finally, with a grunt of satisfaction, he located what he was searching for and held it up for Osoba to see.

"It's a pen Professor", the android remarked doing his best to conceal any tinge of disappointment in the tone of his voice.

Malinowscy shook his head, causing a lock of grey hair to fall over his eyes, brushing it away absently with a hand he said,

"It writes like a pen, Osoba. Indeed it functions like a pen. Until that is, one desires to use it's other action. It then can be used as a short range needle gun"!

"Neuronic"?

Malinowscy nodded.

"Then I would gratefully ask you to show me how to use it Professor? Such a device may indeed be of some help in a tight situation. Without wishing to sound overly dramatic it could conceivably be used in a life threatening scenario".

"My feelings exactly Osoba. Then we were always bound to agree though weren't we, for it was I who programmed your electro-brain"?

The old man proceeded to quickly show the android the function of the little weapon. He had only the need to do so once for Osoba had eidetic memory. Then presented it to his artificial protege. After that initial reception he found a second item, that would be of equal aid to someone slipping into enemy territory. Two hours later, after they had caught up on what they had been doing since they had parted, the android left the professor, wearing different clothing to that which he had entered in, he made his farewell and left Caralis F for what, he hoped, would not be the last time.

On the return tube the sun rose up into the thin air of the pink sky, it was smaller than any Earthman would be familiar with, but fiercely bright and bringing with it a dramatic shift in temperature. The ultra violet filters of the polarized sides of the tube promptly cut in, to save any danger to the passengers. Osoba gazed at the beautifully ruddy landscape littered with large and small boulders, red with rust and wished he had not agreed to the assignment. He did not relish an off world task, especially one on a grim and distant place that was the moon Callisto.

Plug had been right however, he was a patriot and even if he was not, Malinowscy was. The professor had said he must go, must save the lives of Polish miners. So that was that. He rendezvoused with Król who had packed two bags, one for each of them.

"They contain only the sort of things Polish miners would have on their trip", the professor explained to him.

"Oh, how will we be able to blow up the German mines then"?

"We will be staying with other a Polish family of miners", Król smiled, "What do you think they use to open up new seams"?

"And you know some of them enough to enlist their aid"?

"I know enough", the professor assured, "The family we will be staying with will be able to put us in touch with the right individuals who can supply us with all we need. Now get out of those clothes and into these".

"I'll change everything but the jacket", Osoba agreed, "That was from a dear friend and he *is* Polish".

Król examined the jacket with a keen gaze. Then after an instant, seemed to arrive at his decision before declaring,

"It looks Polish enough, very well wear it, but the rest of your stuff stays here. Now then when does the rocket leave"?

"Tomorrow, but not from here".

"Not from here"?

"There are no rockets going sun outward from Dryas Professor, you didn't automatically assume there was did you"?

"I now realise I had not given the matter much thought".

"We need to get a tube to Hesperus, over to the east, do not worry, we will make it in time".

"This rocket from Hesperus", Król asked, "Where does it fly to, on Callisto"?

"There are only two rocket bases on the entire moon at present Professor", Osoba told him having gleaned the information form his memory banks,

"One is at Numi-Torum in the south and the northern one, at Geirvimul Catena".

"Are you going to keep me in suspense"? Król chuckled

"We are going to Geirvimul Catena Professor. Where are your friends"?

"Well I suppose you have been doing your reading", Król admitted. The north is mainly German, the South Polish, so when we get to Callisto we will need to also travel initially to Pekko, which according to you is in German territory"?

"The border does not exactly run straight through the equator Professor", Osoba smiled, "I can see why it is a good place to be situated however".

"Your German will prove invaluable", Król noted, "I will have to be mute following a stroke, when we go through German rocket control I think. Just remember, I am Uncle Bede then".

"I will not make a mistake", the android promised, hoping his human co-conspirator would be equally faultless. The strange duo took a moving walkway to the tube station and after a thirty minute wait managed to get aboard one that luck would have it was going directly to Hesperus. The journey would take two hours in total calling at Simoentis S, Ascanius, Scamander, Scamandri S and finally Atalantes D, before arriving eventually at Hesperus. The professor took out an i-pad and began to read, while Osoba decided to get some rest and put himself in sleep mode.

After less than the allotted time Król suddenly woke the android,

"What is it Uncle"? he asked the professor, as he checked his internal chronometer at the same instant. It had been only just over an hour, thus they would be somewhere between Ascanius and Scamander.

Król nodded forward and Osoba saw three youths standing in the single isle of the tube, rather than remaining seated,

"Trouble", he told the android,

"They got on at Ascanius. They've been working their way down this segment, I think they are demanding *donations* from the other passengers".

"Well we are not the Constabulary", Osoba noted, "Put in a call and constables will get on at the next stop and sort the matter out".

"Oh I think that's already been done", Król agreed, "What I mean is, they will reach us, before the tube reaches Scamander".

"I see", Osoba mused, "Are you ready then"?

"Ready"?

"To refuse to give in to their demands. You take the one with bleached hair, I'll take care of the other two".

"They might have weapons"? Król objected.

"Weapons, yes, you mean like the Germans on Callisto"?

Król shrugged, "Point taken, very well, I'll do the best I can".

They waited. Carefully checking their own weapons as discretely as they could. Two seats in front of them were empty, so the trio were quite suddenly approaching.

Reasoning that attack was the best form of defence, Osoba, who was seated next to the walkway, suddenly dived from his seat. His needle gun was in his hand in the same instant. He felt Król at his shoulder. The foremost and largest of the youths, who was just ahead of the other two managed to exclaim,

"What the...."!

Osoba shot him. The youth fell back against his fellows, body contorted in pain that racked his body from head to toe.

The remaining duo acted with admirable swiftness, they parted and allowed their leader to fall behind them and then darted forward. Both had knives in their hands. Osoba's other target kicked out with violent haste and sent the android's gun spinning from his grip. In that same instant Król fired at the bottle blonde. His reaction was almost exactly the same as his leader's. The remaining youth lunged at Osoba's chest with the knife. With a speed, of which, a human was not capable, Osoba caught the youth's wrist and twisted sharply. He was rewarded by the sound of bones snapping and a scream of pain from his erstwhile attacker. The knife fell from useless fingers and then Król shot him too.

The segment of the tube was suddenly alive with the sound of applause.

"Come and get what they have taken from you", Osoba requested of them loudly,

"Do not worry for your safety, they will be incapacitated for some considerable time".

A fat sweating man was first, he waddled up to the fallen youths giving one a stout kick for good measure.

"The frenger took all my money", he grunted, bending over the blonde and going hastily through his pockets.

"Take only what they took from you", Osoba warned, "If there is a short fall for anyone, my Uncle will be questioning each of you, is that understood"?

It was, the passengers were all too willing to comply.

When the tube finally coasted to a halt at Scamander, three uniformed constables jumped aboard. It did not pull out of the station, as it would have usually. The constables were all dressed in royal blue, the colour of Mars Constabulary.

"Constabulary", one of them yelled superfluously, "What happened here"?

The fat man seemed to have elected himself spokesmen for the entire segment. He began his narration with considerable animation, ending,

".....and these two were magnificent, inspector. Took the frenger's down like lightning, before they could menace or rob the rest of the segment".

The sergeant, for such was his rank, not inspector, eyed Osoba and Król,

"Hmm. It is not normally advisable for citizens to take matters into their own hands, but it would seem you saved 'us' the bother of controlling them, who are you gentlemen"?

"Professor Bede Król of Uniwersytet Katowice", the old man began, "And this is my nephew Izzy".

"I'm assuming you want to press charges"? the sergeant noted their names into his pad.

"I'm afraid we can't sergeant", Król explained, "We're on our way off-world and might be gone some time".

"I'll press charges", the fat man blurted, "I'm Basidore Bloameinpudge, I'm in plexi-glass; my card".

"We'll need additional witnesses", the sergeant said loud enough for the rest of the segment to hear.

There were no shortage of volunteers; crime was a rarity, a sensation, on Mars.

The sergeant and his two men recorded various names and addresses into their mini-pads and then tie-wrapped the still insensible youths.

"Will we still make the rocket"? Król asked Osoba. The android made a quick calculation,

"It will be tight Uncle, but I think we will if we rush once at Hesperus".

The nearest of the constables had overheard their conversation and he told the duo, with a smile on his face,

"I'll ping ahead to the rocket port gentlemen, it'll wait for you if you're late, not that much trouble for the heroes of Scamander".

It was a good omen and the two of them both settled down to a nap, when the tube had finally resumed it's journey.

THREE

"YOU HAVE FLOWN before"? Król asked Osoba, as the duo took their seats. All around them was utter chaos. Some of the miners had exceeded their weight allowance and a steward was demanding they remove certain things from their only flight bag. He repeatedly instructed them that if the bag would not fit in the box beneath their seat, then it was too large or too bulky. There were exclamations and frequent curses in both Polish and Standard.

"I have not", the android confessed, "Is this usual at the beginning of a journey"?

Król nodded, "Weight is the critical factor in determining both duration and manoeuvrability of the rocket. If there is too much weight on board, the flight could ultimately crash into Callisto, or miss it altogether and go onward into space and eventual asphyxiation.

"Why do they take such a risk for an extra shirt or some dubious food stuff"?

"There are no arcades where we are going, all supplies are rationed, some of these miners are doing a three year contract, wouldn't you try to take a few extras"?

"No. I would not".

They waited.

It seemed their journey was to be delayed at every turn. After eighty minutes, the head steward was finally satisfied and the airlock was sealed. A voice came over the intercom,

"This is Captain Grorutandoss, I am going to be your pilot for flight Ca2619 to Geirvimul Catena rocket port. I would like to thank you for taking the flight with Sledzic Linie Rozluzniajace today and the stewards and cabin crew wish you all a comfortable journey.

Please remain strapped into your seating pads at all times as this vessel does not have gravitational control. We should be at our destination in forty five hours, so you will need to use the vacuum toilet facilities located next to your seat. Instructions for use are in the basket, set into the seat in front of you. The stewards will also offer you freeze packed Dodo-prot a selection of non alcoholic beverages and med-cig's as they are wearing magnetic boots.

At no time should you attempt to join them, you 'must' remain strapped in. Failure to do so will incur an instant fine of one hundred universal shillins. Now it only remains for me to wish you a trouble free flight, most customers take the opportunity to catch up on some sleep, but do not become distressed if you find you cannot, it is a side effect of weightless travel. The sound of the cool-drive rocket will also be quite loud in the cabin, this is quite usual and nothing to be alarmed about".

"We should have gone first class", Osoba muttered to the professor.

Król chuckled, "There is no first class to Callisto, Izzy. Not even Verfolgungswege has that facility yet".

"Two days of this Uncle, it will be a wearing experience".

"Agreed, but think how wonderful cold-fusion is, making this journey even possible? Remember nineteen sixty nine. Then until thirty two thirty five the exploration into space was totally static"?

"The dark space ages, yes I have access to that, now I think I shall put myself into sleep mode and see if I can miss some of the interminable monotony".

Since the speed of his attack on the tube which had alerted Król to Osoba's nature, neither had spoken of it. Yet both of them knew, it was a strange situation.

The old man nodded and Osoba did as he had suggested. Unlike the humans aboard, once he had activated deep sleep, he was almost powered down and little could reactivate him. The internal clock in his circuits brought him back to conscious thought and observation of the ship once more, thirty hours had passed. He glanced over at Król, the old man looked exhausted.

"How are you feeling Uncle"?

"Tired almost beyond endurance Izzy", Król admitted. "I've not been able to get any proper rest and my back is absolutely killing me".

Osoba hailed a steward, who clunked over to them eventually, aided by his magnetic boots,

"My Uncle cannot sleep and he is in pain with his back, can you give him anything please"?

"How long have you been awake sir"? the steward wanted to know.

"I've had no proper sleep at all", Król told him. Even his voice sounded fatigued.

"You silly man", the steward smiled, "Why didn't you let me know before this, I'll get the onboard nurse to come and see you".

The onboard nurse was slim, blonde and had the most perfect teeth Osoba had ever seen on a human. The android repeated what he had told the steward. She assured him she could make the old man comfortable. She also gave Osoba a smile that was both open and indicative of attraction. Beltraynial Malinowscy had made Osoba as handsome as just about any man alive.

She returned a few moments later with a high powered sub-dermal pressure spray,

"What is in it please, nurse"? Osoba asked, Król looked like he had got to the state where he did not care.

"Lubie", she answered, "It's both a soporific and analgesic in one. I'll give him two cc's and see how he progresses".

The transparent chamber of the spray revealed the liquid to be royal blue in colour.

"Lubie", Osoba repeated, "But that's made from Mars Lichen is it not"?

She nodded, as she rolled Krol's sleeve up, "Yes but in it's refined state it's nothing like Snufz, don't worry' your comrade will not suffer any lasting side effects from this".

"Uncle", Osoba corrected almost absently, as he took in the girls attraction, "He's my late father's brother".

The sound of the spray acting was heard and Krol closed his eyes almost at once,

"You don't look like a miner", the blonde observed,

"No. We are on our way to visit family, I am Izydor", he held out his hand.

"Floare", she responded, holding his hand slightly longer than was necessary. "Will you be staying in Geirvimul Catena long"?

"That depends on how Uncle Bede is feeling. Are you Polish, Floare"?

"Floare Górnik", she told him, "Your wife is not making the journey with you"?

"I am not married", he told her and then added, "Nor seeing anyone at present neither".

"Me too", she told him with just a little too much haste, "This job makes it hard for me to meet nice men".

"Nursing"?

"Flight Nurse. I tend to get the long runs too, as I speak Polish, working for this company it's not often they do any other run".

"I see, well, let's see how Uncle gets on and maybe you can show me the sights, such as they are"?

He was rewarded with the most dazzling smile possible, "I'd like that, though the sights of Geirvimul Catena can be done in about an hour. Well I'll leave you now to get some sleep yourself, see you in a while Izydor".

She clumped away on her metallic boots and Osoba took some protein, before setting his internal timer once again. He was going into sleep mode. Once his circuits were reactivated, the rocket would hopefully be descending to Callisto.

The change seemed join-less to Osoba, but when he checked his internal chronometer, further duration had passed and the sound of the rockets indicated braking and descent. Added to which, vibration was almost at the limits of endurance. Endurance for a human that was, the android could have withstood a far greater G-force on his duridium body. Krol still seemed to be under the soporific drug Lubie, so Osoba let him remain so. After approximately twenty minutes, there was a sudden shaking vibration of a few seconds and then a soft thump and the motors quickly died to a faint hiss.

Comically, despite being given no such directive, the rest of the passengers threw open their harness' and began scrambling into the overheard lockers; where their flight bags were stowed. Osoba could not see the logic to this, after all, the airlock had not opened. Beyond it the airtight umbilical, that would connect it to the rocket port, had not been sealed either. He remained in position. The captain finally told them they could begin disembarking,

"Uncle", he said then, "We are on Callisto, please wake up"?

As if by the hand of some unseen magician, the old man opened his eyes thankfully looking far more relaxed and refreshed than previously.

He did not speak, causing Osoba to ask, "You are mute until we get to Pekko"?

The older man obliged him with a nod.

The wait to get out of the airlock seemed interminable. Whilst in truth it was only a few minutes. When the duo finally reached it, the crew were at it to wish them a good stay on Callisto. As Osoba passed Floare Górnik, she rewarded him with another dazzling smile and passed a tiny strip of foil to him,

"My e-mail", she explained, "Ping me when you are settled in wherever you are staying".

Krol gave the android a quizzical glance, but could say nothing of course.

Their first stop was custom control. The officers at the booth were dressed in German army uniforms. Over their head read the sign, 'Benutzerdefinierte Steuerung'. It was immediately obvious that the occupants and controllers of the German sector of the moon, had no desire to speak Standard.

"Drogen, Waffen oder andere verbotene Gegenstände"? the uniformed officer in the booth demanded of Osoba and Krol. He was asking if the duo had weapons or drugs, or anything else they could be delayed over.

The android switched to faultless German, with no hint of an accent,

"Just personal protection weapons, for which, we have carrying permits, sir".

"Show me", the soldier demanded. That took ten minutes or so. Then he demanded to see their inter-planetary visas and passports. Through out the whole procedure, Krol said not a word,

"What is wrong with the old man"?

"Nothing sir, apart from the fact that he is mute".

"Very well go through".

As they proceeded past the booth however Osoba heard the officer mutter, "Beschissen Poles, diluting the gene pool once again".

As soon as they were out of earshot of anyone Osoba told Krol.

"I have checked for tube runs to Pekko. One does not go until tomorrow, the service is not as regular as that which we are used to on Mars, so we will need to find a boarding house for overnight, come Uncle".

They took a moving walkway which groaned and squeaked as if it were to grind to a halt at any second. Beyond the towering plexi-glass walls of the spoke, there was nothing but nigrescent night, the sun being on the far side of Jupiter's satellite. As they proceeded however, the vast circumference of the home world began to crawl into view, a crescent so huge it would have taken Osoba's breath away, if he had breathed! The polarised surface of the spoke suddenly activated, reducing the radiation to Earth normal, from ten times higher.

Stepping off the walkway they found a suitable place for their purpose, after but a short walk, the Bergleutebleiben, or Miner's Stay. Once inside their room Osoba could finally switch back to Polish and have a conversation with his companion.

"I don't like this Izzy", the Professor told Osoba at once,"

But if there is no tube, it's unavoidable. The Germans do not like us, I will feel much more comfortable once we are with friends".

"I'm going out tonight after dinner", Osoba told him then, head bent over his pad.

"Seeing the sights with the Polish nurse, from the rocket".

"An unnecessary risk", Krol sounded annoyed.

Keeping his gaze fixed on the Teutonic furniture and ornamentation.

"Perhaps; but it will kill some time and you can get some more reading done".

Krol glanced at the clock on the room's wall, "Two eight two, twenty two. What time did the desk droid say dinner was"?

"Two eight four", Osoba told him, "It is going to take me a while to get used to a three hundred and eighty four hour day"

"You just have to split it up into twenty four hour chunks", Krol told him, "I am going to shower and change before dinner, I suggest you change your clothes at least, so as not to arouse suspicion that you're a cyborg".

"I wonder how long it would take her to come to that conclusion if I never told her"? Osoba wondered with a curious tone in his voice.

"The instant you did something humanly impossible," Krol answered,

"Your speed on the tube, against the louts for example. It was beyond anything that a man could have achieved".

Osoba said nothing more, there was nothing more to be said. He changed some of his clothes even though there was actually no need.

As the Professor showered he asked,

"What about the point seven though"?

"To what decimal do you refer"?

"The point seven. You said to split the clock up into twenty four hour chunks, but Callisto's day is sixteen point seven Earth days long"?

Krol laughed, "Machines, so literal minded. There is of course, the occasion realignment that lasts only a couple of minutes. Worry more about careless talk with the girl. I know you are enamoured, but remember the importance of our mission"?

Once the Professor was towelling himself dry Osoba suggested, "I could give dinner a miss"?

"Not a good idea", Krol did not surprise him, "German agents and constables will be everywhere, observing every movement of Polish peoples in their cities".

"Cities", Osoba smiled.

Krol told him, "Geirvimul Catena may seem primitive to you nephew with your Mars standards, but to a Callistonian it is still a city".

"Very well I will get my hair wet as if I have showered and the change into fresh clothes should suffice and by then we can drift down to dinner".

The dining room was cramped. All such spaces on a moon that had little atmosphere of it's own were of a similar dimension. Due to the presence of water on Callisto though, the creation of oxygen was easy to manufacture. Callisto had initially required the importing of vast amounts of nitrogen gas, which had been deposited as its atmospheric buffer.

Then bacteria had been introduced, to help add nitrogen by converting ammonia found on the surface. The ammonia became nitrates, then even more nitrogen. After that, almost half of the entire Earth's supply and reserves of a potent green house gas, Sulphur Hexafluoride had been sent to Callisto. The moon had an abundance of water-ice, and after the greenhouse gases began heating Callisto, the water had melted to form vast lakes, the Oxygen part of the atmosphere had then been created by electrolysis of some of them. The Callistonian day, sixteen point seven times longer than Earth's, was eventually hoped to create an atmosphere thick enough to distribute heat from the day to the night side.

That was still decades away however and so for now the miners were forced to live in domes and mine in pressure suits. This made the process of extracting more minerals costly, dangerous and time consuming. As Earth had now exhausted it's own natural resources however, there was no alternative. It was thought that the day would come when Callisto would be the centre of the solar system. However with it's low temperatures of minus one hundred and ninety three degrees Celsius and highs of a balmy minus one hundred and eight degrees, much work needed to be done on it's weather system, which still did not in fact exist.

Krol remained silent and Osoba made all the orders in German. The food was predictable, if nutritious. Dodoprot breast with hydroponics potatoes and carrots. For desert mele-cake and white sweet sauce. The choice of beverage was between green beet-wine, red beet-wine or beet beer. Water was the most expensive.

Osoba placed just enough food into his mouth and digestive tract to avoid suspicion. He was able to taste with receptors in the roof of it, not dissimilar in function to those of a man, but he rarely actually needed food. His micro-pile supplied over eighty percent of his energy. He kept glancing at his Callistonian wrist-chrono.

For he had pinged Floare after his shower and arranged to meet her outside the giant chrono in Geirvimul Catena's central square. Their rendezvous was to be at two eight five hours.

Krol suddenly gripped his arm and though he could not speak, his eyes flashed the advice 'Be careful'! Osoba nodded and then said,

"I'll leave you to your reading now Uncle, I'm going to stretch my legs Guten Abend".

Krol grimaced at the last two words spoken in German. As Osoba hastened out of the boarding house, a German seated in the reception area glanced up from his pad and made a mental note of his movement, something the android, with all his receptors of various kinds, did not notice.

FOUR

THE HUGE CHRONO that hung over the central square of Geirvimul Catena was a series of bright red L.E.D's shining out of a fuliginous background. So powerful that they cast a flaming glow over the false ground that was tarmac on top of plexi-glass. Across this even at the late hour carts hustled and bustled and moving walkways snaked their meandering way from one spoke of the spider-web to another.

How this differed from Mars however was the establishments that lined the perimeter of the square. Drab and containing far more modest and far more practical wares than the red planet. Those on foot walked with a peculiar gait in the low gravity a sort of half hop and stride, most of them had the extra heavy boots that stopped one from suddenly and accidentally jumping too high.

Osoba saw Floare at just about the same instant she spied him and was rewarded by a dazzling white smile. She had put her hair into a pony tail and changed into clothes of pale blue. The colour perfectly suited her complexion, which was very pale. Of course the current fashion was for ladies to be as pale as they were able. Radiation was nothing but damaging to the skin and also indicated that one toiled for a living. The well to do were all as white as alabaster.

As she came toward him, gliding rather than walking, he felt a curious sensation at the bottom of what would have been his guts. As though something very light was fluttering inside him. He quickly accessed his vast memory bank for a suitable greeting,

"You look very lovely Floare, so good of you to agree to meet me".

"Thank you and it will be my pleasure, although it will not be a very long tour".

"Well maybe then we can go for a drink of some sort, so that we can talk".

He offered her his arm and she looped her own inside it,

"This way then, at least the tanner will be quite interesting I hope".

She showed him the local tanner, who made strong boots and aprons for the miners. The duo then progressed to the electrician's, who created the various lighting devices for the miners too and then on to the iron monger who sharpened the cutting tools for the miners and so on and so on. Were it not for mining, the town would not exist. This was no surprise to the android and he likened the place to an old wild west frontier community.

They passed chiefly unnoticed, but when any German did ask them what they were about, Osoba slipped easily into faultless German and was several times mistaken for one. Finally they had explored everything, including the food markets and ladies items. For some miners had brought their families to Callisto, they went on to the tea rooms.

"I want to thank you for whiling away some time in a more interesting way than usual", Floare told him as they entered,

"Normally stop overs on Callisto are a pretty dull affair as we wait for refuel and other checks".

"The pleasure has been all mine droga pani", Osoba returned, meaning every word, "To be escorted around Geirvimul Catena by the loveliest maiden in the town was greatly flattering to me".

"May I have Earth tea, do you think", she smiled then; it was expensive.

"You may have what ever you fancy", he responded. The firm had given both he and Krol more than enough shillin to cover expenses. He ordered for them and then asked her,

"So how long do you intend to be a stewardess Floare"?

"Oh, crumbs, I've no thoughts at the minute", she confessed,

"And the remuneration is good so.......".

The conversation continued until the staff started to pack up the rooms for the night and clearly wanted them to leave. Reluctantly they did, departing the rooms as most of the lights in the stores were starting to wink out too. They had not spent as long with each other as they wanted however,

"Why not come back with me to the Bergleutebleiben, the bar should stay open as long as we wish to buy drinks"?

Floare seemed to think about it for but a second, before agreeing,

"Just a couple of drinks then Izydor, you are travelling tomorrow, I do not want to make it too late".

Arm in arm they returned to the lodging house and sure enough the lights over the bar were still on. Osoba ordered two Earth Rums which were exorbitantly expensive, but his time with the beautiful girl had made uncharacteristically reckless.

"Do you think I might see you on our return journey"? he asked her as he sipped the rum,

"There are only two vessels that do the run from Mars to Callisto, so it would be fairly likely", she smiled, "But tell me are you not on Callisto to stay"?

The soft and colourful level of illumination in the bar was designed to be romantic and the evening had been intoxicating to the android. The rum was working on his brain pathways too and he told her without a qualm,

"Oh my Uncle and I are only coming to visit Callisto for a short while. We are going to Pekko tomorrow, to visit some of the family and are likely to return to Mars after a few weeks. Then I presume, we must do so via Geirvimul Catena or Numi-Torum".

"I never do any flights too or from Numi-Torum", the blonde told him,

"So I hope you decide to return to here, which of course is much closer to Pekko. Do you intend to go farther afield"?

"Perhaps", Osoba went on quite naively, "We have been told to visit Orestheas mines and the town of Lodurr".

"You have a very spread out family, or your Uncle has"?

"Uncle Bede is a geologist, family are not at those two locations and they are subject to change anyway".

He missed the slight look of disappointment, at this revelation

"And when you have visited the deep south, do you think you will then come back to Pekko"?

"I think perhaps I will talk my Uncle into it", Osoba smiled.

"For I have a highly motivating reason so to do".

FIVE

THE TUBE TO Pekko was not up to the level of comfort as the Mars transport had been. Instead of upholstered seats, there were simple wooden slatted benches. The journey proved that the tube itself did not have the suspension of those on Mars either. The vista through the sides of the circular conduit was less awe inspiring than on Mars too. In all a disappointing experience.

There were no stops to relieve the monotony of endless dark charcoal vistas. Jupiter was overhead and they could only see it by craning their necks at a less than comfortable angle. The light from it was meagre and the sun was still beneath the horizon, so the tedium of the transfer was never ending. When the two of them exited the airlock at Pekko, Krol was extremely stiff and Osoba felt his batteries were low, this was the closest he became to tired out.

Then a lone figure separated himself from the crowd, a boy of perhaps twelve Earth years strode awkwardly toward them,

"I believe you may be my great Uncle Bede", he said to the two of them. Osoba had both bags one on each shoulder as the professor was close to collapse. What startled the two of them however was that, though he spoke to them in Polish, he wore the crisp uniform of the German Youth League".

"I may be", Krol replied carefully, "But do I know you, young man"?

"I was a baby when last you was on Callisto", the boy returned, but he did not smile, "I am Wolnosc Krol. Am I addressing Bede Krol? My mother has sent me here to greet you and take you back to our apartments".

"Your mother being Sonnenschein Krol"?

The boy nodded and Krol smiled and took hold of his hand,

"Yes I am your great uncle then, your fathers uncle, how is Wytrzymalosc"?

The boy slid his hand from the old man's grasp, plainly unhappy with the contact. His face twisted with distaste, as he replied with stark honestly,

"He is a drunk, great uncle. He's been a drunk for years but clearly he's not yet drunken himself to death. I'm sure you remember his appetite for alcohol"?

Krol's face then took upon it a look of sympathetic sadness, "Yes Wolnosc, I do remember Wytrzymalosc liked to drink. Your mother, she copes"?

"Of course", the boy brightened, "For she is Teutonic".

'That explains why young Wolnosc is in the German Youth League', Osoba thought to himself.

"Oh where are my manners", Krol was saying by then, "Wolnosc, this is a nephew by the other side of the family; Izydor".

Osoba gave the boy a respectful nod, avoiding contact and the boy returned the gesture,

"The apartment is a walk from here only. Are you ready to begin it"?

"Just about Wolnosc", Krol agreed with a puff.

With that the boy turned on his shiny heels and lead them away, at what could only be described as a military pace.

They entered the apartment, a simply and modestly furnished affair and immediately a florid stout woman jumped up from her seat and coming to Krol, threw her arms around him.

"Uncle Bede", she gasped, "It has been too long, it's so good to see you, how have you been".

"Well thank you Sonnenschein, how Wolnosc has grown, you must be proud of him".

A cloud seemed to pass over the mother's face at mention of the boy, but her words belied her mien,

"Of course I am, uncle, he is a fine boy".

"Ja und soon to be a Korporal in the Youth League", the boy returned, somewhat awkwardly as it was plain German was not his mother tongue. Changing the subject Krol said to the woman,

"This is Izydor, he it the son of my brother in law and my nephew on the other side of the family".

Though Sonnenschein looked momentarily puzzled by that, she smiled at Osoba and welcomed him,

"Good to met you Izydor, you are to stay with us and get to know the family".

Krol looked about then asking, "Where is Wytrzymalosc"?

"He will be propping up the bar at the Zielony Kolczyk for this hour and many after it", the boy noted with distaste.

Ignoring him, his mother asked, "Now; will you unpack and bath and then I have some gulasz for the two of you. Wolnosc please show your great uncle and cousin to the room they will be sharing. I hope you like it uncle, we did not have rooms enough to billet you separately"?

"That's fine", Krol returned.

The boy sniffed, obviously having escorted the two of them to their apartments was in his opinion, the end of his duties, but he did take them through a winding perspex staircase up to the second floor of the apartments. Once they were inside and with none other, Osoba turned to Krol,

"I like this not at all professor".

"The boy"?

Osoba nodded, "You never told me your niece was German", he complained,

"Nationalised Pole", Krol explained, "She took citizenship when she married my nephew and Pekko is in the Polish sector".

"Just", Osoba noted consulting the map in his memory banks, "In a peninsular that could be easily cut off and absorbed by the Germans".

"Perhaps that is what young Wolnosc thinks will happen"?

"No, I do not think so. I think the uniform, the mentality, all that is German on Callisto appeals to young Wolnosc. Of course the Germans will be only too happy to accept him into their embrace, there is nothing more satisfying to a fanatic, than a conversion".

"It will get even more complex once the Romanians arrive and seek some territory of their own, neither of the current residents can police their entire hemisphere".

"By then hopefully, we will be gone", Osoba returned, little knowing at that point that only one of them would!

They unpacked, bathed and went down for supper. To their disquiet Wytrzymalosc had returned from the bar and was not dozing like a good drunk, but seated in a chair with a belligerent look upon his sour features.

"Ah! Here are the scroungers, come to get some free food", he sneered as the two of them came into his sight.

"Shut up Wytr"! Sonnenschein scolded and the shortened version of his name suited the drunk very well.

"They are family, not scroungers and you only call them that because you're after more money for drink".

"We can pay if it is problematical", Osoba offered, "I have....."

"Charge family", Sonnenschein cut him short, "No grand nephew, you will stay with us and there will be no charge".

"Let him pay if he wants to", Wytrzymalosc argued, "What will you pay the head of this household young man"?

"Head of the household, pah", Sonnenschein's voice was filled with bitterness, "You have not run this household for years Wytr; now go to bed before you make even more of an dummkopf of yourself".

"Frenging Germans", the husband cursed at this, but he began to rise from his chair as the airlock suddenly sighed open. In walked the young Wolnosc, in his uniform and this caused his father to hasten and be out of sight as quickly as possible.

"I haf gut news", he puffed out his chest as he seated himself beside Osoba, "My promotion was confirmed at this evenings meeting, I am now a Korporal in the Youth League of German-Callisto".

As his mother placed some stew before him Osoba said,

"Glückwunsch Herr Korporal".

"You mock me sir"! the boy seethed, offended.

"Nicht so, ich freute mich über deinen ersten Befehl (Not so, I was pleased for your first command)", Osoba persisted.

Suddenly the boys eyes lit up with the fire of enthusiasm bordering on fanaticism,

"You speak German cousin, yet I thought you a pole, explain, but then also promise to teach me some while you stay with us"?

Osoba forced a laugh and then returned, "I speak several languages Wolnosc, but I remain a good Pole".

"Do you also speak Romanian"? The boy wished to know,

"For if you do you could be of great use to the Germans, who intend to keep the half of Callisto they already have".

"Sau de serviciu pentru sectorul polonez care doresc sa pastreze ceea ce au si ei ", Osoba demonstrated and then translated,

"Or of service to the Polish sector, who wish to keep what they have too".

"The Poles are weak", Wolnosc argued,

"Yet the Germans are strong".

"And yet you are strong", Osoba flattered,

"And are a Pole".

"Not when I am eighteen", the boy informed,

"I can then apply for German-Callistonian citizenship and I will".

"Enough talk", his mother requested, "Let us have the rest of the meal in quiet".

They did, but the tension in the air did not go away. Not until the boy confessed tiredness and went up to his own room. Then Sonnenschein let out a sigh of relief and told the two of them in almost a whisper,

"You must guard your every word in front of him".

"She knows of our mission", Krol told the android,

"Whom are we to meet my dear niece and when"?

"He is known only as the Moth", Sonnenschein told them with total seriousness,

"He will meet you tomorrow in the square, or one of his men will take you to him. He has the materials you need".

"Do you trust this Moth"? Osoba asked.

"I have arranged the rendezvous, he knows who I am and my position in this, so yes I do Izydor".

"Then once I have helped you clear away and cleanse the pots, we should go to bed", Osoba offered.

"I will let you help me on the condition that we then share a glass of Polmos, the best Polish Vodka from Earth and toast the success of the mission"? Sonnenschein offered.

"Deal", Osoba smiled.

SIX

THE SQUARE WAS not busy, few were moving about. So when a man dressed from head to toe in black took up a position beneath the huge red chronometer, the duo knew it was either the Moth, or the man who would lead them to him. Osoba strode out, the professor in his wake. They both stopped beneath the chronometer and the android addressed the man,

"I see you favour black, is it the fashion these days"? Osoba asked the question.

"It is and it also suits my mood", the man returned, exactly as rehearsed, "I will take you to the Moth. Who are the two of you"?

With a sardonic smile on his face Król told the man in black, "You may call me the Hound and this is the Hawk".

Osoba smiled, the nomen the Hawk suited him very well.

"Alright then if that is how you want to be regarded". agreed the man in black, "Come with me Hound and Hawk".

The bizarre trio ducked into a shop that sold potted plants of the indoor variety. Some of the community raised such for recreation, using UV lamps, to supplement their need to photosynthesise.

The proprietor merely gave them a tight nod and allowed them through his shop. Into what looked to be his living quarters behind it. The man in black moved a Welsh dresser, which glided smoothly on casters and beyond it lay some Perspex steps. The three of them descended under the surface of the moon. Their way was softly lit by small and amber L.E.D.'s, the sloping surface of the stairwell was as black as the clothing of their guide. Then the well flared out into a sub-Callistonian chamber, at the centre of which, was a simple unadorned desk. On the surface of the lone piece of furniture was an angle poise L.E.D. lamp. The strange trio placed themselves before the desk, the light was in their eyes throwing the figure seated behind into silhouette.

"Don't move", the man in black commanded and stationed himself as Osoba's side.

Król peered into the light, "I see now why your code name is the Moth", he observed wryly, "I am the Hound and this fellow at my side is the Hawk. You know what we have come for"?

"Plastique Four", came the rumbled reply. Either the Moth had a deep baritone, or he was speaking into some sort of sound altering computer programme that disguised his natural tone.

Osoba switched to infra-red vision and got a shock. The outline of the Moth, the body language and hairline indicated that Król was in conversation with a woman!

"And detonators and timers", Król continued, oblivious as to Osoba's discovery, "We could also use two blast rifles and night scopes for said. We would also require backpacks to carry all the equipment".

"You do not look like a saboteur, Hound. Is Hawk strong enough for the two of you"?

"Yes", Król responded simply, "While I possess the knowledge of where to place the explosives, to do the most damage. So, can you give us with what we need to accomplish our mission yes, or no"?

"It is easy enough, but very expensive. There will not be a problem if you have the price. If not, then sadly we will be unable to do business".

"How expensive are you suggesting then, Moth"? Osoba asked, speaking for the first time since they had entered the dim liar.

"Do you intend to make profit on freedom fighting for our own miners"?

"So you too have a voice, the muscle of the group", Moth noted.

"To answer your question, we make nothing. For it costs dearly to smuggle onto Callsito and some have lost their lives attempting it, no greater price can be paid for the cause than that, as I'm certain you will agree. We see that the families of those who do die are supported in the right way, everything costs my dear Hawk".

Osoba thought the Moth's form of address toward him was strange and possibly a clue, but he said nothing. Finally the Moth asked them,

"What will the strength of your donation to our worthy cause be then, gentlemen"?

"You want us to name the price"? Król sounded surprised.

"That is not the usual way these negotiations are settled".

"Well let us say we need to be unconventional for the moment then and so why not"?

Even with the voice tailoring programme the tone was one of sardonic amusement.

"If it is a fair and generous sum, it will be accepted".

"Very well". Król took up the bargaining conversation, "For the supplies we require, we will give you ten silver shillin, ninety nine percent argent in vacuum packed sachets. Of course you will not see the coinage other than by vid image, it will be transferred directly into the bank account of your choice, by direct transfer once we have your account number"?

"Agreed", the Moth was evidentially expecting a lower offer, "Seven five seven four, five five five five, two eight eight two, seven five seven four, three three three zero. That is the twenty digit number of our account, do you wish me to repeat"?

"Not necessary", Osoba told the shrouded figure. "I have a superb memory".

"In that case, when can the transfer be conducted"?

Król pulled the ditty bag that had resided over his shoulder, he tugged it over his head and opened it to slip out a pad. His fingers tapped it to life, he explained,

"Within seconds", this seemed to eminently suit the Polish saboteur.

"You are absolutely certain you do not need the number again, we do not want any mistakes", the basso rumble noted, but Osoba then demonstrated his memory,

"No need". He repeated it to Król, just as it had been instantly stored in his memory banks.

They heard the Moths fingers tapping a similar device and he was apparently satisfied, for he instructed the man in black,

"Get enough Plastique Four to destroy the bulkheads of three mines. Detonators for said and timers, two blast rifles and night scopes and get them two further power packs for the rifles. Oh and do not forget their back packs. Will that be satisfactory gentlemen"?

"It will, but we don't want it now", Król told the Moth, "It must be smuggled into the apartment we are staying at, during the quietest hour of the night".

"We could have the boy eliminated"? the Moth offered, thus demonstrating the efficiency of the group's intelligence.

"That will not be necessary", Król replied swiftly, "He's family, no matter where his loyalties lie".

He could not know as he spoke that such would be a decision that would prove disastrous for one of them!

"Then our business is concluded, you will not see me again", the Moth told them then, not that they had *seen* him the first time.

"Good luck".

It was by way of a dismissal and the man in black took Król gently by the elbow and guided him toward the stairs, Osoba mentally shrugged and followed his mentor out the way they had come.

"Now we have plans to make, a schedule to construct", the professor rubbed his hands together.

"I will tell you of the three targets I have only just determined, once we get back to the rooms".

A short while later the professor whispered to his comrade,

"We will have to take three separate evenings to have hope of concealing the explosives upon our persons", Król began. "Our first target will be Vanapagan, the furthest away over to the north west. If we are successful we will pull back then to Maderatcha. Finally the largest prize, we shall put Großtiefreich out of commission".

"Großtiefreich"! Osoba echoed, "Probably the most guarded mine on all of Callisto"?!

Król's eyes glinted with enthusiasm, "The very same, but first, tonight dear nephew, we set off once the Moth has delivered our supplies, for Vanapagan".

"There will be no tube at that hour, uncle, how do you think we are going to get there"?

Król chuckled, "We're not going by tube, but by buggies, in space suits".

"You have access to these and did not tell me, why did you keep the details secret"?

"Why in case we were compromised of course. The suit you wear will be a spare for me as it turns out, for you do not breathe do you"?

"No. Let us hope that after the raid 'you' are still doing so professor", Osoba quipped darkly.

Under cover of low light, for the interior of the dome still kept a twenty four hour cycle going for the convenience of the inhabitants, three figures emerged from the front of the store that sold potted plants and slinked over to the apartments, where Wolnosc was sleeping. They stole inside, there to meet two space suited figures, who were planning a short trip to the local outside airlock, where prepaid buggies were waiting for them. One figure cracked the seal on his helmet and pulled it free,

"You've reached your customers, I am the Hound. Come with us, we are going to take the entire shipment to a place where the Germans are least likely to find it"

"Where would that be, Hound"? A third figure in navy coveralls asked.

"Outside", the Hound told them, "Not here though, we have outer transport. You will load it and then you will never see the supplies again. Tel the Moth we are satisfied and grateful and say good bye to him on our behalf".

The man in coveralls agreed to do just so and followed the two suited men to the local airlock. He and his duo of comrades helped load it into the airlock and then the Hound sealed the inner door in readiness for cracking the outer hatchway. They slunk away then, for the light was so subfusc, they could barely make out the outline of the buggies, as they rested peacefully on the slate grey landscape of the moon.

Król sealed his own helmet, then the outer lock was cracked and thrown open. It took barely two minutes to load the buggies and reseal the doorway that kept the air inside the bubble.

"Outer lock sealed"? Osoba heard the tinny question through his helmet's headphones, "We don't want an alarm going off in about three minutes as I would estimate"?

"Sealed and checked Hound", Osoba assured, with a certain irony.

"Good; then follow me, I have set a course East north east, for Vanapagan. It will take us some hours to get there".

"As you know professor, I do not tire. Go as swiftly and for as long as your vitality endures and I will be with you, but do not push yourself too hard on the first mission".

"Acknowledged", came the tacit reply and Król's huge tires kicked up spurts of dust and miniature debris as it suddenly accelerated and raced away. The brake horse power of the buggies fourteen hundred cc engine was a staggering two hundred! The acceleration flung Osoba back in his own seat when he placed his foot on the accelerator and the grey ground of the moon began to speed away beneath the duralite chassis. At that sort of pace, the journey would not be as long, as Osoba had initially expected.

What he had also not expected, was just how long Król could drive before stopping for a rest. Obviously with the suit on, he needed no food nor waste removal, the suit did both for him, so his only reason for any interruption in their journey was fatigue.

"I don't want to sleep in this tin can", the professor's voice crackled over the headphones in Osoba's helmet,

"But it's still a fair lick to the mining town of Vanapagan".

"Have you any contacts once we get there"?

"No, that's where your German comes in Izzy, and I go mute once more. Now, before we continue, bury one third of our supplies here and make an entry into your memory banks. This is how we hide the explosives and what not, till we return and once more need them".

The android did as directed, progressing at a leisurely pace with his task, to allow the old man to recuperate as much of his strength as possible. Then they sped onward once more.

SEVEN

VANAPAGAN WAS MUCH bigger and more impressive than Pekko. Beyond the town, the vast domes of the mines towered over both them and over shadowing the dwellings, like some huge plastic beast. It was a great place to hide two buggies, in the inky shadows the light from Jupiter created, when interrupted by such structures. Finding the nearest airlock they waited until all was quiet and then entered, stashing their suits behind a convenient bulk head. Now it was up to Osoba to pass them off as Germans, until Król was rested enough to complete the mission.

The hotel was called the Plötzlich Finden, which was apt, for Osoba chanced upon it quite suddenly. The entrance hall or vestibule seemed bigger than the entire interior of most establishments in Pekko. One thing they had to concede to the Germans, they were great engineers and builders. Osoba walked over to the desk while Król waited behind.

"I would like a room for myself and my uncle please"? he asked the woman behind the reception counter, in faultless German.

"Certainly Herr...."?

"Herr Król", Osoba lied, it passed more easily for German and Król had given him forged papers some time previously. "The mute gentleman is also Herr Król, naturally".

"How long do you intend to stay Herr Król"?

"Only overnight, we are on our way to Aziren".

The girl requested the price of their stay,

"Seventy two grote please Herr Król"?

Osoba handed over a shillin piece,

"Keep the change for yourself my dear", he instructed, thus placing her on his side, it never hurt to have a friend; anywhere!

Though the shillin was universal, some nationalities still split it into unique lower denominations, the Germans were no exception to this.

"So we wait", the professor told him when they reached their room, "We go at Three three six".

Osoba nodded, "Then I will go into sleep mode until shortly before, try and get some rest professor, I will wake you at three three five"?

The room was dim and barren of hardly any adornment, making it all the better for rest, lacking distraction.

Król nodded, causing the android to marvel at the old man's vitality. He would keep a close watch on him however, for he might just be running on adrenalin and fail quite suddenly. Never the less, at the appointed hour, the old man sprang to his feet with an eagerness to get on with the mission, matched only by Osoba's own.

They left the Plötzlich Finden, hardly anyone noticing their passage at such an hour (it equates to midnight Earth system) and walked to the area where the town ended and the mine began, the exact same place where the airlock was and the explosives were stashed.

The two of them had practised their next few moves, back on Mars and they proceeded barely without thinking. Packs checked, thrown onto backs, slow trot commenced, no talk, no light, until they came to the head of the mine.

Almost at once their luck ran out.

"Hör auf, was machst du hier (Stop what are you doing here?)", the sentry's voice shattered the peace of the sterile air inside the vast bubble.

"Aha gemeiner Soldat, you have passed this evening's exercise, well done. Your name please so I can pass it on to the Über Kommandant", Osoba tried.

"Put your hands in the air and don't move a muscle if you please"? Came the ordered reply. He was not fooled for an instant. "You, the old one, take that rifle from your shoulder slowly and let it fall to the floor. Try anything and I shoot your young friend".

Król slowly did as he had been bidden. Then the German commanded Osoba to follow suit. Once the second rifle was down, he returned his instruction to Król,

"Now the back pack, no sudden moves, please to remember who is the one armed here. Fail to do exactly what I say and I will open fire, you believe me ja"?

"He cannot answer", Osoba thought to distract the soldier, "A childhood illness Callistonian Saline-Mockpearl, from the seas here you may have....."

"Halt deinen Mund", the soldier barked, which Król understood all too easily. "Now you, the one with the runaway mouth, take off your back pack and do it very carefully".

Osoba did as instructed, then asked, "I have a pen may I keep that"?

The fact that he had asked the question, caused the otherwise hidden object, to become an issue.

"What sort of a pen"?

"It has some family significance, see, if you press this button so, it......".

Despite himself, the soldier leaned slightly forward and the needle hit him on the left cheek. With a look of utter astonishment, he sighed and his knees gave way. Osoba rushed forward and gently lowered him to the floor.

Taking up his pack and blaster rifle, Król noted quietly, "Remind me to never ask you to sign anything, I presume you got that from Malinowscy; a neuronic needle gun in miniature"?

Osoba nodded and commanded, "Go mute again, we have some charges to set and have your blaster at the ready, the closer we get to the stulm".

From that moment on however their luck held and Król set the charges at the stulm, while Osoba kept out a sharp eye, his blaster rifle at full readiness. Then they were racing away as quickly as the elder saboteur could manage. Back to the airlock, into the suits and on the buggies.

The ground seemed to buckle beneath the tyres of the buggies and there was a sound like a dull thwump and as they twisted in their seats, they saw the destruction they had created. The great dome of the mine of Vanapagan split and caved inward with a might whoosh of escaping air. Król examined his feelings, he felt no guilt, merely patriotic fervour, two more sites yet to destroy before their mission was over.

The return journey was to be to Maderatcha, after picking up their buried supplies along the way. This time they had to be extra vigilant however, just in case Germany had something in the air, that could spot their buggies. Such was very unlikely though, even with cool fusion, space flight was very expensive and as yet the settlement had no air force. It would have had to consist of space capable craft, over the airless skies of Callisto.

At least it was only half the distance from Vanapagan to Maderatcha, as it had been on the original journey out from Pekko. They performed the same ritual as before, hiding the buggies in the deep shadow of the mines, their suites in a convenient bulkhead. They were racing against time now though. For in thirty hours the moon would begin to turn it's face toward the sun. Then there would be no shadow on Callisto for almost seventeen Earth days. For though the sun was a fifth of the diameter as seen from Earth, it was still very very bright.

The duo walked as casually as they could through the town of Maderatcha and finally found somewhere to stay; the Grabensuchmann (the German who searches and digs).

"We need a double room for but a few hours please", Osoba asked the man at the reception desk.

"Papers please", the young man demanded looking at the two of them with some disdain. Evidentially he was wondering what two men dressed in simple miners clothes were doing at the quite select hotel. He examined those which were handed over to him, with longer scrutiny than was necessary. Then, with his next question, Osoba knew exactly what was going on.

"You heard of the explosion last night, at Vanapagan".

"Why no"! Osoba managed to gasp, "I hope no one was injured. Tell us please, what happened"?

"The dome was shattered", the youth told them with heat.

"The atmosphere lost. They are still digging out the dead, the rescue workers in space suits. It will take months to recover from the disaster, according to reports. Months for replacements to arrive from Mars and then the mine itself must be reworked".

"Of course", Osoba agreed, "As geologists we appreciate the problems only too well. Who would do such a terrible cowardly act of atrocity"?

"You ask me that when we are at war with the Poles"? the youth was astonished, the glint in his eye suddenly reminded Osoba of Wolnosc.

"I believe they are sub-human. Even retaliation would not aid the production here in the north, I think the Kaiser will sue for peace, a cessation of hostilities, to agree some sort of peace talks".

"Such will take time though surely, the Polish Cesarz may not even agree"?

"Our Kaiser has been outflanked by the Poles, who would have thought they would have escalated hostilities so rapidly and so violently"?

"Terrible, terrible times. Alas now, my uncle tires, you will excuse us, if we go to our rooms"?

Once inside, Osoba asked the professor, "What do you think? Should we continue"?

"Of course", Król was obdurate, "The victory must be crushing and complete, especially as the Romanians are on their way".

"Very well", Osoba agreed woodenly, he was thinking of the dead; the families of those who had perished. War was a filthy business he decided.

"I will just see what the net has to say about last night's explosion", surely someone would speculate that it was some sort of accident"?

Osoba found plenty of news from Earth. The Imparat of Romania was expressing grave misgivings for the rocket soon to be launched from Constanta bound for Numi-Torum. The King of England had personally expressed his sadness upon hearing of the explosion. Finally the Franco-Scot alliance headed by the recently elected Ceann-suidhe, one Thighearna Piere McDonald had demanded an official enquiry, headed of course by the Thighearna himself.

On the southern continent the explosion had rated nothing more than a mention in the Kingdom of Austrazealand, something which may well have annoyed his Highness up in England. King Darren the first was frequently annoyed by his antipodean subjects. While over to the west, the governor of Canada had made the appropriate noises in response to his Monarch's netcast.

The only other mention the destruction of Vanapagan had merited was by the Governor of Zulushire. The relatively new colony of England, down in the continent of Southern Africa, which also mined important minerals and the shares in such companies as Minegland and Yorkshare had enjoyed a rise of seven sestertius per unit.

Osoba closed his pad in some ire. The last thing he hoped their sabotage would achieve, would be to disturb the interests of the English Empire. With their wealth and political influence, they could easily turn the peoples of Earth against the Polish. Yet he was resolved to continue what the two of them had started and put himself into sleep mode for a few hours.

Once Król had showered and eaten, they commenced to repeat the entire procedure of the night before. Both hoped this time they would pass unnoticed into the right area to set the explosives. It was not to be so easy though, for now that one act of terrorism had been perpetrated against the German Empire, their military machine was on alert. There were soldiers everywhere.

"Perhaps we should rethink our strategy", Osoba asked of his friend and supervisor. "Maybe the explosion at Vanapagan was enough to bring about concessions for the Polish mines and miners"?

"You think we should only strike once and allow them to get over it in time"? Król was incredulous. "No Izzy, we hit them and we hit them so hard, they will never take the rights of the Callistonian-Polish community for granted, ever again"!

"No more talk then, Bede, my friend, let us see how far we get before we encounter guards this time".

The professor glared at such defeatist talk, but sure enough, as they squirmed forward down a supply conduit, the instant they emerged a soldier challenged them.

"You two, what were you doing in there, papers and answer me"? Then the German spotted their back-packs and blasters.

"Freeze. I have you covered. Now you, old man slowly remove your back pack and then the rifle".

The German military was still stretched pretty thin it seemed, for at no time did he attempt to call a comrade, or use his throat-mic. Perhaps his was a quest for personal glory and advancement? Osoba watched as Król did as directed and then the soldier told him to follow the old man's example. Slowly he did as directed.

In a fraction of a second though he had twisted an upper button from the coat that Malinowscy had given him and tossed it at the German soldier's face. It promptly burst into a cloud of neuro-gas and Osoba caught the German's corpse, before it fell dead to the floor.

"Now I see the attachment to that coat", Król chuckled, "Do all the buttons have the same function"?

"That would be telling, professor", the android returned and then, "Give me a hand to get his uniform off and then I will get into it myself".

"Shall I wear the coat"?

"It goes in my back-pack, your reactions are not good enough to use it to advantage. Now hurry, soon you will be my prisoner, on our way to the Verwalter der Mine".

"It will not be long before his body is missed, even if we ram it into a conduit", the professor objected.

"Then let us not waste any precious moments debating the issue"? Osoba reasoned.

Within minutes they were once more chanced upon by a patrolling soldier, "Who is he"? the German asked Osoba.

"I caught him loitering at the east bulkhead", Osoba told him, "I am taking him to the Verwalter der Mine for interrogation".

"One moment gemeiner Soldat", the other's hand went to the trigger of his blaster, "I do not think I know you"?

"You do not", Osoba agreed readily, "I was brought in from Rongoteus garrison this afternoon, this mine is in the Orange Sektor".

"Orange Sektor"? the German echoed, as Osoba knew he would.

"Forgive me I have said too much. Not everyone has been briefed yet. You will be told about the state of heightened alert at you next break, no doubt. Now, I must take this man to the Verwalter der Mine".

"Perhaps the Über Kapitän would be better"?

"And perhaps it is the way of every gemeiner Soldat to question the actions of every other here in Maderatcha", Osoba suddenly flared.

"Evidentially we have greater trust of our comrades in arms, in Rongoteus garrison. Now if you will excuse me".

"Of course", the other backed down at Osoba's apparent anger, "Apologies comrade, we are in difficult times for Callistodeutsche".

Osoba nodded and this time they reached what Król thought would be a suitable spot to stick the Plastique. It was the work of seconds to sink in the detonator, the timer and hide it out of sight. Now they had to get out through the airlock, where their buggies were before the explosion happened.

The duo tried not to run. Such would have proved disastrous, rather they strode as quickly as they could without raising any undue attention. Several times at distance, a soldier saw their passage and Osoba boldly saluted them. Each time they were rewarded with an answer in kind, the uniform was actually aiding their escape. Until......

"Is this the couple you described gemeiner"? a voice barked.

"Ja mein Über Kapitän, that is them".

Osoba fired, even before the German's had time to command them to stop. The captain was thrown from his feet, his chest a ruptured ruin, as the blaster did it's grizzly work. The private who had reported them froze for the merest instant, his face contorted in horror and shock. It was the last expression he would ever wear, as his head burst open like an overripe melon.

"I think I under estimated your reflexes uncle", Osoba remarked.

"They made a fatal mistake", Król said sadly, "They took a moment to gloat, thinking we would surrender. I always say, if you have to shoot; shoot, don't talk".

"An admirable maxim uncle; so let us get the Hades out of here".

The buggies were already speeding away when the ground buckled slightly and the blast wave hurried them along a little. They had but one remaining target, the pride of German mining; Großtiefreich!

EIGHT

A N ANDROID IS not supposed to have human feelings as such. They are constructs of a durinium endo-skeleton, interwoven with nylo-planyon muscles and a circulatory system of pseudo-plas piping, all padded out with acto-flesh and pseudoskin. Their eyes are electro-receptors, their voice issued from an incredibly sophisticated micro speaker. They can smell and feel, thanks to a network of receptors that work very much like the real thing in a mammal, or other higher animal and they can think, reason, and learn from experience, by virtue of the electron brain housed logically enough, in their durinium skull.

They are not programmed to possess feelings however. Certainly they have an immense memory bank, from which to draw and thus make the best logical choice, which can appear to be a decision. They are not however capable of instinct, insight, but most importantly they have no premonition.

Yet when Osoba accompanied Król to Großtiefreich, he had a feeling of foreboding!

His circuits did not appear to be working quite at optimum, a self diagnostic showed there to be no reason for this. Yet his brain was confused by a flood of emotions.

He mentioned none of this to the professor. To do so, might cast even greater doubt on the mission. Above all, Król wanted to render Großtiefreich incapable of mining for some considerable time., All he had spoken about that evening, was the Romanian decision to blast off for Callisto after all. The Imparat of Romania had ignored his misgivings and the rocket was launched from Constanta bound for Numi-Torum. The arrival of a third sovereignty on Callisto would only make things more difficult for a peace process. Großtiefreich had to be disabled rapidly, if it was to be disabled at all.

The duo had their blasters at the ready when they scrambled from the conduit that had lead them to the mouth of Großtiefreich Miniery. Soldiers were patrolling in pairs and the chance of success this time seemed less than one in two. Yet Król had a glint in his eye, a set to his jaw that brooked no argument, there would be no turning back, until the task was completed to his satisfaction.

Almost at once, they ran into one of the myriad patrols. Król fired only a few fractions of a second after the android, such was his fervour. The German soldiers had no chance. At least the element of surprise still lay with the two of them; just. Dragging the bodies to as little cover as the tube way allowed, the duo pressed on without speaking. There was no point in conversation, their purpose was mapped out, they knew what they had to do.

Two hours before a sunrise that would herald a day of some sixteen point seven Earth rotations. Almost seventeen days of no darkness, no where to hide! They had reached the very spot that the geologist had calculated was the main load bearing column of the dome. The crucial support for the sphere overhead, that held the air in and the frigidity of space out.

When.

"Stop right there and drop the weapons", a voice ordered from behind them.

Osoba felt utter astonishment. For the voice was that of a woman, the voice of Floare Górnik!

As instructed, little doubting that disobedience would result in anything short of death, Osoba and Król let their blasters fall to the lower surface of the tube.

"Now the back packs", the nurse instructed.

Only when the android had obeyed her, did he turn and regard the duo that confronted them. The other member was none other than Wolnosc Król, great grand nephew to the professor himself.

"You betrayed us"! Król spat, "How could you do such a thing to your own family"?

"It was not as much the boy's doing as you think", Floare contradicted, "For you see, you already know me old man, know me as Moth and you were betrayed as early as your arrival in Geirvimul Catena and by none other than your nephew here".

As Wolnosc turned to demand some sort of credit, Osoba remembered the old adage, if you have to shoot; shoot, don't talk. With every ounce of his unnatural strength he vaulted at the pair slewing in the air to crash against both of them, horizontally. All three of them smote against the bulkhead with some not inconsiderable force.

Of course the impact did nothing to the android, but it totally winded the boy and the snapping sound that came from Floare Górnik told him that at least one bone had broken.

Everything then happened at once and in a couple of seconds. As Osoba was climbing hastily to his feet, Król was reaching for his fallen blaster once again. Górnik remained unmoving, but Wolnosc was made of sterner stuff, he fired his own blaster pistol and it hit the backpacks with a huge blue flash of incendiary destruction. Król then purposefully shot his own great nephew!

Osoba went over to the smouldering ruin, that was what was left of the backpacks, while Król covered the still inert Floare Górnik. A quick examination revealed that while the Plastique and detonators had survived, the timers were melted to uselessness.

At that moment Floare opened her eyes, wincing with pain,

"How did you do that"? she croaked.

Osoba replied with grim satisfaction, "You are a good double agent Moth, but you made one miscalculation, you did not realise that the man you flirted with and toyed with, before betraying, was in fact, an android. That was a miscalculation that will cost you your life I am afraid, a pity to destroy such beauty, but then, I am a patriot".

Król looked up from his own inspection of the timers,

"We cannot do it now Izzy", he said glumly, "There is no way to get to safety and explode the Plastique".

"You can get to safety Bede Król", Osoba countered, "And you will, now go, leave the Hawk with the Moth, I will give you twenty minutes if I can".

Król considered what Osoba was suggesting; opened his mouth to speak, closed it again and gave the android a nod of admiration. Osoba was making up for the indiscretion he had committed in Geirvimul Catena with the nurse who was a German agent. He was making up for it by paying the ultimate price, the end of his existence.

Then with his blaster at the ready Król turned and raced back to the conduit without a single backward glance.

He was in his suit, in the buggy, racing across the harsh and airless terrain of Callisto when the explosion rent the quietness.

THE FOURTH STORY

ONE

T HE ELITE CLUB was so elite that it only had five members! The reason being that only those five individuals were thought elite enough to merit inclusion in the group. They met monthly, or more frequently if any two members wished to call an interim gathering. They met chiefly for an exchange of information and views and occasionally they simply met to share a good bottle of rum, snuff a little snufz and simply enjoy the company of those who were their equals in every sense of the word.

The meeting place was the Executive Suite of the Grand Hotel in Scorpii, which as everyone knew was the grandest under-bubble hotel in the solar system.

The oldest member and founder, was Professor Bede Krol the Polish Geologist and Scholar. He boasted some eighty Earth years, yet was still sprightly and alert for his years. Each month he was joined by his four friends who were, in no particular order; Chief Constable Heiter Starhoven of Mars Constabulary; the surgeon; Grandios Vul Grande - Soil Man of all Mars and Lord Aubrey Saint-John Willow of Yorkshire, England.

Between the five of them they boasted considerable influence and power. Power so extensive as to rival that of 'Corporation', 'Orang-U-Can' and 'We Can Make It For You'. Not that such was always apparent by appearance. Though Grandios Vul Grande was always resplendent in the newest and highest of fashion, Lord Aubrey was nothing short of scruffy at times, belying his vast wealth. Heiter Starhoven usually came in uniform and Krol and the surgeon tended to wear what on Earth would have born the appellation, 'country wear'.

On this particular occasion Krol arrived in the Executive Suite first. This tended to be the case the majority of times, for he was a very punctual man by nature. He also took pleasure from preparing the table. Bringing with him rum, glasses, bowls and of course the snufz. In addition the surgeon smoked med-cigs, so he usually brought a pack along out of simple hospitality.

He had just finished setting everything out to his satisfaction, dimming the L.E.D.'s to the right level when Grandios Vul Grande Soil Man of all Mars arrived.

"Bede".

"Grandios Vul", the professor responded, he never addressed Vul in any other way, for his, of all tasks on Mars, was the single most important. The recycling of every type of waste into something much more useful. On Mars, under the bubbles, nothing was ever truly wasted and soil men were the workers held in highest regard as a result.

"Can I tempt you with a glass of rum"?

"From"?

"Barbados; Grandios Vul, it came at no little expense".

Vul smiled, picked up a glass and held it out to the professor, just as the door to the suite opened and in walked Chief Constable Heiter Starhoven.

"I hope the duty has been paid on that, Bede", Starhoven joked, "You know I am never off duty".

Bede chortled politely, Starhoven used the same tired quip every time the Elite Club met; he never meant it, or at least that was what he lead them to believe. While the professor was pouring a second glass, for the chief constable, the final two members of the quintet arrived together. The surgeon and Lord Aubrey Saint-John Willow of Yorkshire England.

The latter two took their seats and some time was spent in the pouring of drinks, the lighting of various tobacco products both safe and otherwise, the simple enjoyment of being in opulent surroundings and then Lord Aubrey took it upon himself to take the chair, just as he always did.

"If I recall", the Englishman began. "We had dispensed with our usual exchange of news and views in favour of something more fanciful. To wit, the telling of the most fantastical story each of us had experience of in our equally long and eventful pasts".

"You recall directly my Lord", the surgeon agreed. "For it was you yourself, who had set the proverbial ball rolling the first month with your yarn regarding the Bombay Emerald".

"Yarn sir", his Lordship spluttered in mock indignation, "Yarn! I'll have you know every detail narrated before this august gathering was the absolute truth, so help me".

"And then we heard the case of the Murders in Eumenides", Vul continued, "Told us by the Chief Constable, followed by my account of the Plague of Thirty Three in Pyrighlegethon".

"Indeed, indeed", Lord Aubrey rescued the chair, "So that leaves just you professor and our good friend the surgeon, who have yet to entertain us with an account of some notable event in their past. Which of you shall it be gentlemen"?

The surgeon glanced over at Krol and raised an eyebrow and the latter took the bait.

"I shall go next with my friend's permission"? Krol asked and the surgeon nodded his agreement. "As I am to go fourth, I will begin with the simple title; The Fourth Story".

"Might it just concern your exploits on Callisto by any chance"? Grandios Vul interrupted instantly.

Krol had a sudden far away look in his eye, as he disappointed the other four, "No. I am not quite ready to narrate that particular exploit yet my dear friend. No this goes back much farther than that, to my youth in fact, but before I tell you of the details in those days, there is a certain introduction to the story that must be told. So sit back, take your rum and I will tell the Fourth Story".

TWO

I WAS AT Tritonis S rocket port, when the second chapter of the story begins, but really though it's the second part of the tale, it makes more sense to tell it firstly. I had received a strange e-mail from Earth, from Kraljevo to be precise, which as most of you will be aware is in Serbia. Before I saw the signature at the bottom I knew who it was from however, the Internet protocol had told me all I needed to know.

It was from someone I had not seen for nearly forty Earth years, a friend from university one Villutyre Milinkovic. I see some of you raise eyebrows at the name, yes the very same Villutyre Milinkovic who for several years was head of distribution for 'Corporation' and thus one of the most powerful men in the solar system. The message had been brief and simple;

"I must see you, meet me at Tritonis S on the fourteenth, Vil".

Milinkovic and I had shared a room together when we had both attended university at Katowice in Poland. We had not parted on the best of terms for reasons that will become apparent as I continue my tale. However, I had to admit to some intrigue. If only to see how the years had treated the youth who had possibly been the most handsome in his class.

It was one of those searingly bright days at Tritonis S and foolishly I gazed through the dome of the bubble, as the rocket made it thunderous descent. So much so that by the time Vil was walking toward me, the corona after image of the sun was still disturbing my vision.

"Bede", he croaked to me and instantly I knew something was very wrong indeed. I blinked several times and took in the nature of his features. he was still undoubtedly Villutyre Milinkovic, but his features were knotted in pain, wan almost grey of hue and he actually looked on the verge of death.

"Get me to the executive lounge I have something to tell you and there is not much time", he said, as he shook my proffered hand. His was cold and clammy.

"What is it"? I asked. "The journey? Do you need a doctor"?

"I am beyond doctoring", he wheezed. "Please just get me to the lounge".

So, there being no other logical alternative under the circumstances, I took his arm and guided him to his desired location. He let out a gasp and threw himself down upon one of the couches there. Fortunately there was no one else in the room, so we had total privacy.

"I have to clear the books, Bede", Vil told me then. "We both know I wronged you in the past and though you forgave me, it was still unjust, but the cosmic scales have a way of achieving balance of their own volition and my tale will prove it so".

"Let me get you medical attention old friend", I urged, "Then you can tell me aught that you desire".

"No", he lurched forward, gripping my wrist so as to deter me. His grip was strong and determined despite the poor condition he evidently laboured beneath. "I will tell you what I came to tell you and then you can fetch a doctor".

"Very well Vil", I consented, for there was no help for it, "Tell me your tale".

This was the story Villutyre Milinkovic related to me.

THREE

I NEVER REALLY liked you when first we were roomed together Bede. You were everything I wasn't. Smart, industrious and despite both of those; poor. I on the other hand had come from a reasonably well off family, I had gone to university simply because I did not know what else I was going to do with my life and I was a poor student as a result. There was of course another difference we exhibited. You were short, plain and not especially confident, I was tall, good looking and confidence oozed out of my every pore.

So though we were room mates and shared quite a few hours together, I admit I sort of looked down on you. I know you didn't suspect any of this, it suited my purpose to leave things that way too.

Then came the evening which shaped our lives for many years to come. It began when we were told we were to make room for another student. The bunk was brought in, one of those with the desk beneath it and the two of us were instructed to make space for a third man's study material, though of course we did nearly all of it on our lap-tops in those days. Remember lap-tops, replaced of course by our pads now.

Anyway the new guy arrived and I got the shock of my life, when he introduced himself.

"Hello", he began with a grin, "I'm Milinkovic, I hope the three of us will be firm friends".

"Milinkovic", you laughed, "The chances of that are next to zero, I would never have bet on it no matter what the odds".

You were something of a gambler in those days weren't you Bede?

"Milinkovic", I echoed as I took your hand, "That is my name, is this some sort of wheeze"?

"Wheeze"? he repeated, "Why no, that's my name sir, Villutyre Milinkovic".

"Now I know this is some sort of prank", I barked in anger. I was quick to anger in those days. "Stop this before my head starts buzzing".

"*He's* Villutyre Milinkovic", you explained to him, "Who told you to use that name"?

"It *is* my name sir". Milinkovic persisted. "Perhaps the university housed us together because the computer made an alphabetical match"?

"It's more likely that the computer thinks the two of you are the same student", you remarked, "What is your field of study"?

"I'm doing a post-grad thesis on E.S.P". Milinkovic replied, "What are you doing sir"? He asked me.

"Business Studies and Volume Distribution. You know what, I think I'm beginning to believe you, but if you're lying....."?

"I'm not, my name is Villutyre Milinkovic".

"I'm Bede Krol and I call this chap Vil, so you're going to have to get used to answering to Kovic, what do you say to that"?

"Kovic", he tried it for sound, "Sure, you can call me that, if it's so important to you. Now if you don't mind, I'm going to get settled in".

"Settle away", I agreed, "I'm going out with a girl. One Roupetala Clocoding to be precise"

"Why are you still stringing her along"? you asked me, "You know you care nought for her"?

"Nought for her", I laughed and in truth I knew you were right, "Nought for her, Bede. You're spending way too much time on your pad, why don't you get yourself out for the night too".

"As a matter of fact I am meeting Zanastârc Trentavoria this evening", you announced to me.

"You're out of your league and you know it", you warned me, "There's no way her Uncle will let you, a poor Pole from Katowice, become part of the Trentavoria empire".

"I know", you sighed, "But I love her and whilst she is willing to see me, what else can I do"?

"Trentavoria", the then named Kovic mused aloud, "Isn't that the name of the family that......".

"Owns the major holdings in Corporation", I finished for him, "Yes we know".

"Vil"? you asked then, "Stay in tonight, do some studying, don't hurt poor Roupetala, she's an honest girl".

"I like her when she isn't", I laughed and did not care what my remark did for her reputation, that was the sort of blackguard I was in those green salad days.

So I got ready to go out, in my crisp white polo collared button shirt and Edwardian frock coat of black I cut a dashing figure even if I say so myself. I glanced as my name sake a few times. I had no need to worry about him. Like you Bede he dressed in lounge pants and lumberjack shirt. He resembled me in one detail alone. From then on you and I thought of him as Kovic, a pale imitation of the man who's name he shared.

I was ready well before you. You were labouring over a shave, remember, it was before depilatory pills were available. I quite liked the bald chin but hairy head look, much preferred it to the tonsured one the pills created.

Anyway I left our rooms, that were on the third floor and took the stairs downward to the exit. In the lobby I almost physically ran into Zanastârc, we virtually collided, as did our fates. That first meeting set in place a series of events that changed our lives for ever.

"Sorry", I beamed at the blonde and beautiful creature before me, "Totally my fault".

"That's alright" she smiled and with that one gesture made my decision that I wanted her. Wanted her more than any other girl I had ever met.

"I've not seen you in this block before, are you perhaps lost, or maybe waiting for someone"?

"My boyfriend", she told me and it was as if I had received a blow to the solar plexus.

"Boyfriend"?

"Yes Krol. Bede Krol, do you know him"?

I set my face into one of regret, marvelling at the same time, at my own powers of deception,

"Oh, he did not send you a ping, you do not know"?

"Know? Know what"?

"He's got a upset stomach and cannot meet you this evening. You must be Zanastârc Trentavoria".

"I am. How........".

"I'm Villutyre, his room mate".

"Oh! Right, nice to finally meet you Vil is it? Well I had best........".

"Listen Zanastârc", I cut in, "I'm just going for a rum myself, alone as it happens. Please join me, if only for a single drink"?

"That's gallant of you but.....".

"No it's not. I would much rather have a drink with a beautiful girl than sit at the bar on my own. Please say you'll join me. I'm sure Bede sent a message, I can't understand how you didn't get it"?

"Well maybe just one drink then", she said with the most delightful of smiles, "And it's Anna if you don't mind, I'm not so comfortable with Zanastârc".

"I will call you Anna then", I agreed offering her my arm, "If you will call me Vil".

To my delight she took it and I took the first step that would lead all three of us down very different paths of destiny.

We went to the student bar, a spacious domed building with a transparent dome. Anna seemed to like staring at the stars.

"One day, I'm going off world", she said as I passed her a rum. "I'm worried about Bede, do you think he'd mind if you took me to your room"?

"That's not a very good idea his condition is not, well conducive to polite conversation. Both ends, if you follow".

"Oh! Strange that he did not message and tomorrow we are going to a sort of posh dinner dance and it's couples only".

"I doubt he will be better by then", I lied smoothly, "But it would be an honour and a pleasure to deputise for him in the event that you find yourself stuck".

"That's kind. You have no other plans? What would your girlfriend think of you going with me"?

"I'm not seeing anyone at the moment so that's not an issue", lies tripped off my tongue as easily as you told the truth Bede.

We enjoyed a very pleasant evening. I was in my suave and gentlemanly role, one that fit me easily when I wished it so. Roupetala Clocoding never entered my mind and neither did you. I knew you'd be waiting for Anna in the lobby for some time and when next we met I never told you why Anna had not been available for your rendezvous. I got her to agree to take me to the dinner dance and from that night on we saw one another every night for a week. Then in answer to your persistent messaging, she replied that she was seeing me instead. She knew I was something of a rogue. Yet she found me entertaining and exciting and it was the end for the two of you. I expected a big row remember, but that was not how things turned out at all?

"I'm sorry Bede, it's just one of those things that sometimes happen with people our age. I'm sure Anna will tire of me soon as well".

"And what about Roupetala"? you wanted to know.

"I'll explain to her when next we run into one another", I said glibly.

"You are a rat Vil", Kovic suddenly lifted his head from his own work, "You act without thought of consequence to yourself nor others".

"I don't believe I asked for your opinion", I reminded him, "If Bede is taking the situation like a gentleman, what has it got to do with you".

"I am merely making an observation", my namesake said very calmly and something about the way he spoke and the way he regarded me, made me keep any other remarks I had to myself.

I was walking through the grounds a couple of days later. It was spring as I remember and the birds were chirping, the sun was shining, all the plants were in bud and I realised that I was, at that very moment, content. Then a voice shattered the feeling with the very first syllable,

"Vil"! I turned, she went on, "I've been looking all over for you. You don't answer my messages, you stood me up. What is going on"?

"Zanastârc Trentavoria and I are going on Roupetala", I said as I turned to regard her, "Whilst you and Bede are being left behind. Is that clear enough for you"?

She was momentarily dumbstruck and I chose the opportunity to begin hastening away. Then the stupid girl actually started following me.

"Wait, wait, we need to talk about this", she said. "What we had was special, how can you just finish it by cheating on me"?

"It might have been special to you Roupetala", I told her quietly, "But to me it was anything but. Now will you stop pestering me, we had some pleasant times, but now they're over, move on. Why don't you ask Bede out, he's at a loose end at the moment and you can be fun in bed".

"You blackguard"! she seethed then, "You used me".

"I think my dear, that we used each other", I corrected her, "Let's admit that there were some fun times and go our separate ways".

"You are a handsome man Vil", she said then, "But your mind and personality are ugly".

"Then you are well rid of me", I told her and increased my pace hopefully away from her.

She trotted after me,

"I can't help but love you", she started to cry then, just like all stupid women do when they are feeling sorry for themselves,

"If I can't have you I won't have anyone, I'll kill myself Vil".

"If that is how you feel I regret our previous association", I said with as much decorum as I could muster, "But I don't love you, so you see your plight is hopeless".

"Do you want me to die"? She screamed then and heads began to turn in our direction. I walked back to her and looked her straight in her rather ordinary brown eyes,

"Just because I do not share your viewpoint", I said to her very quietly, "It does not instantly mean that I am labouring beneath a hearing impediment. Now, you are causing a scene which my current girlfriend might hear of and it might cause her some distress. So I suggest you leave the area, as you are not a student of this university and if you intent to kill yourself, you do it with the minimum of fuss and above all quietly".

I must confess as to being curious regarding the expression on her face at this directive. The pallor of her skin was also less than usual, but I had no intention of investigating such phenomenon and turning on my heels yet again, I strode away; my dignity intact. At that instant I noticed two things.

One was that Roupetala Clocoding was no longer following me. The other was that Villutyre Milinkovic was at my shoulder matching my stride pace for pace.

"Oh, good afternoon Kovic", I addressed him cordially, "What brings you on this path at this very instant"?

"I think she meant it", he remarked seriously, "If you don't intervene I think she really might harm herself".

"She is nothing to me, why would it concern me in the slightest"? I asked him.

"Do you really mean that", he asked me gravely. "Is that truly how callous you are Vil"?

In a flash of inspiration I asked then, "You're not one of these new Solarchurch converts are you Kovic"? I asked him, with a laugh,

"What is it they believe, that god was an astronaut"?

"No I am not", he returned very calmly and the way he had about him I always felt cold creeping down my spine when he did.

"Well what ever you pursue or believe will you please go and do it"? I asked him, "Because I do not seek nor want your company".

The following day we were in our room supposedly working, although I was playing with a deck of cards. When my pad pinged. It was a message from Zanastârc and read thusly,

'Thought you should know that Roupetala Clocoding was found dead in her apartment last night, by her sister, who was visiting because she was worried about her. I believe you mentioned that you were once acquaintances, my sympathies dear; your Anna'.

As I was wiping the message I glanced up and Kovic was staring at me, saying nothing, just staring. I had to go out for a long walk then to get some air and clear my head. I did not go to the funeral. It was poison the coroner ruled.

Things were quiet for the next few weeks, you thrust yourself into your studies, while I continued to see Zanastârc and pay the odd student to complete study assignments for me. Then came the day I learned how strapped you was for shillin.

"If I am very careful", you were telling me, "My grant will just last to the end of my degree and I can go into the area of work I find so fascinating".

"You only have just enough", I laughed, "What sort of figure is that Bede"?

"Oh, one hundred shillin not counting the sestertius".

"Who counts the sestertius", I laughed.

"Bede does", Kovic's voice was in my ear like the annoying buzz of an unwanted insect. Sometimes I wished he would go and take poison like the girl he felt so much sympathy for.

A couple of hours later we were playing nine card brag and I suggested half in jest,

"Do you want to make it interesting Kovic, say put a wager on each hand"?

The gambler in you could not resist looking up from your pad and I spotted it at once,

"Sorry Bede, but you don't have the collateral to be in a man's game".

"I might win, in which case I would not need any money", you almost whined back, but Kovic had to point out,

"A good gambler only ever plays with what he can afford to lose Bede and you can't afford to lose any of your savings. Sure Vil, I'll play a few hands with you, for twenty sestertius a hand".

"Twenty sestertius", I laughed, "Even Bede could afford to sit in for a few hands with those phenomenal stakes".

It was just enough of a goad to rile you into an erroneous decision and as I expected, you retorted, "Deal me in. I'll decide when I have enough money to win, or to lose".

I saw Kovic frown, but to be fair to him, he said no more and merely dealt the cards. An hour later with me dealing occasionally from the bottom of the pack to secure constant victory I had cleaned you out; you fool.

"I'll accept a bankers draft at your convenience Bede", I told you. "Then to show you how fair I can be, I'll help you pack".

You made the transaction on your pad without a word and then glumly left the room, no doubt to clear your head and reflect on your ruined education, now that you could no longer pay for the last year of your studies. Kovic waited until you'd gone to say slowly,

"I saw you dealing from the bottom of the pack, Vil. You've taken his girl, now you've taken his money and his education, why did you do these things"?

I was without a solitary regret as I replied,

"I'm a winner Kovic and I don't care what I have to do to win. He's a loser. That's life, there are so many losers, don't waste your time feeling sorry for Bede Krol".

"On the contrary Vil, it's you I feel sorry for", he told me as he too left the room and that twisted my gut a bit I have to confess. I had some extra cash though and I had Zanastârc, so the emotion was fleeting.

Not long afterward, you were forced to leave the University of course, due to the fact that you could no longer pay for the final year of your course.

My romance with Zanastârc progressed as I had intended it would. I knew I would not get my degree, I hadn't done enough work. I also knew though that Zanastârc's uncle would get her fiancee and eventual husband a position in Corporation, she was my ticket to riches and the lifestyle it would bring me that I craved.

I had been right; that there was no way the head of Corporation would let a poor Pole from Katowice marry his niece. I was not a poor Pole though, my family were well-to-do and I was a Serb, not a Pole. Apparently when he found out about our romance, there was some resistance to the match, but Zanastârc was quite a dynamic character in her own right and we continued to see one another. Then we got engaged and the old goat knew when he was beaten. So much so that when we were married a year later, he footed the bill and also paid for our honeymoon in the luxury resort of Arago on the Moon.

More importantly though, he found me a position in Corporation, with promise of rapid promotion, just so long as I remained married to his niece. There's nothing quite like nepotism is there? So for a short while all was rosy. I was wealthy, with a brilliant job, I had a beautiful wife and a huge mansion in Calahonda, Spain.

I did not believe anything could possibly go wrong for me.

How wrong I was! How thin the line we tread between ecstasy and misery, between faithfulness and deceit. One fine morning I was walking into the office at Corporation the happiest I man could be, when only ten minutes later, my life turned an unsuspected corner and the accident happened. My secretary was just bringing in my morning tea, when the silly cow tripped over her ridiculous high heeled shoes and dumped the whole drink into my lap. I wasn't burned; maybe it would have been better if I had been. At least then I might have been taken to hospital instead of flitting back to the mansion to get a change of shirt and breeches.

The instant my flitter pulled onto the drive I had a suspicion. For the pool guy's busted up old ground car was in the way. It was a Tuesday and he was not hired to be there on a Tuesday. Perhaps there was an innocent reason for his presence, I told myself as I vaulted up the curved stone driveway, past the beautifully clipped lawn and the magnificent fuchsias that were resplendent in their immaculately cared for borders. I pressed the thumb plate and entered by the back door. Something told me not to use the front as I usually did.

Creeping through the silent ground floor rooms, I reached the stairs and slipping off my genuine hide loafers, eased up them in my stocking feet.

I heard them, before I pushed the door open. Zanastârc was panting and making noises of ecstasy that she had rarely made with me. The door swung back easily on it's superior quality hinges to reveal my wife's bare back, the bed sheets wrapped around her exquisite ass. She was riding the pool guy and as

I simply stared in dumbfounded shock and fury, she went for the big one and screamed out her moment of supreme pleasure. I did the gentlemanly thing. I waited for her to finish and then I growled from deep down in my throat,

"I'm going to frenging kill the pair of you".

Had it not been for the seriousness of the situation I might have found it funny how swiftly Zanastârc dived from the pool guys loins and hunted bare assed for her discarded knickers. His face too was farcical, his expression told me he believed my threat and he grabbed up his own fallen clothes and vaulted toward me. The idiot thought he could rush past me through the only door and I would simply let him by.

My fist impacted his solar plexus with every ounce of my strength and he let out the most unusual of sounds before falling at my feet writhing in a vain attempt to draw breath.

"Don't Vil"?! Zanastârc screamed, "Don't hurt him, please"?

Now had she laughed and told me he was nothing more than a casual frenge and meant nothing to her, I might have some how found it possible to forgive her; eventually. After all I had banged at least three of my past secretaries, but to find out that she actually 'cared' about him. 'Cared' about him when she was married to me, me Villutyre Milinkovic, well that was just simply more than I could stand.

It also presented me with something of a quandary. Should I divorce her, I doubted my Uncle-in-law would continue to support me and further my career in Corporation. However, she had frenged another man and try as I might, I couldn't forgive her. The pool man took to his heels and it's a bit obvious to say, but I promptly dispensed with his; ah services!

Zanastârc hastily dressed, while I walked calmly down to the magnificent galley kitchen we shared and made myself a peppermint tea. Whilst I was sipping it wondering how I would get rid of her, she joined me and seated herself on the far side of the bar which ran along the centre of the room.

"What can I say Vil"? she began rather obtusely, I thought. I didn't answer, never talk too much when you have the upper hand.

"We have been growing apart ever since you started putting in long hours at the office".

I could have added that a goodly proportion of the time I had been putting it into three of my secretaries too, but you don't talk when you've got the upper hand.

"I was bored Vil, bored I tell you".

"I wondered if she had lifted this dialogue from one of those dreadful day time shows she watched on the net-casts. I let her go on.

"I feel dirty now, now that it's come out, but also kind of relieved you know? Perhaps now we can start over and work on building something lasting? What do you say"?

I finished my drink, walked over to her and gave her a peck on the cheek,

"I'll have to think about it Zanastârc. I want you to know I'm no longer angry, just hurt. You've fired a deadly barb into my heart and I fear it will split in two".

Then I left with my dignity in tact and also rather pleased with my dialogue, perhaps I had a back up career as a writer for those very shows?

Anyway I was feeling much better an hour later. I had my latest secretary, Beaunosentia, thrown over the desk face down, her knickers around her ankles and her frock around her shoulders as I porked her from behind. My orgasm was one of those angry ones you have from time to time you know; or maybe you don't Bede.

I still had the problem with my whore of a wife, I was thinking on it, when the secretary, who had regained her breath and her under things and was back in the office outside, announced on the intercom,

"Some one asking to see you mister Milinkovic. He doesn't have an appointment, shall I send him away? He says his name's Kovic"?

"Show him in", I directed with a smile, wondering what my namesake was doing there. I'd not seen him since being expelled from university, for banging the Dean's sister (older, but one saucy minx). Fortunately the detail had been kept very quiet and Zanastârc, nor her uncle, had ever heard about it.

The door opened and in walked Villutyre Milinkovic, looking exactly the same as I remembered him, still resembling me, without being anywhere near as good looking.

"Now then you old eater of other people's leftovers, how in Hades are you doing"? I greeted him.

He gave me one of those enigmatic smiles of his, remember, then asked,

"Jam on it Vil, mind if I sit down"?

"Make yourself comfortable, what will you have to drink? And I mean a drink-drink, this is a cause for a mini celebration"?

"Is it really"? Again that mysterious smile

"Well no not really you bounder of the first water, but have a drink anyway and tell me what brings you to Calahonda"?

As I walked over to the cabinet carefully, for the rough ride I given Beaunosentia had left little Vil a bit sore, he told me,

"In a way 'you' do Vil. Go on then; I'll have a vodka, if you're having one"?

"Having one? Of course I'm sinking one, this is the best kept mini bar in the building. Do you want Russian, Czech, Estonian or Ukrainian vodka"?

"Russian please".

"So what do you mean when you say 'I'bring you here, are you after a job" I asked him, as I handed him the glass. To my great surprise he nodded,

"Yes, can you offer me anything, or get me an interview"?

"You can start in the mailing room in about ten minutes if you want"? I joked and then he cut the laugh short in my throat.

"Very kind, thank you".

"Eh? No you plank I was joking, the mail room only pays fifteen a week, I can get you something better than that. Why do you need me though, surely you got your degree"?

Draining his glass he rose and placed it back in the bar,

"The mail room will be fine Vil and it is not me who needs you, but the other way around".

I believe my mouth was still open when the door closed behind him.

Dismissing it as temporary insanity on his part I returned my attention to the problem of Zanastârc and how to be rid of the whoring bitch, yet still retain my relationship with Trentavoria and Corporation. The conclusion I came to was inescapable; Zanastârc had to die!

I see that shocks you Bede, but when you think about it, what else was I supposed to do? Forgive her, ride the saddle that lout of a pool guy had been in? I don't think so.

Whilst I was contemplating foul and ruthless murder, I heard about you and your heart attack. I hope losing that slut of a wife of mine, to me, was not a cause of that Bede, more likely your stumble on the way to academic success; which come to think of it, was my fault too wasn't it?

Anyway I heard of your move to Mars for the lighter gravity, your completion of the course by net and eventual professorship after a few years and realised I'd only caused a hiccough not a fatality. By that time I was a grieving widower.

I'm not given to acts of violence really and it usually leaves tell tale evidence, so that ruled out weaponry for me. I also eliminated the hiring of a hit man, also risky. That left me with fatal accident. I was mulling over how to achieve that when fate brought the answer to me, into my very office no less. It came in the form of a visitor and that visitor was the famous world renowned biochemist Professor Baadareina Hoyle.

Hoyle was frinselling up about his delight at creating Dodoprot and his sadness at being involved in Snufz. I was listening with half my mind and both my eyes three quarters open, when he got onto the new craze of 1in2 cigarettes. I might have to clarify here for you Bede, while Snufz was the mind bending and addictive narcotic cut with tobacco and originated on Mars, 1in2's were worse! You see when Hoyle spliced the lichen on Mars with yeast, it made a culture than when cut with one quarter of tobacco, created Snufz. Taken nasally it was a mind expanding hallucinogen and quite addictive narcotic.

Then some buffoon tried cutting it half and half with tobacco and the effects bizarrely, were much worse. Millions became addicted overnight, there were several fatalities. That was when my attention suddenly perked up.

"This is all very intriguing Professor", I lied, "But tell me; what would happen if someone took one hundred percent pure Snufz"?

Hoyle blinked and stammered, "Such w-would be fatal Vil why would anyone want to d-do such a thing"?

"Tell me something else", I asked him, "Could you create a cigarette that looked like and tasted like a 1in2, but was in fact pure Snufz"?

"Ever the academic, the fool considered this and then began, "Yes I could...... but such would be a deadly weapon Vil, or an instrument for murder".

"Yes", I agreed, "Murder is what I want if for, when can you have a couple ready for me"?

"Ready for, for you? Why; why would I do that"?

I looked at the middle aged, balding man of no great stature and no great looks. Yet because of his wealth and position he was married to a beautiful blonde pneumatic trophy wife.

"I suspect you would rather make a couple for me, than watch a net-cast of your Bonitaru sat astride me;

riding and going for the big one".

I waited for a while for the information to sink in, he paled and asked,

"You mean you would seduce Bonny, sleep with her just to injure me. You would not do that, could not do it".

"Are you willing to bet I couldn't"? I wished to know.

He suddenly sagged in his seat, a bead of sweat running down his domed forehead and burying itself in his brow,

"When do you want the 1in2's"?

"1in1's", I corrected, "And soon Baadareina, very soon".

Do you know, at the instant he gave me them, I also decided it might just be fun to frenge Bonitaru anyway. Only once Zanastârc was dead of course. Mrs Hoyle could comfort me in my hour of need, help me get over my sad loss!

"I've been thinking about you and the pool guy", I told Zanastârc that evening, as we ate dinner. Usually such events were now conducted in total silence so she was shocked that I had spoken to her. "Anyone can make a mistake and that was what it was, wasn't it"?

"Well yes", she returned carefully. She really was pathetic, the sad slut.

"I bitterly regret it Vil".

"I know you do", I lied and managed to take her hand across the magnificent mahogany dining table we owned, I could almost have brought my meal back up over it

"I forgive you Anna. To make it right, I think we should have a party".

"Party"?

"Yes, invite all our friends, all of them, show them how happy we are together, we'll have it here, at the mansion".

The look of relief and sadness, the mixed expression on her face really was nauseating, but to my credit I enthused over all her preparations. Encouraged her to throw herself untiringly into the whole venture. I made certain the Hoyle's were on the list too, it might be fun to lay the ground work of Bonitaru's seduction on that very occasion. In the mean time, I didn't go without, I made certain of that. I'd grown tired of Beaunosentia and promptly sacked her, she'd cried the poor bitch, but then female tears had never moved me much.

I hired a replacement, Santina, with her long curly brunette hair, superb ass and the best tits I'd ever seen on a girl, she was occupying my frenge time nicely and she could do things with her mouth that would make a prostitute blush.

The day of the party arrived and she was the last person I would have invited though. You know how it is Bede, you have to compartmentalise your women. The wife, the mistress and the maid. Although in my case the maid, Raeca had also a place in the mistress section, having dutifully spread her legs a time or two for me, when the need required it.

Through out this period Kovic had visited me on more than one occasion, he had become quite the comic, since university,

"Your slide into depravity Vil, has surprised even me", he told me one day over a vodka, "I knew you'd end up in dark times and actions, but by thunder, you're surpassing yourself".

"What the frenge do you know about it mail boy", I'd laughed. When he'd gone though I asked myself was I truly depraved? No, I reasoned, just a proper guy's guy, who knew his own place in the order of things and the place women played. Round about these days I read on the net about your marriage to Elizaveta, the good wholesome Polish girl who had been living in Medusae F when the two of you had met, on one of your lecture tours of Mars.

I was pleased for you, thinking it would certainly help you stop being so uptight if you cleared your tubes once in a while.

I digress though, the party. It was certainly an elaborate affair, which was of course, exactly what I had hoped for. I had managed to get Bonitaru Hoyle away from her stooped and pathetic excuse for a husband and carefully laid the groundwork for a future liaison, then slipping upstairs to the master bedroom, went to the drawer where the 1in1's were. The room was almost dark, but the blinds were open and dull moonlight spilled in sufficiently for me to reach the drawer and the cigarettes, without turning on any lights. I was just taking them, ready to slip then into an inside pocket, when the door opened and a silhouetted figure intruded into my personal space.

"Who the frenge's that"? I barked, in what I hoped was sufficiently menacing a voice to deter any thought of violence in the intruder,

"The party's downstairs, you don't have to be up here, when we've three ground floor water closets".

"I came to ask you something", Kovic began. "Is this something you really want to do Vil"?

"Kovic, you frenging imbecile, I didn't even invite you to the party, get out of my koofing house"!

"Not until you've answered me", he persisted. "Up until now your mischief and thoughtlessness toward others has been on a rather disgusting level. Now though, you're going to escalate even that, there can be no coming back from it".

Totally unbidden, Roupetala Clocoding suddenly entered my mind. I could see her trusting and faintly moronic features as clearly as I see you now Bede. I didn't like the effect Kovic was having on me, the evening and my plans. From the drawer I felt for, rather than looked for, the needle gun, my fingers closed around it first time.

Levelling it at Kovic's chest I told him calmly,

"I could shoot you as an intruder, mail boy and none would condemn me, so I suggest you get the frenge out of my house".

"What needles do you have in that gun"? he asked, he did not sound kowtowed by either my threats, nor the weapon.

"Neuronic level one", I told him honestly enough. "True they would only disable you, but the effect is said to be excruciatingly painful. Now, moron, do you want to experience it, or are you leaving"?

He shrugged, turning to go, then over his shoulder he actually thought to advise me,

"If the gun's for home security, level one is not a good idea. The assailant might have recovered before the constabulary arrive and attack you. You really should get some level two needles".

When he left I thought about the latter and resolved to do just that. Or maybe the new level three's, which injected a neurotoxin into the bloodstream and caused those hit by it, to die in about three days, of painful septicaemia They seemed the cruellest of all to me and I liked the idea.

Pocketing the cigarettes and putting the gun back in it's place, I went to rejoin the party and to locate my dear sweet wife, she whom was soon to be, my '*former*' spouse.

I found her looking a shade forlorn, perhaps she thought that if she engaged any men in conversation, I would accuse her of flirtation. I might have too; before I killed her.

"Anna how is the party going, are there enough canapé's how are the drinks going down"?

"Don't worry", she said dully, "Raeca has everything under control".

'She lost control last night'! I thought to myself with a smile

"I'm not sure you're having the best of times", I noted then, "Do you want something to help you cool-out and take the edge off everything"?

Her brow furrowed in confusion, "I don't know......"?

"I've a couple of 1in2's in my pocket, got them from one of the mail lads", I told her with a wink, "You'll have to go outside to smoke one though".

"1in2's"! she gasped, "They're illegal Vil, what do you think uncle Magnus would say if.....".

"Who do you think created Snufz in the first place", I reminded her, "Okay if you're not interested I'll share with........".

"How many have you"?

"Two"?

"Alright I'll try it, will you take me on the road, if it's a bad trip"?

"No one that's smoked one of these babies has ever complained". I was able to tell her with total candour.

I was standing very close to her, almost an embrace. Touching parts of her body like that, old stirrings started, she was still beautiful and very desirable and then I remembered the noise she had made when she cum on the pool guy. I slipped her fifty percent of the deadly cigarettes I owned and advised,

"Go in the front, there's less chance of anyone seeing you then". Some of the guests had spilled out into the rear grounds, Bladdered on my booze. Once anyone found Zanastârc's body the party would be over.

I waited.

Twenty minutes passed, didn't anyone want to go out for a med-cig?

I waited some more.

Finally a small group decided to go out for a smoke, the scream of horror heralded the end of the party and the end of my marriage. I rushed out to portray the grief stricken husband and almost burst into hysterical and ironic laughter, Zanastârc was floating face down in the pool.

The next few days were very busy ones for me. I had to show the suitable grief and shock, in front of uncle Magnus. He ordered me to stay off work and then told me he would be making all the arrangements for the funeral. I was thus in the mansion and could not really be seen out for a while, looking too happy.

I lasted two days and then on the third, whilst Raeca was bending to dust a low table, I managed to cup both her rather satisfactory breasts in my hands at the same time.

"No maestro es demasiado pronto", she objected in Spanish (No master it's too soon)

"I'm lonely", I told her, "Before the accident there was only you anyway, we were as a man and his wife, for there was no longer anything else for me".

"The overdose of drugs was very sad", she adjusted her brassiere, "You had no suspicion"?

I shook my head, "And now I just want to be with someone who understands me", I told her, that crap usually worked fine with the less intelligent ones.

"Just give me some comfort darling, the inquest is tomorrow and then after that there is the funeral. I want to feel alive Raeca and you do that for me".

So she did and the verdict at the inquest was death by misadventure and then I returned to work.

I was in my office, wondering if Santina would like to be spread eagled on my desk, when who should walk in but the numero uno, the big cheese himself.

"Villutyre", the old goat wheezed. Magnus Quintilius Trentavoria was not a particularly large man by stature, but when it came to status he was a giant. I bet he had been awesome and unstoppable in his prime, now he was in his late seventies and the years were beginning to slow him down. Not the steely glint in his eye though, that still burned with a resolve that bordered on fanaticism. I had to admire him.

He seated himself on the edge of my desk,

"I'm glad you're back, how've you been holding up"?

"It's the early evenings that're the hardest M.Q.", I lied. I always called him M.Q. he seemed to like it.

"That was when we ate dinner together and I would tell her all about my day here and she would tell me all about her day shopping, do you remember how she loved to shop"?

"Hhm, quite", the old goat was never able to handle talk about feelings. It was a wonder to me how he had managed to father his daughter at all; if he had! That would have been funny, the heir to Corporation a bastard. One bastard following another it would be then.

"Drink M.Q."? I asked then, just to fill the gulf that had threatened to sink our little tête-à-tête.

"I'll have a Brandy, if you've got one".

The old pillock knew I never kept the French filth, couldn't stand it,

"One vodka coming up", I said cheerfully, smiling inwardly to the twisting of dissatisfaction of his already pursed mouth.

"You may be wondering what I've come to see you about"? he began then.

I'd presumed it would be something to do with his will, to wit my being written out of it, now I was no longer strictly one of the Trentavoria clan.

"Business M.Q."?

"Yes", he surprised me. "Have you heard of Marslip Inc:?

I dredged what I knew of the freight firm to mind, "One of the companies under the ownership of Drorb Makers-Guild isn't it"?

"For now", the fire in the eyes burned like a furnace. "Corporation is going to make a merger and acquisition strategy for buying it using little or no capital up front and I want you to spearhead it"?

The old goat had surprised me. He thought that a promotion would help me get over my grief and he was giving me a plumb assignment to prove myself.

I nodded, trying to look more confident than I felt,

"You can rely on me M.Q. and thank you for this opportunity".

"And before you ask. it's fifteen thousand per annum more". He drained his glass, "Oh, there's one other thing too, I'm giving you an assistant, someone who's on the up and up in Corporation. A dynamic fellow who has impressed all those he's worked for in the very short time he's been with the company. You'll remember him, you gave him his big chance here and he hasn't let you down. Take him under your wing Vil, teach him some of what you know and introduce him to plenty of people in distribution".

I was dredging my mind as to who he was talking about, when he shouted through the unclosed doorway,

"Come on in Tyrean". As Villutyre Milinkovic walked into my office Trentavoria was saying,

"Strange coincidence too, with the names I mean they're very similar, Villutyre Milinkovic, Tyrean Kovic. Well anyway here he is Vil".

I rose from my desk and shook his hand, knowing my smile would be glassy, we both muttered some platitudes, until the old man left.

"Which wall would you prefer me to be seated at with my desk in front of me"? *Tyrean Kovic* asked me then.

"What is your frenging game Kovic"? I wanted to know.

"Why a merger and acquisition strategy for buying Marslip using little or no capital up front", he smirked and I thought to myself,

'I still have a 1in1 left, carry on agitating me Kovic and see where it gets you'!

I was single again though, still well off, still young enough to have a great time and why should I let him get me down?

The next few months I did everything I wanted. I won't go into detail, but there was very little I didn't try and very little I didn't enjoy. It was around about the same time of the Martian Plague. I watched the net for you and was pleased to see you managed to survive it. It was a shame about Elizaveta but I reasoned that you were young enough to re-marry if and when the fancy took you.

It was Kovic who began to figure more and more in my life.

I did not want it thus, but after the merger, Trentavoria assumed we were a team and he seemed to have moved into my office permanently. This meant my office romances, such as they were, had to be discontinued. I also grew to resent just about everything that was ever uttered by him. In short he got under my skin in a way not even the pool guy had.

He had to go!

I ruled out a second suicide by misadventure, to coincidental; even the Spanish police might work that one out.

No, it had to be good old fashioned murder and I developed a plan over the next few weeks. Kovic made it easier too, for his constant nagging increased and with it, my resolve to do a serious doings, namely his demise.

For some time I had used a retreat, a second property I had in Kiunga, Kenya. It had been cheap to build, the servants worked for very little still accepting KSh (shillings) divided into Cents, rather than shillin, it did not rain in winter and you've never had a really good frenge, until you've had some charcoal pussy; believe me!

As a shillin is currently two hundred and thirty seven Kenyan Shillings, you can imagine I was a rich man when over there.

"We've been working hard these past couple of weeks Kovic", I said to him one day, "Do you fancy the weekend at my retreat"?

He looked up from his work, "I always expected you would have another property, but didn't know where it was"?

"Kiunga, property over there is amazingly inexpensive. We could go to the national parks, or just cool-up what ever you prefer".

"You have no other assignations this weekend then"?

"It's not like that", he could annoy me over the slightest things, "I'm making you my first choice as to who to spend some down and level time with"?

"Then I shall be pleased to accept", the imbecile finally fell into my trap.

I had the location, nice and quiet, I had the means, the needle gun and some level three ammunition, I had the motivation, I hated the frenger and I had the man".

We went down to Kiunga in Zanastârc's air flitter, the Honda Air P5 Cruise, which of course was now mine. I determined to have it re-sprayed though, for being white it would surely attract all the flying insects once we landed, green and brown camouflage would suit it and me better. I was dressed in camouflage safari gear while Kovic had opted for khaki which was also suitable.

When we landed Abdi came running out to meet and greet. Abdi Churchill Blair was my servant/butler, his teenage daughter Chausiki served as cook maid and when I was in the mood, bed wench.

"Salamu bwana have you luggage to take inside? What about this other bwana"?

I had always instructed Abdi to speak in a mixture of Swahili and Standard, it added to the exotic air about the place.

"This is Bwana Kovic", I told him, "Kovic meet my butler and general man about the place; Abdi Churchill Blair".

Kovic smiled at the appellation and nodded to the Kenyan.

"Yes we have some luggage but I need something else", I told my mtumishi. "For later this evening I would like you to get me a mzuri vijana msichana (comely young girl) I think you know what for. How much will you need"?

Abdi thought about it and asked for two thousand KSh, I could have bought a girl many thousands of times over, with the change in my pocket. I threw him three thousand shilling notes and advised him to keep the change if he matched the order precisely. Of course this conversation went over Kovic's head, for he did not speak Swahili. I spoke enough as to be understood by Abdi, but it was a pigeon mixture at best.

We went in the house, had lunch and amazingly Kovic *started* again.

"You need to look at your life, Vil and decide just where you are going", he began, "You're on a down ward spiral that is just going to end in disaster".

"Strange", I countered, "But I fell fine about my life and who I am".

His lecture went on, even when I took him to the national park and showed him such bizarre creatures as, Buffalo, Lions and Elephants. I mean, Elephants, have you ever seen such a huge and strange beast? To me, Rhinoceros and Giraffes look like they're from some other planet, which is strange because they look weirder than the Piscmarsalis and Ardentemcancmarsalis of Callisto.

Kovic just kept going on about my soul and I was thus resolved after one more night, to put him out of *my* misery!

We went back to the house for dinner. It was to be with Chausiki and the girl Abdi had gotten for Kovic, her name was Zawadi, she joined us for dinner. She was everything I had ordered for him. In other circumstances I might have made use of her credentials myself.

"Who are you my dear"? Kovic asked her. She smiled a perfect white smile with her excellent white teeth,

"I kwa ajili yako".

"Well miss Yako can you please get off my lap"? He asked her, as we were served desert.

"Her name is Zawadi, she says she is for you", I explained to him, "I got her for you this morning".

He looked shocked, "She's a comfort girl you mean"?

"I'm not sure if it's professional", I laughed, "But for this evening you've gotten lucky Kovic and I must say very lucky, in my expert opinion".

"I don't want her", he objected, "Please ask her kindly to leave, Vil"?

In frustration I bid Chausiki good night and taking Zawadi by the hand bid Kovic good night too and went to bed with the new girl. He'd made a big mistake, Zawadi was worth the money twice over.

At about three in the morning I awoke, the girl slumbering peacefully by my side and knew why my slumber had been disturbed.

Somehow my internal clock had decided it was time!

I arose, threw on a cotton robe and taking the needle gun out of the bedside drawer loaded it with a level three needle. Easing my way out of our room and into his was no problem in my bare feet and while he slept on top of his own bed, I aimed the gun at Kovic's thigh and fired!

FOUR

A T THIS POINT, my old adversary; for in truth I could not call him a friend, ceased his narration.

I guessed, "You felt a searing pain in your thigh? One that has not diminished, since but grown stronger and stronger and soon it will be too much"?

Villutyre nodded once, his handsome features bathed in sweat, then he smiled, suddenly gripped his chest and having made a tremendous effort to complete his narration for my benefit, promptly died in front of me.

That my friends is the fourth story, make of it what you will.

FIVE

GRANDIOS VUL ASKED, "We're not expected to believe that such a fanciful narrative is true are we"?

"Make of it what you will", Krol smiled, "It is the Fourth Story".

"I found it fascinating and repulsive in equal measure and thank you for the entertainment", the surgeon said, finishing his drink,

"Now I must bid the rest of you goodnight until next month, for I have a very early operation in the morning".

Krol showed him to the door, while the other three chatted between themselves.

"Was it true"? The surgeon asked, as he walked through the door.

"Does it matter"? Krol asked, "It was my story and next month it will be your turn".

"Goodnight then", the surgeon made his exit and Krol rejoined his friends.

"I think we have time for one more drink", Lord Aubrey suggested, "Shall we make it vodka for a change"?

IF YOU WANT IT, WE STOCK IT

ONE

VOORHEES PON WAS just settling
back with a nice cup of peppermint tea
and having a moment, gazing out of the french window when his pad pinged.
Since the vast planting programmes of a decade ago Russian Lichenvine and
Lichenbamboo forests had proliferated in the lowlands and now the bubbles
of Mars were a thing of the past. Huge greenhouses still existed everywhere of
course and estates were extremely conscious of the thermal properties of their
buildings, but it was said that some hardy individuals could now make short
journeys without even the small compact oxygen cylinders on their backs.

The vast network of tubes that had hither to connected the cities were now
equally lengthy and impressive rail lines, but for shorter journeys flitters were
in use. Pon even had a small and compact garden next to his condo, or at least
his quarter of the land, which he shared with his three neighbours. He had
planted Lichenlavendar, Lichenevening Primrose and some Lichencarrots and
Lichenradish. In the evenings he often went out in his thickly fur lined hooded
coat, to smell the fragrances.

The ping was from the controller and finishing his tea, he reluctantly
locked up and slipped quickly into his Honda Silk Stream E250. Such a short
journey from interior to interior no longer had the need for oxygen at all, the
atmosphere of Mars was now breathable for very short periods!

When he entered Plug's office, he was once again forced to peer through
the smoke of many thousand med-cigs and it did not help that the controller
had photophobia and thusly kept the illumination very low. The fact that the

walls were dark stained wood did not make matters any easier. They had began life as shiny mahogany, now years of nicotine had dulled their sheen and darkened their colour, to a muddy rendering that was both unnatural and ominous.

"You sent for me sir"?

"No", said a sharp and high pitched voice from the corner, "I did".

The seated individual, that Pon had totally missed in the gloom was a marunt, a Martian runt, one of those born after the plague of some years past. Unlike neither a midget nor a dwarf, the marunt had perfectly normal growth in certain areas of their body and dwarfed areas in other. How they were distinct from the other two groups however, was that the dwarfism seemed random in any given group, making for the most bizarre and deformed people that existed in the solar system.

"Who are you"? Pon asked, ignoring the other's infirmity.

"I am Fongelturn Dorba" the marunt rose to his full height, of some one hundred and seven centimetres, "I am a detective".

Plug remained silent so, hiding the amusement out of his voice Pon replied, "A detective"?

"Oh, I know I'm short", the marunt acknowledged, "But I have nerves of duridium and the heart of a hero".

"Then why have you come to the agency", Pon wished to know, "Unless you're looking for some sort of goofy sidekick"?

Dorba giggled, more a titter than a laugh. "That's funny mister Plug, you told me he had a sense of humour".

"Yeah, I'm a regular wow a minute, but you took me away from a golden moment, near my garden, mister Dorba, so is there any chance you might get to the point before Explorer Once returns to the solar system"?

"I've been hired to do a job, but to tell you candidly I major in divorce work where my, ah infirmities are a positive boon, for this little assignment I need someone to take my place, act as me, if you will".

"And what is the job"? Pon asked, he did not like how his controller had remained silent throughout the meeting, thus far.

"For attending a party in my name, I will split the one hundred shilling fee with you fifty, fifty", Dorba offered

"That's tempting", Pon noted, "A party eh, so what is the job, might it be bodyguard by any chance"?

"Sort of, sort of", the marunt agreed, "The party sir is being run by Alovar Hornrunner".

"The owner of, 'If You Want It, We Stock It'? Who is threatening Hornrunner's life"?

"No one, that's the bizarre situation. The assignment is to protect his nephew Arlvo".

"So someone is threatening Arlvo's life? Why not just cancel the party"?

"It's not that straight forward", Dorba continued. "You remember Alovar's brother committing suicide some six months ago"?

"I seem to recall reading the podcast".

"Well obviously he was Arlvo's father and Alovar, to try and make life a bit more glamorous for his nephew is throwing the party at Arlvo's mansion; to cheer him up so to speak".

Pon was confused, "So who actually needs protecting and from whom"?

"Arlvo, from himself! The head of the firm is hiring one Fongelturn Dorba to make certain his nephew does not commit suicide, at his own party".

"Why would he do so, at a party"?

"Can't you think of a few good reasons? Rum, Vodka, Pills, Snufz, 1in2.....".

"I get the picture, the evening sounds like it's going to be a real wheeze".

When the marunt had gone, having made an arrangement to meet Pon at twenty hundred hours that evening, Plug finally broke his silence,

"Look after both the job and our diminutive detective, Pon"?

"Okay, who is he"?

"He's the grand nephew of Governess Winterstone of Idaho"!

TWO

THAT EVENING THE strange duo were speeding toward Isidis Planitia, the western equatorial region that had recently recorded a record high temperature of twenty two degrees centigrade at thirteen hundred hours. The Honda was making good time, despite Dorba's obvious nervousness. Pon pulled her up outside what could only be described as a very impressive structure indeed.

"Well, this is it, you want me to pretend to be you, so what will you be doing".

"I'll stay in the flitter", the marunt said firmly, "Keeping an eye on the exterior and monitoring who comes and go's. You have your earpiece, so I can keep you informed".

"That's the plan"? Pon regarded the marunt. His head was small and his ears very small indeed, his eyes and ears were in proportion to his head though. His arms and legs were small, but his feet were tiny and his hands of normal size so that they looked way too large for the rest of him. The overall effect was more disquieting than frightening, Pon accepted all, for what it was.

"Yes, that's the plan", Dorba agreed and Pon climbed out the side of the flitter and made it to the front door without any oxygen. At his signal the airlock hissed open, to reveal a butler dressed in tails and white bow tie.

"Your invitation sir"? the man requested, a white gloved outstretched hand. Pon handed him the foil print out.

"Come in mister Dorba", the butler smiled, having perused it, "Director Hornrunner is expecting you".

Pon was not prepared for the opulence of the interior of Arlvo's mansion. All was glittering Mar's crystals in azure, crimson and turquoise, lit by cleverly concealed L.E.D.'s. The floor was of exquisite marble, in a tasteful very pale grey, the walls covered in works by Stormglund, Roxbrough, Jennterers and even an occasional and almost priceless van-Haaser.

Waiters were on hand with trays of h'orderves, cocktail snacks, small sandwiches and the choice of drinks was endless, even trays of med-cigs were being handed out, so presumably the building had an extraction and purification system.

Pon took some snacks and then an Earth rum, he was just enjoying both, when a beautiful blonde approached him with a crimson smile. Beauty was nothing unusual in the thirty third century, when everyone had augmentations in their early teens, but it was something about the way that this girl conducted herself that had Pon entranced from the offset,

Good evening", she said simply. Pon replied in kind.

"I'm Ava Vine-Flentine and you are"?

"I'm Fongelturn Dorba and I'm looking for Alovar Hornrunner".

"You say you're Dorba", she looked momentarily puzzled. "Well then let's go and find the Director for you".

She walked before him, or rather glided and the surgeon that had created her ass, was a craftsman. Pon drank in her perfume, as it trailed behind her divine body. The room they entered was filled with people dressed in clothing that would have cost more than Pon made in three months.

"Aah there you are Director", Ava Vine-Flentine crooned, "Fongelturn Dorba, Director Alovar Hornrunner. Now if you'll excuse me gentlemen".

She drifted away, but her perfume lingered after her.

"So, you're Dorba", Alovar Hornrunner's voice dripped with haughty disbelief, "Your voice gave a different impression of you, over the net-mic".

"You know how we private det's are", Pon returned smoothly, "We use voice subfuscation technology as a matter of course, security you know".

"I see", the arrogant older man did not sound like he believed the glib explanation, "Never mind that anyway, you have your assignment, are you ready"?

The way he regarded Pon was like a chill wind, blowing across a grave yard, there was not a trace of humanity left behind the business man's grey eyes.

"I'll keep Arlvo in my sights, sir".

"You need to do more than that", Hornrunner snapped, "You need to keep him alive"!

"I'm presuming the suicide of his father has badly effected him, that's why you're so worried"?

"Even more, I've heard him say he's contemplating it".

"Has anyone else heard him behave in this way".

"What in Hades is that meant to imply".

Those gathered around them began to melt away at the old man's indignation, it seemed Alovar Hornrunner was a man to be feared.

"The more people he's told, would indicate how determined he is", Pon was not uncomfortable when he was doing his job and he did it well.

"Miss Vine-Flentine; if you must know", Alovar reluctantly informed him then. "And I consider that to be enough"!

Unkowed Pon persisted, "How does Ava fit into this little picture, mister Hornrunner"?

"It's Director Hornrunner, or just Director, *'mister'*Dorba and I think you're being just a bit mupefluint".

"It all adds up to useful background, but if you don't want to tell me I'll try not to be mupefluint again", Pon promised, wondering what the word meant, so many new ones cropped up every year, it was impossible to keep up with them all.

"Very well if you must know", the director bridled, "Miss Vine-Flentine is an old friend of the family. Oh, there's Arlvo now, I'll call him over".

He did so, with the sort of command and gesture one would give a pet dog. As he was introduced to the nephew, Pon could see the family resemblance, they exchanged nods and then Arlvo asked,

"Are you enjoying the gathering, mister Dorba"?

"It has already had it's moments", Pon smiled, "What about you, are you having a pleasant time"?

"Not really", the youth looked sad, "These functions get to be a bally bore after the first few".

"You must forget about your father, my dear late brother", the director urged.

"How can I, when you keep belting on about him, at every crawl", Arlvo suddenly flared in his young person's vernacular.

Ava Vine-Flentine suddenly saved the rather embarrassing scene, she had appeared once again and asked Pon,

"Mister Dorba, would you accompany me for a moment".

Gallantly, Pon agreed "Of course, do you need some assistance"?

"This place is too hot and stuffy, the gathering of so many bodies, you know. Would you grab one of those oxy-tanks and come into the garden for a breath of frigid air"?

Pon placed his glass on a convenient table and followed her out. The air was frigid indeed and they would not be able to stay out long, even with the oxygen. The two of them stood for a second admiring the beauty and hardiness of the Lichenalupes, the night perfume of the Lichenastocs.

"They smell marvellously, don't you think", she said, as if reading his mind.

"I think you smell better", he smiled his best smile.

"Oh but that is just perfume. I'm pleased you noticed it though it's 'Promesse de Soie Sous'.

'It would be French', he thought, *'They don't think any one else can make a decent eau de toilette'*.

"And do you Ava, promise in silk under your outer garments"? Suddenly Pon worked it out, old friend of the family his elbow, she was Alovar's mistress and she had an agenda for bringing him out, into the very thin night air of Mars.

"We should go back in before you get hypothermia", he ordered seeing the goose bumps on her arms.

"I could do a med-cig before we go do" she crooned.

"That's illegal, now the government are terra-forming and you know it", he replied.

She gave a deep throaty laugh and asked, "And you've never done anything illegal, gone over one twenty in your flitter"?

"I don't have any cigs with me, as it happens", he lied, "And I can see you couldn't have any concealed under that frock, so I'm going in. If you don't follow me, I'll bring you one out".

Pon did not like the way the evening was shaping up, he always trusted his gut in such situations and right then he had a belly ache. The whole set up felt wrong, it felt like a *'set up'* in fact. He slipped inside and avoiding the rest of the party goers began to silently slide from the main hall and examine the surrounding chambers; one at a time. Then he found the right one. It was obviously some sort of study, judging by the computer set up and wall maps of Mars, company charts and graphs. Pon spied through the quarter open doorway, just in time to see Alovar offering his nephew a slim white cylinder. It was either a med-cig, a cigarette, or a 1in2!

He stepped inside,

"There you are Dorba", the old man looked as guilty as sin, "You appeared rather suddenly".

"Mind if I have one of those"? Pon asked, nodding at the thin white tube.

"Of course not, I'll get another from the pack".

"You can have that one" Arlvo said almost absently, "I never really wanted it".

The director looked confused and then suddenly brought it forward toward Pon snapping it in half, as it caught on his Edwardian frock coat.

"Oh, I'm dreadfully sorry", he blurted, "Let me get you another, from the pack"?

All his arrogance had suddenly evaporated, Pon knew his instincts had not let him down. He was a betting man and he lay odds of ten to one the he'd just stopped Alovar Hornrunner, director of 'If You Want It, We Stock It', from giving his nephew a 1in2!

The director fumbled in a desk drawer and offered Pon a med-cig, he took it, thumbed it to life, whilst the director did the same.

"I trust you have a filtration system for this", Pon said as he drew the tobacco into his lungs.

"I don't know the sort of people you usually encounter in your work Dorba", the director had recovered his composure, "But nothing illegal is going to take place on these premises".

'Murder's illegal' Pon thought, but instead replied, "Just checking director, I'll have this and then you and I should rejoin your party Arlvo".

Once again Ava Vine-Flentine found them,

"Here you are, come on the cake is going to be served and I've asked for some Jarre".

"Music to drift to", Pon noted, "Quaint".

"I see you found some cigarettes", the tall blonde beauty breathed, in her rich contralto, "Give me one of those, director dear".

"I've an idea", the director said as he passed the girl a cigarette, "Why don't we go for a drive and then come back when the party has livened up a little"?

"I wouldn't say no", Pon agreed, "In addition to the stars, Earth and Venus will be visible in the night sky if you know where to look, does your flitter have a clear roof"?

"I've a Toyota Royce Hp400", the director returned stiffly.

"Why don't you ride with me, Arlvo"? Pon suggested.

"No", the director returned, just a shade too quickly, "There's something I want to discuss with Ava and my nephew, you follow in your flitter, what ever it is; if you can keep up"?

"It doesn't matter if I lose you", Pon promised, "I have sat-nav, so I'll find you all back here if that happens".

'I don't like this one little bit', the private-det thought to himself, *'The old goat hires you and then it would seem he wants to get you away from the very youth he's hired you to keep out of trouble. How does the girl figure in this too? Do I believe my gut, or have I become a bit hackneyed, with all the dirty dealings and doings I've had to work with in the past'?*

He had no choice but to follow the old man's plan though, he could not very well ignore the suggestions of the man paying his fee. So they finished their cigarettes and going back out into the other guests, slipped out through the airlock and Pon ran to his Honda.

"Follow the Toyota", he instructed the real Dorba, "I've a ping to make to a mate of mine, at the Mars Planet".

He snatched up his pad, as, without a word, Dorba gunned the motor and the flitter shot forward,

"Sorry", said the marunt, "I'm not used to anything with this horse power".

"Well he's got more, so stay in low gear and race the engine if you have to, but don't lose him", Pon instructed.

Then he connected with Tellman T. Moorhelm at the net-cast address, "It's Voorhees".

"Oh, hiya Voorhees", came the reply on his earphone, "What's cooking"?

"I'm after some information", Pon began, "On the suicide of Bralis Hornrunner".

"That's an easy one matey flip, where've you been these past months"?

Pon grimaced, "What the story Tellman"?

As Dorba did his very best to keep the taillights of Hornrunner's Toyota in his sights, Pon listened to the report from his friend,

"Okay, so the guy tops himself by overdosing on Snufz. Seems the coroner was none too happy, but that was his decision, with the evidence he found".

"Was there a will"? Pon wanted to know.

"Yeah, left the whole pile of vazumah's to his son, Arlvo. The kid's no businessman, so his uncle, the great director Alovar, has been taking care of his interests ever since. He owns forty eight percent of stocks in 'If You Want It, We Stock It', while the kid's now got forty eight percent too".

"Who owns the other four"?

"Someone called Ava Vine-Flentine has one percent and the other three are with, yes you've guessed it Magnus Quintillius Trentavoria".

"Interesting". Pon mused, "Hey thanks, Tellman".

"It's all on the net you old tart", the news man joked, "I guess you've been busy right? Is there some other story connected to this, I smell something"?

"If I find anything out, you'll get the scoop Tellman and thanks".

He cut the connection, but as he did, he heard a second soft ping, someone had hacked their conversation! Someone had been listening to the skype, Pon looked at the speedometer,

"You okay Dorba"? He asked the little marunt, who had the Honda up to one sixty.

"This is great", came the excited reply, "One hundred and sixty kilometre's an hour and no vibration, I'll have to get me one of these".

"Just keep your concentration on the road", Pon advised, "And don't lose that Royce".

"Man oh man what a flitter", Dorba enthused, "That Toyota has to be three hundred horse power easy".

"Four", Pon replied, quite admiring the marunt's driving abilities. Little chance of doing some planet spotting, at these velocities.

"What happened at the party"? Dorba wanted to know.

"The girl tried to keep me from the job, something fishy is going on", Pon replied. "Then I caught Alovar trying to slip a 1in2 to his nephew. I intervened just in time and the old goat then suggested this drive".

Dorba suddenly braked, "He's cut his speed, what's he up to"?

The two of them heard the train at the same instant, the whistle warning of it's arrival at the crossing. The Toyota accelerated away at a speed the Honda was not capable of.

"Don't even try and follow him" Pon snapped, "We'll never make it, the train would wipe us out".

It roared past an instant later, Alovar, or who ever was driving the Toyota, had successfully given them the slip.

"What do we do now"? the little man wanted to know, "Why hire us to keep an eye on the nephew, only to deliberately get him away from us, it doesn't make sense"?

"Maybe he didn't think you would be so thorough", Pon mused, "It would still be a sort of alibi if Arlvo ends up dead tonight. Right! The only thing we can do is get back to the kid's house and as quickly as *I* can! Get out and swap places with me"?

THREE

I F DORBA HAD thought that he could drive quickly in the Honda, then Pon showed him how it was really done. The flitter may only be able to hover fifty centimetres from the surface of the road, but it fairly flew back to the mansion of Arlvo Hornrunner.

Pon pulled up around the rear of the property this time, the instant he dived out and trotted to a rear exit, he noticed the noise level of the party, which had increased and there were more lights on, on all three levels. Excellent cover then for one who wished to undertake some nefarious doings. Meanwhile, noticing a side structure, possibly some sort of greenhouse, Dorba picked up his mini oxygen and decided not to wait in the flitter a second time.

Pon melted into the throng and searched it carefully, with his keen gaze. Of the trio he sought, there was no sign, they were not in the main hall, where the party was gathering full swing. He knew he could not possibly have beaten Hornrunner back, in his less powerful Honda, especially with the delay at the railway crossing, so he must once more diligently search the property room by room.

He had seen every room on the ground floor and proceeded to the second, when he found Ava in what was undoubtedly her bedroom, she had a full glass of rum by her side and was smoking what smelled like a standard tobacco cigarette. At his appearance she looked neither surprised nor startled.

Mister Dorba, come in"? She crooned in her rich contralto, "Or may I call you Fongelturn? I'd shorten it to Fongel of course", she giggled at her own humour.

"That sort of sounds like fondle doesn't it? Do you fondle, Fongelturn"?

Despite the superfluous nature of tarrying, Pon found himself taking a seat on the chaise longue beside her,

"It has been know, on certain occasions", he smiled.

She lifted the bottle of rum (Earth) and produced a glass from beneath the table,

"Drink"?

He nodded, "And I'll take a cigarette too if you have one, as long as it's not a 1in2".

From her beautiful eyes came the flash of annoyance,

"They're illegal, Fondle, what would I be doing with one of them"?

"So's driving at over one hundred on the open road".

"I was not at the controls, Fondle".

"No, I guess not, just out of interest, where are the director and my charge"?

"Aren't they at the party"?

"No".

She handed him his drink, "Well never mind, we can have our own little party here".

Pon thumbed the cigarette she gave him, but it did not ignite, she clicked a lighter and set it going for him. It was real tobacco and he inhaled deeply savouring the full flavour, before saying with exaggerated care,

"So what's the plan Ava, you seduce me, we have sexual intercourse and Alovar meanwhile is free to murder Arlvo while I am in the building as a sort of alibi"?

Her hand whipped up to strike his face, but he caught her by the wrist and then rose carefully,

"I'm going to find the two of them before someone ends up dead. If sexual intercourse is still on offer, I might swing back this way later".

To his surprise she smiled at that,

"You think yourself one smart det don't you, Fumble"?

Pon strode from the room and began to conclude his search in earnest. He exhausted the second floor and was then on the third, as he softly crept toward the room that would terminate in an outside terrace. He could hear voices, so he flattened himself against a wall and strained to hear the conversation between uncle and nephew, carefully peeping through the side of the lock too.

"I'm sorry Uncle but even with the oxygen I'm freezing out here, let's go back inside".

"Just a moment longer Arlvo I've got the Earth in focus now, come and have a look through the telescope".

There was a pause then,

"Don't push against me like that, the rail's not high enough to be a safety".

Pon drew his needle gun and rushed through the airlock,

"Get away from him", he barked at the director.

"What in Hades is the meaning of this, Dorba"? It was Arlvo who made the demand.

"I was hired this evening to stop '*you*' committing suicide".

"Suicide? Me? I've no intention of taking my life, just because my father did. Have you lost your reason"?

"I think the plan was not a suicide, but a staged one", Pon spoke quickly and confidently, "In other words Arlvo; your murder"!

"That's totally preposterous Dorba, you're fired", the director finally regained his composure.

"Before I go then, do yourself one favour Arlvo, check all the pockets of your frock-coat will you, Humour me for just one second".

After a short search the nephew drew forth a slim plastic packet,

"Just some med-cigs.....no wait, these aren't my brand, they must be tobacco....but how did they......"?!

"They're neither Arlvo", Pon cut him off, "They're 1in2's! I saw your uncle slip them in your pocket as you leaned over to look through the telescope. You were going to take a nose dive from the first floor with those on your person, the conclusion to the constabulary of Mars would have been obvious".

"I need to think about this", Arlvo sounded confused, "But inside, before we all expire from lack of oxygen, or hypothermia".

As he pushed past the detective however, Alovar produced a blaster,

"Drop that toy, Pon, this is ten times more powerful and deadly".

"So you knew I wasn't Dorba all along eh"? Pon asked, letting the needle gun fall from his hand onto the plush carpet.

"What's going on here"? Arlvo demanded, "Has everyone gone stark staring mahulie"?

"You know Hornrunner", Pon said with some irony, "You have a big car and a big gun, are you trying to over compensate for a shortage in some other area, should I ask Ava"?

"You will not get me to make a mistake now I have this trained on you", the director said smugly, as the airlock hissed too behind him.

"What's going on uncle"? Arlvo squeaked yet again, "Why would you put those Snufz narcotic cigarettes in my pocket"?

"He's finally beginning to work it out, Hornrunner", Pon told the glowering director, "With you out of the way Arlvo, how much stock in 'If You Want It,

We Stock It' does your uncle plan to come into? So, Hornrunner, why did you not reveal my true identity when you knew I was not Dorba"?

"I've seen your agency on the net Pon", the holder of the gun returned, "I didn't really care who you were, you would still serve the same purpose".

"Okay, you've got the blaster, what's the plan now"?

"Well let's see", the director seemed to be savouring his moment of power.

"You want me dead Uncle, why you eater of other people's leftovers......"!

Arlvo threw himself at his uncle, but the taller heavier man simply crashed the butt of the blaster against his nephew's skull,

"Go for that needle gun and it's curtains for you", Hornrunner barked.

"I've already got some curtains", the det replied acidly. "So now what, you seem to be winging this Hornrunner".

"I pick up this needle gun firstly", Hornrunner said, bending swiftly and backing away from Pon, before he could react. "Then I shoot you with a needle, put the gun in Arlvo's hand and toss him out the airlock and off the balcony, onto the paved driveway beneath. It will look like he managed to get a shot off, as you threw him to his death. I presume these are neuronic level one at the least"?

"Level two actually".

The director smiled, "That's even better, the lethal ones, so there will be no witnesses to tell any other tale. Except for the one I will logically come to, of course. For the Chief Constable of Mars constabulary".

"There's just one little snag Hornrunner, I don't have a motive for killing Arlvo"?

"Oh but you do, the oldest motive in the book, money. You see I asked Arlvo to transfer one hundred shillin from his bank into the agency's this afternoon. I told him it was a loan and would repay him next week. Three of my staff overheard you complaining it wasn't enough for looking after the; as you put it, boring little creep".

"Three staff in your employ"?

"On fantastic wages for what they do and willing to commit perjury any time I so desire. Suspicion will never fall on me, for I have the email asking your agency for an agent to protect Arlvo this evening".

"Just one moment", a thin high pitched voice was heard by both of them then and as Hornrunner turned his attention for the merest moment, Pon dived at him hard and low. He heard the 'phut' of a needle pass just over his shoulder and then he was rugby tackling the director to the floor. The needle gun was still in one hand and the blaster behind his back. Pon grasped the wrist of the hand holding the gun and twisted with every ounce of his strength. He was rewarded by the sound of a dull crunching noise at a bone snapped and Hornrunner let out a scream. The needle gun fell from numb fingers. Pon climbed up and quickly rolled the all but insensible Hornrunner over, pulling the blaster from the waistband of his breeks. He tossed it to Dorba who caught it neatly with his relatively huge hands.

"I'd say the party's over wouldn't you Fongelturn"? Pon smiled.

"Apart from the one they'll have down at the Mars Constabulary Station, Voorhees".

FOUR

T HE GUESTS WERE gone and so were the constables as Arlvo and Pon were sitting in the now quiet main hall of the mansion. Both were smoking med-cigs and while Pon had Earth rum, Arlvo curiously had a Martian-Vodka. It seemed he preferred it.

Blowing smoke up into the air Arlvo noted,

"It's going to be a big job running, 'If You Want It, We Stock It', I could use a good man for security and who knows you may have some business acumen if you try. What ever the agency's paying you, I'll double it, what do you say Voorhees"?

"Somehow I don't think I'm cut out to sell things Arlvo", Pon returned honestly enough, "But if you want a good man for your security you could do worse than hire Dorba".

"He did save both our lives didn't he"? The new director of 'If You Want It, We Stock It' mused rubbing the lump on his temple.

"That's not such a bad idea as that Voorhees".

The private-det drained his glass and stubbed out the end of his cigarette.

"So, time to turn in", Arlvo noted, draining his own glass.

"Good of you to put me up for the night", Pon said.

"I couldn't let you drive home after all the drink you've put away. Nearly all the bedrooms are not in use, take any one that takes your fancy".

"Thanks, good night", Pon agreed and slipped up the stairs in his stocking feet. He did no searching though, but strode straight to one bedroom in particular, a bedroom of all azure walls and deep blue drapes, a bedroom that he had been in before. Opening the door he turned on the ceiling illumination. The rise in lighting caused Ava to stir and sit up in bed. Her negligee was of royal blue too and it hinted at the magnificence of her breasts.

"What are you doing in here"? she demanded.

"I told you I'd return remember"? Pon smiled lasciviously.

"Oh darling, I'm sorry", Ava crooned, "But that's all off now, so you go and get yourself a nice bed somewhere else".

"I told the police I didn't think you had anything to do with the attempted murder tonight", Pon said then, starting to take off his shirt.

"Of course when all the excitement settles down and I have time to think about it more carefully, certain details might come back to me".

"You'd do that, rat me in, Pon, because I won't play ball with you"?

"Ball wasn't the game I had in mind Ava", Pon started to remove his breeks, "And call me Fondle, I'll show you how appropriate a name that is, in a moment or two"!

NYJORD

ONE

WHEN COOL-FUSION WAS finally refined into cold-fusion, the resultant reactor meant that an engine of hither-to incredible power could finally be constructed. Space flight became hyper-space flight and the distance a vessel could travel grew exponentially.

The Moon, Mars and Callisto had long since been colonised, but now mankind could look to the stars and commence a search for a second world, that would be as close to the Earth as would not matter. The huge electron telescope swept the milky way and Proxima b was believed to be the best initial target. The construction of Explorer One was tendered out and thanks to the wealthy of the country of Texas, became the location for it's creation and blast off. This also meant that Texas had the distinct honour of supplying the captain for the voyage.

Explorer One would only be able to carry eight crew. To make it larger would result in the absorption blanket never withstanding the massive peppering of minuscule particles of space dust that it would receive and the vessel's very integrity would then be compromised. The rest of the world put forth candidates to supply crew members and were forced to pay for the privilege. The crew had to meet certain requirements; they must be single, physically fit and with no family, or none that they cared about. For who knew how long Explorer One would be gone in one second per second time on Earth? Plenty had theories, but that was all they were and could be until the journey was done.

Each of the crew must be the very best in their field of expertise and the eight areas required, were mapped out by a team of multinational scientists.

Explorer One was ready for take off on November the twelfth, three thousand two hundred and thirty five. An auspicious day, for it was also the day when Mercury, Venus, Earth and Mars were in exact alignment in their orbits around the sun. The launch was trouble free, if the Texans could not build a rocket, no on could. The crew withstood the G-force of launch and escape from Earth's gravity and then the captain had only to wait for Explorer One to be clear of Mars and he could initiate the hyper-drive.

They spent the thirteen hours checking and rechecking instruments, the doctor monitoring the vital readout's of the crew. There were to be no surnames on the ship, such would be a thing of the past on a new planet. So as they had trained together, the four men and four women had come to know one another by their first name alone, or sometimes their speciality.

The men were Captain Merle (Texas), Engineer Willy (Germany), Military Darren (England) and finally Construction Aldo (Italy). The female crew compliment were made up of, Doctor Lin (China), Biologist Sita (India), Geologist Wera (Poland) and finally Psychologist Tyra (Republic of Scandinavia).

During the first few hours Doctor Lin was almost as busy as the captain, checking the bodies of the rest of the crew. Then Captain Texas' (as he had come to be know) voice came over the head sets of the other crew members and he said,

"After hours of hysterical inactivity, we enter a field as yet unknown, crew members, no one has ever been where we are going now. I'm going to activate the hyper-drive after a brief countdown. Without it our journey would take forty years, by using it we will be in hyper-space for five months and at the end of it, if the computed calculations are correct, we should find ourselves in the Proxima System. Very well; ten, nine,...."

He counted down in seconds and then engaged the cold fusion motors. In his view screen the stars abruptly disappeared, what they were replaced with no one had known, until then!

Texas gazed at the strange swirling motion of dun and slate. It pulled at the eye and he glanced away. When he looked back, the formless motions of grey nothingness pulled at his vision once again, causing him to look down at his instrument panel. The dials and indicators all told him that Explorer One was in hyper-space. A voice came over his earpiece.

"Can we try loosening our harness yet captain"?

Before Texas could reply, the doctor did so for him, her sing song voice advising,

"Very slowly Darren. You may weigh nothing, or you may weigh more than a planet, this is new territory for us and a rash action could be fatal"!

Texas twisted in his bucket seat to regard the military man from England. Sure enough he was slowly undoing the strapping on his harness. Uncertainly and with considerable caution, he put his booted feet to the decking and rose to a standing position.

"Are my readings normal, doc"? he asked.

"Absolutely, what are you doing"?

"I'm standing up, my magnetic boots are on the decking on the bridge".

"How do your arms feel when you lift them"?

Texas watched as Darren waved his arms about,

"I think this may come as a surprise to just about everyone, but I feel I'm in One-G"!

"Wait"? Willy asked from his own harness in the engine room,

"Checking", then after a pause, "Confirmed gravity inside this ship is one-G".

"That's incredible"! Geologist Wera gasped, "The gravity of mankind's home world, what are the odds"?

"The math for calculating that has not yet been developed", Sita, the biologist reasoned.

"We will meet in the galley then", Texas told the crew, none of them had eaten for thirteen hours.

It did not take long for the octet to unstrap themselves and assemble in the area, which was to be both gallery and general meeting area, most of the vessel was otherwise pretty cramped, with almost every square metre serving some sort of function. Texas almost felt guilty for being tallest and heaviest among the men, his passage cost the vessel the greatest energy.

"Are you monitoring any strange anomalies when it comes to crew physiology doctor"? he asked Lin.

The Chinese woman shook her head,

"All is normal, as though we are hardly moving, as opposed to hurtling through the vacuum of space at an incredible velocity".

"And the engines Willy? They are functioning exactly as they should"?

The German looked up from his pasta salad, the fresh food would run out in just a couple of months and he was making the most of it.

"Ja, captain, the German technicians who built the propulsion system have excelled themselves".

"I just hope the rest of the voyage is like this then" Texas said for them all.

"Well, crew go about your duties, those of you who have none yet, help those who have, dismissed at your discretion".

He left the galley firstly, Tyra followed him out,

"There's just one thing captain"? she began and when he nodded, continued, "The one variable we cannot be prepared for starts now".

"And that is"?

"The psychological effects upon the crew of months of hyper-drive. Now I know you personally don't hold much with that sort of thing, but I'm on this voyage for a reason".

"I'm not trying to devalue your function in any way Tyra. Begin detailed analysis of all the crew, at your convenience".

The Scandinavian nodded, "And the crew includes you too sir".

"Of course it does, is that all"?

"For the moment yes".

TWO

FOR THREE WEEKS Tyra the psychologist wondered why she had been worried. Then, on the first day of the fourth week, the first incident happened.

She was having lunch with doctor Lin when Aldo burst into the galley looking agitated,

"Bloody German", he spat out, "I'm the second best qualified to be near the engines and he damn well knows it".

"What's happened", Tyra asked.

"He told me I was *'tinkering'* with the engines and to get out the engine area, or he'd do violence upon me".

"Do violence upon you", Tyra repeated, "Was that his exact wording"?

"Frenge"! the Italian exploded, "What in Hades does the wording matter"?

"Suffice to say, Aldo, that it does to Tyra", Lin pointed out, "So answer the question".

"I will do violence upon you", Aldo repeated, "Yes that was his exact wording".

"So he's trying to control his ire, but having difficulty", the Psychologist noted thoughtfully. "Thank you Aldo, I'll go and have a word with our Engineer".

By the time she had left and walked the short gangway toward the back of the vessel however, Willy seemed his usual jovial self.

"Hello Tyra, what brings you back here"?

"Why? Do you mind if I come to see you"?

"No, not at all"?

"And do you mind if Aldo comes back here and helps with the engine calibrations occasionally"?

"Mind, Hades no, I could do with a bit of company".

"And he had no memory of the outburst at all when I questioned him further, captain", Tyra reported not ten minutes later.

"We are in cramped conditions solitude is virtually impossible to achieve and added to that we don't know what will happen when we cut the hyperdrive. Cut it, for the first time in history"!

"You don't need to emphasise that to me", Texas said with feeling, "For all I know we could find ourselves in totally uncharted space, all is just theory; until we actually do it".

"And it's worrying you"?

Texas smiled, "You can stop with the analysis for a second Tyra, anyone in command would worry with what I've got on my plate".

"I'll keep observing and keep you posted captain".

The following day Darren came to see the captain,

"I've a problem sir".

"Of course you have", Texas responded tiredly, he had not been able to sleep for thirty six hours, by his wrist chrono, the ship's chrono made no sense at all.

"Aldo has been to see me and made a serious accusation against another member of the crew, it's something you should sit in on and the thing is, I know he's lying".

"What has he accused Willy of and how do you know he's lying"? Texas guessed.

"He claims the engineer threatened him, with a needle gun"!

"And you know he's lying because the armoury has never been opened and only you and I have keys"?

Darren nodded, "Can I leave it with you"?

Texas nodded mutely and once the military man had left, pinged Tyra,

"I need you to sit in with me in a meeting, I'm going to have it with Construction Aldo, I want you to psych evaluate him as much as possible while we are talking; ten minutes".

The psychologist nodded and Texas then pinged the Italian and asked him to come to his ready room. Ten minutes later all three were seated in comfortable chair sipping peppermint tea.

"I know you'll suspect I've asked you here for a specific reason, Aldo", Texas began.

"Sì, Willy threatened to kill me", the Construction man replied, getting immediately to the point.

"He did so with a needle gun and you went to Darren with this information", Texas said before adding, "When you should have actually come to me"?

The Italian nodded, "I wanted to know why Darren gave Willy a needle gun"?

"That's the problem we have with your story Aldo, Darren didn't, the armoury has been locked since we blasted off from Texas, no one has been in it".

"I believe you tell me what you think is the truth captain", Aldo conceded, "But you see I think Darren and Willy are in this together, to get rid of me".

Tyra spoke for the first time, "What reason would they have for getting you out of the way Aldo"?

"That is obvious signora", Aldo replied with a broad smile to her. "With the best looking man out of the way, they have a better chance with you ladies, especially you and Sita".

Tyra had the presence of mind to blush, Texas said carefully,

"This is a scientific expedition Aldo, we are not a colony ship. It may be years before mankind has the chance to begin colonisation of a planet outside the solar system".

"So you don't think any of us will hook up, during the stay on the Nuovo Mondo"?

"Nuovo Mondo"? Texas asked.

"It means New World captain", Tyra explained, "It's what Aldo wants to call Proxima b's planet, if we find it".

"No one has yet decided what I will officially call the new planet", Texas told the Italian. "I might have us draw lots for that honour, it will keep our minds occupied for the next few days. What do you think Tyra"?

"It's a great idea", the psychologist smiled, "In the mean time, I'll spend some time with Aldo and treat him for Hyper-drive psychosis, the first recorded incident".

"I'm not crazy signora", Aldo protested.

"Yet there was no needle gun", Texas pointed out, "Could not have been, so you'll have some sessions with Tyra, that's an order".

Three hours later the crew were assembled in the galley and all seven names for the new world were listed. They were; Nuovo Mondo (Aldo), Nyjord (Tyra), Proxima One (Texas and Darren), Neuerde (Willy), Nowa Ziemia (Wera), Brahma (Sita) and Sheng (Lin).

"To make it more interesting I will draw out one suggested per day and that name will be eliminated", Texas told them.

He made the draw while the others watched on in perfect silence and to his and the Englishman's dismay eliminated Proxima One.

Over the next two days Nuovo Mondo and Neuerde were also drawn and then Tyra came to see the captain once again, her pretty face drawn in worry,

"What is it this time Psychologist"? the captain wanted to know.

"It's Aldo, I can't find him for his appointment".

Texas laughed, "You can't find him, on a ship this cramped"?

He flipped the ship wide intercom toggle and asked the Italian to report to his ready room, they waited ten minutes and then Texas broadcast a second message,

"All crew find Construction Aldo and bring him to my ready room please".

"Please"? Tyra asked.

"They're all stressed, a bit of courtesy won't hurt, for a while".

Once again no one showed.

"All crew meet in the galley at once". This time he was not courteous. Five minutes later the seven of them were together and the Italian was still missing.

"This is impossible", Darren said, as military, he was in charge of security, "We've been in every cupboard, even if they're too small to hide a full grown man".

"He must be aboard", the German was adamant, "My instrument show none of the airlocks have been opened, he could not have killed himself by jumping into hyper-space".

"I'm getting afraid captain", Lin said, if he's neither eaten nor drunk since his disappearance, he can only survive about three days.

"Even if that's the case, how come we can't find his body"? Wera wanted to know. It was unusual for her to speak.

"Captain", Tyra suggested, "The draw"?

There was nothing else to be done but eliminate Sheng!

THREE

THE CREW BEGAN to have nightmares and hallucinations. Sometimes they saw and spoke to Aldo, sometimes they saw dead relatives or figures from public life. At times they had conversations with one another that moments later, one of them could not remember being involved in.

Texas called Tyra for a private meeting,

"What are we going to do"? He asked instantly, "We are on the verge of insanity? Only you seem to be unaffected by hyper-space, how do you do that"?

"I question nothing and accept everything", she replied. "Just go with the flow and believe that we are all fine and the mental aberrations are the result of hyper-drive emanations. Like the normal gravity, you've accepted that even though none of us expected it".

"You mean the seven of us might be floating around in here and thinking we're walking"?

"All is possible when you cannot believe the evidence of your own eyes and ears", Tyra nodded, "And it's eight of us, not seven".

"He's been missing five days".

"Or; we only think he has, mass delusion".

"So that's your best advice, just let every illusion take place and not worry about it in the slightest"?

Tyra nodded, "And what ever you do don't touch any controls, let the automation bring us back into normal space, once it kicks in itself".

"Alright then, go and call a galley meeting and tell them the same. The only trouble is in five months time will we be mental cabbages, or still the crew that left Earth"?

"It's all new", was all the psychologist would answer.

The ship sped through the grey void at a speed incalculable by normal physics. It was bending space, taking a short cut by travelling through the bend from one end to the other. On paper it made Einstein look like a fool, but then it was thousands of years since he had postulated his law of relativity and all was relative. e no longer equalled mc squared, the answer was zero and infinity at one and the same time. Up was down as well as up, there was no north south east nor west, the minute was not divided into sixty seconds for there was no hour, no day, no time. Would there still be reason?

Finally the crew began to settle into the same unspoken pattern, they remained in their bunks or eating or voiding. They did not talk though, not by choice, to one another. If they saw someone they knew could not be on the ship, they refused to answer them. They said little of anything, it was almost as if the vessel was manned by nuns and monks who had taken strange vows. No one saw Aldo, but they refused to think about it anymore, he was either gone, or still among them, or both, or neither. Their logic became the acceptance of illogic. Nothing made sense and yet at the same time it was all unquestionable.

They slowly grew four months older even though no time had passed and at the same time the eons had sped along, whilst they existed outside of time, space and matter. Then; finally, a soft buzzing sounded throughout the ship and it dropped out of hyper-drive. Texas raced to the pilot's chair, Willy to the engines, the others took places in their cots, strapping themselves in.

"Stars", Texas said to himself, whilst weeping with relief and he turned on all the ship's sensors. They had made it! The vessel was in the middle of a star system of planets. He activated all the navigational and scientific instrumentation Explorer One possessed and almost at once data began feeding into the computer. Fifty minutes later he called the crew to the galley, the first to arrive there was the Italian!

When Texas arrived everyone was excitedly talking at once, as they drifted around the room. Aldo was the centre of attention, but as the captain appeared before them, they fell silent, he had data to give them.

"Firstly may I just say it's a pleasure and a relief to see our construction man back with us".

There was short applause and Aldo said for maybe the tenth time, "I was with you all along and can remember all our conversations".

"Which you never had", Willy cut in, the laughter was one of supreme relief, as much as humour.

"Okay crew pipe down", Texas said sternly then. "We're now going back to functioning as trained, so listen to the data the computers have given us, regarding Proxima b".

Total silence, as Texas described the Proxima system.

The star had a gravitational system of bound planets similar to Earth's sun. The computer had recorded an age of four point eight billion years, so it was a little older than the Solar system. Again a familiar figure, most of the system's mass was Proxima b itself with the orbiting worlds not adding up to fifty percent altogether. It was slightly hotter than Sol, but not so much so, that it burned the planets around it to a crisp.

Their were only six worlds, three were primarily composed of rock and metal. In other words, Earth like in construction. The other three were gas giants and substantially larger than the inner ones. Unlike the solar system there were no planets of ice. All the planets except for one, had slightly elliptical orbits that lay within a nearly flat disc, (the ecliptic). One of the gas giants aberated from the ecliptic though and could possibly have been captured from Proxima Centauri. So the belief that Proxima b had been a planet was finally exploded and it had proved to be a star in it's own right. How the existence of Proxima Centauri effected the planets of b, was still being calculated by the ship's computers.

Then came the data the crew had been most eagerly anticipating. The nature of the planets and the possibility that one of them could sustain life. The data was beyond their wildest expectations. The closest planet to the star was very much like Venus, in terms of mass and conditions, the chances of life upon it were very slim indeed. The next two worlds were much closer to one another than anything the solar system had to offer and both had ideal atmospheres, capable of supporting life. Not only that but one of the duo was about the same size as Earth's moon and did indeed orbit Proxima two, in addition to orbiting the star. The crew ignored the two gas giants and the wandering planet, they were like Saturn in nature and not capable of life as accepted by conventional theory.

After the last elimination drawer, Nyjord had remained un-drawn and so the computer had been ordered to call the second planet by that name. The smaller orbiting world however Texas told them was therefore the name that had been previously eliminated last; Brahma.

The data then told them that Nyjord had an atmosphere consisting of seventy percent nitrogen, twenty two percent oxygen, point seven percent carbon dioxide, and the rest a series of other gases, one of which the computer did not recognise. It was therefore very breathable indeed, in fact the crew would feel very energised by the extra oxygen. Added to that, the gravity of Nyjord was only eighty percent that of Earth, so the crew would feel like supermen. Brahma had an almost identical atmosphere, but half the mass and gravity, therefore forty percent that of Earth. It's mass however meant that if water existed on Nyjord, which the reading said was more than eminently possible, the waves would be like constant tsunamis.

"Can we go down onto Nyjord and not die at once, captain"? Darren was the first to demand.

"Data is still pouring in, but radiation is much lower than Earth's, the oxygen is rich and the gravity comparatively low, so after some orbiting photographs, if all looks well then I think I'll pilot her down and then we'll do some more tests.

In the cramped space of Explorer One the sound of cheering was then incredibly loud. Against all the odds the first time mankind had stepped outside the solar system, they very well may have found new space for humanity to live in!

FOUR

TEXAS VIEWED SEVERAL high definition photographs of the surfaces of Nyjord and Brahma, he turned to Aldo,

"Vegetation and water areas look to be about half and half. There are vast lakes and huge forests which look strangely the wrong colour, but I believe I can pilot her down to a clearing. How quickly if all seems well, can you have some sort of camp ready"?

"With the materials given me, it will only take a few hours captain", the construction man promised. "I'm not holding you up with any technical problems".

"What about you two"? Texas turned to Tyra and Sita.

"The mental health of us all is now fine, now that we're out of hyper-space", the psychologist informed.

"Thanks to the exercise programme we've followed, the physical health is also more than acceptable for us all to begin doing some physical and mental work", Sita added.

"So no concerns really"? Texas had to be cautious.

"We're all just itching to try a landing and see the wonders of an alien planet", the Scandian added.

"Get everyone strapped into their cots then", Texas suddenly made his decision, "I'm taking Explorer One onto the surface of Nyjord".

With a ship as cramped as their's, word of preparations went around quickly and minutes later Texas took the computer off line. As far as automatic navigation was concerned, he would not use it but began to fly the ship like a huge aeroplane. The shaking started and ceased again quite quickly as the vessel cut through the upper edge of the atmosphere, then Texas began to really fly the ship. His view screen showed the ground growing ever nearer and speeding beneath them ever swifter and then he began the buffeting braking procedure.

Bizarrely the craft landed vertically with no more trouble than a jump jet. As the engines were cut, the crew broke into spontaneous applause once more.

"Now it's your turn Wera and Sita", the captain said into his throat mic, "The airlock stays shut until the two of you can convince me the risk is minimal".

"Imagine though", Willy said to Darren, "If we had come all this way and then he won't let us onto the planet surface"?

"Oh, I think we'll go out", the Englishman replied, "It's just a case of whether we need full suits, face masks, or nothing at all by way of protection from the atmosphere".

"Seems to me we spend all our time waiting", Willy grumbled, but grumbling was his natural state.

The interior of Explorer One was all grey or blued steel, not greatly dissimilar to the view through the main screen when the hyper-drive had been in use. Whether the crew wished to acknowledge it or not, that dull lack lustre surrounding had effected them all in a very negative way. There was little they could have done about it once the voyage began, but Tyra had written in one of her reports that any future expedition should be in a ship with a soft pink painted interior. The colour of the womb would have had a calming and comforting effect on the very same individuals on their way to Proxima b.

Of course a second expedition would also know there was a worthwhile goal at the end of the months of hyper-space, something Texas' crew could not have known. A more comprehensive library of entertainment would have been another boon, colourful musicals filled with songs and melodies. This crew had chosen mainly science fiction and exploration which, with hindsight had been a mistake. They were already living the topic and it was too much of the same thing. Tyra hit save on her latest report and sent it on it's way to Callisto, never knowing if it would reach there.

Hyper-space radio waves were transmitted using the ships powerful transmitting dish, which resided just behind the absorption blanket field, that had protected Explorer One from microscopic space particles of dust and ice. The trouble was, the waves, though oscillating at a tremendously high frequency, did not have the same luxury and so by the time they reached the solar system, they well have become too corrupted for the computers on Callisto to make sense of them. There may be too much data loss, dropped out or degraded information that a re-enhancing programme could not have enough to work piece together. It was unknown territory, for previously man had sent radio signals into space never knowing if they would reach anywhere. Now the same waves were being accelerated into hyper-space, otherwise they may reach earth centuries after Explorer One's return.

Was there dust and particles of radiation in hyper-space? Was there anything in hyper-space? Or was it, as some proposed, even devoid of vacuum, for vacuum being a positive measurement of nothingness could also conceivably be missing from a phenomenon that was closer to anti-matter, than matter. Could hyper space be total zero, not even containing nothing?

Tyra was thinking along those lines, having just sent off her report, when a voice came over her earplug,

"It's Texas", the captain began, "I'm speaking to three of you at the moment, Tyra, Lin and Sita. The results of the air samples the ship has analysed are in, there does not appear to be any reason why I cannot simply crack the airlock on the ship. The air of Nyjord is totally breathable and so like Earth's, that we should be alright. I'm asking the three of you now if you can think of any reason why we shouldn't do it"?

The Chinese girl piped up, "Bacteria, captain. I need more time to do tests. There could be micro organisms that.....".

"We are all totally inoculated", Sita cut in, "From every bacteria known to mankind. If you tested for another year, would you be any more able to say that this world will never give someone a runny nose, doctor".

"That's a facile comment and you know it, biologist", came the agitated reply. The argument raged in the captain's ear for several minutes more, but then as the two of them had argued one another to a standstill Texas asked,

"Tyra, if we sit in this ship for another couple of weeks and complete a myriad of tests what would the effect be on crew morale"?

"Captain, I think we need to feel solid ground beneath our feet and look up at an open sky and the sooner the better, before someone gets seriously hurt".

All was silent and then Texas came over seven sets of ear plugs. "Crew assemble at airlock alpha, we are going outside. Darren get weapons, Aldo get some materials together for a camp site. Tonight, if all goes well, we will not be in this tin can".

A mere ten minutes later all was in readiness and the seven crew were at the captains side, as he hesitated before the main controls of the starboard side airlock. All of them had a needle rifle over one shoulder, several of them had items Aldo had asked them to carry for him. Texas said finally,

"I believe the very last thing you want to hear from me right now is a lengthy speech, so all I'm going to say before I hit this button is; for the peoples of the solar system, the race we call mankind, I open this lock and claim the territory beyond ; theirs".

Texas pushed the button and four of them crammed into the airlock; himself and the three other men, then he hit the outer door release and the ladder automatically extended down and hit the ground just as expected. The four of them gazed out at Nyjord and their mouths fell open.

FIVE

T HE SKY WAS pink, not blue! The grass beneath it was of various hues, but the overall impression was of red. They looked closer at the surroundings, forcing themselves to remain calm and observing everything they could merely by sight. The grass was mainly red, but interspersed with yellows and the more familiar greens. Dotted within the blades were small white mushroom like growths, then there were the larger plants!

Texas thought of them immediately as fronds, for they were devoid of bark and a silvery blue in colour. At the ends of the myriad stalks on the fronds were huge white flower- like structures with orange centres. For some reason despite everything, he smiled at the flowers atop the fronds, they reminded him of fried eggs. The fronds ranged in size from small bush like arrangements, right up to sky scraping boughs, but they were definitely not trees.

"Alright men down the steps and let the girls see this before we go any further. Darren you're with me, Aldo work the airlock again, Willy follow me".

The two of them stopped at the bottom of the ladders and just stared both lost in thought, trying to come to terms with what they had done. They were on an alien world, one which did not orbit the sun!

Then the duo looked up into the pink sky and as if to cement that knowledge with total conviction, they saw the vast ball that was Brahma. It seemed perhaps three times the size of the moon as seen from Earth, but it was swathed in heavy cloud and shone a soft green and blue of hue.

The two men had to force themselves to breathe, which they were glad to do. In fact both found that if they took a deep breath, it caused an instant feeling of light headedness, telling them the oxygen content of the air was higher than what they were accustomed to. They also noted that they felt light on their feet, buoyant, the gravity was proving to them, that it was less than that of their home world.

The eight of them had been standing in total indecision for several minutes, before Texas said,

"Right to work, we have about six hours before darkness comes, according to the ships readings. The day on Nyjord is twenty hours and we are near the equator, I know it feels hot, it's about thirty Celsius right now, but we must build a shelter before the darkness comes very suddenly upon us. Unless, that is you want to climb back into the ship tonight".

Aldo said, "My turn to take charge, we need buildings and quickly, watch me and then do as I do. I'm sorry but you must take your gaze from the lurid landscape and work. First we connect these rods and make a frame. Then we throw the nylo-planyon over the frame. Then crawling under it we throw the nylo-planyon base onto the ground, Next the tricky part, the catalytic spray, do your best to get it as even as possible, do the last part of the floor as you step out from under the wall, it does not matter which one. Then spray the walls and roof of the structure. Then we can have a break, twenty minutes later the spray will have hardened the nylo-planyon and what we will have is a box shaped rigid, but transparent structure, that could take a needle, yet is incredibly thermal. It will keep cold out, heat in, or visa versa.

Then we mess it up by using the duridium electro-saw to cut a crawl entrance, the smaller the better for obvious reasons. I will cut the crawls and then fit the duralite screwed hinges and thermal rubber seals, I'll also drill the air holes that make certain no one suffocates.

We have four two man buildings to complete in this way and then the darker translucent buildings, one for showering, one for latrine. That's six buildings in six hours, so you must have all done one an hour each, let's go people".

Texas being captain had the luxury of not being forced to take part, even though he would share a hut (as they came to call them) with the military man. The women would billet Sita and Lin together, the rest were obvious. The captain could not tear his eyes away from Brahma, had he made the right decision? Had he landed on the right world?

As the light faded and his teams struggled to complete the shelters for the night, he went back into the ship and pulled up the map of Nyjord. He called the landing spot Dallas. Two of the lakes that surrounded it he named Kendal and Ngoring, over the next few days, circumstance permitting, he intended to honour each of his crew with a named location.

The smell of cooking drifted into the ship and when he went out, it was to see that a stove was over an element and a stew was being prepared by Willy.

Aldo told him proudly, "Four quarters, a shower area once I get the piping up and a latrine, all completed captain, by dusk".

"Excellent work everyone, I leave it to the individual as to who decides to sleep out here and who would rather go back into the security of the ship. However it works out, set up some security, Darren".

The night sky was moonless and both Brahma and Proxima had slipped beneath the horizon, it turned from pink to angry roseate and finally to black and the stars came out. They had not travelled far enough to change the constellations and their familiarity was strangely comforting.

Darren brought the captain a steel bowl of steaming stew,

"Well, we made it captain. How long can we explore before we have to return home"?

"I have absolutely no idea", Texas admitted honestly, "Lets see how events unravel and as soon as I arrive at any decisions, I'll be sure to brief the crew".

"Have you any idea what we will do first, tomorrow", the security man persisted.

"You'll find out as soon as the others", Texas told him, "I've no doubt Aldo will be busy plumbing, while Sita and Wera will want to commence data gathering. That may leave some of us time to go on a short expedition, you'll have to wait and see".

After the meal, it was decided to see if, despite the excitement, they could get some sleep. Texas decided to sleep in the ship, while the others all opted for the new constructions, Darren set up a watch rota and the duo's went into their huts.

As expected it took a couple of hours for everyone to settle down, but once they had, they all got the best sleep they had since being in the solar system.

Texas was up with the dawn, made more spectacular with the rise of Brahma also, he imagined there would be many interesting eclipses in Nyjord passage around it's star. Breakfast was a hasty affair, for everyone wanted to make a start in the shorter day than they were used to. As expected Sita and Wera wanted to start on research and Aldo asked for Willy to help him with the shower and latrine plumbing. This meant that four of them could start to explore the area around Dallas, if Texas thought it safe enough.

"I think two teams of one man and one woman", he told the other three, "Tyra you're with me, Darren you go north with the doctor. Only proceed for four hours and then turn back, that makes it certain for us to be back for supper. Have your needle rifles at the ready at all times. Okay, that's it. Tyra we're going south".

"Off we go then", the captain said to the psychologist and they began to walk south in the calm sunshine. They had no need to fear radiation according to Lin, the output from Proxima would only give them a tan after many hours of exposure. Pink tinged clouds scudded across the sky, but they had yet to experience the phenomenon of rain on Nyjord.

"We're not far from Lake Ngoring are we", Tyra asked.

"No but we will not venture to the shore today, we don't want to encounter the dramatic waves that Brahma must create".

Suddenly both stopped at a faint buzzing sound

"Life"! Tyra was excited, "There, look, it looks like a sort of dragon fly. It must proliferate if there are no birds".

They tried to catch one for a specimen jar, but the winged creature was far too swift for them.

"By Jimminy, look up", Texas said suddenly and as the psychologist did so, she saw overhead, a huge flying creature swooping and wheeling. It was too high in the pink sky to discern it's features and they found themselves hoping ardently that it was not a bird of prey, or carnivorous flying reptile. Fancy coming all the way through hyper-space to be consumed by a local avifauna?

"I suddenly feel like a lab rat", Tyra said, "With very little control over my environment. There could be dangers we have no suspicion of, on every corner of this world"?

"That's why we are single unmatched individuals", the captain reminded her, "We are the ultimate exploration team".

The first day passed too quickly, for in truth they only managed to cover six and a half kilometres before having to start back. There was so much to see, so many recording to make, with their hand cams. They found more insects, both flying and in the red grass. Parasites living on the mushrooms and a white sort of mould growing on the blue fronds. The latter started off as shoots and flowered when only thirteen centimetres or so high. They still looked like fried eggs with their white petals and orange centres and they took to calling the adult plants egg-trees.

The were careful to physically touch nothing that first day, they ate and drank only what they had brought with them. The duo arrived back at Dallas tired and happy eight hours later and supper was on the stove yet again.

After they had eaten they went into the ship with their hand cams and downloaded all the data into the ships computer. Darren and Lin had experienced similar observations, to those of the captain and Tyra, positively no one had experienced an accident or mishap and Aldo reported the plumbing was finished.

"Tomorrow we will form three teams then", Texas told them as they ate. "First team of myself, Tyra and Aldo, second team of Darren and Lin, third team, Sita Willy and Wera. Team three will go east, I don't want anyone going near the lakes for now".

They spent the rest of the evening doing the things people do before going to bed. Chatting, reading their pads, some were writing a letter to Earth, that they did not know would ever reach it's destination. The peace of the camp was abruptly broken by a commotion at the shower room. Darren was there with admirable speed, his needle rifle already at the ready. He got there in time to see Aldo sprawled on his back in the red and yellow grass-like covering, that littered the plain. The Italian's eye looked angry and red and was already beginning to swell and close. Wera was standing over him, wrapped in a towel only. With her damp shoulders and wet hair, Texas suddenly realised how attractive she could be in certain circumstances.

"He came into the shower, singing; while I was in there", she told the now assembled crew.

"I didn't know it was occupied", Aldo protested.

Texas gave the matter a second's thought, it was one person's word against another, despite what he suspected might be the truth.

"I think you got you just deserts Aldo", he decided, "You'd better see the doctor, with that eye".

Still protesting his innocence, he was lead away by Lin.

"He's a frinsle", Wera said, "I'd finished showering and was about to get dried, but the water was still running".

"Still running"? Willy protested, "Don't you realise.......".

"That's enough", Texas cut in, wondering what a frinsle was, "Let's all put the episode behind us and get some sleep, we're all marching tomorrow".

He returned thoughtfully to the ship and pinged the word:-

frin.sle - colloqe (v. frinsle, n. frinsle)
v.t.

1. to lead astray morally
2. to lead into unhealthy sexual practices.

n.

3. a person who practices acts of voyeurism, sexual perversion and debasement

Texas smirked at the definition, thinking, *'Yeah, Aldo probably is a frinsle at that'!*

SIX

T HE THREE GROUPS set off an hour after a spectacular dawn. All of them felt well and rested with the exception of the Italian who complained of headache. The doctor sprayed his forehead and he was forced to set off with the others. Texas lead Tyra and Aldo north, this time making a faster pace in order to cover more ground. The huge winged creatures still wheeled overhead, but they learned nothing more of their nature as they never seemed to decline to lower altitudes.

Texas found himself wondering if an intelligence was behind his fantastic creation that was Nyjord? He could not believe it was a cosmic accident, such was not in keeping with his catholic upbringing. To allow mankind to make their way over the vastness of space, with humanity's incredible technology, was it the work of a greatly advanced civilisation (The Planet Builders named after that sect), or God? This did not mean the crew was safe though, just because a race of beings were advanced, it did not follow that they were humane. Just because God was omnipotent, it did not mean that he could not be harsh at times? Perhaps this was yet another test of faith, or the Planet Builders allowed them here simply out of cold clinical amusement; or simply as an experiment? He was like the lab rat and possibly had just as much control over events, as they.

He was not able to continue speculation down such a dark meandering however, for he suddenly heard a shout. Not only that, but it was a shout of a female and sounded human. The trio glanced at one another, unshouldered their needle rifles and trotted forward, toward the noise that alerted them.

Yet despite searching almost feverishly for ten minutes they found no on. Or; no one that wanted to be found!

"We'll press on", Texas decided.

"I wonder if any of the natural plants of this world are edible"? Tyra suddenly offered. Perhaps just to break the silence and tension that had settled over them.

"I think it safer to stick to our rations for the time being", the captain cautioned.

"You don't seem as chatty as in the past Aldo, any particular reason"?

"No, I am usually quite, quiet", the Italian replied. This caused Texas and Tyra to exchange a smirk and then the American felt a stab of attraction for the Scandian and did his best to suppress it.

The blonde girl scanned the unusually close horizon, Nyjord being a smaller sphere than Earth.

"I wonder if we are the only living mammals on here? Sharing this world with the insects and those huge aerial creatures"?

No sooner had she iterated such conjecture, than they all turned their gaze upward at the sound of movement there. Three great winged reptilian creatures were passing over them. Much lower than ever before. As the Italian threw himself to the ground Tyra suddenly exclaimed

"They look like Pterodactyls"!

Texas gasped, though they were some differences, the name was suitable and the three of them were forced to consider the creatures as such, from that moment onward.

"I hope they don't eat people", Tyra noted aloud, but to their collective relief the flying reptiles seemed uninterested by them.

They continued northward, wondering if further inhabitants of Nyjord would present themselves. They did not have to wait long! As one, they heard a sort of sneezing wheeze just behind the ubiquitous fronds and as they rounded them each was struck with fear, fear of the unfamiliar and the huge!

The creature was massive, fully three and a half metre's high when down on all six legs. When it raised itself up on the back pair, it towered in the pink sky, seeking the orange and white growths that adorned the tips of the blue fronds. It had variegated skin, mainly green, but with hints of xanthic and ochre on it's rear flanks. It's back was mainly various shades of green from lime to deep green. The six legs were not it's most astonishing features however, but it's two barbed tails and it's two long necks, upon which; were two heads!

The head's possessed multi faceted eye's, like those of a fly's. Each head had three horns, two above the head situated like a cows, while the third was from the front of the heads, situated like those of the rhinoceros. The eyes gleamed red, but the three of them fancied it was the reflection of the ground, rather than the beast's pigment. The rear legs were strong and ended in toed feet while the central pair and front pair had more delicate design and ended in sharp claws.

The sound that they had heard was from this monstrous giant! It seemed to make a scream of delight when it founds a particularly tasty and large flower-like growth, which it then conveyed to one of it's two mouths. Texas chose to conclude that the creature was a herbivore, but it may also be omnivorous and he halted in his tracks just like the woman and Aldo.

"What by the sacred laws of Hades is that"? the Italian gasped

He got no immediate answer and there was a reason for the silence of the other two. Inside their head's they felt a curious itching sensation, as if insects were crawling over their brain's and with it came a curious sense of well being, an unquestionable lack of danger. The trio then regarded the closest of the grazing creatures, for there was a herd of them. One of the foremost beast's heads was pointing directly at them, regarding them, with those mysterious, perhaps curious, eyes. Before the captain could comment, Tyra said,

"They won't hurt us, I know this. Do either of you feel it too"?

Texas nodded, pulling out his hand-cam and beginning to rapidly film the bizarre giants. While Aldo admitted,

"I do, I feel content and with no sense of danger, is that thing broadcasting waves of calmness toward us"?

"Yes; of this I'm sure" the psychologist acknowledged. "They must have a rudimentary mental broadcasting system. Not quite telepathy, more like broadcasted empathy

"Care to name them Aldo"? the captain asked the construction man, "Beat the biologist to the drop"?

Aldo smiled, "Well the Latin name would be viridi-ingens vitula-eligans".

"What does that mean"? Tyra asked

"Huge green cow", the Italian explained, "But they should have a common name taken from the Latin.

"What about a Viriligan then", the Scandian offered, "And the plural being"?

"One Viriligan, two Viriligan", Aldo laughed

Texas laughed, "It's a perfect name well done you two and won't Sita be annoyed that we haven't named the placid creatures after some Hindi god"?

They continued to watch entranced as the herd moved at a languid pace and from none of the herbivores did the three of them feel or sense any threat.

"If all the creatures of this far away place are like this one, we have nothing to worry about", Aldo observed in a hushed tone, "I suspect they won't be though".

After quite a stay, observing and filming the Viriligan they continued onward. So calm were the beasts, they chose to wend their way between the herd, for that was the direction they had chosen. To their delight they then came upon a stream. The water was pink, a reflection of the sky. Aldo suddenly dipped his hands in it, it proved to be totally clear and on an impulse, before the captain could stop him, drank some.

"If I don't get sick, then the two of you know it's safe", he said, "Give it three hours to get into my system".

"You should have requested permission from me, before you did it", Texas fumed, but then, other than to tell Lin when they returned that night, there was nothing he could do.

"How do you feel"?

"I feel refreshed, it tasted marvellously, not like that recycled fluid we've been drinking for the last four months".

It looked very inviting and the thought of recycled wastes was not so palatable, but the other two resisted the temptation.

They traversed the stream, heading for a dense copse of the tall blue fronds, the water never touching them for they found some convenient stones, over which to skip and they were sure their nylo-boots would keep their feet totally dry. Entering the copse, they gave a collective gasp of surprise, for the front most were tied and crossed, to lead to a meandering avenue, which continued on into the distance. Between the rows of fronds on either side, the avenue was created by flattened ground and compacted stones.

"This looks constructed", Aldo noted aloud. "By creatures with reason and dexterity enough to use tools".

"Certainly made anyway", Texas added, not willing to let his imagination run away with him just at that moment.

"Do you think it has a purpose"? he asked the psychologist.

"Evidentially", she nodded, "The labour taken to create such an avenue must equate to that"?

"Then it must lead to a village or town, or even a city", Aldo enthused. Tyra countered,

"It may lead to a trap! How advanced do you think those who created it are? Do you think it was made by a race indigenous to this planet, or made by visitors like ourselves"?

The men had not considered that there could be other visitors to Nyjord, but Tyra's conjecture set them to considering every possibility.

The captain had been examining one of the cut bows of the tall fronds and suddenly bending, lifted up something that had previously been concealed by the crimson grass. The Scandian noted,

"That's a broken saw isn't it"?

Texas nodded looking closely at the broken and rusty blade, "I can't tell if this is steel or iron, but it was certainly not used by off-world visitors. With the technology they command, creating this avenue would not have been done by relatively hard labour".

"So an industrial civilization none the less", Aldo pointed out, "Advanced enough to produce iron. Do you think they are the true Nyjordic"?

With his question he had just created the name given to any who dominated the planet; Nyjordic.

"If it's a trap though, what do we do"? Tyra wanted to know.

"It seems an awful lot of trouble to create such an elaborate and labour intensive lure", Aldo postulated.

"It's more likely that this is a trade route, or a theme park for the Nyjordic to view the Viriligan". the psychologist mused,

"What do you think, captain"?

"I think we come back tomorrow, with Darren at the very least, possibly with all our crew and armed to the teeth. Although we obviously come as a peaceful mission, we must be prepared to defend ourselves with deadly force, should the need arise".

So that was that, they returned early, having not used all their time and waited for the others to do the same.

The third team, Sita Willy and Wera had explored in an easterly direction. The morning was free of any sort of event, although tiny black dots filled the pink sky from time to time. The dots were obviously flying creatures, but they were too high up for the explorers to discern any features. They had lunched and proceeded easterly and were almost at the point of turning back for the journey to camp, when disaster struck.

The German had been leading, when from a coppice of fronds, a crude wooden spear suddenly flew through the air and struck him dead centre in the chest. An incredibly tall, seemingly blue humanoid jumped to his feet and whooped in delight. Wera had her needle rifle off her shoulder first and fired without thinking. The humanoid gave a cry of pain and fell back into cover.

"If there are any more of you I have plenty of needles", the Pole cried in fury and her tone must have been enough to conquer any further hostility, for the fronds parted and a lone figure began to make progress toward the two women.

The tall female warrior or chieftess wore a headdress of blue fronds, hanging from a forehead thong that kept her long silvery hair tidy. Beads of various shades of azure and turquoise were wound around one upper arm and also her neck. Cautiously she approached with her incredibly long hands, palms forward, possibly a gesture of peace the two Terran hoped. Slowly she approached the duo and asked them in a deep contralto,

"Akha veruma con diominu"?

"We do not speak your language", Wera replied, "But your tone now sounds conciliatory, tell the others to come out"?

The girl's skin, for she was only young, was blue, like the veins of a human's wrist. Her eyes were a lambent grey and her lips had been turned royal blue by some sort of stain. The race was capable of adornment and of manufacture it seemed. She repeated her enquiry and Wera gestured that the others should come out. It was the work of ten minutes to get her to understand what the geologist wanted.

Finally two lanky warriors emerged from the cover of the fronds, hauling another by dragging him, with his arms over their shoulders.

"You waste your time", Sita told the female, "He's dead, the needle was level two".

Wera pointed to the fallen German and drew a line across her throat, then pointed to the blue corpse the two males were supporting and repeated the gesture. At this the female laid her own spear on the grass and repeated the gesture with her hands and the two males followed suit.

"They surrender", Wera mused aloud, "Obviously the needle rifle has made a tremendous impression on them".

"So what do we do now", the Indian wished to know.

"Get some tie wraps out of your back pack, it seems we have some prisoners", Wera returned crisply. "Tie them with their wrists behind them, we shouldn't trust them, they killed Willy without a thought of consequence".

"What about the bodies"?

"We'll tell Texas when we get back and perhaps return to bury them, if there are no carrion on this world".

"Poor Willy, what a way to end an expedition, when he'd come so far as well".

"Poor us if the ship develops a problem, it may mean we are stranded here for the rest of our lives"!

The instant the trio of Nyjordic were tied, their body language became one of glum resignation to their fate. It did not appear they expected their fate to be good!

Because of this though, they dragged their elongated feet and made the return to the ship one continuous round of prodding and cajoling to get the trio back to Dallas. Finally, as dusk was threatening to plunge them into sudden darkness, they saw the vessel and Darren hurrying toward them, his own rifle at the ready.

SEVEN

THE FOLLOWING DAY Texas ordered Darren and Wera to go and bury the two bodies. Sita was detailed to teach the Nyjordic Standard, whilst at the same time learning Nyjordic. She used a handcam and downloaded every new word learned into the computer so that it could become a Nyjordic-Standard dictionary.

No more expeditions would take place until the nature of the natives was learned. For their part Darren and Lin had learned nothing of interest the day before.

Aldo was currently under the care of the Chinese doctor. He had developed a severe allergy to the flowers, or grass of the planet. Either that, or he had some sort of infection from the stream water he had drunk. Either way his nose and eyes streamed and he soon developed a post nasal drip irritated cough. By the afternoon Lin had ordered him to a cot in one hut, that would now become a hospital, it was the same hut he had shared with Willy!

Sita had wanted to journey to the stream to take a water sample, but Texas was adamant, no more travelling until the strength and proliferation of the natives was learned and mapped out. The others all had various tests to conduct and research to investigate, that could be done on computer, so no one was idle.

Once Sita tired with working with the female, Wera took over with one of the males and then Texas with the other, this rota taught them more than persisting with one couple. By gestures and pointing, after one day they had learned a considerable amount. After feeding the natives and securing the camp, they ate supper and pooled what they had learned.

Sita began, "The natives call themselves the Khela, which I think roughly means people or humans. Obviously they think of themselves as such and we as the aliens. The female is called Valoare, the males Puteric and Vitala. They are related, the males, possibly brothers, I couldn't quite work that one out. I learned their word for sky, world, lake and the Viriligan. That was about it for me."

Wera took up what the day had revealed, "The Khela are currently involved in a tribal dispute over land. I suppose we would call it a war. That was why they killed poor Willy, they heard his approach and though him a Barabora, which sort of roughly translates to brown skin, or dark skin. I learned the Barabora are tall too, just like the Khela. I showed Puteric the map, to try and learn the territory of each, but he had no concept of such, nor of the written word, I think. That was all I learned for today, except for the fact that Puteric spent a good deal of the time and considerable energy gesturing to me that he wanted to ah, to......".

"Tonk you", Darren laughed, "You've gotten yourself a native admirer have you Wera

"Not surprising in a primitive culture", Tyra noted, "Without writing nor any form of other visual expression and with a territorial war in full swing, then procreation would be at the top of the male's list".

"Thanks Tyra", Wera simpered, "And I thought it was because he found me beautiful".

"Speaking of individuals who find Wera desirable, how's Aldo"? Texas asked.

"Getting worse, despite a broad base antibiotic, did you learn anything by your questioning of the last of the natives, captain".

"I think the Khela have encountered it before", Texas began. "When I showed Aldo to Vitala, he muttered the word 'Phleege' before making some sort of superstitious or sacred gesture".

"That helps", the Chinese girl said, "It means it's an infection rather than an allergy, I'll change his medication accordingly".

"What if it's a virus"? Darren wanted to know.

"Then there's nothing I can do but make Aldo comfortable and hope he fights it the best his own immune system can. I don't have the equipment to start trying to treat a virus. Do you Sita"?

She shook her head, "The good news is we know Aldo did not pick it up in hyper-space, now. If the Khela know of the malady it's obviously indigenous to Nyjord".

"Could you make a vaccine from a sample of one of the native's blood", the doctor asked the biologist.

"Just a second", Texas cut in, "Before we go sticking them with needles, we need to know more about Phleege. Puncturing one of them might release it into the atmosphere around the camp".

"We could control the environment on the ship", Sita suggested.

"No"! Texas was adamant. "Remember the Martian plague? It was kept on Mars, the entire planet was quarantined until those who were immune were clear. I'm not risking taking Phleege back to Earth or any world in the solar system".

"The only one hundred percent way of ensuring that is for us never to go back", Sita said glumly.

"Then learn all you can about it while I am studying the manuals on the engines", Texas ordered

"Darren you continue to patrol our tiny border, Sooner or later the Khela may come looking for our three 'guests'. Tomorrow you and Tyra start learning some more Khelac, Wera".

"And what ever you do, don't offer to have a shower with him", the psychologist teased the geologist.

Chuckling, five of them turned in for some sleep, leaving Sita on first watch, the Khela were already asleep, simply laying on the ground where they had been tethered.

In the morning the doctor told the captain, that, in the night, Phleege had claimed it's first victim, Aldo was dead, his lungs had filled with fluid and drowned him. The crew were down to a sextet.

"I'll keep studying the engines", Texas promised them, "The rest of you continue talking to the natives, or doing your own research. We can still make this mission a success. We will keep sending reports back to Callisto, Mars and the Earth, even though we have yet to receive any answer".

That evening Valoare asked Wera if she could speak with the 'chief'.

The geologist found Texas and brought him to the female Khela.

"If you no tie I no run in day, no in not day too"? the tall and quite attractive blue female said solemnly to Texas.

"I cannot risk you returning to your people and bringing others to attack our camp", the captain told her reluctantly.

"I swear by Marahaarha no run", Valoare returned with equal gravity.

"Who's Marahaarha"? Texas asked the Polish girl.

"One of their gods", Wera explained, "The mother of all the gods as far as I can make out, the most powerful for that reason".

Valoare had been listening to them and added,

"Marahaarha bring sun, she bring rain, she make all grow".

"What do you think"? the captain asked Tyra who had drifted toward the conversation and was listening.

"It would be a trustworthy promise", the psychologist offered and then turned to Valoare,

"Swear by Marahaarha and break your oath and the rain will cease, the sun will not shine and your own insides will not carry children ever, do you understand"?

The Khela girl nodded, "Valoare swear and Valoare not run, is so".

"Alright untie her after she has sworn and let her have the run of the camp for tomorrow and then we will speak to the males", Texas decided.

"They won't swear", Tyra predicted, "They're warriors and there is a war on, what would you do"?

"I wouldn't swear either", Texas admitted.

So Valoare was released and then instructed to make supper, which she did. Her duty seemed to enrage the two males though and Sita said to the crew,

"I think Valoare is quite high in the hierarchy of the clan. Their structure is very like the red Indians of old Nevada before they were destroyed and the countries were not separate".

"The bucks would run the instant they were released", Darren cautioned, "I'm also worried their being here might eventually lead to the Khela finding us, we should consider moving sites".

The Barabora might find us too", Lin added, "The war is all over this territory".

Texas rolled out a map of the planet that he had printed out,

"Where do you suggest then, I will take it under advisement".

The crew pored over the map and even asked Khela how far the tribes involved in the war spread through the area, but the girl had no understanding of either. It seemed prudent, if they were going to make a shift, to make it for some considerable distance. They had been enjoying the heat though and so Texas, after listening to everyone picked a spot and called it Katowice.

"Tomorrow we pack everything up and make the jump to our new site", he told them. Just before we set off, we'll let the three of them go".

"No go", the Khelac female implored then, "Go with pinks".

"What ever her set up was back at their camp, it would appear being with us is preferable" Tyra observed,

"She absolutely loved the shower and the clothes we loaned her, perhaps that was it, or perhaps the Barabora were winning the dispute and her eventual fate was not one to look forward too".

"Yes", Valoare implored, "Get Valoare and brother from Barabora".

"Brother", Wera asked, "You mean one of the men has the same mother as you"?

Valoare nodded, "Vitala brother to Valoare".

"Then explain what we are doing to him and Puteric in the morning and ask them what they wish to do. We will be going many many days walking from here". Texas told the Khelac.

By carefully removing the segmented struts within the huts it was possible to flat pack them into the ship. The plumbing was more difficult and they cut it into the largest possible sections Explorer One could house. Then it became time to get aboard and offer the Khelac relocation, if they so desired. Vitala chose to come with his sister and was released to climb aboard after her. Puteric decided to return to the tribe. The airlock was closed the ship's engines engaged and the craft merely acted as a very high powered plane which took them to the west coast of the massive central continent of Nyjord, at the same latitude. Within moments the craft was landing and the two natives of the world ceased their praying to various of their gods.

As they disembarked, Texas told the others,

"In honour of our dear departed engineer I have decided to call this continent Zentrum".

"Can each of us name some others this evening please captain"? Wera asked.

"If the new camp of Katowice is completed by dusk you shall have such an honour", Texas promised. That was how the northern landmasses came to earn their names of;York, Hubei, Hyderabad, Skalo and Warka. There were some smaller islands too, which for the moment remained unnamed on the map that Texas sent back to Callisto and the Earth.

"We have completed a mountain of research, enough for now, tomorrow we shall explore our new area and take two new people with us", the captain decided.

EIGHT

THE BLUE FRONDS proliferated and waved gently in the breeze, for the first time it rained on Nyjord and the rain, unsurprisingly, was pink. Once it had ceased the eight of them set out to explore beyond the camp which they had named Katowice.

The sun kept trying to burn it's way from behind the clouds, but the day remained bright and overcast, a cooler wind was blowing from the east, the sea of Bengal. The actions of Brahma would make the breakers more impressive than any on Earth so they kept inland, but it was possible to smell the saline in the air.

"Nyjord is a paradise", Wera said to Texas as the walked, "Would not the introduction of Terran's ruin it"?

"In some ways I guess they would", the captain returned thoughtfully, "But you've found huge deposits of minerals and other useful resources, of which, the Earth is exhausted, mankind must continue to expand or stagnate".

"And the Khela and Barabora, what do you think will become of those native and primitive peoples", the Pole wished to know, although she suspected she knew the answer.

History does not paint a good picture, when a primitive civilisation is met by a more advanced one", Texas mused,

"Look at the history of my continent, the indigenous tribes were all but wiped out, but what can we do"?

The others had drifted closer to hear the content of the conversation.

"We could stay; here on Nyjord", Darren offered. "Perhaps Earth would then presume we were unable to return".

"There would be a second ship", Sita pointed out. "They would come primarily to rescue us".

"But it would give us time to teach the natives what to expect", Tyra offered, "They could be ready and prepared".

Texas was shocked despite himself, "You mean we go rogue. Against our own race"?

"We would become Nyjordic", Darren offered eying the Khelac maiden, evidentally the thought had certain appeal to him.

"There is just one problem", Lin the doctor pointed out, at the seed of their notions, "If we go native we don't yet know how to conquer the Phleege, it might kill us all, especially once we start ingesting local plants, local animal flesh, if any is edible".

"Then our choice is obvious if we decide to stay here", Texas could not believe he was considering it,

"It's down to you and the biologist, doctor, to create a vaccine for the Phleege, or to build up our own immune system until we are not effected by it".

Lin turned to the incredibly tall Valoare,

"From here do you think you could reach some of the Khela, get them to help us with our problem with the Phleege"?

"We roam further", the Khela girl answered, "To find Khelac. Some witch doctors have good ju-ju".

"We should consider the implications of this action", Texas told them then, "We will talk more about it tonight at camp".

The general consensus of opinion was that Nyjord needed time to realise that mankind was on it's way and one of the best ways of delaying further missions was for them not to return. They voted and it was unanimous, until they heard from the Solar System, they would not lift off planet. This made the Khelac their future, it seemed.

"Might I suggest I go with the two of them on a longer search for the western edge of their territory, sir"? Darren asked the captain.

"I really don't think they will have an antidote to the Phleege", Sita told him then.

Valoare cut in, "Witch doctor has power ju-ju".

"It may be a start, we should let Darren try", Texas decided. "In the mean time we continue research and transmissions to the Solar System".

Before anyone quite realised what she was doing though, the biologist suddenly reached down and plucked a leaf of red grass and promptly place it in her mouth and chewing for only a second, swallowed it.

"Now we can work on a toxin the moment my blood contains pathogens", she said.

"That was a singularly stupid action"! Texas raged, "You're on report. Well, Darren, it seems you and the Khelac are now racing against time"!

The trio set of the following morning. Darren seemed particularly excited to be going on a mission with the Khelac girl, despite her incredible height, he found her attractive and desirable.

"Don't anger her brother", was the captain's parting warning and they both knew what he meant by that.

That day Lin and Sita worked feverishly, documenting the biologist's statistics - hourly. By the end of the day Sita's nose had began to run and her eyes were smarting, she was displaying the same symptoms as Aldo and it would only be a matter of time before her rash act would prove the reason for her demise.

"Maybe I flew too far", Texas mused bitterly, "It's many kilometres from here back to Dallas. A third of the breadth of Zentrum, I should have taken us down in the centre of this section of the continent".

"You can't blame yourself for Sita's rashness", Tyra returned, "We can't leave Katowice now, Darren would not find an alternative site, if we switched, before giving him chance to return. We have to hope that the Khelac are spread throughout this land mass".

"And that the Barabora aren't", Wera added. "Even if Darren finds them and they get their witch doctor back here, '*ju-ju*' is probably just some useless mumbo jumbo. Lin and Sita herself, are the girl's best hope".

Texas looked about, as the fronds rustled in the breeze from the Sea of Bengal, "This world truly has a beauty when one gets used to the different hues".

"Let's hope it doesn't end up being a beautiful final resting place for us all", the geologist replied.

They were awoken in the middle of the night, around fifteen hours, on their twenty hour clock.

"Come out, it's Darren and we've some new visitors for you"?

"Texas rushed out of his hut to see the military member of his crew with four tall, blue figures. He recognised Valoare and Vitala at once. As if reading his mind Darren said,

"Captain, let me introduce Kharos and Khorvos. Their village, which is called Közössé, is only on the other side of this peninsular, we were lucky".

Texas nodded politely to the newcomers who bowed in response, as the rest of the crew joined them. The one named Khorvos had some sort of filaments attached to a strip of leathery material bound around his temple to keep his long silver hair in check. He also had a plaited band of blue leathery material around one arm. So Texas was not surprised when Valoare told him,

"Khorvos witchdoctor, have powerful ju-ju".

"Ask him if he thinks he can help us then and what he would need for his services"?, the captain enquired.

"Already know", Valoare replied without consulting the other Khelac, "We tell of big silver bird come from black sky. Chief want ride and you go Közössé. Witchdoctor help if agree"?

"They obviously regard us as some sort of celebrities, the ship adding to the attraction", Tyra noted to Texas, she asked Valoare,

"The Khelac of Közössé, they are friendly like you and Vitala"?

The tall blue girl nodded, "Always so with Khelac, no fear Khelac, fear Barabora".

"They want us on their side", Texas mused, "And to help us with the Phleege they want a ride for the chief, I think we can cautiously agree don't you"?

"I don't think we have a choice if we want to save Sita", Lin told them then, "The disease is advancing, she doesn't have long left".

"Alright we do what we can", Texas made the decision, "Take Khorvos to Sita and see if any of his superstition helps her".

"And the herbs", the doctor added, "Look he has a ditty bag".

Lin, Valoare and the witch doctor went to the hut that had been designated the hospital.

"What is the function of the other chap, what's his name, Kharos, Vitala"? Tyra wished to know. At first the Khelac girl's brother did not understand for his standard was not as accomplished as hers, but when he did he replied,

"He chief's man, he speak for chief".

"An ambassador", Texas laughed, "Very well the two of you come and have some supper"?

"He no eat in place of Phleege", Vitala explained, "Bring own".

"Then ask him to join us and eat what he wishes, we must begin the process of getting to know all the Khelac".

During that night after imbibing some of Khorvos' heated brew, Sita sat up and announced she was feeling much better. Lin took samples, made sure the Indian was comfortable and then settled her back down for a couple of hours sleep before dawn. She fell asleep herself in the chair, in which, she was keeping a bedside vigil. When the light came with the rising of Proxima, Texas strolled to the hospital tent once he was up and washed and went to see the biologist.

She was dead!

"I thought you said you were awoken by her and she was feeling much better"? he asked the doctor.

"And so she did", Lin agreed, "It's called the early hours bloom".

"Then we are lost, the Phleege will claim us all once the supplies are exhausted, we must return to Callisto and tell them Nyjord is ripe for conquest", Texas was miserable. The doctor suddenly had her hand on his arm,

"Before she died her blood provided a serum, captain, which I distilled and produced partly with her and partly alone. We do not have to go home if we decide not to".

"It may not work"?

"It worked on me, I am ready to inject the rest of you with it".

"What do you mean it worked on you"? asked Tyra who had drifted into the hut to see Sita, herself.

"I administered it intravenously it last night, then deliberately drank some of the collected rain water in one of the gutters, the water tested as being of Nyjord origin and I have no symptoms".

"Do some more tests of your own blood", Texas ordered. Then eat some of the white and orange flowers if you are convinced you are immune to Phleege, only then will I be satisfied enough to do the same, remember only I can pilot the ship"!

The Chinese doctor did just as ordered, while the rest of them tried to concentrate on their own research and recordings. Kharos pestered them for the ship to go to Közössé, as his chief had requested, but with Valoare's help they stalled him.

A second day Lin was free of infection ad announced that tests confirmed this. Wera insisted on being the next guinea pig. Two days later she was immune to Phleege so then the rest of them including Texas were inoculated and they ate the flowers that looked like eggs and curiously tasted; just like...scrambled eggs!

"So if we so desire, we can stay and live with the Khelac and continue our research and especially try to communicate with the Viriligan", Texas said to them that evening.

"Or we can pack up and return to Earth disease free and with armfuls of research".

"Through hyper-space again" Wera shivered.

"Without knowing how much real time will have passed since our departure", Tyra mused.

"Might I suggest the fairest way of deciding is with a vote, captain"? Darren asked eyeing Valoare as he spoke.

"Very well we will vote and I will even allow Valoare and Vitala to vote with us", Texas smiled, knowing it was the democratic thing to do.

So they voted.

AMBITION

ONE

MULLER HAD KILLED seven people before the long arm of the law finally caught up with him. Chief Constable Heiter Starhoven of Mars Constabulary had made a statement to the net-press, when the murderer was finally apprehended,

"This blackguard is not insane, he is simply and unequivocally pure evil. He should be locked up in the highest security institution we have here on Mars and the swipe card thrown away. Today my officers did a great service to the citizens of Kasei Valless, the streets of which, are now a safer place to walk, because of their competent work".

News man Charpy Moonbadger of the Kasei Valless station zero one eight was the only one allowed to interview the serial killer, before his trial,

"How do you react to the statement Starhoven gave to the collected press following your arrest, Hindrodine"? He could not resist asking the fearsome man, of some one hundred and ninety centimetres of height and some one hundred and two kilogramme's in muscle, not a hint of which was flab.

"When I get out of prison, the first to die will be the Chief Constable", Hindrodine Muller had promised.

The trial took place, the jury were shocked by images of Muller's victim's, all of whom, he had killed with a machete in the most brutal and bloody fashion. They were only out of the courtroom twenty minutes before returning to give their 'guilty' verdict. The judge gave Muller seven consecutive life sentences. Muller was taken by flitter to the most secure penal institute on Mars, Csúnabörtön, which was at Argentia Planum near the south pole.

Deputy Chief Constable Inahimo Glissman had been waiting for just such an opportunity. Glissman had been born in the poor district of Lomonosov. Yet he had decided he was going to amount to something, when even at school. He was going to rise to the top of some sort of profession and he did not care who he had to tread on or cheat, to do it.

Lomonosov Infants School was a rough place where only the physically strong and aggressive were never bullied. It soon became Glissman's turn, when an older boy three years above him decided to rob him of his lunch voucher one day. The older boy was taller, heavier and there was no way Glissman could get past him in the corridor without letting himself in for some sort of beating.

He handed the voucher to the older boy, while the cronies around the bully smiled, but then he leaned into the taller child and said to him in a low voice,

"You can loan it today, I'll take it back tomorrow along with yours, for interest".

"I don't think so", the bully laughed, pushing him to the floor.

The next day however, as the bully and his cronies swaggered down the same corridor which led to the refectory, Glissman was waiting for them. From out of the sleeve of his shirt a thirty centimetre ruler slid and without a word he brought the sharp edge down, with a crack onto the back of the bully's hand. Once the bully had finished screaming Glissman said quietly,

"I believe you owe me two lunch vouchers, give them to me now; or I'll do the other hand".

Hurrying to do as instructed the bully snarled,

"Tomorrow I'll have a ruler Glissman".

"I'm sure you will, but then I will have a stick. If you then get a stick, I'll get a piece of piping. If you get a piece of piping I'll get a knife or a broken bottle. Who do you think is going to get fed up first"?

"You're crazy"! one of the cronies noted.

Glissman did the best he could to give them all a wide eyed glare,

"You may be right, so put the word out children, Glissman is not to be touched, unless you want more trouble than you can imagine".

It was the last time he ever had any trouble at school. As he got older he did not become a bully himself though, rather he became popular and the other children and even some of the staff referred to him as 'No nonsense Glissman, the boy who is not to be touched'.

After his teen re-augmentation surgery, he was as handsome as all young men, but with greater assuredness and confidence he was able to talk his first girl into bed at the age of fifteen. He was on the pill, so nothing could come of it and she never complained anyway. There were other girls, but his greatest conquest was at the age of seventeen when he managed to seduce Miss Corffo, the physical education teacher, who was twenty four at the time.

Glissman decided his rise in life must be in the regimentally regulated framework of a services career. He contemplated the Martian Space Fleet, but it was bursting with applicants. Mars had little need for an army nor navy so that left either the fire or police service. Following the incident with the bully years previously, he had discovered he could coerce with speech rather than be forced to violent confrontation and the police beckoned.

His first post as a constable was the streets of Lomonosov; if he could survive there, he could police anywhere. it was during this period that Glissman learned the best way our of a situation, or the best way forward from one, it was not always the honest one. He built up a small group of paid informants, but he also went on 'the take'. If it was easier to accept payment to turn a blind eye to certain crimes that did not result directly in violent death, he did so. He discovered that during this period too, that those above him were in some cases working the same system. This made him dangerous to some who supervised him, by reason of knowledge and the easiest way forward was to make certain of his silence; they made him one of them. He was promoted to sergeant and transferred to Mie. It had taken him only three hundred and forty Martian days to achieve it, approximately half of a Martian year.

He continued with exactly the same policy at Mie and was similarly rewarded in six hundred days with a second promotion to inspector of Cassini. He was the youngest inspector on the entire planet. Within twelve hundred more days Glissman made Chief Inspector, remaining in Cassini. He was then head hunted for the post of Pasteur's station as a superintendent. Glissman had developed a system where the villains of his area of responsibility actually policed one another, with himself at the top. He had, in fact, become a professional law breaker himself.

Twenty hundred days later he was promoted to chief superintendent of Hebes Chasma and it was then, that he became of interest to Starhoven. The chief constable of Mars was intrigued by the meteoric rise through the ranks of Glissman. The apparent reduction in crime where ever he was posted and of course his driving ambition. All of this Glissman was ignorant at the time, until he received a ping on his pad one day inviting him to interview for the post of assistant chief constable of Olympus Mons Constabulary, which was the headquarters of the planet wide police station.

Invited to apply? It was unheard of and Glissman did as suggested and got the job, for he interviewed very well, very well indeed.

That had been a thousand days ago and now Glissman was Starhoven's deputy and right hand man.

He was not however, satisfied!

For he was not at the top, one man stood in his way, his mentor and friend, Heiter Starhoven. So the solution was obvious; Starhoven must be removed. Only two men actually possessed the power necessary to sack him however and they were, King Rövalaát of South Mars and King Iyhyt of North Mars. To be taken from the post would take an act of gross incompetence with disastrous results and Glissman would never do such a thing.

Just as he was beginning to despair that Starhoven would be in his way until he reached retirement, an unforeseen opportunity dropped into his lap. A serial killer began needlessly butchering Martian citizens with a machete. It was the most heinous crime that the planet had ever seen. Starhoven promptly created a task force with one sole objective, the capture and incarceration of the killer. the task force was created under the name Operation Nullify and Glissman was made head of it.

It was a shrewd move by the chief constable, for if his deputy succeeded, he Starhoven would take the credit for Nullify. If on the other hand it failed to apprehend the killer, before public opinion turned impatiently against it, then Starhoven would have the chance to remove Glissman and place the blame on him, by nature of such an action. Glissman was aware of two things, one was that Starhoven, whilst admiring him and being supportive of him, also considered him as a threat to his position. The other was that should he fail to find the serial killer and quickly, that beneath him assistant chief constable Fals Denigerend had ambitions of his own and his target was Glissman himself.

Muller was caught though and within a reasonable time scale and as he was jailed Starhoven made his speech. Glissman considered this a mistake and was deeply gratified when he read of Muller's response.

A daring plan was beginning to form in Glissman's mind!

TWO

T HE KLAXON WAS very loud indeed.
It caused armed men to scurry from
their posts toward a command centre at the very heart of the facility. The men
were warden's of the high security Csúnabörtön Penitentiary, which was at
Argentia Planum near the south pole. One of the high risk prisoners had escaped
from a place that the law thought impregnable!

How had he gotten out of his cell? Only the guards had the correct swipe
card and they were on the other side of the door. Items were only passed
through the door's inspection port and every prisoner in the high security wing
were an eight guard unlock. Yet one convict had gotten out of his cell, rendered
the night guard unconscious and dragged his inert form to the outer door,
opening the next door with his thumbprint. It was then easier for the prisoner
who had gotten thus far, to go through the next two doors. All he needed was
the guard's thumb print; thus all he needed was the guard's thumb.

As the klaxon continued to scream their distress Muller dived into the
waiting flitter.

Glissman managed to take it up and forward at high speed, whilst still
having a needle pistol aimed at the murderer's chest all the while.

"You don't need that", Muller's deep baritone rumbled, as he eyed the slim
snout of the weapon, "If you hadn't visited me and slipped me the swipe card,
I'd still be in there".

"True", Glissman was happy to concede, "But I know it won't take you long to realise that I was part of the investigation that helped put you in there in the first place".

Muller's eye's almost glowed in the dark like malign coals,

"But you didn't head it did you, that was Starhoven".

"You remember our deal"?

"You think I'm a retard, you think I have some sort of retardation? Have you brought me a machete"?

"My dear Hindrodine", Glissman began with a mirthless smile, "It's time for you to start showing a bit more finesse when taking someone's life. I am going to let you have a high powered needle gun with night vision telescopic sights, once you're out the flitter that is".

"Call me Muller and I don't want no gun, I like to use my machete"!

"The machete gets you caught Muller, the gun gives you chance to get clean away before the constabulary arrive. Plus you employed a double negative then, if you don't want 'no' gun, then you must want 'a' gun. Be a good homicidal maniac and take the gun and the money in that envelope, the one you're sitting on".

Muller pulled the envelope free and ripped the top of it open.

Glissman told him, "There's two thousand shillin in there, to give you a fresh start somewhere, go to Callisto or maybe even the new mining operations in the asteroids".

"It's not enough"!

"How can it not be enough, when you were going to do it for free. Now listen carefully and I'll tell you when Starhoven is going to be at his mansion, which he has ludicrously called Olympus. This of course means that you'll know when you'll be able to kill him and get away with it".

It was all set, Glissman rehearsed Muller several times so that he was certain the murderer would get the details right and then he, Glissman, would take the top job on the planet!

Starhoven's pad pinged and he read the message from Governor Sleutel Zárbezár, the colour drained from his features, for it read simply:- *'Muller has escaped, we have not yet recaptured him'.*

He opened a skype and Zárbezár's features swan into pixelised focus.

"You got my message I see", the governor mused.

"I did and I am furious Sleutel, furious I say, how could Muller escape the most secure penal installation on the planet"?

"Easily, he had a swipe card to his cell door. he opened the inspection hatch reached through it and simply swiped himself out. As for the other doors he had one of the guards thumbs. The surgeon says it is successfully reattached and should take, if you were thinking of asking".

"The swipe card, but only two swipe cards to Muller's cell exist and you and I are the only ones who have them"?

By way of answer Zárbezár held up his card, adding,

"This has been in my safe all night, until just now, when I removed it to make certain it was still there".

"Wait", Starhoven asked tacitly and abruptly and went to his own safe, punched in the ten digit combination, with a grim realisation he returned to his pad,

"Mine's been stolen"!

"Then I suggest you look to your own office for the one who is aiding Muller", Zárbezár offered.

"Impossible"! Starhoven exploded, "Only myself and Deputy Chief Constable Glissman know that combination".

Zárbezár nodded with a smile, "Goodnight Heiter", he said and cut the connection.

Starhoven immediately ordered two uniforms posted at his door, then skyped Glissman. The latter appeared on the screen his hair in disarray, his shoulders dressed in a pyjama jacket.

"You're in bed"! the chief constable observed, "Yet it's only twenty one hundred"?

"Well it was my day off chief and I had a headache, so I wiped my forehead with analgesic and decided to have an early night".

"Muller's escaped"!

Glissman looked astonished, "But that's impossible, the only two people that could get him out of his solitary suite were yourself and governor Zárbezár"!

"He seems to think that the piece of information you have just described, should tell me something".

Glissman looked thoughtful and then slowly admitted,

"I don't follow chief, your card is still in the safe, so what is he talking about"?

"My card is gone", Starhoven said carefully. Glissman asked,

"So why did he have your card stolen only to .....oh I get it. He 'had' to have the card stolen otherwise it was obviously he who released Muller, but why"?

It was Starhoven's turn to look confused, "You think he did that?! It was not something I had considered. Why though, why did he want Muller out"?

That bit's obvious", Glissman smiled, "you only have to tell me now if Zárbezár would want you out of the way for some reason; or......"

"Or"?

"Or Muller had money we knew nothing about, or knew someone who would pay the governor to get Muller out of prison".

Glissman was once again satisfied to see his superior look confused, sure enough Starhoven admitted,

"I had not thought there might be so many variables to this, I confess to being lost now".

"Look, chief, let me get rid of this headache and meet you in the a.m. and we'll go over this together, is that alright"?

Starhoven agreed and Glissman cut the connection. Sometimes it was just too easy for him.

THREE

T HE FLITTER SLID to a halt, landing on the gravel roadway and Muller climbed out.

From the driver side of the vehicle Glissman climbed out too. He glanced up, the stars were set in a sky the colour of old blood and the faint sound of lichen-beetles, rubbing their legs together could be heard. He said over the roof of the flitter,

"I kept my word to you, so give me back the swipe card"?

The murderer did so with a shrug. Glissman reached into the hatch-back of the vehicle and pulled out a long range needle rifle with telescopic sights.

"I wanted my machete", Muller sounded petulant.

"A weapon that ultimately got you caught last time", the deputy chief pointed out. "Take this, get him and the promised shillin will be yours".

"Where's the place"? Muller asked, by way of tacit agreement. "You're shaking; are you scared deputy chief"?

"This is not the usual sort of activity I get involved in", Glissman admitted bitterly. "Now look at those two amber L.E.D.'s. They're either side of two massive iron gates, set into an unassailable wall. This is the visage of Starhoven's Noctis Labyrinthus property and he'll be coming here Saturday night, a detail only I know about. Here's some provisions, now I'm going to give you a hand with one of the gates and get you inside. Just remember this Muller get caught and you'll get the firing squad it will be my first action as chief, but get away cleanly and you'll get the money".

"I can handle the gate", the murderer scowled.

"No, you can't they're electrically operated from inside the property or with an electronic key that Starhoven keeps on his person. They're solid cast iron, it will take two of us to force them manually, so come on".

Starhoven had been chief for twelve years and would likely last as long again. Glissman could not afford to wait that long, his ambition burned inside him like a furnace and this was the only way he could fulfil his desires. He could see the scenario in his minds eye, the huge metal gates opening, activated by the chief's key, the flitter easing up the driveway beyond and then Starhoven climbing out. The phut of the needle rifle and then *'he'* was chief. He even imaging his speech, he would not rest until Muller was standing before a firing squad, the very first execution on the planet and instigated by Chief Constable Inahimo Glissman.

The excitement began on the Wednesday, when the swipe card was found in Constable Sulvinger Balek's locker, the search instigated by Glissman of course. Poor Balek had been interrogated to exhaustion, but still sweatily professed his innocence.

It was Saturday morning when Starhoven was summing up his thoughts,

"I just don't think there's any way Balek could have gotten into the safe, no way for him to know the combination, he never visited Muller either, so how could he have gotten the card to him and how could he have gotten it back. Himo; are you listening to me"?

"Eh....oh sorry chief, I was wondering about that too, it's a real mystery. Just like Muller's disappearance, where could he have gone without any money"?

"He must have an accomplice".

"Yet he was a loner, never trusted a living soul before. One of the things that helped us catch him in the first place".

"Maybe we'll only find out when we catch him"? Starhoven mused. "Anyway, we're leaving at nineteen hundred this evening".

"We are? What do you mean *we*, chief"?

"I'm frightened of no one Himo and that includes Muller, but I need your company this evening. It's the gates to my Noctis Labyrinthus property, something wrong with the electric sensor. So the gates have to be opened manually, the bar that slips in place is too heavy for one man, not to mention the gates themselves. So I need you to come with me".

Glissman remembered the bar, even Muller with his kilo's of muscle had struggled with it. Starhoven was speaking again,

"I want you with me anyway, Himo, in case we get any leads over the weekend".

"But I've made a date with..........".

"Cancel it", Starhoven was firm, "What's the problem anyway, you've never turned down a weekend at Noctis Labyrinthus before, it will be as always, good food, good drink and we can get a couple of girls for Sunday night, the best, clean and polite you know".

Glissman was backed into a corner and he knew it, "Of course, I'm with you, I'll pack an overnight bag from my apartment at lunch time".

"The weekend will do you good", Starhoven noted, "You've been looking a bit peaky this week, I think you're putting too much into this case, but don't think I don't appreciate it".

Glissman was not thinking about lunch nor packing as he walked down Olympus Mons main street. The tall conifers were now pumping out sufficient oxygen for some younger fitter individuals to be able to cope outside for twenty minutes or so without tanks. He had his hooded fur-lined coat on, but was actually sweating as he thought about Starhoven's gate. That damned contraption was going to ruin everything and could well get him killed. He could imagine the scene; the flitter pulling up outside the mansion, two men climbing out, Muller using the unfamiliar rifle and firing and he, Glissman catching the dart and ending up very very dead!

They could not go to Noctis Labyrinthus that evening, or Glissman was in mortal danger. How was he going to stop the journey from happening, trying to talk Starhoven out of it would prove futile and look suspicious, there had to be another way. Then inspiration came, the chief's flitter! If it developed a fault mid way that would be enough to cause a cancellation. Turning on his heels Glissman hurried back the way he had come, back toward the police car pool.

"Hello Sezrelo", he said cheerfully ten minutes later.

"Hello chief", the mechanic returned.

"I need something out of the chief's flitter, where is it"?

"Second row, fourth down", Sezrelo replied.

Glissman walked nonchalantly down to the Honda and flipped the driver side lid, none of the vehicles were locked in the police headquarters, there was no need. It was the work of a few seconds to prize the dashboard cover free with his penknife and then he cut the wires to the V.D.U. Starhoven would get inside with him in the passenger seat and then be unable to get any information at all. By the time they called Sezrelo at home and brought him back into work, it would be too late to set off for Noctis Labyrinthus.

Where ever Sezrelo was, when Glissman left the pool, he was not watching what Glissman was doing. Fine, act keenly for the trip all afternoon and then be disappointed when the car could not take them.

At nineteen hundred that evening Starhoven lead Glissman down to the pool and without thinking the deputy chief began walking toward the second row,

"You're going the wrong way Himo", Starhoven told him then, "You're going to my usual spot but I'm not taking the Honda, when Sezrelo did a routine check on it this afternoon, it had a display fault, so we're taking the Toyota".

Glissman struggled to keep from stumbling, the ground seemed to sway beneath his feet. He cursed himself for relying on too simple a wheeze, was he losing his touch?

"You drive", Starhoven told him when they got to the flitter, "Be careful though, there's a great deal of horse power underneath that bonnet".

There were two ways to get to Noctis Labyrinthus from Olympus Mons, one was the a22 that took them through Ascraeus Mons; the other was the a24 south toward Biblis Patera. Glissman took the latter for a good reason, it was a longer journey, enabling him the excuse to request a stop. The chief would normally make the run straight through, but as they got within minutes of Biblis Patera, Glissman complained,

"I need to make a bathroom break chief". He could feel the blood pounding in his temple, he did not want to die. "I'm hungry too, fancy a burger"?

"No", the chief was annoyed, "We can eat when we get to the mansion, can't you hold on"?

"I must be getting old chief but I really need to go and while we're there I could do with a snack at least, otherwise I might get another one of my headaches".

"We were making such good time too", Starhoven returned petulantly, staring out at another tremendous Mars night sky.

"I'll make it up to you", Glissman offered, "I'll pay".

The chief laughed, "Then it's a quarter pounder with cheese and all the side bits they do".

"You've got it boss", Glissman smiled, whilst thinking *You greedy fat blackguard, on the pay you're on you'll let me pay too, I just wish I wasn't with you and you were going to that gate alone'.*

He was not alone though and he could not bear the thought of getting shot with a needle by mistake, he had to make a second attempt to stop their arrival at Noctis Labyrinthus, his life depended upon it!

The Toyota slid into the parking lot of Biblis Patera's 'Eat a Pile' advertisement, the two of them climbed out, as they walked into the burger place Glissman noticed a cyber-cafe over the road, while Starhoven took a seat at one of the double tables the deputy chief said suddenly,

"Order what you want chief, I'm just going over to the cyber-cafe over the road to tell my girlfriend I'm standing her up tonight and it's your fault"!

"What do you want"?

"I'll have the same as you".

"Why the cafe, where's your pad"?

"It's on the fritz".

"You could have made that ping this afternoon".

"And given her time to tell me a dozen reasons why I was not going to be here with you tonight, now it's fate accompli".

"Well borrow mine then"?

"Chief, it's going to be a personal call, you know what I mean"?

"You're going to have to tell her you love her", Starhoven chuckled.

"Just cut me a bit of slack will you"?

"Alright, but don't be long"

'Who do you think you are, my frenging keeper', Glissman though, but instead he promised, "Oh I'll cut the connection as soon as she pauses for breath".

Starhoven laughed again, it seemed he found Glissman's sardonic wit amusing. He strode over to the cafe and slipped a few coins into the nearest pad, he disabled the cam but kept voice only active. Then he pinged Olympus Mons headquarters.

In answer to the reception identification he asked,

"Let me speak to Inspector Eerstpróba", he asked and was told Eerstpróba was unavailable, "Inspector Provýforsøk then", he waited while the inspector came on the connection,

"Hello Provýforsøk, it's Glissman, just to let you know I'm having a burger with the chief, at 'Eat a Pile' in Biblis Patera, just in case you get a break on the where about's of Muller, okay"?

Provýforsøk did not think it likely but he was polite to the deputy chief constable and Glissman cut the connection. Then he waited three or four minutes before pinging the station again, he lowered his voice as deeply as it would go

"Hello cop station, listen I've a hot lead on the where about's of Muller, put me through to the chief constable and fast".

The girl on the switchboard told him in a voice of considerable concern that the chief was unavailable,

"Well give me someone who can take this info and fast", Glissman demanded gruffly,

He got the desk sergeant, who he knew would then go to Provýforsøk, he repeated his message before adding,

"I'll talk to the chief and the chief only about this tonight, say at twenty one hundred hours, just make sure that where ever he is, he comes back to the station so I can meet him in his office then".

Satisfied that the message would have them turning back shortly, he went back over to the burger hall and seated himself opposite Starhoven.

"Did she portion any grief"? the chief asked around a mouthful of beef.

"She's a tart, chief, what do you think"?

Starhoven laughed, "She'll get over it, surely you're not that irresistible"?

"You'd have to believe it if I told you I was, two guys together", Glissman joked back all the while thinking to himself, '*Come on pad ping for Hades sake*'.

Why had the station not pinged Starhoven by now? Five minutes passed; ten, fifteen and still the chief's pad was silent. Glissman talked the chief into ice cream but still there was no peep on Starhoven's pad.

"Okay, I'm done, go and pay and we'll set off again", Starhoven instructed while he puffed on a med-cigar.

Glissman could stall him no longer, perhaps the ping would come once they were back in the flitter? He paid the bill and walked slowly to the Toyota finishing his own med-cig, as he climbed into his seat, Starhoven was plugging his pad into the vehicles charger. Glissman's heart sank, the pad was out of charge otherwise the chief would not have plugged it in, headquarters could only have reached them at the 'Eat a Pile' and now they were driving away from it, the second ruse had also failed to work!

He examined his feeling, the thought of approaching that gate with a homicidal maniac training a needle rifle on him was not something he wanted to do. Indeed he knew he totally hated the idea. In the dim glow of the amber lights either side of the gate, it would like as not be impossible to tell he and Starhoven apart. If it were him with the weapon, he would shoot both men. So how could he expect Muller to use more discernment, more care.

Noctis Labyrinthus was but a few kilometres away when the sandstorm hit. The wind was probably blowing at some eighty kilometres an hour and the flitter's filters were in danger of getting clogged. Glissman was sweating, what was he going to do, subconsciously he began to slow down.

"Put your foot down Himo, this cab can do much better, even in this weather", the chief ordered impatiently.

"I'm just worried the filters might get clogged", Glissman was disgusted to hear the whine in his own voice.

"You know I'm still not convinced about that swipe card business", Starhoven remarked as Glissman reluctantly increased the speed of the flitter.

"Eh"?

"Yeah Balek just doesn't seem right for safe cracking"?

"So what then"?

"The governor still swears he and his guards are solid".

"Well he would do, wouldn't he"?

"I'm going to make it my business to get to the bottom of it no matter what".

"Ooooh", Glissman suddenly feigned pain and gripped his left arm.

"What is it"? Starhoven demanded, keeping his eyes on the road. It was almost impossible in the shrouded swirling sand.

"I don't know, must have a bit of burger stuck in one of my corners", Glissman gasped, "I've suddenly gotten crippling heartburn".

"Look what you're doing"! Starhoven cried, "You nearly took us off the road then, here let me hold the wheel"?

Under Glissman's direction however the Toyota skidded and hit a huge bank of sand that had been blown to the road side. Glissman hoped the old goat had forgotten his seatbelt, but no such luck; he heard him groan just as he was checking himself over,

"Are you alright"? Starhoven asked, in a dazed fashion.

"I don't know, are you unhurt"?

"Banged my damned right knee again, it's going to stiffen up for sure. We can't get out, not till this sandstorm blows over".

"Probably best if I turn the flitter around and get you to a doctor in Noctis Labyrinthus".

"You're joking of course", Starhoven was obdurate, "We're practically there, can you reverse us out and go on, slowly this time"?

"I think it's set in pretty deep", Glissman returned hopefully.

Then they heard a vehicle pull up beside them, saw the flashing amber of highway maintenance, a voice cried,

"Hey you guys okay, I saw you slide off the road, hang on while I attach a tow bar and pull you out".

"Thanks mister", Starhoven chuckled, "Can you beat that for luck Himo, the odds have to be one chance in a million that highway would be coming down this road just when we needed them! The storm's lifting too, or moving on, just let me get to the mansion and I can soak the ache out of this knee".

"Yes boss", Glissman echoed dully, "One chance in a million". Then he thought to himself, *I'm going to die, by the very weapon I furnished Muller with'!*

Within minutes the flitter was winding up the road to the heavy gates at the mansion. Glissman had done everything he could, short of confessing and still they were making the rendezvous with Muller and his needle rifle.

"Right Himo, stop here", Starhoven ordered and climbed out the Toyota with more ease than expected considering his complaints about his knee.

"Come on, we'll get some jollop down you for that heartburn, once you help me with the bar to the gates? Come on, don't act like a child, here, I'll give you a hand. Now come on, we'll lift the ruddy thing together".

Glissman climbed out of the flitter as though he was living the last few seconds of his life. He was shaking uncontrollably, this was not how his hard work and years of planning was supposed to end. He could see no way out though, three times he'd tried to stall this moment and every time that bitch, 'lady luck' had been on Starhoven's side.

He walked over to the gates, every step feeling like his boots were filled with lead and then he was in the amber light, with the chief and Muller would be taking aim. Wondering why there were two men instead of one, shrugging and deciding to take both out to be on the safe side. Glissman could almost feel the murderer's finger squeezing the trigger and then.......

Bang!

Glissman fell, poleaxed.

FOUR

A FLITTER PULLED UP beside Starhoven, the window slid down and Provýforsøk leaned out,

"What was that explosion chief, scared me half to death"?

"Just the Toyota clearing it's flitters", Starhoven explained, "But what are you doing here"?

"We just cornered and arrested Muller", the inspector told his chief proudly, "In Noctis Labyrinthus, where he'd gone for something to eat, a respectful citizen of Mars had spotted him and pinged it in".

"So he's locked up for good this time hopefully"?

"Better than that chief, he's dead, had a needle rifle with him, we had no choice but to put him down and for good".

Provýforsøk climbed out the squad flitter and gaining his feet, noticed Glissman for the first time,

"Say, what's the matter with the deputy"?

Starhoven went over to the fallen body and turned it over, after a few seconds of checking he said solemnly,

"He's dead! He was complaining of heartburn and I wouldn't let him stop, must have been having a coronary"!

"Poor guy, never got to see Muller in the same state before he copped a packet himself".

"We'll give him a hero's send off", Starhoven promised somewhat guiltily, "He was a workhorse was Himo, one of the best, yes if you could say one thing about Inahimo Glissman, it was that he certainly had ambition"!

TIMESTONE

ONE

TONE WIPED THE sand carefully from the bonnet of his Honda. He hated sand, it got everywhere. On the bonnet, on the roof, in the brakes, in the filters. It was a constant job to keep it out of the works of the flitter. He almost wished for the days when Mars had no atmosphere, when the flitters ran through enormous domes and spokes that connected domes, when all was under pseudo-plex. Then he looked up at the beautiful pink morning sky and changed his mind. An icy wind was blowing in from the east, it's gusts had teeth of steel, but he did not mind, it was just nice to be out of the flitter, for Ellis Tone was a flitter cab driver.

His main area was in and around Eos, just north of the equator, in the warm region, where the sandstorms were at their worst. Of course if the fare was willing to pay, he would flit to any area of the cold, dim world. His Honda had already done one hundred and seventy seven thousand kilometres, but the engine of the two hundred and fifty brake horse power of an Honda Slipstream was capable of much more. He stopped his polishing at an interesting item on the netcast, finally the tracking station on Callisto had received a signal from Explorer One, it was good news, the ship was free of hyper-space and was entering the system of Proxima. The next few days or weeks would be exciting times if further transmissions were to be received.

Tone glanced at his wrist-chrono, eight thirty hours, time to drive into Eos and see if he could pick up some fares. He'd had breakfast at his apartment so there was no need for a stop at any cafe's, he could pick up the morning traffic, the morning fares of those journeying to and from home and work. Putting the swiffen back in the hatched back of the Slipstream, he climbed into the driving seat and thumbed the ignition, as usual it caught first time and the purr of the flitter's impressive engine could be heard.

It headed into town. The lights were just going out, the red sky turning to a roseate pink, the tiny sun burning away the morning mist of the lichenfurs. Were it not for the accursed sand, Tone would have wound down his window to catch the inviting fragrance of the pine resin, but he had no intention of getting grit in the cab. Then he saw her!

The back of her to be precise. It was like the back of no other woman on the street. She was dressed in a long frock of burning crimson, her chestnut hair hanging down her back in coiled ringlets. Her legs were stockinged and she actually had shoes of black leather rather than the usual fur lined boots. She must be freezing out in the thin morning air of Mars. Her arm came out a thumb raised and he sighed to a halt precisely at her side with experienced ease. Reluctantly he slid the passenger side window down,

"Are you looking for a taxi madam"? he enquired.

She bent down toward the window to answer him and the red dress was low cut, her cleavage was magnificent, more than that though, nestling between her breasts was a green precious stone. Or at least he guessed it was precious, yet it was only suspended on a leather thong rather than a gold chain.

Regarding him with deep brown eyes she crooned,

"I might be, if you were to take your eyes off my tits for a second".

"Wear a dress like that and you're inviting inspection", he returned unkowed, "Anyway they're quality, what did they cost, five hundred"?

"They're natural if you must know", she said mildly placated, "Would you go as far as Hellepontus"?

"I'll go as far as you want if you have the fare, madam", he offered. Thinking at the same time, *'And as far as you want with your body, for free'!*

She slid into the taxi rather than climbed in, her movements were as lithe as a cat's.

"I want to decide the fare before we set off, no sense in having the meter on all that way, what do you want"?

She deliberately left her lips slightly parted at the end of the sentence, knowing exactly what she was doing. He resisted the urge to come up with an arrangement that did not involve money and quoted a figure instead. She agreed it at once and he took a band of leather and tied it around his head to keep his long hair from falling into his face. Long hair and beards were the fashion with the atmosphere of Mars being so thin.

The Slipstream began to move forward through the traffic and he observed,

"You're not exactly dressed for outside miss....".

"Femefaah", she supplied, "Pericomât Femefaah and my clothing is not actually any of your concern, nor my lack of luggage before you ask".

"Do you want me to call you Pericomât? Or miss Femefaah"? He wondered why the name sounded vaguely familiar, had he heard it before, on the net?

"You call me Miss and I call you Cabbie", she returned quite frostily.

"You don't even want to know my name"?

"Why should I"?

"Well, Hellepontus is a long way, who knows what might happen"? He hurried on, "What I mean to say is supposing there's a motoring accident and you cannot even tell the rescue services who I am"?

"Alright Cabbie, what's your name"?

"Ellis Tone, or Cabbie if you prefer".

"I prefer", she returned sardonically.

She was like all beautiful women, Tone decided, aloof and seemingly unapproachable. Initially that was, press their right buttons and they'd come across and how.

"I'm single, thirty two", he began "You"?

"I'm the fare", she retorted, "Just keep your eyes on the road and your mouth shut and we'll get along just fine".

"Alright lady, no need to be rude", he returned, "Silence is fine, some passengers just like to talk that's all, but if you don't, then no problem".

They sat in silence for a few kilometres and then she admitted,

"I was a bit brusque with you, I've things on my mind", and she suddenly took the stone from it's delightful resting place and massaged it between her finger and thumb. He risked a glance at it and it seemed to oscillate slightly and shimmer from verdant to azure, from turquoise to teal and flickers of energy seemed to come from it.

'Ridiculous', Tone thought, *'It's only a stone, bet it isn't even worth much'*?

In truth he could not have been more wrong, for the stone was beyond price.

"Your name sounded familiar", he risked then, "Have I heard it before"?

"I don't know, have you"?

"Well you know how it is on Mars, there are few generic surnames, everyone likes to be unique and I doubt there is more than one Pericomât Femefaah on this world right now"?

"Actually you're wrong there", she said and her smile was enigmatic, her eyes glinting with some mystery.

"What do you mean"?

She seemed on the verge of speech and then, it was as though she changed her mind. Instead she told him quite suddenly,

"I'm twenty seven and there is no one special at the moment".

"Oh", he was surprised into being short of a reply for a second, so he asked instead,

"Would you like the net on for a while"?

"How far are we from Pyrrhae Regio"? Was her response.

"Seventy, maybe eighty minutes".

"Alright then. Not the news though, If I hear anymore about Explorer One I'll just scream, put a music site on".

'Maybe I'd like to hear you scream'? Tone thought somewhat lasciviously, but instead he asked,

"Musical preference"

"Twentieth century seventies progressive music, the site is ULHK I believe? Do you want me to ping it for you while you're driving"?

"Are you kidding me"? Tone was bowled over by the choice, "It's only my favourite station, what are the odds, just click on the icon".

"You're into ancient electric music"? She actually seemed to begin to defrost at this revelation.

"Not just into it miss, I'm in a band that plays it, my bass guitar is in the back of the hatch. The band's called Râulatura, you might have heard of us, we're on the station sometimes".

She looked thoughtful,

"Râulatura; Râulatura, do you play a track called, 'The Kingdom of the Fool'"?

Tone gave a whoop of joy, "That's us, what did you think to it"?

"Well firstly I did not appreciate the whoop", she chastised him, "But the track, yes, I liked it, it reminded me of Galleon, do you know them"?

"Yes, I do and I like them, I have some of their sticks".

The net suddenly blared into life and she hurried to turn it down,

"This is Riverside", she said, "I love their stuff".

The rest of the journey to Pyrrhae Regio passed in the wink of an eye as the two of them exchanged musical information. As the flitter sighed past the first sign for the town she asked him,

"Can we stop at the first roadside cafe, I need to freshen up and could maybe eat something".

"Absolutely", Tone agreed, "I'm thinking along the same lines".

The first one they came to was Mother Guska, run by a Bosnian family. Tone was always happy to stop there, in case Lamija was on shift. She was the owner's youngest daughter and very lovely, with a face that would rival Pericomât Femefaah's.

He pulled the flitter up to a stop and rushed out of the taxi to open the passenger door. He need not have hurried, she had waited for him to do exactly that. Together the two of them set themselves against the sand and wind and strode as swiftly as possible inside the Mother Guska.

"Where would you like to sit"? he asked her.

"I don't care", she told him quietly, "Now, the ladies rest room".

Lowering his voice he told her where it was and chose his usual spot in the middle of the front row, against an enormous treble-glazed window. From this vantage point he could keep an eye on his flitter and see who was coming out of the kitchen. To his pleasure it was Lamija who came out to take his order, she offered him one of her albescent smiles, her hair bobbing in pigtails that day,

"Ellis, how are you doing this day", she asked him in accented standard, for she had grown up on Earth in Bosnia.

"My day just got better, thanks to your lovely smile Lamija", he began, "Now when are you going to let me take you out, I ask you often enough".

"And I have to tell you the same reply", she returned as part of the ritual, "My father he is strict and you must firstly ask him if you can take his daughter out. Now Ellis, what will you have today"?

"I'll try a lichensteak today my dear Lamija", Tone began, "With lichenspuds and lichenpeas and to drink I will have Earth tea and now you must wait a second, for today my fare is in the rest room".

As he finished telling the pretty girl this, Pericomât Femefaah glided out of the end of the cafe and approached them with her sensuous walk. Lamija's face fell and she was plainly kowtowed by the more mature woman's stunning beauty and figure.

"I've just ordered", Tone told her as she slid into the seat opposite him. He wondered how he was not going to spend the entire meal staring at her breasts.

"What will you have"?

"Two dodoprot eggs poached on lichentoast and a cup of caj please".

Lamija was suddenly delighted, for Femefaah had asked for Bosnian tea,

"With you as soon as you would hope", she smiled with the phrase that all the staff used on receiving an order.

Femefaah looked around, there were only two other couples in the place and both one man and one woman. Both of the men were looking at Femefaah, annoying the women they were with,

"I suppose that thing becomes tiresome after a while"? He asked her.

"Thing"?

"Drawing the unwanted attention of men all the time. Even in a time when everyone is augmented in their teens you are exceptional though Miss. Which is especially impressive as you are natural".

"You may call me Peri", she suddenly decided, "And I'm not natural one hundred percent".

"Oh, I thought when you said that your.....I presumed that......".

"They are and most of my figure, although I've had a buttock lift once. During teen-aug I had lips thinned, nose made smaller and eyes bigger. My tongue was lengthened too and before you make some lascivious comment, I had a lisp. What about you"?

"The usual; you know", he twitched, penis girth and length were nearly always increased, "Then hair thickened and made lighter and eyes increased in verdency".

"That's all"?

"Yes, why, what else did you think....."?

"If that's all then you were already handsome".

"Thank you that's the first compliment you've paid me".

"You're a reasonably good bass player too, but Râulatura need a better vocalist, he almost spoils 'The Kingdom of the Fool', were it not for the long musical break".

I'm beginning to fall for this woman and I know nothing will come of it' Tone thought to himself, 'There is something totally intriguing about her though, *I just can't put my finger on what it is'*

The food arrived, Lamija gave Tone a sort of hopeful signal smile, it seemed she would not mind if he really did ask her father if he could take her out. They wanted nothing else, when she asked, so she had retreated back to the kitchen.

After a few mouthfuls and the food was excellent, he asked her,

"So why are you gong to Hellepontus, business or pleasure"?

"To save my life", she replied simply and dramatically.

"Do you want to tell me about it"?

"Not really, you tell me about the band instead, how is the new drummer fitting in"?

It seemed she knew far more about Râulatura than she had initially indicated. He was happy to talk about it and the meal flew by. He paid the bill, she let him, he said goodbye to Lamija and they left after he had visited the gentlemen's rest room. Once again they were in the flitter and travelling through Pyrrhae Regio. The sky ahead looked sullen,

'Filled with frenging sand I bet', Tone thought, *'I hate frenging sand'!*

"Want to see if there's more news of Explorer One"? he asked her

"Put ULHK back on", she ordered. Pericomât Femefaah was used to getting exactly what she wanted. Tone guessed any boyfriends she might have had would only last while ever they did exactly what she desired, but the rewards?!

He tried not to think about her as she might look naked, spread out on a bed, waiting for him to join her, to pleasure her, but it was not an image he could dispel easily. To possess someone like Pericomât Femefaah was something most young men aspire too but never realised.

They passed through Pyrrhae Regio. Tone took the A57 north west to Vulcani Pelagus and as he did so Femefaah became slightly more animated,

"Do you know this area Peri"?

"I grew up around here".

So was she going home to visit family, but if she grew up around Vulcani Pelagus why continue on further west and north to Hellepontus? No point in quizing her, she only revealed that which she decided to share and when she wanted..

So he listened to the net, watched the sky for sandstorms and drove carefully because something told him this might well be the most important drive he had ever undertaken. He had almost slipped into what he called 'auto-drive' that state when one drives without consciously thinking about it when she suddenly cried,

"Slow down"!

He glanced at the speedometer, the flitter was only going at seventy two kilometres an hour, hardly disturbing the dust beneath the drive's curtain.

"I want to scrutinise this part of the journey", she explained, "It's very important to me".

Tone eased off the accelerator, dropped the Honda down to thirty two, they could almost get out and run as fast. The area was a dense plantation; row after row of lichenfurs, designed to extract carbon dioxide from the air and give off oxygen in it's place. In between the rows were the fertilisers and energy-store tanks, that produced nitrogen and other constituents and organic compounds. When all of these were mixed by computerised tanks, spilled out onto the surface of the planet, an atmosphere breathable to man was the result. The air was thin, due to Mars poor gravity, but it was breathable at warm periods in the Martian day. Few people were brave enough to go out at night without very thermal clothes and an oxygen tank.

"Stop the flitter"! Femefaah demanded suddenly and with total urgency.

It was not difficult for Tone at such a slow speed. Without warning Femefaah jumped out of the flitter at her side and took two hesitant steps forward and then seemed to freeze. Tone joined her swiftly and his eyes were drawn to the strange stone resting between her glorious bosom. It seemed to be pulsating; shimmering with a myriad shades between green and blue. Once again the woman took the stone between finger and thumb and began to massage it. Suddenly Tone was alarmed to feel the ground shift beneath his feet. The air before them acquired a type of blue haze and his guts told him of a feeling of swift motion. Yet the landscape assured him that they were not moving.

"What's happening Peri"? he demanded and felt that the woman would reply to his request for information. He had a right to an answer.

She turned to him with a half smile,

"We are moving", she told him and then went on hastily, "But not up, nor down, nor east nor west. In fact not in any direction, but in when".

"What do you mean", he was naturally confused, "What does moving in 'when' mean"?

"We're going back when into the past", she said, "To the same spot as this was, but now to the past spot".

"You're not making much sense", he remarked coldly, certain it was some bizarre trick that was being played upon him and then suddenly the haze vanished and the illogical feeling of movement stopped.

"Where are we"? Tone asked.

"Exactly where we were before", Fcmefaah responded, "But not when we were before. We have moved back-when and soon it will be for a good reason".

Before Tone could make any further enquiry or complaint, a small girl darted from out of the area where the pines and tanks were and began to dash across the road. A flitter appeared from up the road, travelling at pretty fast speed and the girl was running into it's path. Femefaah dashed forward, snatched the girl up and the two of them fell at the roadside as the flitter flashed past, tyres squealing as the driver was braking furiously. He stopped farther up the road a ways and climbed hurriedly out. As he passed Tone, he cried,

"Did I hit them, I braked as soon as I saw her, she came out of nowhere"?

"And so did you", Tone complained, joining him in his rush toward the fallen couple.

"You were going way too fast, what sort of speed do you think you were doing? The limit on here is a hundred and twelve and you were doing closer to one forty or so".

"Well it's a Beemer", the young man returned by way of an excuse, "They're made to go that speed".

As they reached the woman and girl, they were climbing to their feet, Tone could see that though covered in sand, they were otherwise unhurt.

"Take your Bavarian motor and get out of here before I make a note of the number", Femefaah virtually spat at the young man. He did not need telling twice. He left the three of them and fairly dashed back to his flitter.

Tone looked at the girl, her features were vaguely familiar. She resembled Femefaah in no small degree. Perhaps the nose was bigger, the lips slightly thicker, the eyes a little smaller, but the resemblance was unmistakable and then Tone thought he had it!

"Your daughter"?!

"Whoth thtith", the girl asked and as she did so, the jewel at her own chest, resting on it's cord of leather glowed and shimmered just like Femefaah's.

"The taxi driver", the woman told the girl, "You'll remember him, when you think about this later. Now go home to your parents and never, ever run out into the road like that again, I'll only be here once and now you're on your own".

"Alright then, bye lady, good bye mithter, thank you for bringing her here".

"Just a second"? Tone asked in wonderment, "What's your name little girl"?

"Pericomât", the girl said, "Pericomât Femefaah, but my friendth jutht call me Peri".

As Tone's world seemed to shatter into a myriad pieces of unreality, the little girl ran home to her parents. To Femefaah's parents.

TWO

"YOU KNOW NOW", was all the woman said, "You know that it was me, as I was, when a child".

"The stone helps you travel through time"?

She nodded. "At that age I could not fathom it's function. Indeed I only did so a couple of months ago. Then I started going over my life, my memories and I realised I had been back into my own time three times, twice to save myself and once to give myself the stone and complete the circle".

"But there were two stones"? Tone had no choice but to believe the evidence of his own eyes, accept that the stone could do exactly what the woman claimed it could.

"If you went back and gave yourself the stone, you would not have it now"?

"As an older woman than I am now, I was old and bent and seemingly over ninety years old, to the little girl you just saw me save".

"So you are going by your memory and by doing so you made certain you were here today, to save yourself from being run over".

Femefaah nodded. Waited for Tone to digest this information and then told him,

"And now we have a date with my teen self, in the town of Vulcani Pelagus".

"How can you be sure I'll help you, now I know what you're doing. I have friends in my own time, I don't want to end up in my salad years thank you very much"?

"I'll get you back once I've completed the next task", she promised, "And I know you'll help me, because I remember you being there in Vulcani Pelagus".

"This is not fair", Tone complained, "You remember me, while I know nothing about you. You should have told me all about this before we left Eos".

"And you would have believed me"?

"Good point".

"And I only remember you being there, very little else, as for what happens after the second visit, it's as new to me then as it will be to you".

"You've never visited the future, to see if Explorer One returns"?

"I told you, I've only just learned how to go into my own past, I have to complete the circles or I will simply spring out of existence".

"My head aches".

"No it doesn't you're just being difficult. I need you to help me and you do, but I want you to know I appreciate it". She flashed him a winning smile, he bathed in it for a few seconds before turning back to their flitter.

"Can we stay in this when, till we get to Vulcani Pelagus then"? He asked her.

"Why"? She wished to know as they climbed into the vehicle.

"Less traffic", he smiled. He gunned the engine and started back down the A57, before asking her,

"So how long do you think it would take you to learn how to go fore-when".

"I've not given the process much thought, but now I seem able to direct my thoughts into the device I doubt it would take me much longer than having the will to do it".

"You know that level of technology and on such a tiny scale is way beyond the abilities of humanity, so where did the stone come from"?

"Either from alien technology or from human technology in the far future I guess, who knows"?

"How did you get the stone".

"From an older version of myself, so the answer lies there if anywhere, or any-when".

"And you're not curious to find out"?

"One thing at a time, first I have to save myself from getting kidnapped in Vulcani Pelagus".

"That's why your name sounded familiar"! Tone suddenly remembered. "You were the only person years ago not to be kidnapped and murdered by the serial killer Zabójstwo Kradacós"!

Femefaah nodded and then Tone remembered something else,

"But you were not saved by an older woman, but by a mysterious stranger who after the rescue simply melted away and was never seen.......just a minute, oh no, I'm no hero Peri".

"You will be, you know you will, it happened and I'm taking you there and then".

Tone was not impressed by the way he had been manipulated,

"Now just one ruddy minute Peri, it's one thing to watch you save yourself from being run over, but Kradacós was a homicidal maniac and I'm not even armed".

From out of her handbag Femefaah pulled a slim needle pistol,

"It's loaded with level two needles so be careful", she said simply.

Tone thought about it. Then he glanced at her breasts and then her legs, he knew he would succeed, he 'had' succeeded, so he asked carefully,

"So say I do this for you, you learn to use the stone and see the future, will you be able to see how we work out"?

"Safely of course".

"No, I mean how '*we*' will work out, you know, if the two of us, end up well, together"?

She smiled, "A bass playing taxi driver and me, do you remember who I was, who I am"?

Tone tried to do so, he cast his mind back to the reports, wishing he'd paid more attention at the time, then it came to him;

"You're *that* Femefaah"! he gasped. "Daughter of Afceri Femefaah, the owner and M.D. of 'Take One of These and You'll Feel Better', one of the biggest pharmaceutical firms on Mars".

"The very same Ellis", she returned using his first name, he liked how it sounded on her tongue,

"It's not likely that father would approve of you, not very likely at all is it"?

"Well"! He hesitated, "Love sometimes wins out, despite various pitfalls and setbacks".

She laughed and he was entranced by the sound, but then she spoiled it by pointing out carefully,

"I don't love you Ellis and soon you'll have saved me and then we won't see one another ever again. So I suggest you resign yourself to that notion".

"What if I say I won't help unless you agree to marry me"?

She frowned, "Blackmail has never been a good platform for a happy relationship Ellis".

"What about a compromise then"?

"And just what do you have in mind now"?

"I'll risk my hide against Zabójstwo Kradacós on the condition that you come and see Râulatura and afterward have a drink with me"?

"I was going to do that anyway as a matter of fact, so deal", she laughed.

"Really"?

"Yes, I like the band, the music and you, well you're a bit like moss aren't you"?

He was nonplussed, "Moss"?

"Yes, you grow on one, given enough time".

They played some more music then pulled into Vulcani Pelagus at around twenty one hundred hours, she told him,

"We have several hours to kill, it happened at twenty four fifteen if you remember and the whole thing was over before twenty four thirty".

"What do you want to do then"? He was hoping she might suggest getting a room, but no such hope,

"It happens over from that restaurant there. Firstly I need to bring us forward in time and then we go into the more recent version of the place".

He waited while she rubbed the stone once again and they remained in the flitter. Although the brake was on he felt the same disorientation, the same seeming movement and then she suddenly declared,

"We should be in the right period now. Let's go get something to eat".

The appearance of Vulcani Pelagus had changed, there were more flitters, more people the buildings were taller and brighter. The restaurant had changed it's name, it was now the Pelican Umede, Tone followed the beautiful woman into the establishment, all the while enjoying the magnificent sight of her ass moving as she walked.

"It occurs to me that I should ask you the date"? he told her as they waited for a waiter of some sort, "But what would be the point, this isn't a final stop is it"?

"I'll return you to your own time-when", She promised and then fell silent as a young man approached and asked them what they would like. They ordered food and then waited once again for it to arrive.

"You do know how to aim a needle pistol"?

"I guess you point and pull the trigger", he was deliberately blaze' about it, "Obviously I hit Kradacós, because I 'did' hit him didn't I"?

"Your logic is inescapable", she smiled. "So tell me some more about the band, where you hope it will end up, what your personal ambitions are"?

It distracted him until the food arrived. Fortunately, for the Pelican Umede was not the most salubrious of establishments. It could do with, what the interior designers called, a 'face lift'. In certain areas the dull yellow walls were starting to peel, the skirting had been washed so often with disinfectant, that the colour was practically absent from the first three centimetres. Above, the ceiling was starting to turn a faint nicotine brown from all the med-cigs the customers had smoked in the place over the years. Even the pseudo-plas top of their table was cracked in a couple of places and the edges were starting to lift from the steel beneath.

Their time passed slowly, because they were waiting for it to. They had several extra cups of lichentea and that resulted in several trips to the bathrooms. Finally the lights flickered, indicating that the place was closing down, they had been it's only occupants for, the last half hour. They walked out into the biting apparently airless night and she shivered. Gallantly Tone removed his jacket and draped it around her elegant, creamy shoulders.

"Thank you", she said and slipped into the deep shadow of a building, "Hurry now, I hear myself arriving, are you ready"?

He could hear the soft click of high heels on the pseudo-stone pavement,

"As ready as I'll ever be", he whispered stepping into the light of the overhead L.E.D's that were the streets illumination.

A young woman, wrapped in a heavy coat, approached, a flitter appeared suddenly, as if from nowhere and screeched to a halt in the space between them.

Tone saw the bulky figure of Zabójstwo Kradacós struggle out as rapidly as his size allowed. Zabójstwo Kradacós, who Tone had seen so many images of on the net, Zabójstwo Kradacós who Tone knew was dead.

Zabójstwo Kradacós who Tone was about to kill and make him dead again.

The homicidal sadist rushed toward the coated younger Femefaah and she screamed, for she recognised the menace in his purpose and body language.

"Stop"! Tone heard himself cry and as he did so, Kradacós grabbed Femefaah who began to struggle and kick at him. He was immensely strong though and held her in a vice like grip. Ludicrously Tone had time to think, 'Steady with her they're too magnificent to bruise', before crying out again,

"Leave her alone", and he pulled the pistol.

"I want this one", Zabójstwo Kradacós growled and it was as though the voice was coming from an animal that was not used to talking.

Femefaah struggled out of her coat, but Kradacós threw it down and grabbed her again, her dress ripped and Tone was treat to the impressive sight of one of her breasts. It bobbed and jiggled as she struggled and despite the situation, Tone found himself being aroused by the sight.

"Last warning", he cried and remembered reading those had been the final words of the mysterious stranger that had never come forward, even when Afceri Femefaah, the owner and M.D. of 'Take One of These and You'll Feel Better', one of the biggest pharmaceutical firms on Mars, had offered him a substantial reward to do so. Of course he couldn't come forward, he had been up-when Tone realised then.

He fired and despite the fact that the two figures were still locked in a desperate struggle, the needle hit Kradacós in the upper arm. It's poison was admirably swift, Kradacós gasped for breath as Femefaah tore herself free. His lungs had been shut down of course and the action on his part was futile.

Stupidly he clutched at his throat and then the venom in the needle reached his heart; he was dead before he crashed to the pavement.

Femefaah rushed forward and she was suddenly in his arms and the embrace felt wonderful; all pneumatic and heady with perfume.

"Thank you", she sobbed over and over again. Finally, reluctantly he pulled her to arms length and with exaggerated care covered her naked breast saying from memory,

"He'll hurt no one else, now, you'd better go inside that restaurant before it closes down and fix your make up. You are very beautiful you know".

Through the streaked foundation and running mascara she asked him,

"You've to come with me, my father will want to........".

"I'm so sorry but I can't", his regret was sincere, "I've a vital appointment that I '*must*' keep. You're a brave girl, go and do what I say and the owner will ring the constabulary for you".

"But I need your email or some sort of contact, you don't know who I am, who I'm the daughter of"?

"I really have to go now, good luck".

He half pushed her toward the Pelican Umede,

"Hurry before they lock up".

She stumbled reluctantly away and he joined Femefaah in the shadows,

"Well done, come on, we have to get back to the flitter and into the future, so the constabulary doesn't find us".

"I could stay", he teased, "Get your gratitude and become your lover, perhaps even your contracted husband"?

"No you can't", she remarked, "Because you didn't, now come on"?

THREE

"WE'RE BACK IN our own time"? "Yes", she assured, "Back where you belong Ellis".

"So we need somewhere to spend the night"?

She shook her head and the beautiful chestnut ringlets cascaded across her milky shoulders,

"No, we drive through the night, through Noachis territory, we have to be at the outskirts of Hellespontus by dawn".

"Why? Another rendezvous"?

"Yes the last one, then I'll pay you your quote for the journey"?

"I'm not sure I can drive all night when I should be sleeping".

"Then I'll take my turn at the controls".

"Are you going to tell me the detail of this next meeting"? he almost demanded.

"I can't Ellis", her voice was suddenly softer, "For I don't know myself, all I have is this scrap of foil that I found in my apartment a few days ago".

"Take the wheel then while I read it"? he asked of her and she did.

Dear Pericomât,

This is your older self. You will know that it's possible, because by now you have just learned how to use the 'Temporastone', the green stone you wore about your neck as a child.

On the twenty fifth of this month you must take a series of actions that will make certain you continue to exist. I will detail the actions you take and you must follow them to the letter....

Tone went on to read the instructions that detailed what the woman had to do in order to secure her continued existence. The bulk of it concerned the actions of the last day he had spent in her company and knowing what it contained, he skipped to the part that was events yet to take place...

...You must get Tone to drive through the night, so that we can rendezvous on the outskirts of Hellespontus at zero six hundred twenty, on the twenty sixth. You will see a sign by the road made from pseudochrome. It will be a tall pole with a circle of tubing on the top, the sign will be but a kilometre out from the city. There I will meet you and your actions and mine will secure my existence until I am ninety seven. Fail me and I simply flicker out of existence and then your fate would by like the rest of humanity's, fickle and with no self control. I look forward to meeting you again (the first time was when I gave you the stone as a child) Pericomât. Good luck, but you won't need it!

Pericomât.

Tone looked up,

"All this just to seal two circles, it seems rather pointless, you could have used the stone for far greater things".

"I 'will' do once I've met the older me", she assured him, "I've only just learned how to use it, but now, once this little escapade is over, I can do so much more, till I become the person who wrote that message".

"You might need a side kick", he suggested with a smile, "You've learned already that the stone takes more than one person through time when you manipulate it"?

She grinned, "Who knows I might at that. My older self will tell me if I ask her, no doubt".

"You'd consider me"?

"Oh you meant yourself"? she teased him, "I was thinking of a female side kick".

He assumed a look of hurt and she admitted then,

"You're still growing on me like moss, Ellis. Let's wait and see what my older self has to tell me".

"And if she tells you nothing"?

"Then I'll make a decision at the time, but not before".

He turned the tables on her then,

"Your younger self was incredibly beautiful Peri".

She scowled but kept her eyes on the road, he wondered how many years had passed since the incident; in truth she looked slightly more mature, but was equally lovely.

They drove through the night taking turns to doze and then take the controls. The flitter's seats were not designed for prolonged rest however and when they pulled up outside the town limits of Hellespontus, both of them were tired and stiff limbed. Femefaah immediately dove into her purse and pulled out a small wad of shillin,

"Your agreed fare", she told him simply and to Tone it felt like a dismissal. He eyed the sign, the hoop above a pole that told them that this was the agreed spot, then realisation came to him and he observed,

"There was no mention that I would actually be here, just get you here, so my usefulness to you is over"?

"You can stay if you wish", she condescended, glancing at her wrist chrono, "In a few short minutes the question will be academic anyway.

Tone did something that would seal both their fates then; he decided to see the scene out, remain to take the girl into the town if she wished it.

Zero six hundred and twenty hours arrived and the stone at Femefaah's breast began to flicker and glow, even though she had done nothing to make it behave so, it could only mean one thing and promptly a very old woman appeared before them.

The ninety seven year old bend figure was clutching a needle gun in her gnarled hand and it was pointed at Ellis Tone!

"Get down"! a man's voice cried out the urgent warning, as Tone threw himself instinctively onto the sand, Tone heard a needle gun phut, as it was discharged and he glanced up in horror to see the needle had hit the present day Femefaah!

"No"! he cried, but it was too late, she glanced at Tone in abject horror and then fell to the dusty ground.

He twisted his head around just in time to see the old woman simply wink out of existence, stone and all. Of course, she could not have existed if her younger self was dead. Climbing to his feet Tone regarded the man with the raised needle gun, he strode toward him several steps and then halted in utter astonishment.

The last man he had ever expected to see, he who was guilty of the murder of Pericomât Femefaah. The man was Ellis Tone!

"Why did you kill her......Ellis, you my older self"?

The older version of Ellis Tone explained,

"The old woman had a needle gun aimed at you and was going to shoot. If I shot her, then her younger self would in turn have time to shoot me; or you. So I did the only thing I could. I shot the younger Pericomât Femefaah knowing her later self would then cease to exist. Be certain of one thing; it saved your life".

"Why was the older version of her going to kill me"?

"Can't you guess? She was old enough to know both your future and her past"!

"I'm lost", Tone admitted, "You'll have to explain why you feared for my life"?

"In 'my' past Pericomât Femefaah and I got married. From that moment on things went down hill, her father hated me and then the arguments began, she was torn you see, torn between her love for me and her devotion to her family and it caused so many rows the two us made a private hell for one another. Eventually we dissolved the marriage, but it took twelve years and as the woman you think of as young and beautiful - grew older, she became as bitter and twisted as her body. I knew she and her younger self had rendezvoused here on this date and I suspected what she planned. She planned to kill both of us with one shot, just as I killed both of her with a single needle".

"Why didn't you come back and warn me before we got married then"?

"Because the stone was only mine as a result of this rendezvous, it was also selective in what it let's me do, as you will discover when you take the stone from Pericomât Femefaah's neck. It takes a while to work out how to operate it, there are no controls and no instructions".

"I don't want the stone", present-Tone replied, "If I have to rob a dead woman's body for it".

In answer to that the future-Ellis held up the stone from around his own neck,

"But you take it, look, I have it still and it enabled me to save your life, the circle is complete you cannot break free of it".

"Where did it come from, who created it"?

Future-Tone grinned, "Don't you want to work anything out for yourself, go and get your stone, our stone".

Despite himself Tone went over to the dead form of the lovely woman who he would have fallen in love with, in another circle and gently took it from her. When he turned to tell his older self he hoped he was satisfied, it was to discover he was alone on the plain outside the town.

SITUATION CRITICAL

ONE

S AUL CHOSTAMURE WAS sitting in his office filled with the ennui of inactivity when his pad pinged. He was feeling so lethargic he almost regretted the intrusion and then shook his head to clear out the cobwebs. It was a message from the agency, finally he had an assignment. The boss didn't bother to summon him on this occasion and he could see the reason why as he read the mail. It simply told him he had a bodyguard job at the Daily Solis Planum. The news-net service that operated out of Chostamure's local area. He slipped the pad into it's cover and turning off the L.E.D.'s on his way to the door, strolled down to his flitter.

The Skoda's fine blue bodywork was once again covered with dust, damn the constant sandstorms of Mars. Still he was lucky, living on the Planum where storms were less frequent, he pitied the poor drongos who had chosen to make their homes in Schiaparelli, where the winds were constantly causing the rusty debris of the planet to cover everything almost daily. It took him twenty minutes to clean the flitter's filters, but it was a necessary precaution, no sense letting the dust start to get into the interior, or worse starting an overheat of the Skoda's micro-pile engine. After a quick flick around the vehicles skirt, he tossed the brush back in the hatchback and climbed inside.

The two hundred brake horse power roared into life the first time he threw the toggle. Skoda's might be a little slower than the Japanese flitter, a little less stylish and with fewer unnecessary frills, but their engines ran for ever and they broke down less than any other make on the red planet. As soon as the flitter was underway, Chostamure put Aupi at the controls [the auto pilot] and opened himself a can of Orang-U-Can. He knew it contained caffeine, he knew too that it was filled with sugar, seven point three grams per one hundred millilitres to be precise, but apart from it's taste, that was why he drank it. It had made Drorb Makers-Guild a very wealthy man, years ago when he had first created it and now the Makers-Guild family empire almost rivaled Corporation for power and wealth.

He turned on the flitter's net-speaker as he drank his beverage, a second message had been received from Explorer One and the news was absolutely fantastic. The vessel had not only survived hyper-space, but it had also achieved orbit around a main class planet that the team had called Nyjord. The news went on to pronounce that around the new world another smaller planet orbited too, rather like a living breathing moon. The team had decided to call that world Brahma.

Of course all this might have happened years ago in normal space time, there was no way to know how the data behaved when it too was shot through space at incredible speeds. So it was the year thirty two thirty seven on Mars, but on Nyjord the calendar was a total nonsense and how long would it be in the solar system before Explorer One returned, the crew roughly the same age as when they had left? It was all beyond Chostamure's powers of imagination to even comprehend what was possible and what was not.

The Skoda suddenly bleeped and he turned Aupi off, preferring to park outside the offices of Daily Solis Planum manually. He debated whether to take his small oxygen tank, but it was only a sort walk to the door and the lichenfurs were making the atmosphere more tolerable every day. Sliding out, he was in the building in less than twenty seconds and found himself in a magnificently impressive hallway of great height, topped by a domed plexi-glass roof. The floor was an unbroken surface of light grey marble and the walls, which soared upward, broken by two tall columns, were beige emulsioned plaster. The building must have cost an absolute fortune and it just went to prove there was shillin in news.

Chostamure walked over to the sole piece of furniture in the great space and his foot steps echoed almost without pause as they bounced around the vast unbroken surfaces. The desk was something of a disappointment, but wood was vastly expensive and so the curved and smooth black plexi-plas was no real surprise. Behind it was seated a pint sized blonde, her hair in ringlets, her eyes shadowed in pale blue, her lips a scarlet slash. In other words the sort of girl, of which, fantasies are made.

"Can I help you", she squeaked, her voice as diminutive as her form.

"In more ways than is decent actually, but that's not why I'm here at the moment", he quipped.

She simpered, not the sort of girl to be stuffy about the occasional flirt,

"What I meant was is your query general or do you have an appointment sir!?

"Sorry. Yes I'm expected, the name's Chostamure, the agency sent me".

The little blonde made some adjustments on her pad and then confirmed,

"Oh yes, I've found you", she told him, "You're here to see Wellington Booth, the editor".

"Wellington Booth"!, Chostamure echoed, "Do you have a lisp miss....."?

"Tangmouse", she finished for him, "Koreen Tangmouse".

'You couldn't make this up', Chostamure thought to himself. Then asked,

"And where do I find mister Booth's ah; booth, Koreen"?

Tangmouse giggled, not a particularly unpleasant sound, before answering,

Take the lift to the very top floor, that's the fourth, tallest building in Solis Planum you know, anyway mister Booth's office is clearly marked, along with the reporters, mister Hope, included".

Thanking her, Chostamure walked over to the lift and thumbed it, wondering who Hope was, while he waited. It would not be long before he was to find out. The lift sighed open and in he climbed and asked for the fourth floor, the highest in Solis Planum! It was a very swift ascent and he almost fell onto the requested floor seconds later. This time, beneath his feet were the sort of carpet tiles that were actually tougher than granite and equally unattractive. These were a sickly mustard colour, leaving him to wonder why carpet tiles never came in nice colours. Tramping up and down them were busy staff and he asked the first he encountered to direct him to the editor's office. It was at the end of the corridor, furthest from the toilets, closest to the kitchen, he could see the reasons for such a location.

The corridor itself had no windows but a solid strip of light came from the ceiling, artificially illuminated for the candescence was a pale blue, rather than a deep pink. Chostamure pushed his way through and tapped on the door marked *'W. Booth. ed'*. Inside was a grisly man, with enormous bushy eyebrows that gave his huge round face the look of an enraged owl. Beneath his boho shirt was a mighty gut that hung over his loons, perhaps his location nearest the kitchen was not to discourage staff usage except at regulated breaks after all?

"Are you Wellington Booth"? Chostamure asked. The simple enquiry seemed to illogically enrage the man.

"Now let's see", he began in an outside voice, not suited for interiors, "It says W. Booth on the door, I have a green editor's cap on my head and there's a picture of my wife on the frenging desk, so who in Hades could I be but he? Oh, and one crack about wellington boots, or the duke of Wellington and you go out the window".

In a chair opposite his desk another figure suddenly rose to his feet somewhat uncertainly and said in a slurred voice,

"If you're in one of your blackguard moods Wells, I'm going".

"Sit down, Hope, you useless Snufzhead and wait till your guard arrives".

"I'm not having a guard my dear editor so that is that ", Hope objected with an attempt at outraged dignity, one that his slurred speech spoiled completely.

"I'm sorry to interrupt your tete-a-tete", Chostamure finally managed to cut in, "But I'm Chostamure from the agency and if I don't get some sense soon, I'm gone".

"The agency"! Booth roared, "Why by Beelzebub didn't you say so in the first place man, come in come in. Drink"?

Hope suddenly fell back into the other chair leaving Chostamure with nothing to do but stand,

"I would love a cup of Earl Grey if you have it, editor"?

"What by Satan's burning arse, is Earl Grey"? Booth cried, "I meant a proper drink you dimwit, Vodka,

Rum, Snutz"?

"I'll have a snutz if you're offering", Hope said eagerly.

"You've enough of that stuff in your addled brain already you hopeless piss-head", Booth, rattled back. Well Chastamure, what'll it be"?

"A small vodka then please and it's Chostamure, editor".

As he poured the drink the burly and belligerent editor stormed,

"Annoying isn't it, to have your name crucified all the time? You know I almost changed by name to Sandal? I wouldn't have helped though would it? All the fault of my imbecilic father, Wellington indeed, I ask you"!

"What did you send for me regarding, editor", Chostamure persisted.

"To look after this useless cretin here", Booth finally seemed to be getting to the point. "Our esteemed 'Arts and Drama Critic' and total piss-head Derby Hope".

Chostamure resisted the urge to make a pun out of the art critic's name, instead he requested,

"Define look after, please"?

"Well for one, see he comes to no harm until after tonight's show and for another keep him away from Snufz and 1in2's. He needs a clear head if he's going to write a review in the morning".

"Tonight's show"? Chostamure asked.

"Over at the Solis Planum Theatre", Booth roared, taking a serious slug of his own drink, "Some eater of other people's leftovers has written some turgid drama about the human condition and managed to get Clorise Starburst to star in the frenging thing".

"Clorise Starburst from Earth"?

"You think there's more than one"?

Hope suddenly piped up, "*Treading Softly on My Id*, probably a right piece of night soil as well".

"Just in case you had not guessed; 'Treading Softly on My Id', is the name of the play", Booth explained, "The writer's a new boy, one Darcy Pontoprime".

"There's a frenging nom de plume if ever I heard one", Hope cursed.

"Now listen moron", Booth stormed, "Try and get that night soil out of your brain for one night so that you can write a nice positive review for once in your miserable career. That's where you come in Chostafume, take him somewhere, get him sobered up and showered and dressed in clean clothes. Here; here's fifteen shillin to do it okay"?

"I'm a bodyguard, not a nanny", Chostamure objected as he took the notes from the editor's pudgy hands.

"For thirty hours you're a nanny", came the reply, then came the clincher, "Do a good job and you get a bonus and a free advertisement on our site for your agency".

"I'll do my best then", Chostamure began "Or I'm not the nanny I think I am".

TWO

"I AM NOT taking another detoxify pill and that is final", Derby Hope promised and pursed his lips into a thin line.

"Do you want to force it into his mouth; or hold him down while I do it"? Chostamure asked. The question was ridiculous, Hope must weigh twice that of the trim and tiny Koreen Tangmouse.

"I still can't believe mister Booth let you enrol me for this task", the girl squeaked, "Do you know how many words I can type a minute"?

"I'm sure it's an impressive figure", the bodyguard observed sardonically, "As is yours Koreen, but right now you're on the pill, if you'll excuse the expression".

With that he punched Hope right in the solar plexus and while the critic was gasping like a fish out of water, the receptionist forced a detoxify pill into his mouth. Then his mouth was forced shut until he swallowed.

"He's swallowed", Tangmouse observed, forcing Chostamure to bite back a retort.

"Get him stripped off and into the shower", he said instead.

"Are you kidding me"? Tangmouse objected in almost hypersonic.

"I'm not stripping a man", Chostamure said, "Come on Koreen, don't tell me you've never undressed a guy before"?

He earned a glare for that and she wavered,

"I'd better get a really enthusiastic plaudit for this when you see my boss again"?

"It's in the bag", Chostamure promised, "Now get his clothes in the other one, over there".

The second pill did the trick, but nothing for Hope's personality. He sobered up in the foulest of moods. Chostamure looked around at the devastation the visit of the critic had created in his flat. Before he could feel any sort of dismay however, there was a tremendous banging at his airlock and the agency man wondered if they were being raided by the Mars Constabulary. A man of medium height and a shock of brunette hair, that waved about his head as though it might become detached from his scalp at any moment, gusted into the apartment, like some sort of malign whirlwind.

"Where is he"? he demanded in fury.

"Just a moment mister", Chostamure began, annoyed at the unauthorised intrusion, "Who the ruddy Hades are you and what makes you think you can come busting in here, like you own the frenging place"?

"I'll tell you who I am", the angry intruder began, as though he had a choice in the matter, "I'm the poor eater of other people's leftovers who writes plays for that blackguard to mercilessly crucify, that's who I am".

"So you're Pontoprime", Chostamure reasoned correctly, "Well I'm the owner of this apartment, dolt, if you don't watch your manners I'll throw you out on your ignorant ass".

"Hello Darcy", Hope grinned, "What weak diatribe have I got to look forward to this evening".

"You see, you see", the playwright squealed in a combination of outrage and justification. "He's decided to pan me and he hasn't even gotten to the performance yet".

"I believe that's a critic's right", Chostamure observed, "Unfair as it might seem".

In desperation Pontoprime glanced around the room and his scrutiny fell upon Tangmouse.

"Every drama I've ever written, he slashes at like some demented Visigoth", he said to her and then fell silent, before asking quietly,

"Are you an actress my dear"?

Tangmouse simpered, "Why no, I'm a receptionist".

"And which one of these reprobates is your boyfriend, please tell me it's not the talent less never-been Pontoprime".

Tangmouse blushed, "Neither, I'm just helping mister Chostamure get mister Hope to the opening night on time".

"So you're single then, unattached"?

"Just a minute Pontoprime", Chostamure cut in, "Before you're finished trying it on with my assistant, I'd like you to get out of here".

Pontoprime held his hands up palms forward,

"Alright, alright I'm going, once I've just said this. You give my newest work of dramatic art another slaying Hope and I'll kill you, so help me".

"Kill"? Chostamure echoed, "That's a pretty strong threat mister Pontoprime, one Solis Planum Constabulary would be interested in hearing about, would you like to rephrase"?

"I have no problem finding the right words; lackey", the playwright seethed as he also made for the door, "He should never have gotten the job, everyone knows he's a Snufzhead, now I'm going. Come back stage after the show my dear, I may have a part for you in my next production".

"A position for her more likely", Hope retorted, "On her back with........".

"That will be enough of that"! Chostamure cut him off.

Twenty minutes later the three of them were in Chostamure's Skoda, heading for the Solis Planum Theatre. The agency man-come-bodyguard heard Hope's tablet ping.

"Aren't you going to answer that mister Hope"? Tangmouse asked.

"It will just be another demand for payment from my landlord", the critic sighed resignedly.

"The Daily pays you enough sir". She sounded jealous of his salary.

"Not when you've got a Snufz habit to support", Chostamure quipped, "Now, we're here and on time, so just you behave yourself Hope".

"Have you a cigarette"? the critic asked hopefully

"Yes thanks, I prefer my own brand anyway", Chostamure returned sarcastically.

"I meant could I have one of yours", Hope persisted.

"Yes", Chostamure agreed, "I know you did. So you behave yourself until the end of the first act and I might let you have one during the interval".

They parked and strode into the theatre, surprisingly it was packed to capacity. Perhaps the throng had come to see for themselves, the next production Hope would mercilessly pan. Or maybe the crowd were mainly Clorise Starburst fans. Chostamure guided Hope to their seats, which were situated in row zero, good seats then.

Chostamure took zero fifteen, put Hope at his elbow and asked Tangmouse to take zero seventeen. An expectant hush filled the auditorium as the lights dimmed and the curtain went up. The scenery was of a meadow, the stage covered with artificial grass, behind which was a backdrop of trees and a blue sky, obviously the play was going to be on Earth then. Suddenly the audience burst into spontaneous applause as they recognised a statuesque blonde dressed in a frock of white decorated with yellow flowers. She was facing the male lead, she was Starburst and she was forced to wait to deliver her opening lines.

"Oh Algenoni, you cut out my heart with a spoon and dished it up to me on a plate and thought I would eat it because you had added relish", the beautiful blonde began.

'*Oh steaming wahoolis, Hope's going to have a field day*', Chostamure thought. The callow youth replied, his hand flying dramatically to his forehead,

"It's no good Bevermeria, no good I tell you, it died and is lost and nothing you say can re germinate it".

Chostamure heard a soft snoring at his left, he glanced at the critic and almost let him be, but that was not what he was there for, so he whispered to Tangmouse,

"Give him one in the ribs will you Koreen, it may be tripe, but he's got to endure it, if we do".

At the first intermission Hope complained,

"I need a stiff drink"!

"You can have an Orang-U-Can", Chostamure told him, "And sip it slowly because you're only getting one, you're not getting the chance to slip to the gentlemen's rest room during act two, so as to miss some of this".

The unlikely trio went to the lounge and just as Chostamure had brought the drinks a balding man of medium height and darting eyes suddenly approached.

"Hope"! he enthused, but it was obviously synthetic fervour, "How good to see you on opening night, are you enjoying my production"?

"This is the producer of that debacle we have just witnessed", the critic told his two minders, "Benifico Barsoom".

Chostamure suppressed a grin, didn't anyone in theatrics ever use their own name.

"Well, Hope, you didn't answer me"?

"I didn't want to upset you Barsoom".

"You're not enjoying, Treading Softly on My Id"?

"Terrible title, I would have preferred Rex or Rover, being as the play is a real dog", Hope retorted with professional relish.

"Now listen Derby", Barsoom began desperately, "I got your favourite actress to appear in this, at no little expense, I thought you liked Clorise Starburst".

"I used to", Hope agreed, "But not after this debacle. She needs to sack her agent for talking her into appearing in this mulexcra, the only way it could be improved would be if there was a nude scene, show the public her tits, that's what they'd like to see".

"It's not a titillation", Barsoom was outraged, "It's a study in human emotion".

"Well I'd sooner watch a human motion", the critic retorted coarsely.

"Now you listen to me Hope", Barsoom replied desperately, "I've put all my own funds into this production and if you ruin everything with your obtuse cruelty, I'll........I'll..."!

"What will you do"? Hope asked totally unmoved.

"I'll frenging kill you"!

"You need to get in the que then", Tangmouse observed, which made Chostamure laugh despite the potentially fraught situation. It seemed that everyone was lining up to take Hope's life, and the critic did not give a lichen.

As the three of them took their seats for the tortuous second act an incident occurred that brightened Chostamure's evening considerably. The lights had gone down when a sweet smelling brunette suddenly seated herself in the bodyguard's lap. Then she turned and her fragrant and delightfully soft breasts were pushing in his face as she whispered,

"Excuse me but you're sitting in my chair".

"Actually I'm not", Chostamure returned, "But you can stay there for a while if you wish my dear".

"Yes you are", the soft bundle protested, "I have my stub somewhere in my handbag, seat zero zero fifteen".

"This is zero fifteen", Chostamure whispered into her pink shell like ear. "Don't worry I'm sure we can get comfortable if we squeeze together".

"Zero fifteen; oh. I'm so dreadfully sorry, I'm at fault, please forgive me"?

"I do already, you're not going are you"?

Without an answer she was squirming away and left him to the torture of the second act. The second was as bad as the first, until the backdrop suddenly gave way as one of the characters went through a hardboard door and the resultant movement brought the whole thing down onto the actors. The crowd broke into hysterics and Chostamure leaned into the critic,

"See, it's picking up now. Or should I say falling down".

Hope made no response, his head was firmly on his chest.

Asleep again, Chostamure thought and nudged the critic. He slid sideways and forward and fell into Tangmouse lap.

"Hey no chance", the receptionist squeaked, "Get back up Derby".

Even in the dim light however, Chostamure could see the needle sticking in the back of Hope's neck,

"He can't hear you Koreen", he observed dryly, "He can't hear you because he's dead"!

THREE

CHOSTAMURE HAD GONE to the producer and ordered him to bring up the lights and cancel the rest of the show,

"What, what are you trying to do to me"? Barsoom had wailed, but when Chostamure had told him and that if he did not ping the Constabulary, he would, the producer had reluctantly followed his orders. No one had been allowed to leave the building until the Constables had arrived. Then after much arguing and time wasting, the public had been let out, but several individuals had been kept behind. The suspects!

These included the cast, Barsoom, Pontoprime and to his dismay Chostamure.

"Sergeant Litseinik", Chostamure began, "Why are miss Tangmouse and I still being kept here"?

"Because Tangmouse worked with Hope, Chostamure", Claudius Litseinik of Mars Constabulary told him,

"And where ever you happen to be people turn up dead".

"Now that's not fair you know the nature of my work sergeant. As for Miss Tangmouse, she's a receptionist at Daily, she had no dealings with Hope until today".

"Listen Chostamure, you do your job, let me let me do mine. You were supposed to be protecting the deceased, so you've either frenged up, or you're in someone's back pockets and I haven't yet found out which. You were sitting next to him and he gets a neuro-needle in the back of the neck, talk about opportunity. As far as motive goes, whazumas are the oldest motive in the book. Do you want to confess, it'll make you feel a whole lot better"?

"So you want to pin it on the closest person and go home to your fat wife do you"? Chostamure asked in anger. "What about the other suspects"?

"Okay loudmouth", Litseinik flared, "Which suspects"?

Chostamure turned to Barsoom,

"The producer for one, both miss Tangmouse and I heard him threaten Hope with murder".

In answer to Litseinik's glare Barsoom retorted,

"I've been in the bar all night, ask any of the bar staff. T'wasn't seated next to him when he was murdered"!

"Who else wise guy"? the sergeant of constabulary demanded of Chostamure.

"The writer, he threatened Hope whilst he was in my apartment, once again miss Tangmouse was a witness to the incident".

"I was backstage all the time and have not been out from there", Pontoprime told the sergeant smugly, "You can ask any of the cast, sergeant, of course all the cast can also alibi one another with the same reason".

Litseinik glared at Chostamure,

"That leads me back right to the place I started Chostamure, right back to you, or maybe the girl. But I think you the more likely of the two".

"Why would I want to kill Hope, sergeant"? Tangmouse asked quietly, "Or am I in someone's pay as well as Saul".

"You're easy", Litseinik smirked, "Jilted lover, or you were spurning unwanted attentions, or the deceased was".

"You need to get you mind out of the toilet Litseinik", Chostamure flared at that. "And no one is eliminated, anyone could have walked down the isle when the lights were down, sneaked up to Hope and........wait a minute, the brunette"!

"The girl who sat on your lap by accident", Tangmouse asked.

"Oh"! Chostamure noted, "You saw that, Koreen"?

"What are you two cooking up now", the sergeant demanded, "How come the alibi's you seem to have, depend on the other every time"?

"Because we've been together since this morning", the agency man told him.

"You have"! another suspicion gleamed in the constabulary sergeant's eye at that revelation,

"Of course, you're in it together, how about it Chostamure, are you banging the cutie"?

"More talk like that Litseinik and I'll bang you", came the heated response. While the girl merely flushed and the agency man had time to think,

'She likes me, file that away for future reference Saul old friend'.

"There was a brunette who fell into my lap", he told the constabulary sergeant. "She claimed her seat was zero zero fifteen. This happened just before we found Hope dead".

"How convenient", Litseinik was not sounding convinced so finally Chostamure said,

"This has gone far enough, I am being paid by Wellington Booth from Daily and so is miss Tangmouse, neither of us have any reason to kill a man who was earning us our pay, that's easy enough to check isn't it"?

"Go ping Booth and ask him to come down here", Litseinik told his constable and then turned back to the gathered group,

"No one can leave for the moment, you can get soft drinks from the bar and you can all ping if you wish, but the doors are covered by my officers so I suggest you remain in the theatre".

"I'm going to freshen up, Saul", Tangmouse told Chostamure and her make up was indeed streaked with tears,

"Okay, I'll go get us a drink each", he agreed and strode away from the sergeant with exaggerated locomotion. He was just walking back, having drunk his own drink and taking Koreen hers, when he was approached by a stunning blonde dressed in only a semi diaphanous dressing gown.

"Mister Chostamure", Clorise Starburst began, "May I have a private word with you? My dressing room perhaps".

"Of course", Chostamure crooned. He was a big fan and Starburst was a lovely as her on-net images. He followed her slowly admiring the movements of her buttocks in the shear gown, her body was as heavenly as her face.

"Come in and please sit down", she asked him, indicating a small sofa that the impressively large room coped with easily. "Can I get you a proper drink"?

"Thank you but no, if the sergeant smells it on my breath..."?

"I understand".

She then seated herself beside him and he could feel the heat from her divine body.

"I have something of a problem I think", she began, "And you might be able to help me mister....ah, I don't know your first name"?

"It's Saul".

"Well Saul, this is my problem".

She began, leaning into him and then it hit him in a flash! The pad in his Skoda!

"I sent Derby a ping earlier and I was wondering if you would know where his pad is"?

"One of those sort of ping's"?!

"Well, yes, you see mister Hope and I were *'friends'* and I am relying on your discretion and the possible retrieval of the pad? The thing is we had a rather senseless quarrel earlier about the play and he pinged me to tell me that if the play stank, he would certainly net as much. I'm afraid that infuriated me at the time and I pinged something I didn't really mean, you know how it is? Well now I would really like to get my hands on his pad and remove the last message I sent. Would you get me the pad, if you find it that is"?

"I'd have to read the ping first, I mean the constabulary are involved now".

"Please don't. I wrote it in the height of anger, and I can swear to you that the anger has passed now and the message is nonsense really".

"I'm sorry but I can't promise anything", Chostamure returned and was frostily and promptly shown out the door. The first person he ran into was Litseinik.

"How long did it take just to ping the editor of Daily"? the sergeant demanded, "And what's my chief suspect doing wandering around and coming out of actor's dressing rooms. Why don't you save the town the cost of a trial Chostamure and tell me why you and the blonde bimbo did it? Or were you working alone and the poor air head just happened to be in your company"?

"Hello hello", a familiar voice suddenly boomed.

"Booth"! Chostamure exclaimed, "Thank you for introducing me to a new experience, to wit, being happy to see you. Now will you tell this flat foot who I am"?

"I hired you to protect Hope and keep him off the......ah, and keep him focused on his job and you bungled it Chostamure, so I don't think of you as a competent body guard that's for sure".

"What better way to get close to the man you're going to kill, than to get hired as his bodyguard", Litseinik reasoned and he took hold of Chostamure's elbow, "Come on matey, we're going down to the station".

"Ah, before you take him sergeant", Booth suddenly interjected, "I'd like him to give me Hope's pad, he may have made some preparatory notes regarding tonight's performance".

"So you want the pad too", Chostamure said suddenly thoughtful, "That's one popular piece of kit, sergeant, he's not the first person to ask me for it this evening".

"Oh", Litseinik was a better constable than he seemed on the surface, "A pad and two people are keen to see it, where is it Chostamure and who was the other person who was interested in it"?

As the trio had been talking two women had approached. One was Starburst, the other Tangmouse, Chostamure said,

"The other person was her, sergeant and she's left some nasty threat on Hope's life on it. Get your constable to escort miss Tangmouse to my flitter and you can see for yourself, it's on the back seat Koreen".

"Damn you Chostamure", Starburst ranted and rushed forward to rake him with her finger nails. Litseinik released Chostamure's elbow with one hand and batted the actress away with the other.

"Now everyone settle down", he demanded, it froze the group for an instant. "CONSTABLE".

Litseinik was joined by his second in commend, he instructed him to do just as Chostamure had suggested and ordered everyone else to stay exactly where they were.

"I'm so disappointed in you Chostamure", Clorise Starburst told the erstwhile bodyguard.

"I'll second that", Booth added voluminously.

"Know what guys", Chostamure remarked, "I can live with it".

Tangmouse returned with the pad and gave it to Chostamure, despite the fact that several hands were outstretched to receive it. They waited with bated breath, while the former bodyguard accessed the messages and then he read aloud,

Dear Derby, Following our heated words of earlier I realise it is over between us. Your ego is bigger than our relationship, bigger than my career. I will not let you trample on it Derby, if you write your usual scathing review of my performance or even the production that I am now in, you will not live to regret it. The truth is I have met someone else, a man who is not liable to stand idly by while you ruin me, I have met......"!

"Give me that pad", Booth suddenly lunged toward Chostamure grabbing the pad and then turning on his heels sprinted away with admirable dexterity and velocity for one of his size. Litseinik dashed after him and the sergeant was in much better shape. It was only a matter of time before the editor was caught.

Booth raced across the otherwise empty stage and vaulted up the ladder at it's side behind the curtain and up onto the cat walk. Those underneath watched in fascination as Litseinik almost caught the Daily man, for a second they wrestled and then Booth let out an unholy scream and fell over the guard rail. No one that heard it would ever forget the bone crunching sound Booth's body made as it impacted the stage.

As the constabulary sergeant climbed back down to their level, Chostamure walked over to the heap that was now the dead editor and tugged the pad from his nerveless fingers.

He told the still puffing sergeant,

"As you suspect Litseinik the letter goes on to name Wellington Booth as miss Starburst's new lover".

"But how could he have murdered Hope"? the sergeant wanted to know, "He wasn't even in the building"?

Starburst had collapsed into a ruin of tears at that point. Chostamure pointed at her,

"She's been giving the performance of her life all evening sergeant, there's your murderer, Booth was only afraid of the scandal, he had motive, but no opportunity. Search her dressing room and I think you'll find a brunette wig and some pins to hold it in place".

"That's ridiculous", Starburst wailed, "I was on stage remember"?

"Not between acts and you weren't in every scene either", Chostamure contradicted. "You made a couple of mistakes that gave you away Clorise. One was that when you stumbled into my lap you had not thought to change your perfume, the very same fragrance I smelled when you cosyed up to me in your dressing room a while ago".

"You said two mistakes" Litseinik was missing nothing.

Chostamure smiled, "When she fell into my lap she treat me to a face full of bosom, then later she pressed against me in her dressing room, trying to coerce me into giving her the pad. I never forget the size and consistency of an impressive pair of tits".

"Constable", Litseinik barked, "Go and turn miss Starburst's room upside down, you're looking for a brunette wig".

"That won't be necessary sergeant", the beautiful blonde actress said suddenly and a needle gun had appeared in her tiny hand, "These are level two neuro needles so I wouldn't advise anyone getting in my way".

"The very same neuro-toxin that killed Hope I'm guessing", Chostamure noted.

"Don't be a fool woman", the sergeant warned, "You'll never get out of here, the Constabulary have a ring around the building and where would you go"?

"She's a good actress sergeant", Chostamure pointed out, "She can play many parts and wear many costumes, she just might succeed".

FOUR

"HAS THERE BEEN anything on the net today",? Tangmouse asked Chostamure. She threw her dusty coat on the back of the agency man's favourite chair and then was in his arms. After a lengthy embrace he told her,

"Nothing, the hunt is still going on".

They hesitated for a second, both remembering being locked in the actress' dressing room along with Litseinik. By the time they had managed to call for help and be found, Starburst was long gone.

"Booth's replacement was announced today", she wiggled her way to the kitchen, telling him who it was and he pretended to be interested, while she clattered around preparing their evening meal. She called back to him,

"They haven't picked a replacement for Hope though".

"Well it's a high risk job", Chostamure smiled. She came back to him,

"Dinner won't be for forty minutes, what do you fancy for desert"?

He raised an eyebrow to that,

"What do you think I want"? He asked her.

A CURE FOR CANCER

ONE

T
HE MOST SALUBRIOUS hotel on the entire planet of Mars was in Scorpii, the most splendid of rooms in that hotel was the Executive Suite and the suite itself could be found in the Grand Hotel. For each of those reasons, or combination there of, the suite was rented once per month for a very select gathering. It was the monthly meeting of the Elite Club, at least that was the appellation assumed by the five members who formed it. Each of the quintet was a hugely respected figure and expert in his chosen profession and field. For several months previously, once per Earth month, had all the five been able to find a single evening, that was clear in their busy calendars, the members had met.

The purpose of the club, if it could be said to possess one, was mutual respect and admiration from each, for the four other members. Sometimes the five met to exchange news, other times to express opinion, always it was primarily to enjoy one another's company, for each of them considered the other four their peers, in reputation, adeptitude and mien. Of late they had developed a curious habit too, the telling of a story. Whether it was fact or fiction, they did not care, entertainment was the chief goal.

Four of them had regaled the others with a narrative, on four consecutive meetings, only one had still to do so. The quintet also shared a love of quality things, particularly the gratification of the senses, especially one of taste. They all loved good rum, they all occasionally partook of the frowned upon drug known as Snufz and they all liked to smoke; whether it be tobacco, medically safe cigarettes, or less frequently tobacco and Snufz combined in a heady mixture known as 1in2.

The founding member and oldest of the group always arrived first. He had assumed the position of setting up the room for the arrival of the others. He brought the taste sensations they desired, though occasionally he let one of the others pay him for doing so, lest the expense become his alone. His name was Professor Bede Krol the celebrated scholar and geologist who originally came from Katowice Poland Earth.

Krol swiped the lock of the tall impressively wooden doors to the suite and let himself inside. At the centre of the dressing room of the suite, the staff of the Grand had placed their customary table and tall winged back chairs of real leather. Taken from Earth cows, no less. The chairs were all studded with buttons, very comfortable and only differed in one respect, each had been stained a different colour. This was deliberate, each of the Elite club had purchased their own chair and had it stained to their taste. Once their meeting was concluded, staff would ghost into the room and before cleaning it, place each chair lovingly into storage for another month.

The professor's own chair was a delicious deep oxblood of hue and as he passed it's back he flicked imaginary dust from it's tall back with his gentleman's kerchief. One of his simple pleasures, as he who arrived firstly, was the placing of the chairs, it was he who decided who should be seated with whom and opposite someone else. Sometimes he deliberated over this simple arrangement for close to fifteen minutes. After some thought he decided he would like to be opposite the surgeon that evening, for it was the latter's turn to entertain the others that night. With the fifth tale thus far. So the deep blue leather chair was placed opposite Krol's oxblood.

Between those two, to Krol's right, finally went the gold leather chair of Lord Aubrey Saint-John Willow of Yorkshire England. To the professor's left was then the brown leather chair of Grandios Vul Grande Soil Man of all Mars and finally next to him and on the surgeon's right, Chief Constable Heiter Starhoven of Mars Constabulary, would be in the black leather chair.

The five men, in their various professions and more importantly in their sphere's of influence practically ran the red planet. Only the business corporations of Earth and Mars had more financial and political clout. Krol placed five glasses on the table, one for each of them, to these he added two packs of med-cigs, two packs of cigarettes, a box of cigars, three bottles of rum, a box of Snufz and twenty 1in2's. He was just about to glance at his wrist-chrono when the door opened and in came Grandios Vul Grande.

"One time I'm going to get here ahead of you Bede and decide who sits where", Grande quipped in good humour.

"And when you do Grandios Vul, you will indeed have that dubious honour", Krol smiled back, "Have you seen any of the others in the lobby"?

"No", the immaculately turned out soil man replied, taking his position in his brown leather chair and breaking the cap of the first bottle of rum with a metallic crunch.

"How have you been this month past old friend"?

"Not too good actually", Krol admitted, "My arthritis has been particularly bad since the balmy weather started here in Scorpii".

"Balmy", the soil man chuckled "The mean temperature for the last few days has been sixteen degrees".

"Well my arthritis doesn't like sixteen degrees then", Krol atoned with a smirk, "And the Quintroxibiotin is not helping as much as it used to".

"Perhaps a word with our surgeon friend and a change of medication might prove fortuitous"?

"Good point, I suppose it's entirely feasible that I have developed a certain resistance to Quintroxibiotin. Anyway what of you Grandios Vul, have you been enjoying your customary rude health? I note you say nothing of retirement yet and you must be pushing ninety"?

"I'm eighty seven next birthday", the Grand Soil Man of all Mars admitted, "Were it not for my second heart and lung transplant I would feel old, but medical science continues to push back the years for mankind".

The door opened then and a rather dishevelled looking individual entered the room dressed in boho shirt and heavily creased linen drawstring pants. His long hair was held in place by a leather thong, dangling from which were several wooden beads. His beard could have done with a clip and he looked momentarily out of place when compared to the two earlier arrivals.

"Ah; Lord Aubrey, shall I pour you a rum", the dandy soil man greeted the peer of Yorkshire, England, Earth.

"Dashed kind", the English peer assented and seated himself somewhat heavily in his leather chair that was golden in colour. "My knee replacement is giving me a bit of jip at the moment wot".

"Do you take anything for that"? Krol was suddenly very interested.

"Only some little blue capsules", his Lordship responded as if that did not count.

"Blue you say", Krol wished to clarify. Lord Aubrey Saint-John Willow of Yorkshire England, looked perplexed by the request for additional data.

"Yes, yes, blue, would you rather they were a different colour my dear Bede? Have you some peculiar aversion to that particular wavelength of the spectrum, eh wot"?

Krol chuckled, "None at all, I was just wondering what the medicine was. Do you know the name of the drug my dear Aubrey"?

His lordship waved a dismissive hand before his face and then muttered, "The bally name of the drug, oh I don't know, I think it's got a zed in it though".

"Zeliomylythsin", Grandios Vul supplied, to the surprise of the other two both. When they regarded him with a curious stare he merely supplied,

"I read up on these things from time to time".

"Well perhaps before our friend the surgeon arrives, you can advise me on which to take then Grandios Vul? Krol wished to know, "Should I continue with the Quintroxibiotin, or ask the surgeon for a script for Zeliomylythsin".

"I think you should ask our surgeon friend for *'his'* advice, yourself", Grandios Vul said.

"Ask the surgeon for advice regarding what pray", a voice from the door wished to know and the fourth member of the Elite Club had arrived.

Without asking, Lord Aubrey poured the medical man a rum and thumbed a med-cig into life for him. The reason he did the latter was so he could take a pinch of Snufz and then light a cigar himself.

The surgeon seated himself and was consulted on the matter regarding Krol's arthritis, his reply was,

"Quintroxibiotin is the best available medication for arthritis Bede my dear fellow and it takes far more years than you have been taking it, for it to lose it's usefulness to the patient. On the other hand if you would rather try Zeliomylythsin, I can script you some, but I guarantee you would soon switch back".

Lord Aubrey had evidentially lost interest in the matter, for around his cigar he asked,

"I wonder what's keeping Heiter, it's five past and I've never known him to be longer than seven minutes late and that was when that damned bounder Muller was on the loose".

"Perhaps a case of similar weight and magnitude then"? Krol suggested, "The subject of a future narrative perhaps"?

"Speaking of which", Grandios Vul added, "Who's telling their tale this evening"?

"I have that honour", the surgeon replied. "But I think we can wait a while longer, Heiter would let us know, if he was not going to make it".

"If he's remembered that it's tonight", Lord Aubrey added darkly, "You know my theory about Heiter, his memory's going, time he retired".

The group fell into an uncharacteristic silence at this. They sipped their drinks and smoked their various choices for a few moments and then Krol decided to ping the desk, he read the reply that came almost at once and shaking his head confessed.

"No one's seen him in the lobby, we may have to begin a precedent and start without him".

"Or perhaps we could exchange news and views for a while, after all we're not totally dependent upon the story telling are we"? Grandios Vul offered.

"Absolutely not", Lord Aubrey enthused, "But even so if the fellow's not going to show, then it's bally bad form for him not to let us know, wot"?

"Any more news of Explorer One then, anyone"? Krol wished to know frowning at the English Lord.

"Apparently technical data and research material", Grandios Vul replied at once. "I would love to see some of their information on microbes and the like".

"You've not read the latest then"? Krol was keen to impart news, "They've found new life forms, huge dinosaur-type creatures apparently with three pairs of legs and get this.......more than one head"!

"Surely that would be a Siamese sort of creature"? Lord Aubrey entered the speculation, "It's unprecedented in Earth history. Isn't it"?

"Save for unnatural variations due to radiation", the surgeon told them, "The creature concerned must be some sort of cosmic mutation".

"Just think of it, your own mind having to share experiences with a second being sharing your body"? Grandios Vul mused.

"Well it won't be a reasoning being, an actual thinking creature, or it would be insane", Lord Aubrey predicted, "Wouldn't it"?

"We only have experience of the solar system to draw on", Krol returned, "How can you possibly know my dear Lord Aubrey"?

"Well I know one thing", the peer replied, "I'm ready to hear our medical friend's tale and I don't care that Heiter is not here. I'll give any man fifteen minutes, but then it's a matter of bad manners if you ask me".

No one was asking him, but it was also patently true that the peer had a point, therefore the surgeon finally agreed,

"Poor Heiter does appear to be delayed, I'll make a start and can always recap if he gets here soon. I find it strange that our earlier conversation was about ailments for it ties in nicely with the yarn I have to narrate to you this evening, I call my story, 'A Cure for Cancer".

"Aah a science fiction yarn then", Lord Aubrey noted with a smile of enjoyment yet savoured.

"Well it concerns science certainly", the surgeon conceded, "But as to whether it is fiction or not, that is for you, my dear friends, to decide".

TWO

I WAS WORKING with a female student of mine, a quite brilliant young woman who was bound to go on to greater things with the right tutelage. I see you look at me that way gentlemen but it wasn't like that, well; not to start of with at any rate, Milred Preenstone had earned her place at my side by sheer dedication to matters medical and exemplary academia. She had passed out of every course she had ever undertaken, first in her class, with honours.

She was short, standing only one hundred fifty five centimetres in her stocking feet and weighing a paltry forty five kilogramme's. She kept her hair unfashionably short, cut like some men and wore the dowerest of clothes I had ever seen a young person dress in. No, Milred was all about career and everything came second to that one goal in her life. When she joined me at Red General hospital in Scorpii I don't think she had ever enjoyed a single romance. Indeed she once told me, she would only consider marriage or even living with a young man, when she had firstly distinguished herself in her chosen field. Her field being diagnostics and the development of vaccine. She was thirty one when I began to take an interest in what she was doing, in addition that was, to being one of my house doctors.

I was in the Red General cafeteria one cold and blustery afternoon when she asked if she could join me at my table. This was unusual, my reputation usually afforded me the distinct advantage of being able to eat alone, but on this occasion there were no other vacant seats and anyway Milred was no shrinking violet when it came to rubbing shoulders with anyone eminent in their field.

"Do you mind if I sit here"? she asked me simply and was already pulling out a chair, before I could find any reason to object.

"Not at all doctor......."?

"Preenstone", she offered simply, not bothering with a first name.

I nodded politely and returned to my pad. I was reading a paper on the plague of twenty nine, I'm sure you will all remember it.

"Such a sad waste of life". She said and then apologised, "Oh, sorry I do think aloud at times, one of my bad habits, please don't let me interrupt your reading".

She had managed to read my pad upside down. I turned it to standby and asked her,

"It was sad in many ways, but mankind is already eleven billion in number, do you not think it is time nature thinned us out a bit............ah miss.........."?

"Preenstone", she was forced to repeat and this time I committed it to memory. She held out a hand and I took it, my own wrapping around it easily, she was so petite.

I offered her my first name only and this prompted her to say,

You can call me Preenstone, if you wish, sir, I don't insist on doctor, especially not from one as eminent as yourself".

"I would rather call you by your first name and you must never call me sir, again", I joked and she chuckled at that. She even had tiny teeth, but at least had thought to have them veneered, they were perfectly straight and brilliantly white.

"Very well", she agreed. That was the day our professional association and friendship began.

"And what might you be reading at the moment Milred"? I asked her and she told me in great animation.

"It's my dream to eradicate all disease and I plan to start with cancer".

"A tall order", I noted. "That particular malady has haunted mankind for centuries. Wouldn't you be better starting with the common cold perhaps".

"A virus would be tougher", she argued, "And anyway it's not fatal, merely an unpleasant inconvenience at times. Also I rather think the pharmaceutical companies would put obstacles in my way, cold remedies still enjoy fabulous revenues".

"How far have you gotten with your research then"? I found this tiny and brilliant creature totally intriguing I don't mind admitting.

I am unable to find the cause of cancer, why it suddenly starts to attack certain bodies while leaving others alone", she admitted to me, "So what I am working on instead is a super tonic for the body's immune system. As you know our immune system protects our body against illness and infection by generating responses to bacteria, viruses, fungi or parasites. It is nothing more than a collection of reactions and responses that the body makes to damaged cells or infection. We call it the immune response".

I nodded and was instantly interested, "Please go on"?

"Well normally in a healthy patient the immune system is important, but to the cancer patient it becomes even more vital, because, cancer can weaken the immune system and added to this initial attack, conventional cancer treatments may weaken the immune system still further. Ironic when it can help to fight the disease. Cancer can weaken the immune system by spreading into the bone marrow. The bone marrow makes blood cells that help to fight infection. Weakening of the immune system happens most often in leukaemia or lymphoma. But it can happen with other cancers too. The cancer in the bone marrow stops the bone marrow making so many blood cells. Chemotherapy, biological therapies and radiotherapy all attack the very system crucial to the body's defence by causing a drop in the number of white blood cells made in the bone marrow. High doses of steroids, which are another treatment can also weaken our immune system while we are taking them".

I found myself nodding more and more to this intense presentation.

Milred continued, "Because Some cells of the immune system can recognise cancer cells as abnormal and kill them, I am proposing to create a chemical stimulant aimed at it, to cause it to be strong enough to defeat even the most virulent forms of the disease. I am working on creating a 'muscular' innate immunity. Immune mechanisms that are always ready and prepared to defend the body from infection. Who knows it may be the cure for all infection, but I am currently targeting cancer. I am sure you are aware of most of this yourself doctor"?

"Some, but your presentation was impressively precise, so how much progress have you made"? I asked.

She looked saddened, "I'm at the commencement of my work, I need the help of a suitably expert mentor.

"So you have yet to find a way of building up neutrophil counts"?

She shook her head, but was impressed that I knew enough to ask the right type of question, I went on,

"In effect what you need, Milred, is a working vaccine containing a small amount of protein from the disease. It would not be harmful in itself, but would allow the immune system to recognise the disease and combat it once it met it again. The vaccine would have to use tiny amounts of cancer to create a live attenuated vaccine".

She agreed, pointing out, "And finding human volunteers to agree to such research would be very difficult indeed, we would have to start on mice say".

I chuckled, she presumed I was going to be the mentor she required, but even so I found myself pointing out to her,

"We will need a high concentration of B cells and T cells, those white blood cells involved in the acquired immune response, lymphocytes. The lymphocytes made in the bone marrow, like the other blood cells".

"Antibodies with two ends", she agreed "One end to stick to proteins on the outside of white blood cells. The other to stick to the germ or damaged cell and help kill it".

I agreed, "The constant end and the variable end. So your cure will be concentrating on ultimate immunotherapy. What have you started with Milred, the usual substances"?

She nodded, "Interferon, Interleukin 2 and monoclonal antibodies, primitive as they are, we haven't moved forward on this in centuries. I've already dispensed with Rituximab (Mabthera) that recognises CD20 protein on the outside of some lymphoma cells. Bevacizumab (Avastin) targets growth factors that help blood vessels grow and Trastuzumab".

"You actually want to start from the ground up, with something totally new"?

She nodded, "Will you work with me on it"?

"It would be a tremendous amount of work", I pointed out,

"I'm impressed by your research and enthusiasm, but I have my other duties here at Red General, part-time will be my input, at best, will you settle for that Milred"?

She nodded, a delightful smile playing across her features, "Indeed I will", she agreed.

THREE

I WAS AT home in my own place when the door chime sounded, it was twenty hundred hours and I was not expecting anyone, no one had pinged to tell me they were coming. I went over to the door therefore in some curiosity and looked at the monitor. It was Milred and she looked upset, her features draw into a knot, her eyes red around the rims. Opening the door I saw she had been crying, her lovely eyes that were usually so filled with the fire of research were puffy and inflamed.

"Darren's dead", she sobbed and then I found her in my arms sobbing on my shoulder.

We had given Darren cancer and then regular doses of our own preparation 'Antoxultiplus'. Obviously it had not reaped the correct reward, eighteen months of research and work, a failure.

Our first of several.

Milred and I became lovers.

Six months later Darren II died and we recognised our second failure.

A year after our first, we had our third failure with the death of George and had to scrap Antoxultiplus III.

About this time I had another visitor to my home. The monitor showed me a short man with brown hair and a goatee beard. Puzzled I opened the door.

"May I come in", he began, "I'm from D.I.I.T.."

I opened the door wider to allow him entrance, "I'm sorry but the acronym means nothing to me", I admitted.

"The drug intervention and investigation team", he clarified, "I'm investigator Pruchoo".

I examined his identity card, "What does your team want with me"? I asked, offering him nothing by way of hospitality.

"We understand you are conducting research on a vaccine", Pruchoo began, "I'd like to discuss the nature of that work, doctor".

I was not a doctor, but a mister, but I let the distinction pass, I did not like the sound of D.I.I.T.., nor did I like the look of one of it's investigators.

"I have not requested funds for any of the research", I told him, "It's thus a private enterprise, have I broken some sort of law mister Pruchoo"?

"There are sometimes higher authorities than law, doctor", the little man responded darkly, "As I'm sure your good friend Heiter Starhoven will tell you, if you ask him".

"I'm not sure I like the sound of that", I returned coldly, "And I'm certain I don't like your tone investigator, nor your prying into my private life".

"Then I suggest you grow up, doctor", Pruchoo snapped, "This is Mars and there are certain things you must recognise, whether you like the sound of it, or whether you don't".

"I'd like you to leave investigator", I returned then, "And I would be most gratified if you would not visit me at my home, ever again".

Pruchoo turned on his platform heels and as he departed, urged me in a menacing fashion,

"Cease the research, doctor. Or you will see me again and the venue will not be of your choosing, but mine".

When I told Milred later of the curious and in some ways ominous visit, she responded pretty much as I had done, with anger and a determination to continue with our project.

We flung ourselves into it with even greater vigour and determination. Six months later Antoxultiplus IV was ready and we firstly gave Darren III cancer and then administered the immunity enhancer, after two months we gave Darren III a thorough medical and his cancer was gone, we had found a cure; or at the very least a cure for mice.

The next step was obvious, a step up in the animal hierarchy. George II was a frog, Antoxultiplus IV worked on him. Darren IV was a dolphin, Antoxultiplus IV worked on him and then our greatest success was in curing George III, he was a male chimpanzee.

"It's obvious what we should do now", Milred Preenstone told me one evening, as we lay lazily together on a double cot, both of us quite naked, "We need a terminally ill human who has the very worst of prognosis and ask them to volunteer to try Antoxultiplus IV".

"Convincing a dying man that he has one last chance won't be difficult", I replied.

"Or woman", she countered, "The subject could just as easily be female, one for whom, Trastuzumab has proved ineffective".

"I'll leave the choice of subject to you", I told her, "We can be ready as soon as they are".

Milred found a subject, a tall graceful woman in her mid seventies, Antoxultiplus IV could give her another thirty years especially with successful organ transplantation.

"This is Selini Dyrotomes, Milred said by way of introduction, her life expectancy is one day to one month as given her by doctor Knelph at Blue General".

"I know Knelph", I said, as I shook her hand, "A good man, a fine oncologist, please be seated miss Dyrotomes".

We ran through all the usual questions and then submitted Dyrotomes to an armada of tests, Knelph was on the button, the poor woman was riddled with metastases. The cancer had invaded just about every major organ in her body.

"Before we proceed", I said to her when the vaccine was ready, "I need to tell you that without Antoxultiplus IV, then Knelph gave you a pretty accurate estimation of the time you have left".

"But I feel no pain", she responded.

"That's because of the morphosnufz that is coursing through your system", I explained, "In it's purified state when Snufz is filtrated and synthesised with morphine, it becomes the most effective pain killer mankind has ever seen. Were I to take you off it, the result would not be pleasant. Now you must be certain that you are receiving the very best advice, so take a couple of days to digest what you have been told today and we will see you on Thursday".

"To Tartarus with that", Dyrotomes made us laugh, "Bang it in doctor, I want to be cured"!

So I took a syringe, the first of three and ah...banged it in.

Within two weeks Dyrotomes was free of any cancer and was as fit and spritely a woman as any I had seen, of her years.

Together Milred Preenstone and I had created a cure for cancer.

FOUR

I WAS PREPARING the paper that would officially announce our development to all Mars when investigator Pruchoo of D.I.I.T.. arrived in my office without announcement. This time the little weasel was not alone, flanking him on both sides were two huge individuals, guards of some sort, no doubt.

"Get out of here the three of you", I commanded firmly, but in truth I felt no deep conviction, I knew they would not simply do as I demanded.

"May I introduce my two associates", Pruchoo whined, "Mister Slyne on my right and on my left mister Glolibe. They are interrogators, doctor and they are here to take you to the ...ah, facility".

"I'm going no where with any of you, please leave this office before I call security".

In response to that the 'heavy' who Pruchoo had called Slyne made his way around my desk with a velocity I would not have suspected in one so large. He produced a spray from his coat and promptly sprayed it into my face.

"What the.......", I believe I managed, before falling face first onto my desk, totally unconscious.

I awoke in a plain concrete room of approximately eight cubic metres. I was in the centre, securely fastened to a metal framed chair, by plastic tie-wraps. In one corner of the ceiling was a globe protected camera. I must have been watched, for only seconds after I had regained my senses the steel door behind me opened and in walked Pruchoo and Slyne.

I immediately noticed that the bodyguard had a hypo-spray in his pudgy fist.

"You're awake", began Pruchoo in a matter-of-fact fashion, "Good, we can begin. I understand, doctor that you have created, along with your little assistant, a serum that will herald the doom of mankind"?

I shook my head and replied in a more defiant tone than I felt, "No. I and my assistant have created a cure for the deadly disease you call cancer".

"Same thing, doctor", the D.I.I.T.. man began, "Let me illuminate you. The current population on Earth is twelve billion. Add to that the fifty million on the moon, the thirty million on Mars and the five hundred thousand on Callisto. Consider then that one third of them already do not have enough to eat, forget other necessities for the moment. What you are proposing is the end of the continued reduction of that figure, the continued growth into old age. Imagine if you will what that will mean in ten years, twenty, a century. All those very old and non producing billions depending on the young. What do you think the result of that will be"?

"You seem to have all the answers", I noted, "So tell me".

"It will mean war, doctor. Destruction of property and other vital resources, as those who '*have*' fight those who '*haven't*'. It could mean the end of mankind on Earth certainly, possibly the other planets too. For almost every power now possesses nuclear arms. The war could spray poison into the areas of habitation, fallout that would last for ten thousand years and all because enough people aren't dyeing. Dyeing of cancer".

"I presume you're going to tell me the solution to this problem that has not happened yet, is to cease my research"?

"Don't take me for a fool, doctor. You have completed said and have a cure. You have also hidden the formula. We searched your office most thoroughly, it was not there. We need to know where you have secreted it and if doctor Preenstone has a second copy. We then need an assurance from you, once it is destroyed, that you will never seek to reproduce your research"?

"I'm sorry, agent, but I can't help you".

"Perhaps Preenstone will be more co-operative"

"You harm a hair on her head and I'll kill you, Pruchoo. If you don't believe anything else I've told you, believe that"!

"The formula, doctor", the agent of D.I.I.T.. was unmoved, "Where is it"?

"Rot in Hades"!

Pruchoo nodded to Slyne, who approached, as the agent explained,

"Mister Slyne here has something to help you co-operate with us, doctor. Have you heard of Agotox Three"?

It sounded ominous, but I was ignorant of neither it's effects nor composition, I tacitly shook my head, not trusting myself to say a word at that point.

"Well", Pruchoo began and I could see he was beginning to enjoy himself, "It works on the central nervous system. It's actually a stimulant, it heightens the body's sensitivity to stimuli, in this case, the area you are to consider is one of pain. Now, one last chance, tell me all you know of the formula and if more than one copy exists"?

I remained mute and Slyne gave me the injection in my upper arm.

"It's very fast", Pruchoo informed me, "Almost instantaneous, let us see".

He signalled to the camera and the door opened almost at once, to allow Glolibe entry, pushing ahead of him a trolley, containing various metal instruments, the uses of which I could only too well guess.

"I am a respected physician here on Mars and you cannot expect to mistreat me and get away with it, Pruchoo", I tried then. "Release me now and we'll say no more about it"?

In answer the diminutive agent of D.I.I.T.. offered me a mirthless smile and with exaggerated movement picked up a scalpel from the tray.

"Last chance doctor. or would you rather I directed my request to your lover, doctor Preenstone"?

"She knows far less than me and has no copies of our work", I assured him vainly, "Leave her alone"?

"I may have to bother her if you do not help us", the agent grinned. Then he approached and from my shrinking figure, strapped as I was in the chair, he carefully cut the back of my left hand.

Molten fire coursed up my arm and into my shoulder. I think it was the worst pain I have ever experienced in my life. I grit my teeth and shook my head, but at the back of my mind I knew it was only a matter of time before my resolve would crumble and I would tell them where the cure for cancer was.

Two more tiny incisions and I was screaming myself hoarse in absolute agony. After the third one I blacked out. I was brought around almost at once however, by Slyne, who threw a mug of cold water into my face.

"Shall we continue, doctor, or do you now want to tell me what I want to know"? Pruchoo asked calmly.

My obdurate nature would only have resulted in more agony and the same inescapable conclusion. So I told him where to find the formula and agreed not to repeat the work, then I demanded,

"You have what you want, release me and miss Preenstone at once; do you hear me"?

"Once we actually '*do*' have everything, you will be released, doctor, soon, very soon".

"And doctor Preenstone"?

"One thing at a time doctor, one thing at a time".

"Remember what I've told you, if you've hurt her or harmed her in any way, I will hunt you down and I will kill you".

"Really, doctor"! Pruchoo grinned, "What about the Hippocratic oath"?

Two hours later Slyne entered the room and offered me water, I drank gratefully from a plastic bottle,

"What's happening"? I asked hopefully, not expecting much of an answer.

"He and Glolibe have gone to take the files from your mainframe at Hewlett-Dell-L.G.". He told me.

"And doctor Preenstone, is she alright"?

Slyne rose to leave,

"Tell me"? I cried. When I got no answer, I screamed out the demand,

"TELL ME"! I still got no answer, other than the metal door slamming shut behind him.

The next time he entered, he sprayed the knock out solution into my face and once more I dropped into the inky pit of unconsciousness.

When I came too I was in my office. It was almost as if the entire incident had not happened. With two terrible exceptions! One was the absence of all my research on my pad, my cloud and my link up to the central database. It had all been password protected of course, a password I had given Pruchoo once the pain had become unbearable.

The second exception was even more of a horror. I pinged Milred; no answer. I drove to her apartment, even though she had rarely used it once we were together, she was not there. Then I tried to ping her mother, no answer. In the following days I tried to contact any members of her family that I knew about, like Milred they had simply disappeared. She and her entire family were gone, obviously a message to me, I too could be made a non person, by the D.I.I.T.. at the whim of the evil agent Pruchoo.

I had made him a promise however!

I had promised him that if he harmed Milred I would kill him and I like to keep my promises.

So I contacted an agency. Got myself in touch with one Fongelturn Dobra, who, as it turned out incidentally was a Marunt. Curiously despite his dwarfism, he came very highly recommended.

"I need you to find someone for me", I told him. I had given up on Milred, I knew she had been permanently removed, "His name is Pruchoo, he works for D.I.I.T.".

"I know of the agency", Dobra admitted, "And my advice is to keep well away from them sir, they are bad news".

"It's too late for that advice", I returned, "Do you want the job or not, I'll give you three hundred"?

At that figure all the Marunt's reservations evaporated and he left me with an assurance of ultimate success. I knew I could not bring Milred back, but I could have revenge and that would make me feel a whole lot better.

I made no effort to duplicate the research she and I had done together, my heart was no longer in it and I knew that D.I.I.T.. would have plenty more employee's, so development seemed moot. The only thing I wanted, while I waited for Dobra to return to me, was to know he who was responsible for Milred's demise would pay with his own miserable life.

The day came gentlemen, when I learned where on Mars, Pruchoo had an apartment. I waited patiently, there would be one superb opportunity. One night, when he stayed in the place and alone. I dressed all in black, parked well away from his abode and strode toward it on foot. There was a rear airlock and I bypassed the code with the help of a chip given me by one of the tech boys at the hospital.

Pruchoo was on a couch, watching a baseball game when I calmly entered his living room, having moved almost silently through the apartment in a pair of Hitachi Air-Tread's.

"Hello investigator", I said, from over to his right, near the doorway. He vaulted to his feet, his hands darting to a low table, upon which, was a laser pistol. I caught him with the anaesthetic spray just before his eager hand grasped it's butt. He fell insensible to the decked flooring.

It was the work of seconds to lift him and take him into his kitchen where I tie-wrapped him to a chair and waited for the effects of the spray to wear off. As he came too, I was most gratified to see fear register on his once proud and cruel features.

"How did you find me. How did you find this place", he squealed.

"It's I who will be asking the questions today investigator", I told him with ill disguised relish. "Tell me directly to avoid any pain, what happened to doctor Preenstone"?

"I didn't do it", he began somewhat desperately, "You must understand I have superiors, I just follow orders and do my job, distasteful as the duties might sometimes be".

"You remind me of certain accused from history", I returned, "Have you ever seen the old films of the Nuremberg trials"?

He paled, "You're comparing me to the Nazi's who created the holocaust, I am not an evil man, doctor".

"You tortured me and enjoyed it", I observed, "Under the guise of simply following instructions. Now, don't make me ask you again, where is doctor Preenstone"?

"She's gone", he admitted, "It wasn't me who conducted that assignment".

"Assignment"! I cried into his frightened face, "You call murder an assignment".

"Look, doctor, you have to try and see the bigger picture here, the eradication of cancer would threaten every human being currently alive. You know that, don't you"?

"So gone, means murdered, killed; is that correct"?

"I have money, powerful friends in high places, we can work something out, doctor. Release me and let's discuss our options"?

Then I really began to frighten him when I informed him, "You are out of options Pruchoo. Remember what I told you if anything happened to her, well, I'm a man of my word".

"You have spent your life saving others, doctor. You have taken a binding oath, you are not going to risk everything over me, are you? If you're found out it would ruin a glittering career, ruin the rest of your life. Be sensible, you've frightened me, I'm sorry about your girlfriend, but now it's time to see sense".

I looked out of the airtight window, "You know Pruchoo, one of the things about airtight apartment's is that they're sound proof too. No one will hear you scream"!

He began screaming five minutes later, then mumbling and begging and finally whimpering like a wounded animal. It took him three hours to die! I left the way I had come, no one saw me.

FIVE

"THAT IS THE macabre tale for this month my friends", the surgeon ended, "And now you must excuse me, I have an early surgery in the morning".

He left them stunned to total silence and only when he was gone did anyone speak.

"That horror story has to be fabricated, doesn't it"? Grandios Vul asked his two friends.

"Of course it was, that's why Heiter did not show, he knew we would question him as to the validity of such an organisation as D.I.I.T.". Lord Aubrey reasoned, "Not only that, but if he believed the tale, he would be forced to arrest our surgeon friend for murder".

"What do you think professor"? Grandios Vul asked Krol.

"I think we have time for one more smoke and one more glass and then our meeting for this month is concluded", the professor responded mysteriously.

"If it is true", Lord Aubrey persisted, "Then we should feel sympathy for our friend. To lose something and someone in such a fashion is tragic indeed".

"You know something", Grandios Vul pointed out then. "I don't know our medical friend's name"!

As it turned out, neither did his two comrades.

FELIS CATUS QUAERERE

ONE

THERE WAS A constant moaning wind and the red dust crackled against the flitter's windscreen as Tone, seated in the driving seat, smoked a contemplative med-cig. It had been a slow morning and the afternoon was not threatening to be any better. It was not a holiday, but the sandstorm was keeping all but the most determined indoors. Three times that morning Ellis Tone had been forced to brave it himself. To clean the windows of his taxi and brush the filters that stopped the engine being clogged.

It was not that he needed to work any more and the taxiing was now merely an amusing hobby. For since he had acquired the time stone, he was a wealthy man. It had been easy, once he had leaned how to focus his mind and operate it. All he had to do was go forward twenty four hours and learn the result of the latest Dodoprot race and then, returning to his own time, place a sizable bet on the winner, no matter what it's odds.

Of course such incredible luck was soon picked up by the bookies and he was forced to go farther afield to place his bets. He now had a palatial country home in Maraldi, where the air was almost always frigid, but he often used hotels and roamed all Mars to do his occasional taxi runs.

So when his stone suddenly began to shimmer and he felt the curious bluing of his surroundings, he was intrigued and drawn straight way from his ennui. He knew what it meant, someone else from either up or down the time stream was coming to join him. The first time it had happened in fact since his older self had saved his life.

A bald figure suddenly popped into the ether in the passenger seat of his vehicle. He was dressed in a gaudy turquoise jumpsuit that was body hugging and he appeared to be carrying no weapon. Tone had a needle gun near his right hand but did not go for it, for the chrononaut put his hands up in a gesture of surrender and said,

"Noli timere ego habeo propositum domi noces".

"Is that Italian"? Tone asked, "Because if it is I cannot speak it, can you speak standard"?

"Videtur enim male got nefas esset mihi in investigationis quadrigis", the chrononaut muttered to himself, "Nunc mihi unum quaeso uti translatione ego fabrica".

From his belt he unclipped a slim flat object that looked similar to a compact and spoke into it, after barely a second his voice came through a tiny speaker on it's side,

"Understand me know do you"?

"Yes, that's standard, what were you speaking before"""? Ellis asked.

Since owning the time stone himself it seemed quite normal for this stranger to appear before him and he did not question it.

Once again the chrononaut spoke into the compact device in what sounded like Italian to Tone, and the words came out the speaker,

"Apology. Research assured operator of this time spoken Latin. Device can supply your language".

"Standard", Tone told him, "I speak standard, I've never heard of Lotin"

"Ancient Earth language it. Research thought spoken until sixtieth century".

"The sixtieth century"! Tone gasped, "Just when are you from and who are you"?

"Name be Seven G Nine Seven Two", he in the turquoise jumpsuit informed Tone, "Seven G Nine Seven Two from year seven thousand two hundred and fifty nine".

"The seventy third century"! Tone gasped, it was a date that carried a number only, it was totally beyond his imagination.

He noticed then, for the first time, that Seven G Nine Seven Two was not only totally bald, but he also had no eyebrows nor even eye lashes.

"You must tell me all about the seventy third century", he demanded, "What mankind has achieved, the inventions, the advances in medical science, have you reached the stars, colonised the galaxy"?

Seven G Nine Seven Two listened to the little box pip and squeak in no doubt what was his own language, rather than Latin and then replied for it to tell Ellis Tone,

"Must be careful to preserve integrity of time stream, cannot answer, though one day Tone may journey up when".

The box seemed to be getting better at grammar, the longer their conversation continued, no doubt it possessed a learning programme in it's core.

"You know of me", the taxi driver gasped, "In the seventy third century"?

"We know of stone", came the reply and the time the box was taking was growing shorter too.

"So can you tell me why you're here"? Tone asked, "You've not come to take the stone away I presume as you referred to the possibility of my future use of it"?

"I am on a mission to locate and take an animal back to the year seven thousand two hundred and fifty nine", Seven G Nine Seven Two told him, "An ancient prehistoric creature that has been extinct for centuries. It is our intension to create a menagerie for the public to come and enjoy".

"There are no pre-historic animals on Mars, Sev. You don't mind if I shorten your name to Sev do you"?

The bald traveller nodded his permission, but then countered, "That depends upon your understanding of pre-history Ellis. I may call you Ellis; yes"?

Tone nodded his own permission and then asked, "So in the seventy third century, what area of man's history is thought of as pre-historic".

"Before the year three thousand five hundred, is generally regarded as prehistoric" Sev's compact informed, "The first half of man's rise in advancement".

"So being as I'm in thirty two thirty nine, then I'm a caveman"?!

"We know you do not live in Martian caves", Sev returned and it seemed to Tone that a slight smile played across his thin lips, "But you live in primitive times Ellis, you are therefore regarded by historians as primitive, apologies".

"Fair enough", the taxi driver consented, "But prehistoric animals were the creatures who lived on Earth millions of years past, how can you hope to find one here"?

"My mission is to locate a member of the Phylum: Chordata; Class: Mammalia; Order: Carnivora; Family: Felidae". Sev informed.

Tone picked up his pad and input the information,

"A cat"! he exclaimed. "That covers quite a few animals, Sev. From a sabre tooth, to a tiger, to a house cat. I have to tell you that your chance of finding any but the smallest is slim on Mars.

"Size is not an issue", the chrononaut replied

Try telling that to my girlfriends' Tone quipped inwardly and then asked, "And I suppose you require my help in securing your specimen"?

"If you desire to keep your stone", the reply was automatic and without menace but, even so, Tone was on board at once.

TWO

FELIX HUNTING-GREY WAS a self made man. He had come to Mars in twenty three (three thousand two hundred and twenty three) with nothing more than a burning desire to build his own company and a pocket full of cherry stones. It had not been easy making the farm he had bought on Earth, situated in Ganges Chasma, a success. The red dust had to be made fertile for the Lichencherries and to achieve that he had used his own manure; his very own waste. The smell had been terrible and the neighbours who were kilometres distant, had complained constantly to the authorities. Hunting-Grey had been visited by none other than Grandios Vul Soil Man of Mars. The passion with which he had spoken of his project had won the most powerful soil man on the planet over and he was allowed to continue, despite the never ending complaints.

After several setbacks however, the mutant trees had finally flourished and Hunting-Grey had harvested his first crop of cherries. He set about manufacturing the juice from them and creating the delicious beverage Marvio Delicio. The drink was an unmitigated success and Hunting-Grey reinvested the profits back into the care and propagation of the trees. He expanded the farm, buying out several of his neighbours and the estate expanded. He was able to increase production and float his company on the share market and business went from fair to good, to excellent.

Hunting-Grey's wife Abatha had provided him with two children during this time, a daughter, Foella and a son two years later, Tordale. Felix also brought his brother over to Mars to help him with the ever expanding business,

Moorcliff Hunting-Grey became head of sales at Marvio Delicio. All went splendidly for several years, but finally, matters began to change.

If Kelix cast his mind back to the very first fly in the ointment, it was when the seven year old Foella had come to him one morning, as he sat reading the stock market on his pad.

"Daddy" she began in a pleading voice, "I want a pet".

Kelix raised an eyebrow, "A pet, what for darling"?

"For my very own", the girl misunderstood.

"Why do you want a pet though"?

"Because Ava Vine-Flentine has one and she brought it into school and it's brilliant. It moves on it's own and it eats things and it's like a person, except for it sometimes soils when it shouldn't".

"What sort of pet does she have"? Felix thought the idea ludicrous on Mars, when pets could not go outside because of the terrific cold and barely breathable atmosphere.

"Oh it's a hamster", Foella said casually, "But I don't want one of them, they're too small, you can't really stroke them and if they get cross they nip you".

"Then it's probably not really a very good idea at all", Felix offered hopefully.

"But I still want a pet", the girl persisted, "I've been looking on my learn-pad and I want a cat"?

Kelix put down his own pad and said carefully, "Do you know how much a cat costs Foella"?

"Oh hundred's", the girl responded casually, "But you're rich and it would make Ava so very jealous".

"I'll look into it and let you know", the managing director of Marvio Delicio tried.

"I shall wait for your decision then daddy".

Of course that was not the end of it. Foella Hunting-Grey was as obdurate as her father once she had a notion in her head and Kelix was finally forced to cave in and dip into his pocket, the cat cost a ridiculous five hundred shillin to bring from Earth and when it arrived it was already six months old.

Clawdius Maxipus was pure white, had golden eyes and lived up to his name almost at once. Foella came running to Kelix after an hour, crying and with three scarlet wounds on her arm.

"He clawed me daddy, he clawed me and I don't want him, I hate him". Foella never went near the cat again and Kelix named the animal appropriately. Further Clawdius Maxipus became Felix' cat and would not allow any other members of the family anywhere near him. Foella and Tordale were openly afraid of the huge white feline, while Abatha was forced to take antihistamine tablets as she found out at once that she was allergic to the creature.

When Kelix had suffered a stressful day at work he liked nothing better than to seat himself before the fire at night with a pipe full of med-bacco and Clawd (as his name was shortened to for convenience) purring away on this knee. That was when a second problem began in Kelix' life. Abatha began making greater and greater demands for money for expensive clothes and cosmetics that she did not really need. She had not returned to work after the birth of Tordale and she grew bored. Her answer to her boredom was to go therapy shopping and Abatha was very bored!

There began to be drains on the company profits. Foella and Tordale both attended expensive public school, Abatha continued to be a drain and then Moorcliff became ambitious. Kelix' brother was beginning to make noises that he should play a greater role in the running of the company at the very top level. Compounded to his demands was a request for a pay slip that rivaled Kelix own. The slide had begun and strangely it came to a head in thirty two thirty nine.

Two years before, Foella had reached the age at which augmentation could be undergone, Kelix had seen his daughter about her requests,

"You're fourteen now darling", he had begun, "It's time to think of any improvements you would like done to your appearance. The truth from my perspective, is that you are a lovely young lady and need no augmentation".

"Well Daddy I've some requests", Foella had said. "Firstly I want my nose shortening, secondly I want very bright blue eyes, then I want to be blonde, not mousy and most importantly I want an impressively large but pert bosom".

Kelix could almost see the shillin's adding up. Your nose is fine darling, Your brown eyes lovely and why be blonde, men never respect a blonde quite like they do a brunette, it's always been this way I'm afraid".

Foella glanced down at her flat chest and continued as though Kelix had never spoken,

"I thought an E cup for my frame, that will make me a thirty two E".

"What does your mother thing to your desires"? Kelix asked in desperation.

"Oh '*her*'! I don't really talk to her much Daddy. So can I have the augmentation"?

"All of them darling, you truly are lovely as you are, believe me".

"Yes everyone daddy especially the tits, boys like tits".

Kelix felt an icy finger run down his spine, "You should be concentrating on your studies darling, not worrying about the boys".

"I am Daddy, so please see things my way".

Kelix caved as he always did.

When Foella came out of Red General, he barely recognised his daughter, but she smiled at him and hugged him and he sighed and that evening smoked a pipe and sat with his beautiful cat.

Clawdius Maxipus still had no interest in any other member of the Hunting-Grey household and when Moorcliff came to visit he hissed and arched his back and bushed out his tail in absolute feline fury. Kelix was a little proud of the no compromise stance his cat took to the others and sometimes wished the two of them could swap places.

The date was thirty two thirty nine December eleventh, when the world seemed to come crashing around Kelix ears. He got up that morning, stroked Clawdius as he always did and made his way down to breakfast. Only Abatha was at the table as he arrived and she looked somehow different, her expression and mien were hesitant rather than indifferent, he asked her,

"Is everything alright my dear, you look worried about something".

"I need something from you, something that once given, will ensure you never see me again, the demands for cash will stop and you can while away your time with your precious cat".

"You want to leave Ganges Chasma? I don't understand, why"?

"Well apart from the fact that it still reeks of shit, I've met someone else".

"You're having an affair! Whom with"?

"Does it matter"? she returned stiffly.

"Yes it frenging does, so the thing you need from me, is a dissolution of our contract"?

"Well that's one of the things I also need two thousand, I'm going to set up an art gallery".

Then it came to Kelix, the party several months ago, the artist, what was his name? He remembered him being ten years younger than Abatha as well. He also remembered the way she had disgracefully flirted with him, over praised his work, tried to get Kelix to buy several of his rather abstract paintings that Kelix found nothing to like about.

"Allenon", he started "Allenon Magento, he of the tiny waist and black twirling moustache, what in Hades does he see in you Abatha, apart from my money"?

"The scandal may harm your fizzy drinks", she warned, rising from the table. "If you don't give me the money I will have to take other steps".

Kelix grabbed her wrist, "Just what the frenge does that mean"? He demanded.

She merely pulled free saying, "Get your hands off me Kelix, don't touch me again, ever, or I'll have you taken out of this property and a restraining order taken out"!

No sooner had she left him alone at the table than Foella shimmied in with a second bombshell in as many minutes,

"Daddy do I have your permission to marry"?

Kelix blinked and his features turned ruddy, he asked, "I must be losing my sanity, I though my sixteen year old daughter just asked me for permission to marry".

"Ha ha, very funny", she returned in a pained voice, "Now do I, or do we have to wait two whole years"?

"Foella, do you realise what you are doing with your life", the M.D. asked her, "Who is the boy anyway do I know him"?

"He's no boy daddy, he's thirty seven actually, he's my economics teacher and we are very much in love".

Kelix covered his face with his hands but when he took them down again Foella was still there,

"Mummy says it's fine but the final decision rests with you".

"Your mother has questionable morals, Foella and were I to agree to your proposed union, so would I have, the answer is no. In fact the answer is to stay away from your thirty seven year old tutor, or I will have him sacked".

"If you're thinking he broke the law daddy, he was very careful to wait until my sixteenth birthday before we did it for the first time and since then we've been at it like rabbits, so you might as well let me have who I want".

"No"! Kelix roared thinking he would have a stroke if such crazy pressures continued.

"I absolutely hate you", came the spat reply and Foella rushed out the room in tears.

Kelix left his breakfast untouched and went into his study for some peace and quiet before having to leave for work. Tordale was seated in one of the leather chairs in there,

"Oh, hello son, I don't usually see you before school, is everything alright", Kelix asked doing his best to keep his voice even. Tordale, his son, the heir to the Marvio Delicio empire, the one who had never brought him stress before. This day though, was different,

"No, sir everything isn't alright I'm afraid", his one and only son confessed to him, his features knotted with concern.

"Just tell me then, maybe we can sort it out"?

"I need three thousand sir"?

"Three '*thousand*', how you could possibly need three thousand shillin Tor"?

"We have this card game at school, you see and well, to cut a long story short, it got a bit out of hand, sorry dad".

"Well I'm sorry too, boy, but I am not bailing you out. You're talking about school kids, the lad will not, cannot possibly, expect you to pay anything, never mind three thousand"?

"In most cases that would be true sir, but you don't know who I owe it to and you can call it an advance on my inheritance".

"What do you mean who you owe it too? Who, at fourteen years old could demand a payment of three thousand shillin"?

"Brax Titarang".

"Titarang, a relation of Augternin Titarang no doubt"?

"That's his dad".

"You played cards with a gangster's son and lost three thousand to him"?

"Not all on one day, but ultimately yes".

"Well good luck sorting that one out son, because I've just about had it with this family and you can come up with a solution on your own".

"You don't understand dad", the boy persisted, "If I can't pay, then Brax won't come after me, he'll tell his own father and he'll come to you for the money anyway".

"Tor", Kelix began, "I'm going to work now, we might have to discuss this further this evening. In fact I might hold a family meeting this evening. Now please go to school".

At least the boy had the presence of mind to nod and do as directed.

Kelix collapsed into his own chair and then heard a yowl at his feet, he looked down and found Clawdius Maxipus rubbing against the leg of his boho's. Gently he picked the cat up and began to scratch behind his pink and white ear, the animal rewarded the gesture with a loud purring sound,

"Clawdius", Kelix said to his pet, "What ever would I do without you"?

Twenty minutes later the managing director at Ganges Chasma was dead!

THREE

VOORHEES PON PULLED up outside the Hunting-Grey property and glanced around before climbing out of the flitter. He noted that the country estate was expansive; cherry trees surrounding it in row upon careful row. He noticed the quality of the construction of the building itself and he saw the reason for Kelix' death. It was the oldest motive in the book, money. He also noticed there was more than one flat foot crawling all over the place, so physical evidence was probably not either catalogued, or destroyed for ever.

He buttoned up his frock coat, adjusted his head beads and began to walk toward the drive, he had not gotten more than twenty paces than a constable suddenly barred his way.

"Sorry sir, you can't go in there. It's a crime scene".

"I'm invited by the lady of the house, officer", Pon responded and he held out his I.D. card. The constable glanced it over and said into his throat-mic,

"A private-det is here sir, he says Abatha Hunting-Grey has asked him to call, name's Pon"?

Pon heard a tinny voice reply into the constable's earpiece. The member of Mars Constabulary looked slightly taken aback at the response but nodded to Pon swiftly enough,

"You can go in sir, you're to report to Inspector Litseinik before you do anything else".

"Inspector! He's made inspector, how long has Claudius Litseinik been an inspector, officer"?

"About eighteen months now, sir. You will report to him"?

Pon nodded, "Of course I will and thank you, constable".

He ambled into the impressive building and was met almost at once by none other than the Inspector of the moment,

"What are you doing here Pon, has Chostamure finally been given the heave-ho"? the policeman wanted to know.

"Saul already had a case, Claudius. So I got this assignment".

"Well you're wasting your time", the Inspector snapped, "No evidence and no witnesses. Who hired you anyway"?

"That's confidential", Pon returned, "And there's always evidence, you just have to know where to look for it. How did the deceased die"?

"Level two needle and before you ask, no trace of the gun that fired the shot".

"Does every member of the family have a weapon"? Pon asked glancing at his pad, "The wife and both siblings".

"Who doesn't in this day and age"? Litseinik returned. "They all have one, Talkloom has checked all three, their energy piles indicate that none of them have been fired in the last month, never mind the last twenty four hours".

"Talkloom being your forensic boy"?

Litseinik chuckled, "He's hardly a boy, Pon, he's seventy three".

"Seventy three and still working", Pon mused aloud, "I hope I've given this game up before I get to that age".

"Retirement isn't till seventy five, what would you do with your time anyway"?

"Oh, maybe grow cherry trees who knows. I see you guys are wrapping up, so I presume I can go and talk to the family now"?

"Knock yourself out. They were each in the property when the deceased was shot, none have an alibi and all profess their innocence".

"Sounds like the case might well go cold for you Inspector"?

"Frigid and frenging fast. See you around Pon, say hello to Chostamure for me".

The two shook hands and Pon seated himself in a recliner in the hall until they had driven away. Finally he rose from the seat and went in search of the lady of the house.

The only time he hesitated was when he stopped to admire a Roxbrough in one of the interconnecting rooms. It was a wet street scene, the figures and building impossibly tall and narrow, he liked it.

"Can I help you, what are you still doing here"? a female voice suddenly demanded. Pon turned to see a quite elegant brunette standing before him, she was dressed in an original Jean-Guillaume Archambeault creation in red silk. It must have cost upward of fifty shillin. He held out his badge as he spoke,

"Voorhees Pon, looking for Abatha Hunting-Grey, although I suspect I've just found her"?

She nodded, "And you like my frock I see"?

"Very nice considering it was made by a French poof".

"You're a homophobe mister Pon"? Abatha smiled.

"Not really", the det returned, "In fact I wouldn't mind if every man on Mars was a poof except me".

"Come into the morning room with me"? she chuckled and shimmed her way toward the desired location.

Pon found himself admiring her ass, not bad for a forty year old, the surgeon had done good work.

"Would you like some Calliston tea"?

"I would indeed, being as I've never tried any", the private-det returned, "You've very expensive tastes missus Hunting-Grey".

"I like to try new things", was the reply as she poured him a cup into genuine china tableware. "You'll find the beverage has a curious aftertaste, it's the minerals in the Calliston water and nothing to worry about".

Pon sipped the drink, finding it as described and then noted somewhat bluntly,

"You don't seem very grief stricken for someone who has just been widowed missus Hunting-Grey".

"My husband and I were going to get divorced mister Pon and while I realise that gives me a motive of sorts for killing him, the split was amicable".

"And you've witnesses to that fact"?

"Yes", said a new voice at the doorway, "Me".

Pon turned to regard an incredibly pneumatic blonde with startling blue eyes, "You must be Foella Hunting-Grey".

The teenager came over and seated herself next to him, very closely in fact.

"Guilty as charged", she breathed, "Do you want to interrogate me mister Pon"?

"You must forgive Foella mister Pon", Abatha said quickly, "Her hormones are wild at present, not to mention her biorhythms".

"I was just teasing mother, don't be such a wedgestop, pour me some of that bitter tea will you"?

"Describe your relationship with your father for me miss Hunting-Grey, if you would please"? Pon asked.

"Foella", the girl responded, "We can be intimate, Voorhees. I hated the bastard, does that give me a motive"?

"Why"?

"Because all he thought about was his precious cherries and never afforded me nor mother enough time".

"Foella is simplifying matters", Abatha was quick to point out, "It was more complicated than that".

Pon took another sip of the tea, it was bitter, "And your son, did he have any reason to want his father dead"?

"We all did", the blonde bombshell told him, "But none of us is capable of murder, the case is impossible, Voorhees, you will never solve it".

"Did anyone else have issues with Kelix"? Pon asked beginning to feel that the situation did indeed present him with many difficulties.

"Uncle Moorcliff wanted to run Marvio Delicio", Foella seemed to be enjoying herself. She crossed her legs in such a way as to indicate availability to Pon.

"Foella, please don't make the situation confusing for mister Pon and stop with the ridiculous flirtations, it's embarrassing".

"Have you told mister Pon about your artistic lover, mother"? Foella asked in response, really savouring the older woman's discomfort at mention of him.

Abatha flushed and said in a level voice, "I am having an affair, mister Pon. With Allenon Magento".

"Oh; I know his work"!

"Crud, isn't it"? Foella cajoled.

"I'm no art critic", Pon felt obliged to reply, there was no sense in angering the person who was paying his fee. "I think perhaps now I'd like to speak to Moorcliff, or is he at school"?

"At school with his father murdered this very day? No he's not at school mister Pon", Abatha told him and it seemed as though he might have managed to annoy here unintentionally. Just then he heard a faint purr and a softness brush his boho pants and glancing down it was to see a large white cat rubbing against him. He reached down to stroke the animal, intrigued,

"I wouldn't do that if I were you", Foella cautioned, causing Pon to hesitate, "The little frenger will claw you for certain".

"A cat on Mars", Pon smiled and approached the animal with gentle care, "He has to be one of the only ones for certain".

The cat rubbed against his hand and allowed Pon to scratch under his ear,

"There are nine only on all the planet as far as we were told", Abatha supplied, "And you seem to have made a friend of Clawdius, that's not easily accomplished".

"Claudius", Pon smiled, thinking of Litseinik.

"With a 'w', like the nails of the creature", Foella explained, "Clawdius Maxipus. It would seem you have a pleasing stroke mister Pon, I wonder if you could make other pussy's purr"?

"I'll locate Moorcliff for you mister Pon", Abatha promised somewhat stiffly.

FOUR

OVER THE NEXT few days Pon continued to make more enquiries. He asked for information beyond the immediate members of the family. He was also constantly visited by the teenage nymphet, Foella who quite blatantly offered herself to him on their first meeting. Never one to '*turn his nose up at a freeby, Pon did a rapid and thorough inspection of the girl's goodies'* finding them to his liking. They had become sexual partners but there was not the least romance in it. Pon satisfied a mere physical outlet and craving for the girl while she, at less than half his age, was a flattering convenience for him.

One thing he was not foolish enough to entertain was the notion of her innocence. If anything he thought her more likely to be the murderer than any of the others. There were five suspects on his list and he could not discount any single one of them. The bottom one, was the one he least wanted to consider and the hardest to find to interview. Pon was nothing if not persistent however and he found himself on the right trail a few days into his private investigation.

He entered a bar on the seedy side of Noctis Labyrinthus, having made quite a journey to get there.

"What will you have mister", the tender of the counter wished to know.

"Give me an Earth Vodka and have one for yourself", Pon responded.

"Thanks I'll have the same and drink mine later".

"I'm looking for someone too and was told to try here, do you know where I can find Augternin Titarang"?

The man almost dropped the bottle he was holding, "Who told you I would"? He demanded.

"That doesn't matter right now, can you help me or should I go elsewhere"?

"What do you want with Titarang"?

"I have some payments for him", Pon lied, knowing it more likely that such a reason would get him an interview with the criminal.

"Don't leave here, I've a ping to make, then".

Pon waited and tried to retain his nerve, this was something Litseinik would never have attempted, promoted, or not. After close to an hour three men entered the otherwise quiet establishment and Pon recognised one as the man he was seeking. The other two were veritable giants and the expressions they permanently wore were not pleasant. The barkeeper nodded at Pon and the trio approached,

"You looking for me"? the ordinary looking one asked, his tone was not friendly.

Pon replied, "Yes Titarang, my name is Pon, I'm a priv-det".

"Search him boys", Titarang instructed and Pon was relieved of his needle gun.

"I need no private detective Pon, so what business have you with me"? Titarang came immediately to the point.

"I've been hired to investigate Abatha Hunting-Grey's late husband's murder and wondered if you could tell me your where about's on the thirty first"?

"Why should I, Pon"? Titarang sipped his vodka that had been poured out for him the minute he had entered the bar. "Who is the guy anyway"?

"He was the M.D. of a company who owns Marvio Delicio, his son and your son go to the same private school. His son owes your's a great deal of money and he cannot pay".

"I still don't see why I should answer any of your questions, are you making some sort of accusation against me"?

"On the contrary I'm trying to establish your innocence".

"That's real nice of you Pon, but I don't think I actually care what you think one way or the other".

"Fair enough mister Titarang, if that's your final word, can I have my gun back now"?

"You've some stones coming here Pon, I'll grant you that", the villain noted then. "I was with the boys here on the thirty first, we have a card school every Friday, it was a Friday, right"?

Pon nodded, "I was just wondering how you will get the debt owed you"?

"Were you now? Well according to you I'm owed nothing, it's my son who is owed this apparent debt, however, if you're thinking of disturbing his studies with your fool questions, Pon, I would advise you to forget about it. It would not sit well with me, do we understand one another"?

"I certainly understand the point you are making mister Titarang".

"Good. Oh and one other thing, Pon. If a man is dead, he can't pay his debts can he, think about that one alright"?

"A valid point sir", Pon was pleased to concede.

FIVE

PON WAS JUST sitting down to the tri-vid when the knock came at his door. He put the Martian Lichennuts to one side and activated his pad, looking at the two men outside. They did not look like hit men, but then he realised, what did hit men look like? One of the duo was very tall and totally devoid or hair, the other shorter, dark and tanned. He rose unlocked the door and then reseated himself. When he called,

"Enter"! He had a needle gun in his hand. The door opened and the tanned man's eyes widened in fear. Not hit men then.

"Put your weapons on that low table and then both sit down", the priv-det ordered, without a word the two men seated themselves and the tanned one said,

"My gun's in my flitter outside, he doesn't have one".

"What do you want with me"? Pon asked, "Who are you"?

"My name is Ellis Tone", the tanned man began, this is Sev, we're here to ask you about the cat".

"The cat"?

"The Hunting-Grey cat".

Pon thought he had heard everything in his time, but this was as bizarre a conversation as he had ever had.

"You've come here to ask me about a cat, who sent you, who do you work for"?

"No one sent us and I work for myself", the tanned one returned carefully eyeing the needle gun in Pon's fist.

"You, the bald one, do you speak"?

"I doubt you would believe anything I told you, so I have elected to leave the talking to Ellis", came the reply. He had an accent that Pon could not place.

"So you work for yourself then, Tone, doing what pray"?

"I'm a taxi driver", Tone replied with seeming honesty.

"I'll tell you what", Pon suggested, "You start at the beginning and talk till I tell you to stop, how does that sound"?

"Considering the circumstances it sounds reasonable", Tone admitted, then went on, "We saw the Hunting-Grey murder on the net and noted in the report that Kelix Hunting-Grey left behind a cat. We also read that one Voorhees Pon had been hired by the widowed Abatha Hunting-Grey to look into the murder, so we came to see you. Mister Two here is interesting in acquiring the cat for a menagerie he is starting, that's it sir".

"You want to buy a cat, to put in a zoo"? Pon asked sceptically. "Why don't you buy one from Earth then"?

"Mister Two thought it would be quicker to get one from Mars, as he is from Mars", Tone replied.

"Why didn't you approach the Hunting-Grey's yourself then"?

"We feel you may have, during the course of your investigations, built up a rapport with the family and wish to use you as an intermediary".

"Especially as you are engaging in regular sexual intercourse with the daughter", Two added.

"You see this is why I told you not to speak", Tone accused the bald man, "You've no idea of what's polite in our time".

"This has been fun", Pon decided, "But now it's time to leave gentlemen, if I ever see either of you again,

you'd best be armed and willing to defend yourselves. Do we now have an understanding"?

"I told you we should tell him the truth", the bald man objected.

"So there is a truth"! Pon pounced on the admission.

"There's a truth that you won't believe", Tone replied.

"Suppose you tell me why you're here and let me be the judge of whether it's the truth or not"? the priv-det ordered.

So Tone told Voorhees Pon the truth. When he was done Pon remained silent for a long time and then asked,

"Would you guys like a drink, I know I need one".

"You do not believe us"? Sev asked.

As Pon rose to go to his drinks cabinet he said, "I think if anyone was going to lie to me, they'd have come up with a far better story than that. But time travel, it's not possible is it"?

"Get us the cat and we'll solve the murder", Sev promised then. As Pon was pouring the drinks, he had offered them,

"By going back in time to the instant of the murder and seeing who shot Kelix Hunting-Grey, I imagine"?

"Far too dangerous", Sev noted, "The killer might shoot me too".

"Then just how do you propose to solve the murder"? Pon asked as he poured the vodka's.

"Having read the reports we noted there was an eye witness", Tone said.

"Then the reports were wrong, Kelix was alone, or at least none of the suspects admitted to being present, of course if they were, they would be the murderer", Pon replied handing out the drinks.

"The witness was never interviewed by yourself nor the police", Tone replied.

"Because no one else was in the room", Pon was getting agitated.

Tone smiled, "The cat was with Kelix Hunting-Grey when he was killed. Abatha told the police and you that it darted out when she went to speak to her husband, only to find him dead".

"Oh! Right and I suppose Sev here can speak cat language being as he is from the future"? Pon laughed, "Drink up guys, you're leaving"!

Sev said in total sincerity, "Get me the cat and I'll give you the murderer".

"And who's going to believe three mad men"? Pon wanted to know.

"Believe this", Sev told him, "The evidence you will have will be irrefutable, you have my guarantee".

"I must be out of my mind", Pon said as the flitter roared over the red landscape, twenty minutes later. He was at the wheel and the vehicle was his.

"You're not going mad", Tone replied, "You just want to solve the case and Sev wants the cat and the result of both can be realised once we get to Ganges Chasma".

They were driving through row upon row of cherry trees by nine hundred hours the following morning, Pon told them somewhat superfluously,

"This is the Hunting-Grey Estate, I'll take you up to the entrance and then you can do the talking Tone, alright"?

"No, Voorhees, that's why we asked you come along", Tone persisted. "You know Abatha Hunting-Grey, you know she will be most open to your persuasion".

Pon sighed, "Very well, I'll ask her if she wants to part with Claudius Maxipus".

"Then I will give you the evidence you need to solve the case", Sev promised.

"Yeah, right", the det was not convinced, but he had drawn a blank with his own investigations and was clutching at straws.

He climbed out of his flitter alone, shivering in the frigid air, it was a summery day on Mars. With ground eating strides he made the front airlock and pressed the chimer. It was not long before Abatha appeared,

"Mister Pon, you have something to tell me"?

"I have something to ask you, may I step inside for a second"?

She held the airlock door ajar and Pon got out of the wind, he saw no reason to prevaricate,

"Clawdius Maxipus the cat, I have been approached by an interested party who wished to provide him with a good home. I remember you saying only your departed husband had any love for the animal and I was wondering if you wish to sell him to my client"?

"I presume you're on commission for this little service", Abatha sniffed, "Otherwise this interested party would have approached me himself. No matter, only you can approach the animal at present anyway, what are the two of you offering me mister Pon"?

"Ten thousand"!

Abatha's eyebrows rose in astonishment, "Do you have a bankers draft for that amount mister Pon"?

"I do, in my name, the buyer wishes to remain anonymous".

"In case I missed the dear animal and wanted him back", Abatha's voice dripped with sarcasm. "Well we both know it's more than he's worth, show me the draft and if it looks alright you can take Clawdius Maxipus and good luck to you both. Any progress on your investigations by the by"?

"I expect a breakthrough very soon".

"You do! Well, I will not hold my breath mister Pon. You know where the cat sleeps, this draft looks like the real thing, I will be actioning it directly".

"I will not leave with Clawd until you have", Pon promised.

Minutes later he was back in the flitter. Tone and Sev eyed the huge white feline and Clawdius Maxipus stared right back at them. He rubbed up against Pon, who then, to his consternation passed him gingerly to Sev.

"Not like that", the det barked, "Put him in your lap, support his full weight and stroke him. Then make gentle noises to him".

Sev echoed, "Gentle noises".

Pon demonstrated self consciously.

Sev responded in similar fashion and as Clawdius Maxipus began to purr, the stone that Tone and Sev had about their necks began to glow and to Pon's unbelieving stare, Sev and the cat promptly vanished.

"I told you he was from the future", Tone said with no small amount of satisfaction.

Before Pon could respond with any sort of reply, the bald man suddenly blinked back into existence and this time he was alone,

"Oh good", he mused aloud, "The timing was right, I hate meeting myself when I get it wrong".

"Where's the cat"? Pon asked.

"Being doted on by one of my daughters", the chrononaut told the two of them. Neither thought of Sev as being a father, "Here mister Pon, the evidence to crack the case. I'm afraid the murderer is your lover Foella Hunting-Grey".

Pon gasped as he gazed at the cube in his hand, it was a tri-d image of Foella shooting her father with a needle gun.

"She must have bought a second gun and dumped it later", Sev said, as Tone craned his neck to see the image.

"How did you get this", the priv-det demanded.

"From the only eye witness", the chrononaut told the two of them. "Though Clawdius Maxipus could not speak, the image of what he 'saw', was still in his brain, the extraction was quite painless I assure you".

"Painless, what sort of a machine did you use"? Pon wanted to know.

Sev smiled, "Why it was a cat-scan of course"!

BEYOND HYPER-SPACE

ONE

PATCH WAS WELL concealed, as he peered through the foliage, at the native village. Creeping forward, making as little sound as he were able, he proceeded stealthily forward. The egg trees were thinning out and then suddenly stopped at a huge clearing. At the centre of it lay a collection of rude huts and before him some female natives were gathered around a fire, preparing food. On a sudden whim he decided that this might be the very moment to make contact with his neighbours and decisively, he rose to his feet and walked calmly into the clearing, spotted instantly by the native women. For their part they froze and ceased their chatter and some distance behind them several males suddenly emerged, looking at the strange tall and patchwork giant, as he walked calmly from the undergrowth's entrance.

"I mean you no harm", Patch began, keeping his tone light, "I am a traveller, seeking friends in this world".

One of the men, the one who wore a headdress of feathers and had some beads wound around his arm approached and asked in a strangely stuttering tongue"

"Not from netherworld you are"? He had the complexion of aged wood, as had all the villagers, brown skinned and dark eyed, like the Barabora and yet the down which covered their heads was more like that which grew on a chick, than human hair.

"No, I am from this world and I am very much alive", Patch told him, "But I have journeyed a great distance and am tired. I am the hybrid of two peaceful race's and mean harm to none".

"I Dugazryne of Banteme tribe", the little brown skinned native told Patch then, "What your name, tall of tallest"?

For Patch stood some two point three metres, even taller than his mother who had been Valoare, a princess of the Khela. She who had married the current Chief of their village, Darn, who had come from the sky and who's knowledge was beyond compare.

"My name is Patch; which means these strange areas of pink and blue upon my skin, for I am part human".

"Dugazryne not seen Hu-men before".

"That's right, we have come a great distance", Patch agreed, wondering how much the little Banteme would understand.

"From beyond mountains of Samalla"? he was asked, giving Patch an out.

"Even from beyond there yes", he agreed, which seemed to satisfy the little brown chief.

"Has the people of Dugazryne always been on World"? he asked him then.

Dugazryne nodded, a universal sign of agreement it seemed, "From times beyond Dugazryne's father's father and his father, Banteme have valley. From such times we fight Barabora, Barabora fight us, kill Banteme, but Banteme kill Barabora for this so".

"My group harbour no love for the Barabora neither", Patch responded, seemingly to the native's satisfaction, "We would be friend to Banteme, and enemy of Banteme is enemy of Khela too, Khela is name of my people. I come to ask you to join us, to work with us to mine iron and copper".

"Eye-ron"?

Patch showed the chief his thagomiser, the tall staff that ended with several iron barbs,

"The end of this weapon is made of iron, iron comes from beneath the ground, but it can be moulded with fire and make a spear or arrow point that never dulls. See touch the barbs".

Dugazryne touched the end of one barb and his hand jumped back in pain.

"With iron Khela and Banteme can rid World of Barabora. Will some of you come back to my camp and meet with chief Darn"?

A huge crowd of brown skinned natives had gathered by that time and their chatter had risen to considerable volume during the exchange. It suddenly stilled however and the crowd parted to allow a figure even more decoratively clothed that Dugazryne, to approach their group.

Dugazryne told Patch, "Dugazryne lama of Banteme, but chief Gabom rule all even lama".

When the chief spoke it was in a thin and high pitched jabber that Patch could not understand due to it's swiftness.

"What did he say"? Patch asked the little lama.

Dugazryne seemed surprised at this, but then recovered his composure and drew himself to his full height, which was something short of even Wera's,

"He want know, if you kill Barabora for us with strange arrows and even stranger spear you carry"?

"Tell his excellency, we are peaceful by nature and only attack those who first attack us. If the Barabora task us, or you if we are allies we will respond with deadly force, but we will not take arms against them if they leave us alone".

"Chief not want hear that", the lama complained, but Patch repeated his response and asked that the message be relayed to the chief. This seemed to be to the consternation of the lama. The chief shrugged however, when the words were spoken to him and Dugazryne asked,

"He say you welcome. Even if come in peace. Banteme glad of ally, tonight you stay with us and feast".

"I will be glad to", Patch agreed.

He was shown to a hut and brought fruit, some of which he had never seen before, then once alone, waiting for the night, he stretched out on a blue tendril hammock and thought about his own camp and what he could remember of his past.

When he was a child, he had learned to speak both Khelac and the alien tongue of his father, his mother had explained his amazing heritage. For she, Valoare had been a princess of the Khela, while Darn, had come from the black sky beyond world. That was why his father was pink, his mother blue and why Patch had variegated area's of pigment and had earned his name. His little sister Patchuli shared the same amazing heritage. It also explained why of the camp only Vitala; Valoare's brother, was also tall and blue skinned while the rest of the adults were like Darn.

The tiny group lived peacefully in their village which was called Katowice. They knew of local neighbouring villages of Khela, but the Khela initially friendly toward them, had kept away from the camp and the strange alien temple of gleaming silver, which contained many marvels and mysteries. When Patch was fifteen summers, disaster struck the camp. From out of the sky came the Pteranodon and before anyone could react, Valoare and the couple, Texas and Tyra were gone for ever. Only a year later Lin, the small yellow one, had a fatal fall from cliffs to the west.

The group was reduced to eight. The blue warrior Vitala, his brother-in-law the pink Darn and Vitala's pink wife Wera were the adults. Patch and Patchuli were the adolescents and then there were Wera's three children; the boy Patrice, and the two girls Patchee and Patchomi.

They knew they needed allies, chief Darn had approached the Khela many times, but the tall blue warriors feared the ju-ju of the Silver Temple, that contained many mysteries and strange glowing stars even in the daytime. In desperation Darn and Patch had roamed farther and farther afield and now, he, the son of the chief had been successful! How proud his father would be. it would bring a smile to a face that of late had smiled little. For Darn mourned the loss of his tall beautiful blue princess and their isolation meant he might be widowed for the rest of his days.

He and Wera spoke less and less of their world, that was near one of the stars, they had given up on the notion of being joined by countrymen and women. Their only chance was to find others on Nyjord, which was what they called World. Others to befriend and integrate with.

The Banteme came for Patch then and lead him to the central hut that was the largest of them all. He was conducted into it with great ceremony and some of the natives blew through reed tubes and made pleasant sound by placing their fingers over certain holes cut into them. It was not as beautiful as the discs in the Silver Temple, but it was pleasing to Patch's ear.

They ate and Dugazryne wished to know, "Tell, what station, in your camp"?

"My station? Oh you mean my position, I am the chief's son, the chief is Darn, he is my father".

"This good", the lama seemed very pleased by the revelation, he went on, "This why Gabom want you meet his daughter".

"Oh I see, that's kind of the chief but.......". He trailed off, for the lama had brought forth one of the slim dark maidens, to meet Patch and she was the loveliest of them.

"Strengthen alliance with marriage", the lama told Patch, "Must be done tomorrow. Then you take many Banteme back your camp".

"What do you think to this arrangement, Princess"? Patch asked the dusty beauty before him.

"I do what father tells".

"What is your name"?

"Myra".

"What would you do if the choice were yours and yours alone"?

The beauty looked puzzled,

"Not our way for her to question", the lama explained, "You make Myra happy, she be happy. Agree to this"?

"To cement the alliance between our two peoples I will agree to marry Myra 'after' Banteme have met chief Darn and seen our camp. We are few, but we have very powerful weapons and we will give some of those weapons to your people".

Dugazryne turned to Gabom and relayed this information and the chief nodded his agreement. Patch's mission had been a great success. Tomorrow he would take the Banteme on their three day journey back to Katowice.

TWO

UPON HIS RETURN however, Patch got the biggest shock of his entire life. The Banteme had fallen on their knees and were jabbering prayers, to which ever gods they worshiped. They had not done so at the sight of one Silver Temple at Katowice however; but two! Before he could explain the unexpected phenomenon away, his uncle, Vitala came to greet the entire party. He was carrying a thagomiser and on his arm was a small escutcheon of plaited frond bark. His immense height was also a factor in making him look warlike and magnificent in equal measure.

"More visitors from the chief's star"? Patch guessed.

Vitala nodded, "With four pinks who speak Earther, but with strange accent, different to Wera. I see you were successful in your quest, you bring workers for the mines"?

"And a prospective bride to cement the alliance of the Khela and the race who are Banteme", Patch returned and taking Myra by the arm gently brought her forth to meet his uncle.

"This is Vitala second only to the chief, he is master at arms", he explained to her and to Dugazryne who had regained his feet by that time, "Uncle meet my intended; Myra".

The Khelac gave the girl a stiff nod, but the look in his eye told Patch that he also found the girl a beauty.

From behind Vitala a strange group suddenly began to approach, lead by Darn, four figures dressed in silvery suits that hugged their skin, two were men the other two women.

Patch quickly introduced Dugazryne to his father and as soon as he was able asked to be introduced to the strange visitors from the stars. His father told him,

"Captain Tara Shevchenko, engineer Salur Araz, doctor Amara Kruger and sergeant Patrick Doyle, my son Patch".

"The variation of skin tone is amazing to be sure", the one called Doyle observed while Patch himself was keenly observing the different complexions of the four visitors. Kruger was like ebony, darker even than the Banteme, while Araz was very similar to the brown natives. Shevchenko was the same as his father, but with hair the colour of some of the lightest yellow grasses.

"Now son, you must commence arranging the new workforce, while I have much to discuss with the captain".

"Will you remarry and have more children father", Patch asked and noticed the blonde woman blushed at the enquiry.

"Please do as I say Patch and I will explain things to you better this evening", his father asked.

When the young man had left Darren turned back to the quartet,

"It has not been easy remaining here, but once you have explored a little further afield, you will see the reason for our decision to stay and now you tell me that Explorer Two never returned to Earth, it makes hyper-space look even more hazardous and unpredictable".

"As I said before, corporal, not only did Explorer Two disappear, but no signals were ever received on the tracking stations of Callisto and Mars", Shevchenko reported, "Considering the setbacks you have endured, it is amazing that you and Wera are still very much alive".

"We should begin unloading the equipment captain", Doyle, the Irishman reminded his Russian captain.

"Of course", Shevchenko asked Darren, "Do you think we could involve some of your natives in the procedure, corporal"?

"Tara", Darren began carefully, "On Nyjord, titles and surnames have little or no meaning, there is no need to refer to my rank in his majesty's armed forces, for I have not served him in twenty years now. Please try to be Nyjordic while you are here"?

"Of course", Shevchenko returned politely, I am happy to answer to my given name as I am sure is my crew. So; Darren, the natives"?

"Liaise with Patch, you will find him likeable and willing".

"The variation in skin tone is quite amazing, did you not expect simply a paler blue complexion".

"We did not know what to expect", Darren returned, "You are not put off by it"?

"No no, it seems in keeping with the rest of what we have thus witnessed here", the Russian was candid. "I'm afraid the Scandian decision to re-name Nyjord, Nyjord Prime and Brahma, Nyjord Minor has caused tension between the governments of India and Scandia and hope the message we sent following your response will alleviate matters".

Darren had told the Russian he flatly refused to accept the decision and Texas naming would remain unchanged.

"Tara, get the equipment unloaded and then go exploring, you'll see the beauty of Nyjord. Take Patch with you as a guide, he knows Katowice like the back of his own hand".

"Very well", she agreed feeling dismissed.

Darren - Chief Darn, went in search of his son, the arrival of Explorer Three had not filled him with joy and he realised for the first time how Nyjordic he had become, despite the tragedies and setbacks the group had endured. His son, it seemed, shared his misgivings,

"I have looked at their equipment father", he told the chief, the instant they were together, "I know why there are only four of them, when the ship is the same size as the one that brought you to us".

"You do", Darren was impressed with his son, "Tell me then"?

"It carries fortifications, just like those you described to me, the newcomers wish to turn Dallas into a garrisong".

"Garrison", Darren replied thoughtfully, "There's no g on the end of it. I'm not sure about this, Patch".

"Do we not need a defensive position against the Barabora? More, do we not need somewhere where we can crouch in safety when the Pteranodon strike"?

"We do yes", Darren agreed, "But I don't think that's why Shevchenko has brought the fortifications. Patch they are to protect her and mankind against us, the Nyjordic"!

"Then do we stop them from constructing it"!

"Or", Darren smiled, "Let them do the work, while we see to our mines and the training of the Banteme and then take over the fort, when it's completed".

"That may incur violence", Patch noted.

"Yes", Darren sounded grave, "It may, son".

THREE

THE PANELLING FOR the fortress that was to protect Dallas was made of duridium. Amazingly light, yet incredibly strong. Salur Araz marked out a section of ground that greatly surprised Darren and then began to bolt sections together, it stood five metres high and was anchored by quick setting concrelite; a new type of concrete that set to twice the hardness of previous material and in a mater of two minutes. The panels soon surrounded the rough huts that had been their home for twenty years and then with the help of the three other newcomers Araz unrolled a gigantic bolt of what looked like flexible clear duraplast. Once it was anchored over the entire perimeter of the fort, the Azerbaijani began to spray the top of the cupola with a hardening solution. It would have the strength, though transparent, of metal.

To regulate the temperature inside, a huge generator was attached to an electronic climate control unit. Finally two large duridium gates on massive hinges were hoisted onto their brackets and welded into place. Darren marvelled at the small size of the torch Araz used, but it was certainly adequate to the task. Now all save the two vessels were inside a fortress that could withstand anything Nyjord could muster against them.

By evening it was finished, Shevchenko was watching with Darren,

"You'll lose no more people now corporal", she insisted upon referring to his military rank.

"I am actually a general on Nyjord, captain", Darren said calmly, but irked.

"One of my remits is to have you taken back to Mars for decommissioning then", the Russian finally admitted to him.

"I will not leave my people and especially my children captain, Nyjord is my home and Brahma will always be the name of her sister world".

"That insistence could well cause a war in the asteroid belt of the solar system".

"How so"?

"Scandia has some mining operations on one or two of them. Were the Indian government to insist upon that which you insist, the Indians may well think of taking matters into their own hands and attacking the Scandian's at their weakest and least defensible place, namely the mines in the belt operated by Scandia".

"To change the name would be to ignore the tremendous contribution of our biologist, Sita. It remains as I originally named it. You see Tara I am General and Prime Minister of Nyjord".

"Prime minister", the Russian raised an eyebrow, "There is no government here"?

"By the time you get back to Earth, if indeed that voyage is possible, as it has never been done successfully to date and by the time Explorer Four gets here, there will be one".

"I have a daily report to make", Shevchenko confessed, "Am I to report your attitude in that report corp....ah general"?

"Tara", Darren said softly then, "You must do, what you must do, I must do what I must do. The simple fact of the matter is that even with hyper-drive and the rigor's of hyper-space Earth is four months away. How can mankind hope to claim Nyjord with that sort of gap"?

"You do not acknowledge that Nyjord is a human colony"?

"I acknowledge that the Khela have assimilated we few humans. They are the rightful owners of this world. Them or the Barabora, maybe even the Viriligan".

"The huge reptilian animals? You claim they possess intellect"?

"Get your group together and Patch and I will lead you to them right now, you can then make your own mind up"?

"My report........".

"Can wait just this once".

"Very well I will come with you, sergeant Doyle will accompany me".

"Let me go fetch Patch and then you can meet the Viriligan"?

The quartet were soon assembled and made their way to a designated spot, at which, the Nyjordic regularly met the huge green sextupoid. Within minutes the Viriligan appeared, to the astonishment of the Explorer Three members.

They will not hurt you", Patch told them, his voice little more than a whisper, "They are peaceful herbivore".

"I feel no fear", Shevchenko admitted honestly, "In fact I currently feel a tremendous sense of peace and well being".

"You will", Darren agreed at once, "Those emotions are being broadcast by the Viriligan, "They are empathic".

"We are more than that", a voice broadcast into Patch' head then, "We are telepathic".

"They spoke to me"! the youth gasped in wonder, "They are telepathic father"!

"Spoke, what did they say, I heard nothing", Darren accepted his son's claim, even though he had received no such message.

"They told me they were telepathic", Patch replied and began to walk carefully toward the huge green creature, with careful tread.

The creature he approached was massive, fully three and a half metre's high when down on all six legs. When it raised itself up on the back pair, it towered in the pink sky, seeking the orange and white growths that adorned the tips of the blue fronds. It had variegated skin, mainly green, but with hints of xanthic and ochre on it's rear flanks. It's back was mainly various shades of green from lime to deep green. The six legs were not it's most astonishing features however, but it's two barbed tails and it's two long necks, upon which; were two heads!

The head's possessed multi faceted eye's, like those of a fly's. Each head had three horns, two above the head situated like a cows, while the third was from the front of the heads, situated like those of the rhinoceros. The eyes gleamed red, but the quartet could see that was from the reflection of the ground, rather than the beast's pigment. The rear legs were strong and ended in toed feet while the central pair and front pair had more delicate design and ended in sharp claws.

"You are not afraid" the beast noted in Patch' brain, "That is good, you have no reason to feel any nervousness in our presence".

"Who are you", Patch whispered.

"You have named us the Viriligan, that will suffice", came the broadcast thoughts, "I assume you require a singular name, but I am simply one of the herd".

"But how do you differentiate between one another? Why have you chosen now to broadcast to me, why not my father"?

"So many questions", came the amused response, "But let me answer some for you. We have no need to differentiate between ourselves, we are one, however for your convenience you may think of me as Aaal. I am the head on your left, my brother wishes to remain silent for the purposes of our conversation. I have chosen you for you are Nyjordic while your father is only new to our world, you are now of age Patch and we are willing to think with you".

Patch passed this information on to the others, Darren looked disappointed, the other two sceptical, but they remained silently observing just the same.

"I wish to know all about your herd", the hybrid told the huge reptile, "I wish to know the history of your ah...people".

"Then return to us alone and we will answer some of your ceaseless enquiries", again Aaal's broadcasts were amused, "But for now know that we are suspicious of the humans, those who arrived recently, they harbours feeling of conquest of this beautiful world, 'our' beautiful world".

"I'll do as you instruct", Patch promised and turned back to the others.

"I'll return another time and learn more of these magnificent and peaceful people", he told them.

"People"! Doyle echoed, "They're animals surely"?

"With the power of telepathy"? Darren mused, "I think perhaps my son's choice of nomenclature was correct. Just because the Viriligan do not possess opposable thumbs, it does not mean they aren't advanced and civilised. If that is true then they are to be regarded as people".

"Well I won't regard some overgrown green, two headed cow as people", Doyle persisted, while his captain merely looked greatly concerned at this new development".

As the quartet began to make their way back to Katowice, she asked Darren, "Do you think the Viriligan would make it difficult for our people to colonise Nyjord Prime, corporal"?

"I think the fact that Earth is four months away would make it difficult to colonise this Eden-like world", he noted with a smile.

"And yet the America's was that distance from Olde Europe once", the Russian countered.

He nodded, "Perhaps so, but the barrier of hyper-space is far more of an obstacle than the Atlantic Ocean ever was. Look what happened to the Red Indians once the Europeans arrived in the America's would you see the Khela and the Banteme go the same way? They may be other sentient beings on Brahma as well".

"Nyjord Minor", Shevchenko corrected almost absently.

"You see", Darren pointed out then, Mankind as a race cannot even agree on the naming of these two worlds".

"What would you have me do"?

"Stay! Just as we decided to stay, become Nyjordic, or go on to another star system, as maybe Explorer Two decided to do. Return to the solar system though and it will ultimately result in some bloodshed along the way".

"Are you threatening me, corporal"?

Darren sighed, "Don't be obtuse captain, you asked me what I would do if I was you. I suspect you have already decided what *you* will do".

They reached the fortress in frosty silence and after parting company Darren took his son to one side,

"Get Vitala for me son. When you and Myra are being married, he and I and a few of the Banteme are going to take over the fortress from the crew of Explorer Two"!

FOUR

PATCH GAZED AT his wife-to-be and saw that she was beautiful. From behind him his sister, Patchuli winked and smiled, everyone was happy and the ceremony went without a hitch......

Until.

The sound of a blaster rent the air and every warrior in the compound heard that it had come from beyond the fortress. Patch remembered what his father had told him, as he raced for the great doors, whoever controlled the ships would be masters of the fortress. The duridium walls were not disputed themselves, but those who had mastery of the technology the ships still provided, would remain masters of Katowice.

Thagomiser in his fist, the young warrior pounded out of the doors and decided to turn to his left. Behind him Dugazryne took the opposite direction, having enough idea of basic tactics to meet at the ships in a pincer move. The only trouble was the Banteme followed the lama to a man, leaving Patch alone.

He raced around the fortress perimeter and saw figures in the dim glow of Brahma. One held a needle rifle, some of the others seemed to have their hands in the air. Patch almost collided with his uncle and asked breathlessly,

"What happened"?

"They opposed the chief", Vitala responded, "There was a brief skirmish".

Eyes adjusting to the dimness, Patch could see that the two Banteme were on the ground unmoving, shot by needle fire. Laying closer to the captured group were the inert forms of Araz and Doyle. The two female crew of Explorer Three were the prisoners.

"I suggest you get away from here now, corporal", Captain Shevchenko suddenly said evenly to Darren.

"When we now control the fortress by controlling the ships", Darren noted, "Why would I do that"?

"Go aboard", the Russian told him calmly, "And you will find out why".

"Patch with me, Vitala bind the two of them for now, until we decide what to do with them".

"I'm not going anywhere", Amara Kruger complained, "There's no need to tie me up"?

Darren did not reply though, instead he was striding into the ship formerly commanded by Shevchenko, Patch at his shoulder.

"Hades"! the chief suddenly cursed, "I don't believe she's done that".

Patch followed his gaze and saw the red L.E.D.'s calmly counting downward in what his father had taught him were second, minutes and hours, he asked,

"Is that a countdown to launch"?

"No", Darren shook his head, "It's the self destruct mechanism, she's set this ship to destroy itself with the power of the hyper-drive at it's disposal and in twenty hours".

"How do we turn it off"?

"We can't, only she will know the fifteen digit code to do so. If we try and type it in and get three digits incorrect, the ship explodes at that moment. Our chances of guessing it are fifteen to the power of twenty six, effectively zero then".

"Then we must not guess", Patch decided, "And once we have disarmed, can we reset the code ourselves"?

Darren looked at his son in disbelief, "What are you suggesting Patch, torture the captain to get the correct code? She's just as likely to lie and we'll all go up in a titanic explosion, the like of which, this world has never witnessed before".

"I have an idea", the half-breed told his father, the chief, "Can I have immediate custody of Shevchenko, tied up or otherwise"?

"Of course, before you implement your plan though it's your wedding night you should be....."

"This is more important and Myra will understand, I have a night journey to make".

"To where"?

"To see Aaal".

Understanding dawned on Darren's features.

"Take you uncle for additional security and then go, son and good luck".

Three hours later, guided by the light of Brahma the strangest of trio's reached the herd of the Viriligan. The Russian told the half-breed and his Khelac uncle,

"This is a waste of time, I'll tell you nothing, even if you threaten to feed me to the beasts".

"The Viriligan are herbivore, Tara", Patch smiled.

Then he whispered beneath his breath, "Divine cows hear my thoughts, I Patch of the Khelac people need your help to avoid a disaster that unchecked will kill us all? Are you there Aaal"?

Instantly one of the viridian hued giant beasts spoke into Patch' mind, "Aaal is not with this herd at the moment, do you want to know the direction he left us in"?

"Not necessarily, perhaps you can help me"?

The creature of Nyjord regarded him with it's twin set of multi-faceted eyes, "What disaster and how can we help".

Patch asked, "Who are you magnificent cow"?

The reply contained amusement, "Your need to label us as individuals persists I perceive, give us name's if it pleases you"?

"Then I shall call you Uuum and Ooom", Patch decided. "The female with me has a code that will stop a countdown on an explosive device, that will blast this entire area, killing many life forms. Can the two of you read her mind and get me the code, so that I may stop the count"?

"She will resist"?

"With all her mental strength".

"Then the extraction might damage her intellect, this is a consequence that would greatly sadden us".

"And yet if my father, Chief Darn is right, the area of the blast will certainly kill this herd, along with every other living thing in this area".

"Warn the female biped of the danger if she resists our probing", Uuum/Ooom decided and Patch did so.

"Roast in Hades, alien", the Russian woman cursed, "You cannot have the code, if we cannot have the fortress".

"You are welcome in the fortress, under Darn's rule".

"He who calls an alien mutant his son, do you think I would take orders from him, a renegade"?

"I am his son", Patch was puzzled.

"I meant his *'biological'* son, not the term he uses in affection"!

"Tara, I am his biological son", Patch explained. "My mother was a Khelac and gave birth to me when my father lay with her. The pigment has already been explained to you, why do you question this"?

For the first time some of the Russian captain's composure seemed to melt away,

"That cannot be, we only set off in thirty nine, you must surely be in your late teens, or do you mongrel's grow at alarming rates"?

Vitala growled, "My nephew has seen twenty summers. If you mean thirty two thirty nine, then we number the years as you, since Darn became chief and it is thirty two fifty five".

Shevchenko went ashen, "But, that would mean...........".

"It would mean you were in hyper-space, while twenty years passed in ordinary time", Uuum/Ooom suddenly observed and the whole trio received their thoughts.

While Vitala and Shevchenko got over the shock of being suddenly broadcast too by a Viriligan, Patch tried to understand what this revelation meant to he and his small tribe.

"Chief Darn told me that in hyper-space four months passed subjectively. Tara was it the same for you"?

Shevchenko seemed suddenly capable of thought nor speech.

"Tara, were you and the other three in hyper-space for what you counted as four Earth months"?

Finally she admitted, "Yes, but it must be wrong, if Darren only ....".

"You expected hyper-space to have a constant fourth dimension", Uuum/Ooom noted, "Yet it is not matter. Why then should it behave constantly"?

"We took twenty years to get here", the Russian murmured.

"So it would seem and Explorer Two is taking even longer", the twin headed creature noted.

"How can you, a cosmic cow know these things"? Shevchenko demanded.

"Just because we possess no opposing thumb, it does not automatically follow, that we are primitive", the Viriligan broadcast. "We can travel, but not with our bodies, which are admittedly inelegant and clumsy, but instead with our minds. We can leave these shells and travel to areas you cannot even begin to imagine".

Shevchenko suddenly seemed to collapse within herself, "Then with our current technology we cannot hope to colonise new worlds", she observed sullenly.

"Not so", Uuum and Ooom seemed to broadcast in unison. What they said contradicted the stunned Russian.

"We have been to the system that orbits the star you call Sol. There are many worlds, many moons in that system, they are yet to be colonised".

The gentle giant creature went on,

"It will take more effort, some will need artificial systems, but it will give you time to grow as a race and then one day the stars might not be out of your reach".

"I have an urgent report to make to Earth", Shevchenko decided resignedly. "If you take me back to the ship I will input the code and turn off the self destruct. I can no longer justify the destruction of the fortress".

Then her face suddenly became radiant with a smile,

"Our fortress, Patch"!

THE BRAIN MACHINE

ONE

MICRO-SOLDERING WAS A very precise business and one had to possess very steady hands and great concentration to get it exactly right. A slip and the motherboard could be ruined, the entire procedure started from scratch. This was the flux distributor, probably the most vital component in the entire machine and certainly the most costly. It had cost three weeks pay just for that one tiny part. One constituent of what would amount to his great electronic creation. His hands were steady as the tiny point of the soldering iron dipped forward melting the solder and attaching it just right.

Gleve Orchvestige pulled back in his seat for a moment and took out a rag from the pocket of his overalls. With it he wiped the sweat from his bald head, little caring that the action left a trail of penetration oil on his skin. He allowed himself to smile for the first time in a very long period of time. His was the smile of accomplishment and pride. He had realised his creation, now the only thing that could halt his ambition was if it did not work.

Looking at it with a critical eye he saw a device which resembled a woman's hairdryer in no small degree. The chromium bracket bolted to the chair, the cowl ready to slide down over the skull. How it differed however was the fibre optic wires that festooned out of one side of the cowl, running to a keyboard and screen consol off to it's side. Orchvestige had seen illustrations of olde computers in ancient historical magazines and thought the keyboard and screen looked similar. Of course they had not been used for centuries since the pad had replaced their ungainly and not portable nature.

No matter, that part of the Brain Machine was not designed to be moved around. No the *'subject'* would have to be brought to this remote cave in the upper reaches of the Lomonosov crater. Orchvestige had thought of that and had accounted for it, nothing would ruin his plan, he would have Cylvia for himself!

Cylvia Dortbrooke, was the shapely and beautiful red head that Gleve lusted after and the cause of his heartache. For she was living with his own brother, Darcie. Darcie was everything that Gleve was not. Successful, flamboyant, extrovert, charming and devilishly handsome. He was one hundred and ninety three centimetres and seventy eight kilogramme's of lean defined muscle. He had a shock of thick black hair and his features were clean cut and even, with piercing blue eyes. His augmentation in his early teens had made of him, an Adonis.

In sharp contrast to his brother, who was senior by eighteen Earth months, Gleve stood only one hundred and sixty centimetres, yet he also weighed around seventy six kilos, the bulk of which was around his waist. He was bald with muddy brown eyes and had not been augmented when of age, due to lack of funds on their father's part. Not only did he suffer by physical comparison however, but Gleve was introverted and lacked the social graces to be interesting to members of the opposite sex.

Ironically while Gleve was a successful research scientist however, Darcie sold soft drinks to the users of soft drink machines. It made no difference, the elder brother had enjoyed numerous romantic affairs during his teens and early twenties, while Gleve remained a virgin.

Then into the brother's lives came Cylvia Dortbrooke! Slim, yet shapely enough, pale of complexion with emerald eyes, but with a nature that made almost every man she met fall for her almost instantly. She spoke to Gleve and expressed interest in his work, was always kind and patient with his stuttering drawl and he loved her with all his heart. While she was so gentle and kind to one brother however, she shared the bed of the other.

Gleve Orchvestige needed a plan! His brilliant mind conceded one so preposterous, that no other, save one of his brilliance, could have envisioned it. He used his savings to build the laboratory at Lomonosov crater, using a natural cave for the bulk of the interior, but paying dearly to make certain the outside was a fortress.

One that was also invisible to anyone who was not actively searching for it. He had a generator fitted, so he was not dependant on anyone for power, it was backed up by solar panels hidden in Lomonosov crater, but not hidden from the sun. Then, over a period of time, the equipment was brought to the lab. Sometimes at no greater a trickle than a component at a time. It took him six months to build the first 'hood', seven to complete the second and a further two months to connect everything to a computer, which was in fact a modified android brain in a slim metal case. The brain machine was complete, the only way to test it was to use it on two volunteers and Gleve was going to be one of them!

TWO

DARCIE WENT TO the airlock and glanced through the inspection port, he smiled and swung it open.

"Gleve! Come in, this is an unexpected pleasure, where has my little brother been these past months, I've barely seen you"?

The hunched figure of the scientist shuffled over to the french windows and gazed out at his brother's garden,

"Nili is looking good, Darcie, the government grants are certainly helping with the terra-forming of Mars. I've been busy on a project, but otherwise I'm well enough, what about you"?

"Oh working you know", the elder spanned his arms, "Sales are great as usual, what can I get you"?

"Do you have any Earth tea"?

"I actually have some Yorkshire Tea. Did a deal with a rep some time back and he let me have a few ounces. Let me brew you some, come into the kitchen so we can talk".

The strange duo went through the lounge toward the back of the house and Gleve was treated to another view through the rear window of the property.

"I suppose the lichenferns help with the atmosphere", Gleve observed.

"Yes, Nili council has planted them all over the place. It's not just in the English estates either, the Germans, Poles, Scandians and even the American sections are going as green as the red dust will sustain".

"The artificial satellite ozone layer will help keep all this breathable air from floating away when they come online", Gleve observed, "It's only six months away now".

"Is that what you've been working on"?

"No", Gleve was pleased his way in to the desired topic had come so early in their conversation, "Something far more astonishing, that's why I've come to see you".

"Oh"?

"I have a desire to show my brother the project before anyone else".

Darcie flashed an albescent winning smile and asked, "Will it need marketing"?

Gleve nodded, "And I've mentioned our name to my backers and they're interested", he lied.

"Now that calls for a proper drink, little bro, what will you have"? Darcie went over to a cupboard and opening the door revealed a row of spirits. Unwilling to disappoint him, Gleve said,

"Once I've enjoyed this tea I'll have a small sherry with you. If you have some that is"?

Darcie began moving bottles and from the back of the cupboard produced a half bottle of Tio Nico Cream from Earth.

"Come on then, we'll go in the room, have a cuppa and then enjoy a glass while you tell me all about the project"?

Gleve followed his sibling and tried to sound casual as he asked,

"How is Cylvia, well I hope"?

"She's at work right now, but yeah she's great", Darcie supplied not peculiarly helpfully. "So this project little bro, what is it I'm going to be selling"?

"It's a medical device for scanning for brain tumours and taking them out with an internal laser", Gleve lied glibly, "It will save quite a few lives Darcie and will also be useful as a diagnostic instrument".

"Should be easy to shift then", Darcie enthused, "What sort of salary and commission will I be on do you reckon"?

"The basic is only twelve thousand", Gleve lied carefully, wanting to make it sound realistic, "But Steamans want good figures for this and for every product you sell there will be a bonus of five hundred".

Darcie sipped his drink then he asked, "This is shillin we're talking about, not Marks, nor Zlotys"?

"Shillins Darcie and with that sort of bonus, you should do fairly well".

"In shillins little bro I'll do some serious business. Can you stay, we have to go out tonight and paint Nili with some Orchvestige colour".

"I'm not sure about going mad, but the three of us could enjoy a decent meal at a nice restaurant, my treat".

Darcie reached for his pad, "I'd better ping Cylvia then, let her know, you now how women are with surprise do's".

Gleve nodded, but he had no idea how women were on many topics. He waited patiently while his brother pinged the woman *he Gleve,* desired.

"Hi babe", he heard his brother begin, it was sickening to hear him. ""Guess who I'm with? No go on guess, oh alright then, my big brother and he's just completed a project that makes me his new marketing director. Of course I'm being serious. No it's not some new soft drink. Anyway that's not why I've pinged you, we're going out tonight to celebrate, then he can tell you all about it. He's taking us to dinner, oh, I'll ask him. Where are you taking us bro"?

"I thought Carlo's", Gleve knew the girl would agree to the nicest place in Nili.

Sure enough she agreed and they set the time for twenty hundred hours.

"You can get ready here", Darcie enthused, "You've still that deep blue boho shirt in my closet and a pair of black breeks".

The creator of the brain machine agreed with a nod, it was going to be too easy!

Cylvia looked absolutely stunning in a diaphanous frock of royal blue, decorated with tiny silver crystal beads. The garment was just shear enough to see a hint of nipple on the superbly pert breasts and Gleve tried his best not to stare.

"Keep your eyes off my girlfriends tits", Darcie joked coarsely, causing the girl to wince at her boyfriend's crudity. She really was a stupid creature, preferring Darcie with his crude ways and poor job, to a man with greater brain power and sensibility.

They had lean Dodoprot breasts in garlic butter with asparagus tips and sortees for their main course. Then Darcie had a syrup pudding while Gleve and the girl went for lemon sorbet, for drinks they had a lovely Californian white wine, sweet side of neutral. As they were sipping Colombian coffee Cylvia asked Gleve about the new project and the opportunity it would give her boyfriend.

Gleve told her the same lie, he had fobbed his brother off with. The only difference was, this time he stumbled over his words, tongue tied in the beauty's presence.

"Come on Bro, spit it out", Darcie teased and Gleve was at least thankful to see the girl frown in his defence.

When the fabrication was done, Cylvia remarked, "Well Darcie, this means you'll owe your brother a deep debt of gratitude, I certainly hope you won't let him down".

Darcie shrugged, "When have I ever failed to sell product"? he needed to know.

Cylvia shrugged, "Yes you're certainly capable of selling a bill of goods, that's for certain".

Gleve realised then, that perhaps all was not well in paradise, but it did not deter him from his plan, he had worked too hard, sacrificed too much for him to give up, when he was at the cusp of realising his ambition.

At the end of the evening Cylvia suddenly took hold of his hand and looked into his eyes and said,

"Thank you for what you're doing, Gleve, you're a good brother".

The scientist melted, feeling the softness of the skin of her fingers, so delicate and perfect, he gazed into her beautiful eyes and for the merest instant they locked and then she looked away.

Had he hesitated for the merest moment before that gaze, he could not now, his resolve had just been cast in impenetrable stone, the plan must go on.

THREE

"IT'S SORT OF creepy in here, Bro", Darcie remarked, half in jest.

They were standing in the laboratory, that inhabited the cave at Lomonosov crater. Had not Gleve been the guide, Darcie would never have found the cleverly concealed and fortified entrance. The scientist had deliberately taken the flitter to the rear of the crater and then the two of them had walked to it's only entrance and exit.

Gleve touched the plate that turned on the generator and at the same instant activated the light emitting diodes screwed into the rock ceiling of the cavern. Most of the equipment used to create the hoods was now safely tucked away in huge metal cabinet's that lined the walls, this made the two seats and hoods of the brain machine even more impressive.

"Cream eh"? Darcie mused as he circumnavigated the two seats, "You could have done them in something a bit more inspirational, a bit more imposing, Bro".

"What the scanning devices inside the hoods do, is all that needs to impress, Darcie, not the paint job of the metal casements", Gleve returned, stung by the adverse criticism.

"Don't get upset", Darcie said, looking at the monitor and keyboard, both were mainly black. "I can sell anything, despite what it might look like in a brochure mockup, but I would consider royal blue".

"Paper"! Gleve forgot for the moment that most of what they were discussing was not going to become reality, "You think to print on tree pulp when everyone has pads"?

"Brochures have tactile advantage", his brother explained, "They can be left with potential customers, or even mailed to abodes".

"Mailed? Do you know how much Mars mailing service charges?! No Darcie, this product will sell itself once it appears on the net, believe me".

"I don't really see why you need me then", the salesman sulked and his bottom lip actually stuck out like an infants.

'Hades, how I hate you', Gleve thought, but instead said, "So, are you ready for a demonstration"?

"Sure", Darcie bounced back, "Strap me in and lower one of those crazy hats, I've often wondered what my brain looks like. It's my second favourite organ".

He seated himself in the chair closest the keyboard and Gleve was forced to instruct, "No, not that one, the other".

"What's the difference"? Darcie wanted to know.

"The hood closest the keyboard is the control, I will be under that".

"I thought you were scanning my brain? What do you need to be under the other one for, why not just operate the keyboard"?

"It's complicated, but basically the machine works comparatively", Gleve began, he had expected this very question. "By looking at a healthy brain and it's functions, i.e. mine and then looking at your's, it will see any comparative abnormalities. Of course we hope there are none to see in your case, but this is how our patients will be examined. Don't worry Darcie, take your seat, all will be well".

It was too easy, the dope obliged with a nervous grin on his face and then made the ludicrous comment,

"Of course there's nothing wrong with my brain so there's no need to worry is there"?

"I just think that in order to sell the product, you have to know exactly how it works and how it *'feels'* to be a subject of it, don't you agree"?

"Bang on, Bro, plumb. So, let's do it"?

Gleve lowered the hood onto his brothers head and began to strap him securely to the seat.

"Hey, why the restraints"? Darcie wanted to know.

"Just in case you experience a physical jerk, I don't want you injuring yourself whilst the machine scans you, there's nothing to worry about".

In resignation, the trusting brother let himself be secured to his chair in such a way that he could not free himself, only someone else could do that.

Satisfied, Gleve took his position in the other piece of furniture and lowered the hood onto his own head. The keyboard was before him and he began to activate the brain machine.

The first sensation Gleve felt was a gnawing at the edges of his cerebral cortex, a sort of itching sensation as the electric tendrils of the machine intruded into it. The machine began to sift through thirty three billion neurons, which were each connected by synapses to several thousand other neurons. The machine began to copy the neurons communicating with them and copying them. It ran down his long protoplasmic fibres called axons, carrying trains of signal pulses down his action potentials to distant parts of his brain targeting specific recipient cells. The entire process was then loaded down onto the machine's hard drive.

Simultaneously the entire process had been duplicated in his brother's brain by means of the first hood. Two images appeared on the screen of the computer-plex. Icon's of brains, or rather the patterns of the neurons that made each man essentially himself. Then Gleve began the second process.

The brain wiping!!

This he only did on his brother, leaving his own brain untouched. Once the process was completed Darcie was no longer a functioning human and within seconds his body would begin to shut down. Before that happened Gleve cut and pasted his own icon into his brother's brain and began the process of automatically repeating it with himself. While the neurons of Gleve were filtering down into the brain of his brother, his own were being wiped and replaced automatically with those of Darcie. Gleve lost consciousness and awareness, he fell into a black dreamless period of unconsciousness.

He awoke in the first chair and said calmly but firmly, "That's it Darcie come and undo my straps".

Automatically, still unaware of what was happening, the other figure did as commanded, for Gleve had also imprinted onto those neurons the compulsion to do what Darcie's voice instructed.

Gleve arose to his full one hundred and ninety three centimetres and seventy eight kilogramme's of lean defined muscle. He said quickly,

"Now get in the first chair again Darcie"?

The one hundred and sixty centimetre body that now belonged to Darcie did as directed. Lowering his seventy six kilos, the bulk of which was around his waist into the first chair. Gleve looked at the baldness, glanced into the muddy brown eyes with his own piercing blue ones. Now he was the Adonis, while his numbed and useless brother was inside the husk that the older brother had always hated.

"Go to sleep Darcie", he commanded and the muddy brown eyes closed and the bald head nodded.

Gleve took an intravenous line and slid it into his brothers vein, then he catheterised him, a process he found incredibly distasteful. When he was done, Darcie would live in a coma state for several days, while Gleve would be free to move around in his body, no one could possibly guess that the man they spoke to, would be the creator of the Brain Machine. The plan was an unmitigated success.

FOUR

G LEVE ORCHVESTIGE HAD left the cavern and sealed it so that it was once more a fortress. Not only impenetrable, but also very difficult to detect in remote Lomonosov. He had walked around to the rear of the crater and taken the flitter back to Nili. Without hesitation, he drove back to his brother's house and relaxed with a drink.

He was waiting.

Waiting for Cylvia Dortbrooke to return from work. Waiting for her to return to him, Gleve.

When the airlock opened he could hardly contain his excitement. He rushed to her and took her in his arms and kissed her pationately. It felt just like he had always guessed it would, it felt fantastic. He, Gleve, had the girl of his dreams, she was now hiss.

"My what a welcome", she gasped, "What's the occasion Darcie"?

"I just know how lucky I am", he told her, "To have such a beautiful and wonderful woman as my girlfriend, get a bath and change, I'm taking you out for dinner".

"That's sweet of you, but it's been a long day babe and I'm tired, do you mind if we stay in? I'll cook"?

"No, staying in's fine, and I'll cook while you get bathed and changed". He offered quite amiably.

Cylvia frowned, "Are you feeling yourself"? She wanted to know, "You never cook".

344

"Well tonight, I'll try", he promised, "Just don't complain if it's not perfect".

"Of course darling, you have a go if you feel like it", she smiled and Gleve's heart melted even more.

Gleve went into the kitchen and hunted around for ingredients, fortunately having visited in the past, he managed quite well and once he had the food stuffs, he was quite expert in making something more than edible.

Later, Cylvia drifted into the kitchen and smiled, sniffing appreciatively,

"Smells nice", she enthused, "You're full of surprises tonight Darcie. We both know the reason for the effort of course"!

"Ready in ten", he told her, wondering what that might be, "Go and put some music on sweetheart".

Then it hit!

He was suddenly back in the cavern, securely trussed up into the chair, tubes inserted into his body! It only lasted for perhaps five seconds, but it shook him, it was not something he could account for nor had expected.

"I put on some........Darcie! What's the matter you've gone as white as a sheet", Cylvia was back in the kitchen.

"Probably hunger", he lied, it was something he was getting quite expert at. "I'll be fine once we've eaten".

"Oh, right, well your colour's coming back so you might be right. Be careful with hot pans babe".

He promised he would.

The meal was a delight, Gleve simply watched her eat, consuming little himself. They watched the news on the trivid and then it was time to retire.

I'm going to do her', he thought in triumph, *I'm going to do her as she's never been done before'*. He could barely contain himself. They undressed and got into a knave size bed, but as he leaned over to kiss her, marvelling at the silky smoothness of her naked breasts she suddenly exploded sternly,

"I've been nice, as I promised, Darcie, but there'll be none of that you blackguard rapscallion".

"I don't understand", Gleve murmured in absolute frustration and guilt, "What have I done wrong darling"?

"You're pretending to forget, after only a fortnight you swine", she was incredulous, "Two words Darcie, Jemima Blacklabour".

Darcie's secretary!!

"That was a stupid and terrible mistake", Gleve tried as he thought it at the same instant, "Let's put it behind us, please, I love you, love you more than any man has ever loved any woman".

"Mistake", she echoed coldly, "I suppose your dick just fell into her lady's garden by mistake. More than once too, an incredible mistake, Darcie".

'You supreme fool', Gleve thought, *'You fool of fools Darcie, to cheat on this divine creature, what where you thinking'*

He tried, "Forgive me my sweet, show me you forgive me"?

"Oh I know you've been trying, Darcie," the girl responded, "But I'm sticking to what we agreed, for six months we'll live as brother and sister and then, well, I'll think about it some more".

'Six months! Frenging Hades, how can I wait that long', Gleve's mind wailed. He said, "All I know is that I love you".

"And I love you, that's why I'm still here. But you need to prove to me that you've changed, Darcie and that's going to take time".

She turned over, away from him and went to sleep while he remained sitting up, wondering at the supreme folly of his imbecile of a brother. Finally exhaustion claimed him and he lay down miserably and fell asleep.

He dreamed he was back in the cavern and in the chair, back in his own body, Darcie was standing over him,

"It will not work", the standing brother told the seated, "You cannot pass yourself off as me, not at work. You're no salesman Gleve, you'll be found out and imprisoned. Body stealing has to be against the law".

"I want Cylvia, give her to me, then I will swap us back", Gleve promised.

"And you think she'll want you as you are"? Darcie scoffed and his brother knew that he was right, "Just get yourself a couple of whores and clean out your tubes that way, Cylvia will never be yours".

"She's not your's either", Gleve cried, "Not after what you did, with your secretary as well, it's so predictable, Darcie, why, why cheat on such a beautiful and intelligent woman as she, what were you thinking"?

"Oh come on, you've seen the ebon crumpet, she was gagging for it and I was not thinking with my big head, just my little one".

"You disgust me".

"And you have committed an act of larceny on a new scale of infamy", Darcie observed.

He was never so eloquent in real life and Gleve thought he was dreaming and with a supreme effort woke himself. It was three in the morning!

Six months, could Gleve possibly hope to survive the deception for so long? He knew when morning came he would have to go to Darcie's place of work, take his brother's place and try to fool all his work colleagues. He fretted about it until six and then a buzzing sound from the bed-side chrono told him at least one of them had to rise and he was exhausted.

"Turn it off", Cylvia murmured, "See you this evening, honey".

'Honey; honey'! Gleve's mind raged, *'Why call me a term of endearment if you're not going to let me tup you'?*

He arose and showered, not bothering to depilate his face, his brother should have had the procedure, if he didn't want to wear a beard. Having no appetite he skipped breakfast and walked out to his brother's flitter. Gleve had never driven a Fiat 278HP before and the power of the sports model made him nervous. He took it steadily however and made it into Fossae without incident. He strode into the offices of 'SoftizRuz' as though he was confident, but he was anything but.

He had to consult a board to see where his office was and it was on the third floor, he took the lift up. Exiting he entered through a door bearing his brother's name and who should he see first but Jemima Blacklabour. There was no doubting the Negress obvious charms. With her thick ebon hair and her fine cheekbones and that was before one looked lower and then the enhancements really reaped benefits.

"Morning handsome", she said, gazing at Gleve as she rose and rounded the desk.

Before he had time to think, she was in his arms and kissing him passionately and he felt his brother's body respond in the appropriate manner.

"Your office", she breathed into his ear and Gleve thought,

'Well I missed out last night, why not, after all it will pop my cherry'!

He was half way through doing the business though, when he suddenly found himself being dragged back to the cavern,

'No'! his mind raged, but he still endured a few seconds in the chair, helplessly strapped into place, tubes inserted into himself, before he flicked back to the office.

Jemima, half dressed was looking at him curiously, "What you mean you're not yourself, then who are you"? She demanded.

"It's nothing, I was having an illusion; now where were we".

"I was getting dressed again", she told him coldly, "And you were trying to explain why you only lasted a few seconds, but don't worry, it happens to all my men sometimes. Anyway, right now I have some work to do and you have some clients to visit".

'I don't believe it! I missed it, just how long can my bad luck last', Gleve thought, *'More importantly why these inconvenient flashbacks, the swap should have been permanent'.*

He waited for Jemima to dress and then clicked on his brother's pad, his diary had three appointments,

'Metrochemicals', in Issidis Planitia, 'Binary Coding' also in Issidis Planitia and finally 'Huygens Mining', in Huygens. It was going to be a long day! He had no idea if the appointments were merely for repeat orders, or if he was expected to try and sell SoftizRuz to a new client and he dare not ask. It was certain

Darcie would have known and the last thing he wanted was for questions about him and the state of his mind or memory to begin being investigated.

So he climbed back in the Fiat and drove carefully to Issidis Planitia, which was a thriving metropolis and great investment and building projects were being undertaken there. The sun was shining weakly and with the various attempts to terra-form the planet, the current temperature was twenty two degrees. Taking his last deep breath of dust free air, Gleve left the flitter and strode quickly to the offices of Metrochemicals. He introduced himself as his brother and the receptionist ushered him to a waiting room come lounge, with several appreciative glances at his physique and handsomeness. Now he knew the constant temptations Darcie had been subject too. With Cylvia at home though, he had been a fool to stray, especially in his own back yard.

"Mister Orchvestige", a woman's voice asked, it belonged to a sharp faced thin woman of about forty.

Gleve rose and offered his hand, "Yes".

The woman sniffed and did not take it. "I'm Erin Stridequater, I can give you three quarters of an hour. We already have machines in position and we already have a supplier, but we're always looking to cut down on costs so speak".

It was a grim offer, he was not even ushered to an office, it seemed he was expected to sell to her in the waiting area. Glancing about him for the first time, he spotted the machine, it was a Hitachi Fruitwenty. Gleve glanced at his pad and began,

"I'm sure we can supply some products for you at very competitive prices Mz Stridequater, or may I call you Erin"?

"No, you may not", came the terse reply, "What sort of prices are we talking about, single and bulk if you please"?

Gleve hastily consulted his pad, "Ten cans of Colemar Cherry will only be thirty sestersius, that's only three sestersius' a can"

"Colemar Cherry? You don't do Roamacola, our employees like Roamacola"?

"Roamacola is an Orang-U-Can product ma'am, I'm from SoftizRuz".

"A pity", Stridequater sniffed, "Roamacola is four a can, but the staff are used to it. Does Colemar taste similar"?

Colemar Cherry is cherry flavoured Mz Stridequater", Gleve told her patiently, "Not cola flavoured".

"What else do you have to offer then"?

"For the same low introductory price I can offer you Limezade", Gleve tried, using every micron of his imagination, "A delicious and refreshing fizzy lime flavoured experience in a can".

"Just lime"?

"I beg your pardon"?

"Is it lime only, we currently have Lemlime".

Gleve did not need to consult his pad to know that Lemlime was a Misterfizz product.

"For three a can"?

It's four, but the staff like it very much and I would not be happy replacing it with an inferior product".

Inferior!

Gleve let it go, no sense in arguing with a customer, or not; as the case was rapidly proving.

"I have another delicious offering", Gleve began uncertainly, Orangafizz, twenty cans for fifty sestersius, now that's the best price on the market".

"We already have Orang-U-Can", Stridequater glared at Gleve, "Why on Mars would we go for some cheap imitation"?

"Alright, what about Strawbfresh, Lemonster and Fruitastic cans, only thirty five sestersius for ten cans, they come in a........."

"Thirty five, the price has gone up"!

"Yes, that's because instead of a can the flavours are available in a ....".

"We already have Strawbulite, that comes in a carton and U-Fruit".

From Orang-U-Can yet again.

"Our final offering is an energy drink, we call it Red-Z, after the colour of our home world. It boosts energy and therefore productivity, do you already have an energy drink Mz Stridequater"?

"We have some cans of Protonic, but they don't sell very well", the hard faced woman was forced to admit. "It might be that our staff don't want energy drinks"?

"I've tasted Protonic, have you ma'am"?

"Why no, what are you suggesting"?

"It tastes of lichen and it's made from lichen, I can assure you that Red-Z is infinitely superior in every way and only forty five sestersius for ten cans".

"Expensive then"!

"Not our most cost effective product, but quality. How many can I interest you in as an initial order. I must tell you anything less than two hundred cans will incur carriage costs however".

Gleve strode out of Metrochemicals feeling three metres tall, he had sold two hundred cans to the bitch!

FIVE

GLEVE COLLAPSED INTO a seat. The rest of his day had been a waste of time and energy. His appointment at Binary Coding had been cancelled, had he not received a ping? While the fiasco at Huygens Mining had resulted in zero sales chiefly because the mine did not have a drinks machine.

He lit a med-cig, his hands shaking with fatigue, he'd missed lunch and had not had so much as a drink all day. Darcie's life was not the idyllic existence he had supposed it to be.

Then another spasm hit him. For two seconds he was back in the cavern, trussed up like a criminal and unable to even see daylight. When he flicked back, he began to feel a certain sympathy for his unconscious brother. It was not the easiest of jobs, he had trouble at work and trouble at home and he had a brother who had surpassed him in all but is relationship with a woman who wanted nothing to do with him for half a year. The door way of the inner air lock sounded a hissing movement and Cylvia entered,

"You look beat, bad day"? She asked with a certain dread in her tone.

"Exhausting and disappointing, thank good ness I've you to come home to my sweet", he managed tiredly.

Cylvia looked shocked. "You mean you're not going to have one of your massive sulks and ruin our evening"?

Gleve climbed to his feet, realising it was his mind that was tired, not his super new body,

"No darling, I'm home now and what went on at work was nothing to do with my lovely girlfriend, now then, what would you like me to make us for dinner"?

Later in bed, Cylvia said out of the blue, "I'm beginning to think you a changed man Darcie".

"How so"? He tried to sound casual, but his heart was beater quickly, how could she possibly suspect the truth?

"Your response to your bad day", she reasoned, "It was not how you usually deal with disappointment, your sulk's have been an issue with us for many a month".

"I'm guilty as charged and promise never to self indulge again", he told her earnestly.

"Good night then I hope you can keep to that".

At the end of a tortuous week, Gleve got a summons from Darcie's boss. He tapped on the door with some considerable trepidation and heard the bark to enter through the plastic.

"You asked for me, sir"?

"Sir?! Ruddy Hades it's worse than I thought", came the reply. "I've been getting remarks hither and thither about you Darcie. Strangely conflicting remarks at that. Some say you've changed for the better in your demeanour, your attitude to your fellow sales force, some tell me you have become forgetful and vague regarding details and then, Darcie and then, my once salesman of the month fifteen weeks in succession, there's this weeks effort....."

Obviously the boss was expecting some sort of excuse, that was the reason for him halting mid sentence, but Gleve merely waited,

"You're not going to give me some half assed excuse are you?" The man was incredulous, "Are you just going to stand there and keep shtum"?

"The product has competition sir", Gleve began, "Some times superior competition for quality, sometimes cheaper competition that does not match our own, but the customer is too mean to order better. I tried my best this week, it was not always fruitful".

"Did you use your usual blags? I especially like the one about the competition being possibly carcinogenic".

"Car...I've told customers in the past that Orang-U-Can could give them cancer"?

"What's the matter with you Darcie, it was your own idea, why didn't you use it, do you need a vacation, because you've weeks built up, more than any other employee as a matter of fact".

Gleve seized on the opportunity, "I have been a bit jaded chief. You know what, that's a great idea of yours, could I take some time off please"?

"Get out of here Darcie and don't come back for two weeks", the boss ordered disappointed, but understanding, "When you return, I want the old Darcie, or I may have to consider steps".

"I can't just stroll into work and demand two weeks vacation, Darcie", Cylvia complained, when he told her, "And I know why you're trying and appreciate the effort, but it's simply going to take time".

"That's a shame", he began, as he had rehearsed with himself, "I understand England is very beautiful at this time of year".

"England"? She echoed, just as she knew she would, "England on Earth"?!

"That's where I thought I'd take you yes".

"But we can't afford that sort of vacation"?

Darcie couldn't, but Gleve was not short of money due to his grants for research, he lied glibly,

"I've had a bonus, got the tickets this morning in point of fact, the rocket leaves Biblis Patera for Dishforth - Yorkshire, on Thursday. Now are you certain you cannot get the time off, I could always take Gleve"?

"No! No don't take Gleve", the girl grinned, "I'll get the time off and Darcie, this is a wonderful surprise".

Gleve got to hold the girl for the second time and the kiss was just as good as it had been then.

Gleve drove to Biblis Patera, he was sufficiently used to the Fiat that he opened her up on the motorhigh and sometimes reached one hundred and thirty kilometres an hour when it was safe to do so.

They had their intravenous shots and then boarded a Quinstar Express, both were understandably nervous, for neither had flown before. The take off was smooth however and once in space it was not even possible to determine movement of any sort. At Cylvia's insistence, the moment the green diode told them it was safe to unstrap, they floated for'ard to the stellarium and gazed for over an hour at the stars and the tiny blue and green pebble that was the Earth. Even in that hour it changed from a speck to a marble and they knew that the cold-fusion engine was whisking them to the home of mankind, at a phenomenal velocity.

The longer they were away from Mars, the more Cylvia seemed to relax with Gleve and the more he considered it impossible for him to experience another spasm of brain shift. It was less than twelve hours before they were forced to strap back into their cradles and planet entry began. The engines roared for a brief period, then the next sound was that of the heat shields of the underbelly of the rocket at is scorched it's way into the Yorkshire sky. All too soon there was a dull thump which shook the entire vessel and then the captain's voice informed them they had landed safely at Dishforth and could begin disembarking once the green diode permissioned them.

When the airlock opened Gleve immediately smelled something strange. He was to learn later that it was a combination of tarmac and grass. He also felt movement and knew without asking that it was a wind which was free of red dust. They waited patiently for the other passengers to get off and then leisurely made their way toward customs and border check. It was strange, but they did not feel like alien's and yet they had no Earth citizenship and had only visa's for two weeks. Both of them felt very heavy and sluggish in their movements, Earth gravity was pressing down upon them relentlessly.

A flitter in the bay for such vehicles was waiting for customers and once they had their luggage, which was light, they took one ready for the drive to Northalerton, which was perfectly placed for their stay at the Moors. They booked into the Moor Hotel and then had an hour on the bed, for the gravity would take some getting used to.

"This was an unexpected pleasure and wonderful idea Darcie", Cylvia admitted, "Thank you for doing it. Did you see the sky before we came inside, how blue it was? Did you hear the avifauna, they were so noisy, what a wondrous place Earth is"?

"I agree", Gleve smiled, "It's hard to believe man almost destroyed it in the dark ages of the twenty second century. I wonder how the shield is coming on around Venus' far side"?

"Put the tri-d on if you want, I'm too excited to doze"?

Gleve did and found English Broadcaster Company, or EBC as it was popularly known. The shield was completed. Huge dish shaped foil satellites that would deflect the fierceness of the sun away from the planet's surface. In half a Venus' year that side would turn to face the sun and the green house effect would be stopped. Then the construction of more dish on the night/winter side would be constructed at the same time as the sulphuric acid would be filtered from the surface. it was believed by scientists that the first colonists would be on Venus in the next decade.

"I can't imagine living on a world with six months day and six months night and how cold the winter would be, and how hot the summer, all under bubbles as well, until plants can be designed that can survive such extremes".

Gleve told her, "Lichen from Callisto is already being genetically engineered to create something that can survive the projected winter's of Venus, the problem will be the six months or so that the planet faces the sun. The main problem on Venus will be water. Vast containers of ice will need to be shipped from night side to day, but at considerable cost and it's projected by the corporations that the price of water on Venus will be higher than the price of pure silver".

"I never realised you were so interested in such things Darcie? You've never spoken of such matters before"?

"I'm growing up Cylvia, for you darling and deeply regret some of my past mistakes".

The girl scowled but did not mention the biggest, which was always on her mind, instead she said,

"I hope so Darcie. Well, I feel strong enough to venture out into this wonderful world for an hour or two what do you say"?

They hired a flitter and drove to the moors, ate a picnic and marvelled at the beauty of Earth's raw nature. Fatigue soon gripped them though and they returned to the hotel to shower and have another rest before going down for supper. It was not easy to eat in the oppressive gravity, but they did their best and Cylvia said to Gleve over a glass of superb Italian wine,

"This is the first time I've been happy, Darcie, since I found out".

She had finished the sentence and Gleve said hopefully,

"I never expect you to forget Cylvia, but I do hope you can one day find it in your heart to at least forgive me"?

"We'll see", she promised, but her tone was light and hopeful and Gleve cursed his stupid brother, not for the first time in his life.

When the first inter-planetary spasm hit Gleve he was astonished as much as horrified, he felt the pull, then an easing and then a second pulling sensation with more ferocity than any of the others that had preceded it. He was back in the cavern and not for just a fleeting moment, but for thirty seconds. he could feel, that despite the feed and drainage system that was sustaining his body, that it was weaker, it was the beginning of a decline, of that, there could be no doubt.

Gleve considered his feelings about that. He had always hated his appearance and body, would it's demise upset him? With it's death though, he would be guilty of the homicide of his brother, all that was essentially Darcie, was trapped within that fleshly prison. That afforded Gleve a stab of regret and guilt, but it did not lessen his resolve in any great measure.

He Gleve; was now Darcie. He would leave the pathetic job and set up a lab of his own, do freelance research and make a decent living for he and Cylvia. She would question Darcie's sudden move into the field his brother had previously been expert in, but what could she think? Could she suspect the truth? Was it not too fantastic? Easier to believe his lie, which would be that his brother had been schooling him, before his strange disappearance and that Darcie was honouring his memory by continuing his work. Yes it would all fall into place and Darcie unfortunately, *'must'* die!

SIX

THE RETURN TO Mars was both sad and a relief. They had never gotten tired of walking the moors beneath a sky of blue with white clouds scudding across them. Never tired of the size of a sun that made life possible in all the solar system, they delighted in the appearance of goats, sheep, rabbits and the myriad birds, none of which they had seen before. However, the endless crushing gravity made the whole thing exhausting and as they stepped off the pad at Biblis Patera, it was with a spring in their step and the realisation that they were Martian's!

Gleve got better at being Darcie in that he began to improve his sales technique. Added to which, more importantly to him, his relationship with Cylvia began to improve on a daily basis. The wall she had built between them was being pulled down a brick at a time.

The spasms though, became more frequent and lasted for greater duration, but Gleve hesitated from returning to the cavern, he did not want to behold his own husk, that was beginning to fail. The body that was his brother's prison and would become his tomb. Although he could not kill his own body, he fervently hoped that when it expired, the spasm's would cease; could not, in fact, continue. He vowed never to return to the crater of Lomonosov, for if he did and was spotted, he would be executed for homicide. On Mars, murder rape and aggravated burglary all carried the death penalty. Only on Earth was capital punishment still not used, the Moon and Callisto were in line with Mars and the Poles and Romanians were also committed to continuing it on Venus, once it was colonised.

On the news, which Gleve followed avidly, all the stations were focusing on the preparations for the launch of Explorer Four. Once again it would be a multi-national affair, once again the English were excluded, since the infamy of Corporal Darren who was now under sentence of death for betraying his country and mankind. Darren was known as the Diabolical Nyjordic and the worlds of the solar system were fearful for the fate of both Explorer's Two and Three. Gleve felt a certain sympathy for the Englishman, he had seen the trivid's of the planet that Earth had decreed should be called Proxima Prime and it possessed an alien beauty that eclipsed everything in the solar system save for Earth itself. Had he been aboard Explorer One, he too might have gone native on the distant lands.

He had just turned off the station when Cylvia drifted into their bedroom. He noticed at once that she had used perfume, Lavender Essence, almost a shillin a vase. She was also adorned in a diaphanous flimsy garment that left nothing to the imagination. Gleve could not help but stare at her lithe and desirable body.

"Is this some new punishment, sweetheart"? He asked her, "If so I am tormented to distraction and consider me truly repentant".

"Come here"? was all she commanded and his heart leaped into his mouth.

She touched a stud and the nightdress fell to her ankles, "I am weak", she told him, "I can deny us no longer".

Her mouth was on his then and he cupped her perfect breasts and felt his brother's body respond to the incredible temptation. His brother's body, that was now his!

They fell onto the bed and her hands were suddenly frantic, stripping him of his night attire.

He went to slide down her body, knowing it was what many women delighted in experiencing, but she gasped,

"No, Darcie, maybe later, right now I want you too much to wait, I want you inside me".

He found her wet and partly open to receive him and slid into her with a gasp of absolute delight. They were hurried, fervent and despite his incredible arousal, she hit the big one first and then, unable to contain himself any longer, he spurted himself into her with gasps and a racing heart that threatened to burst.

They lay in each other's arms panting with the violence of their climax'.

"I love you Cylvia", he said, but she remained silent. "I love only you and will do so until the day I die", he added.

Then the spasm hit!

He was in the cavern and his body was wasted and close to death, he struggled to gain each breath. The tube that had been supplying him with nutrients was empty, exhausted. Even without the restraints, he could not have raised himself from the chair in his depleted condition. The cavern had become a tomb. No one could reach it in time, even if they could get past the myriad and complex locking system on the concealed entrance. He felt great pain in his gut, the emptiness of starvation, his limbs were racked with the cramps of wastedness. His forehead burned with fever and his head pounded.

This time a whole minute passed.

With rheumy eyes he glanced again at the chrono on his pathetically thin wrist.

A second minute began to count the seconds................

PLANET OF THE DEAD

ONE

IT HAD BEEN night for one hundred and twenty one days. It had been winter for one hundred and twenty one days. The planet had it's back to the sun and would not turn toward it for one hundred and twenty two days. The world was Venus. It's winter was as long as it's night due to its torpid rotation in the opposite direction to every other main body that man inhabited. Jaklok was a settler, his home land was Romania, the king of which, had sponsored the settlement known as Ember Caves.

Jaklok was an engineer and he kept the generator and other vital systems of the dome running smoothly. He was proud to be in the post, there had been talk that the first wave of settlers were to consist entirely of androids, but the Poles had put paid to that notion. They had landed on Venus ahead of Romania, they had all been human and they had erected the dome at the Nexus.

Poland it was that would be forever in the record books for settling the solar system most inhospitable of worlds. When that world chose to turn itself toward the sun however, that was when Venus would generate enough solar energy to power Earth, the Moon, Mars and Callisto and have some to spare. That was why Venus was so important to man's expansion into space. It was also why any choosing to settle there would earn more in three months than they could previously in a Terran year.

The main function of the Ember Caves settlement was the collection and storage of sulphuric acid, this was then taken from the planet by cargo vessel and sold to the industries that used it. The acid was the most commonly used in industrial applications, these included: fertilizers, pharmaceuticals, gasoline, batteries, paper bleaching, sugar bleaching, water treatment, sulfonation agents, cellulose fibres, steel manufacturing, colouring agents, amino acid intermediates and regeneration of ion exchange resins.

Now Poland and Romania were growing into rich countries as a result of the labours of people like Jaklok.

He had finished his shift and was taking the northern spoke to his habitant when possibly the very first incident occurred! He was on the tube and a man, who had no seat, was standing close by. He was holding onto the stabilising handle that hung from an appropriate rail. He had been pale when he boarded, in fact Jaklok had almost given him his seat until he heard him ask the conductor for a ticket, speaking in Romanian rather than standard. A provincial, a peasant, maybe even a gypsy.

Now his colour had changed from it's former wan waxy complexion, to a very unhealthy grey and he began to cough. Jaklok was glad to get off at his stop which was next on the line. His abode was not far from the station, for no one's abode was as yet. There were just not that many settlers on the world of ice and storm. For when the planet finally did turn it's back to the sun, the twilight area produced winds of unimaginable speed, some even exceeding the speed of the grim world's rotation. Hitting the correct code, Jaklok entered the airlock of his quite splendid apartment. No cramped quarters for the chief engineer of Ember Caves.

As expected Lynlea was in the kitchen making his dinner. She finished before Jaklok, having an administrative post in the dome and therefore started their evening meal, although they sometimes finished it together.

"Evening darling", Jaklok greeted her with a hug and a kiss, almost absently tucking the strand of brown hair behind her ear, as she did hundred's of times per day. That one strand that refused to stay in her head band.

"Evening, it's always evening", she smiled, she looked tired.

"You look like you've had a long day why don't you go and take a shower and I'll finish dinner".

Nine times out of ten she would have refused, but this time she nodded, as though she were almost too fatigued to speak. She went into the bathroom, slipped out of her overalls and had a long sonic shower, water was too precious to waste in bathing. Everyone wore overalls, the freighters had too much precious cargo to make room for variations in garments. Jaklok was glad of it, it was a great leveller, although strictly speaking he answered to no one, not even the bergermeister, who was supposed to be the supreme authority in the bubble. Without the generator and filtration plant he would die with all the others however and he treat Jaklok with grudging respect. Their attitude was one of silent toleration of one another, but they could not be said to like each other.

By the time Lynlea had finished and changed into lounge shorts and singlet, Jaklok had the dinner on the table.

They were having protein stew, a combination of soy, lichen, beets, potatoes and carrots, the flavouring made it quite palatable. No having much expensive water, they drank Martian Lichenbeer which had very little alcohol and therefore did not dehydrate. They ate in silence for a while and then Jaklok observed,

"Do you think you might be coming down with something sweetheart".? He went on to tell her of the man on the tube. She listened politely her eyes dull with either fatigue or the beginnings of fever.

"I think I spent too much time at the console today", she finally offered the explanation, but it did not sound as though even she believed it.

"Tell you what then, why don't you go and watch a bit of tri-vid in bed and then have an early? I'll sanitise the dishes and then watch a bit in the lounge, so as not to disturb you"?

"I won't kiss you then", she agreed gratefully, "Just in case I have something you can catch".

He nodded and went to the steriliser with some of the metal wear, Lynlea had only eaten half her stew and drank very little of her beer. It went into the recycling vent.

When he was finished Jaklok went into the lounge and turned on the tri-vid. The news was all about the disappearance of Explorer Six. This added to two to five, he wondered if it would be the last to leave the solar system, at least for some years. The vessels were either being lost in hyper-space or Traitor Darren was destroying them. News from Proxima Prime, or Nyjord had ceased, so all was nothing better than wild speculation.

His mobile alerted him to a call and he muted the tri-vid, it was Bronlinski, his man on number two purification,

"I'm sorry Jaklok", his voice began, "I don't think I can do my shift, I'm coming down with something and I'm going back to bed", the duty night man told him.

"Okay, get better soon, I'll get the reserve engineer to cover", Jaklok told him and cut the connection. Obviously something was going round. He dialled a number and a female voice answered,

"Yes"?

"This is the chief", Jaklok began, "Can I speak to Roman please"?

"I'm sorry chief, but he's gone to bed, he's got some sort of virus or something".

Brow furrowed, Jaklok gave best wishes and cut the connection, then dialled another number, Transki answered after three beeps,

"I know this is a big request", Jaklok began, "But do you fancy doubling back and covering the night shift, Bronlinski's gone sick and so has Roman. I'll pay overtime".

There was a pause while Transki considered the strength of his bargaining position, then, "Double time chief"?

"Oh come on", Jaklok was momentarily exasperated, "It's not a holiday, the going rate is time and a third".

"Time and a half or I'm not interested"?

There was no one else Jaklok could call, it was Transki or do the shift himself.

"You're a pirate Transki", he was amused despite the situation, "But okay time and a half".

"I'll be there in two hours".

"You'll be there in one hour if you want time and a half", Jaklok could not set any expensive precedents.

"I'll cover for you then chief, but you owe me one".

"Thanks Transki and no sleeping on the job".

"What me"? Transki feigned outrage, then cut the connection.

Jaklok put the mobile down and turned back to the tri-vid. The news was about the peace talks between Scandia and India, it seemed they had reached an agreement and the twin planet to Nyjord was now officially Brahma. Jaklok smiled ironically, what did it matter what the world was called, being as mankind did not seem able to successfully reach it at that moment in time?

He switched stations to catch his favourite cop-show 'M.C. Science'. It was about how the Mars Constabulary captured villains by using scientific technology and the head of M.C. Science always got his man. What amused Jaklok more than the shows themselves however was the lead actor Denver Starmountain, who was just a little too old to be a romantic lead, or any other sort of lead for that matter and despite several augmentations, had gone bald and persisted in wearing the most ridiculous obviously fake wig. It was not even the same shade as the hair around his ears and the back of his head, which he had grown long and wore in a stupid looking pony tail. The whole show was fanciful at best, but Starmountain made it unintentionally funny.

Jaklok was just starting to enjoy the week's offering however when his mobile sounded again, muting and going from play to record, he then took the call, it was another employee going sick. In the next hour the process repeated over and again until finally, unable to cover sterilisation unit seven, he had to ask the day worker to shut the process down before going home. He could afford to do that if it was an isolated incident, but he began to suspect that the illness, what ever it was, was on it's way to becoming an epidemic. Venus could not afford an epidemic, the population simply was not large enough to maintain key processes if over one third of the workforce was effected.

Thoughtfully he rang the medical centre. He was almost about to cut the connection and try a ping, when it was finally answered,

"Hello, Ember Caves Medical"? a tired voice sounded in the chief's ear.

"Chief Engineer", Jaklok began "Have we the beginnings of a medical emergency on our hands, I need to know for the processing plants".

"Hello chief, it's doctor Salik, the answer to your concern is it's too early to say for certain, but things are beginning to look quite serious. Our general practitioner's are being swamped at the moment and I've had to deputise myself. In two cases I've hospitalised patients who are in a more advanced state than the majority".

"Can you give me a run down of the symptoms please"?

"Fatigue, then greyness of pallor, followed by respiratory inflammation, the two more serious now have oxygen masks on, in laymen's terms they are slowly drowning in their own congestion".

"What is it? Some sort of pleurae or pneumonia"?

"Neither of those is airborne, but the symptoms are very similar, it's something new, chief. Maybe even something of Venus in particular".

"So have you given it a name"? Jaklok wanted to know, "In case I need to admit some of my engineers, it will save time in explanation".

"No. Let's see though, I think Venflu would do for the time being, is there anything else chief, I'm really busy right now"?

"Just one more thing doctor and then I'll let you get on with your vital work, I know you have not had the time to start working on a vaccine, what about the Poles, say those in Nexus, have you been in touch with the doctors there"?

"Yes and they have it as well, what ever it is, chief, it's spreading around night-side and I haven't contacted day-side as they are mainly in the satellites".

Jaklok thanked Salik and let him hang up.

Venflu! Where would it all end?

TWO

AKLOK WENT TO bed, no longer interested in the machinations of Blast Favoue, (the name of Starmountain's character), beside him Lynlea stirred, but did not wake. He did not like the sound of her breathing however, she had a wheeze that ruckled as she slept fitfully. Jaklok lay not sleeping himself for a couple of hours but finally exhaustion claimed him.

He awoke at seven forty hours and showered and dressed in his overalls. Then, for a reason he could not explain, he went to a certain cupboard and strapped on a needle gun. it was in a shoulder holster and over his overalls, plainly visible. Ready for the day, as he never had breakfast, he went to Lynlea and shook her to wakefulness her pallor was grey.

"I'm calling the medcent", he told her, "See if there is something I can get you, we have no anti-biotic's in the apartment".

She seemed too weak to argue or even reply.

Salik was still answering the phone, eventually, he must have slept at the centre if at all.

"I can give you a broad spectrum anti-biotic, but I don't know if it will do any good. Try it anyway, chief and then you can let me know the results".

"My contracted partner is not a ruddy guinea pig", Jaklok flared and then thought better of it, "Sorry doc, have you had any sleep"?

"Just come and get a script for quintoxicilin from the front desk it will be waiting for you", Salik sighed and then hung up.

The chief engineer of Ember Caves went to the very rear of his apartment and unlocking the garage went to his Nakamichi Hover bike nine thousand. Instead of using the tube he could be at medcent and then the pharmacy and back to Lynlea in twenty minutes. The receptionist at medcent was an android thankfully, therefore immune to any chance of falling ill, so he got the script quickly and rode to the pharmacy. With the perhaps vital antibiotic in his possession, he broke the speed limit several times on the way back to his apartment, but it was pretty safe, the tube way was practically empty. An ominous sign of the way the virus was sweeping through the small community.

Lynlea did not look well but once Jaklok had given his partner her initial dose, there was nothing he could do, so he went into work. The bergermeister was waiting for him in his office,

"Where in Hades have you been"? The bergermeister was a tall fat figure of a man, something he used to his advantage when bullying those who were afraid of him. Jaklok was not afraid of Bergermeister Drondrew Slavinski.

"What do you want Slavinski"? he asked bluntly.

"An answer to my question would show some recognition of my authority for a start", the bergermeister stormed, Where have you been, it's Bergermeister Slavinski as my form of address as well, Chief Engineer"?

Jaklok said calmly, "Lynlea has Venflu".

It took some of the wind out of the bergermeister's sails, "Ah, well, it's been on the tri-vid all morning, I didn't know they'd named it yet though, or is Venflu something different".

"Venflu is the epidemic that is sweeping through Ember Caverns and Nexus, is there any news from Hall of Whispers or the Juncture"?

"I never saw anything, but it is in Polish Dig Site Four".

"Then it's sweeping all across night-side", Jaklok seated himself heavily in his chair. "So, what do you want, apart from to tirade me over my absence"?

"I need an assurance that all vital life support systems to this dome are going to be kept running. Then I need you to look at Hall of Whispers and the Juncture".

"I can give you no such assurance", Jaklok admitted brutally and with a fair degree of sadistic satisfaction. He enjoyed telling Slavinski certain things could not be done.

This time the bergermeister did not explode in fury as was his want however, instead he seemed suddenly to deflate, he amazed Jaklok by asking,

"Do you feel alright"?

"To date", the chief admitted then felt honour bound to respond, "You"?

"Tired, but I've been up all night, things to do".

"Then don't let me keep you bergermeister", Jaklok was dismissive, but polite.

"Keep me inform....ed, please".

Jaklok managed a nod. After a series of quick mobile calls to those of his team who were still on duty, he determined that he was most needed at Sterilisation. He was there on the Nakamichi in no time,

How's it going"? he asked one of the crew, who's name he did not know.

"The treadle has stopped, the one that feeds the synthesiser pump and then runs through tank four, I can't decide if it's ceased, or if one of the reciprocators has failed and is not monitoring in electronically".

"Have you ran a diagnostic"?

The man nodded, "It was inconclusive, so I'm just going to inspect the mechanism underneath the stoving".

"I'll go and re-align the reciprocators then", Jaklok informed him.

The emergency airlock hissed open unexpectedly and from, it a hulking individual emerged,

"He's not one of us", the worker at Jaklok's side said and then shouted,

"You shouldn't be in here, what do you think you're doing".

"Quality tools", the intruder growled, "Where will I find them"? and his huge hands bunched into fists.

Without a word Jaklok pulled out his gun and shot the man.

"You never gave him a chance to explain himself", the worker complained, "What have you got in the gun"?

"Level two (fatal)", Jaklok told him, "When you need to shoot, you shoot, you don't talk. He was looting, the company doesn't allow it, now get to work".

When he got home, Lynlea was silent and unbreathing. Despite his exhaustion he put on his suit and helmet and taking her out the external airlock buried her in the flat poisonous plain of Venus. He was all the way back inside and unsuited before tears came. Without eating, but after a quick sonic shower, he fell into bed and was instantly asleep.

Jaklok and Lynlea had loved one another very much, but the Romanian's were a practical people and moping around feeling sorry for themselves was not something they were want to do. After all, most of mourning is self pity, the dead are dead, once life has ended so has suffering.

Once awake again Jaklok used his mobile to contact the bergermeister,

"Where the frenge are you Jaklok"? the ruler of the Romanian sector of Venus wanted to know.

"I've just woken up, I had a double shift and then when I finally had to return home, due to exhaustion, had to bury Lynlea".

The news sank into the bergermeister's mentality, "Oh, well, I'm sorry for your loss chief, but we need you at life support. Systems are shutting down all over the place".

"They will be", Jaklok admitted openly, "There aren't enough men to man them. Start to collect all non infected together in one sector of the dome, then I can concentrate on keeping less systems operative".

"That won't work", Slavinski complained, "Some people simply will not move".

"Then they will die one way or the other, tell them that. I suggest you coordinate with the Grand Constable and the doctors at med-cent".

"How do you feel, can you come in and become my personal assistant"?

"I still feel as normal as I could under the circumstances. If I join you however, then '*you*' become '*my*' assistant".

There was silence on the other end of the line as Slavinski digested the offer, finally he offered himself, "We will be an equal part of a duo if you join me, will you do it"?

"Give me time to eat and dress and then I'm on my way", Jaklok conceded. The bergermeister knew he had no choice.

As Jaklok was exiting the sonic shower however sensed another presence in the apartment, whirling around it was to see Lynlea seated quite innocently at the breakfast bar!

THREE

"LYNLEA"! HE GASPED stupidly, "Lynlea"?!

"What's the matter", she asked, looking concerned, "Are you coming down with it"?

Jaklok carefully drew his needle gun and approached the bar, seeing the registering look of fear in the figure's eyes,

"Who, or what are you"? he demanded.

"Jaklok"? she asked, "Please don't point that weapon at me, are you ill or something"?

"I feel quite well, but tired, now I would like to know who you are and why you resemble my wife in every careful detail"?

"Jaklok; I 'am' your wife, you must have the Venflu and it's causing you to hallucinate".

The chief considered this, could it be the correct assumption. He went to the portal closest to the airlock and then swiftly turned to the figure at the bar, the needle gun in his hand and aimed at 'it' once more,

"Please come over here, what ever you are"?

Seeing the steely glint of resolve in his eyes, the figure rose carefully and walked over to the portal, it's carriage mirrored his wife's precisely,

"You see that grave just there"?

"I see a mound of material in an elongated shape", the figure conceded readily.

"That is where I buried Lynlea Jablonski, she died of Venflu and I lay her to rest in that very spot".

"But that cannot be"! the figure gasped and looked genuinely shocked, "I'm your wife Jaklok. Ask me something, ask me something Lynlea; 'I' would know, something only I would know"?

Jaklok considered this. A fake, a simulacrum might not be so perfect as it looked on the surface, it was perfect too, even down to the small mole on the left side of his wife's neck.

"If we had been blessed with a child", he began, knowing what mention of it would do to her, knowing how much she had desired it, "What were we going to call it, if it was a boy"?

"What a cruel question", she burst into tears and Jaklok stopped the course of one with a finger and put it to his mouth, tasting salt.

If this was his wife, then who had he buried, out there in the cruel harsh and poisonous terrain of Venus?

"Well"? he demanded, doing his best to remain unmoved.

"We will call him Werdnum, after your paternal grandfather", she sobbed, "And if it's a girl Eralim after my maternal grandmother. I need to sit down".

She slumped back into place at the bar, while Jaklok's mind could not make sense of what was happening.

He picked up his mobile phone and dialled the medcent.

"Surgeon", came the voice on the other end.

"The surgeon"? Jaklok echoed, "What's happened to doctor Salik"?

The voice informed him, "Doctor Salik died just about an hour ago, of the disease he called Venflu".

"I'm sorry to hear that", Jaklok began automatically, "He seemed like a good man".

"He was", the surgeon agreed, "Who are you, caller"?

"Oh, sorry, yes, we have not spoken before; it's the Chief Engineer, Jaklok".

"What do you need chief"?

"I buried my wife hours ago", Jaklok began and then pressed on resolutely, "And she has just re-appeared in my kitchen, am I losing my mind, or having some sort of hallucination"?

"Another case", the surgeon muttered to himself, then to Jaklok, "You're not the first to report this phenomenon, chief. I don't have an answer for you yet, but what I can tell you is that if you buried your wife, presumably outside the dome and you can see the site of said burial, then that event certainly took place, can you come to the centre and see me in person"?

"I'm not certain", Jaklok said, keeping a careful eye on the hallucination/simulacrum, "Systems are failing all over Ember Caves and I have to prioritise".

"Then I suggest you tell who ever you answer to, if anyone, that the medcent life support system is a priority, the lights keep flickering and the air is stale, should it be top of your list"?

"I'm on my way, mister....er, doctor; what do I call you sir?

"Doctor will do fine", the surgeon replied and then cut-away.

Jaklok took his Nakamichi to the medcent, which was not far away from his apartment, but then nothing was far from his abode. He strode into the interior and past reception without announcing himself and almost collided with a figure in a white coat.

"Sorry doctor, was it you I've not so long ago spoken to on the mobile"?

The other shook his head, "Not recently, but I recognise your voice, chief", he held out a hand of welcome, "I'm doctor Salik".

Ten confusing minutes later Jaklok was with the surgeon,

"My team of doctors and nurses are reappearing with increasing rapidity", the surgeon told the chief. "I know they aren't who they think they are, but they have the exact skills of those they replaced and right now I need them".

"And when you don't doctor, what then"?

The surgeon shook his head, "I don't know".

Jaklok asked, "And why are we seemingly immune to the Venflu? Why haven't we been replaced, along with the bergermeister"?

"Is that all that is left of us? All that is left of the Ember Caves community of pioneers"?

"You should know that better than I, doctor. I don't suppose you can be in every place at once though. I wonder if the Chief Constable is the real one or a simulacrum"?

"There is no point in asking him", the surgeon observed bleakly, "He would be certain of his humanity, as would you and I".

An icy chill ran down Jaklok's spine, "You mean we could be......"?

"I've questioned Salik, he remembers nothing of an illness, the simulacrum have no missing memory, to all intents and purposes they are as those they replaced. I've given Salik a thorough medical. As his supervisor, he did not object to my demanding it, he checks out as flesh and blood and even down to his DNA there is no change from the Salik we have on record".

"The perfect invasion", Jaklok said in a voice that sounded like a hushed voice speaking in an empty graveyard, "They replace us and become us. But what is their purpose, if they behave just as they did before"?

"Maybe just to survive", the surgeon offered, "Perhaps they; rather than we, are the Venuser"?

"How convinced are you that you remain as human as when we left Earth"?

"No grave marks my burial site, the hospital has no record of my illness".

"Doctor, please go into the records and bring up a list of those who fit the second criteria"?

Dread in his heart, Jaklok waited for the names to appear on the screen, the list was frighteningly short, it contained only two names in addition to their own; the bergermeister and an Biotric Engineer called Amiad Hornrunner. The Chief Constable had died and reappeared some few hours later.

"This Hornrunner, he doesn't sound Romanian"? Jaklok mused.

The surgeon accessed his file, "He's Martian, what are you thinking, chief"?

"That I might pay Amiad Hornrunner a visit".

"And the life support system"?

"Ring my office, my workforce should now be Venusered with experts who can get it running at it's old efficiency".

Hornrunner's residence was on the very north western edge of Ember Caves, almost at the border of Polish Winter's Run. The Nakamichi roared down the still quiet tube way and ate up the distance. Above the dome of the tube, the dull sheen of satellite protection dish could be faintly seen. Now such a sight and the coming of the long day would be enjoyed by Venuser, not mankind.

Jaklok could not contain his curiosity however, what made Hornrunner so special, why was he the fourth person only in all Ember Caves to be free of the Venflu and eventual replacement? He pulled the bike down to the flooring of the tube outside a rather large apartment complex and strode to the chime, thumbing it three times rapidly. After a brief pause a tall and slender man in his early thirties answered, by actually opening the lock rather than asking who was without, on the com plate.

"Come in, chief", the man asked, "I've been expecting you. As you already know I am Amiad Hornrunner".

"And you have never been ill"?

Hornrunner smiled, "I've been ill, chief, but not with Venflu. Now what can I get you to drink, I have almost every conceivable beverage to offer. Please sit while I get you something"?

"If you have a Russian Vodka I would be grateful of a measure, thank you".

Jaklok seated himself on a white leather couch, the leather looked like bovine, from a real animal and must have cost an absolute fortune. The room was filled with similarly impressive objects of furnishing and art. The quadraphonic sound system was separates and the stick player was a regal (small r). The amplifier was Black Rox valves and the four speakers Sphere 4.1's. The table upon which, Hornrunner placed Jaklok's glass was Italian Cedar and on the walls were canvas' by Smeel, Prosco and Roxbrough. In every part of the room there was evidence of extreme wealth.

"Thank you. Do you mind if I ask you what exactly it is that you do mister Hornrunner? I have no idea what a Biotric Engineer is".

"My company manufactures the Biotron", Hornrunner told him candidly. Jaklok had never heard of it,

"Just exactly what is a Biotron, sir"?

"The latest line of android, chief, a mechanism that is actually more human than machine, a mechanism that also incorporates biological parts and functions. The Biotron has actual organs, it only differs from a man in that it has a duridium skeleton instead of one of rather delicate bone".

"I get it now", Jaklok concluded, "A Biotric engineer works in biology and electricity".

Hornrunner nodded, "The Biotron are powered by a micro pile instead of a heart, their life cycle is estimated to be three hundred Terran years, they will be the crew of Explorer Eight, when it launches in three years time".

The year three thousand two hundred and fifty two then, seventeen Terran years after Explorer One had left for Nyjord.

"So your presence on Venus, engineer, is to help with the colonisation"?

"Precisely so".

"And how is it then that you remain immune to the threat of Venflu, sir"?

Hornrunner smiled, "Why because I am the prototype, my dear engineer. I am a Biotron"!

While Jaklok digested this startling revelation, Hornrunner went on,

"I had the first stages of lung cancer, so my technicians replaced my lungs with our new bio-engineered model. It seemed silly to stop there, I volunteered to undergo several more, ah..., replacements. When the micro pile was finally transplanted into my chest I was as much machine as man".

"A cyborg".

"Not exactly, cyborg's are part biological, part mechanical. Biotronic organs are biological in nature, simply created artificially granted, but still made of flesh and using blood as fuel. From the success of myself we then went on to create several Biotron from the ground up as it were and they were a great success too".

And where on Venus are they, sir"? Jaklok dared to ask, though he dreaded the answer.

"All three are in Ember Caves, my dear Jaklok, you, the surgeon and the bergermeister have exceeded my wildest expectations of you"!

FOUR

"BUT I REMEMBER"! Jaklok objected, "My wedding day, my first kiss with a girl, my first bicycle. I remember my mother and father, I have a brother in Romania.........".

Hornrunner held up a hand and told the Biotron, "All those were manufactured carefully by experts on Mars and transplanted into your cranial computer, you are only two Terran years old Jaklok, as is the bergermeister. The surgeon is different, he was human once, but certain organs began to fail and he approached me and asked............".

"Never mind that"! Jaklok snapped, "Are you replacing those who died of Venflu, with Biotron"?

Hornrunner's features grew grave, "No. The replacements are Venuser, we are being repelled from this planet. Our only hope of ever making homes here for humans is to approach one of the Venuser and ask to be taken to their leader".

"When do you plan to do that"?

"Not I Jaklok; you"!

"Me! Represent humanity when I am a machine with manufactured false memories".

"Your humanity is the only part of the Earther's left on Venus I suspect. There is no one more human than you".

"You said the surgeon was .....".

"The task is yours Jaklok, all you need to do is decide whom you are going to approach, but I think you know who that will be"!

Jaklok drank the rest of the excellent vodka, then slowly climbed to a standing position,

"Yes", he said, "I know who to approach".

Twenty minutes later he asked her, "Why didn't you tell me I was artificial"?

"It was part of the experiment", Lynlea returned, "Part of Hornrunner's design for you".

"And what of you Lynlea, do you still persist in your claim to be an Earther"?

She shook her head, "No the need for pretence is over, the human called Lynlea is gone, everything she knew, I know however, I am from this world, I existed in my native form, just beneath the surface of our home, our biological engineers surpass those of even Hornrunner. I can never return to my native state however, I am now stuck in this bizarre shape with it appendages and strange senses".

"Just like me then", Jaklok observed bitterly, "We both look human, but neither of us are, strictly speaking".

"Then we must learn to cooperate, my husband. Though neither of us are human, we retain humanity in our memories and our feelings; we are the next stage in the evolution of Venus".

JUDGEMENT

T HE YOUNG WOMAN wore a grey
pleated skirt and a white high collared,
buttoned blouse, she smiled at McMak and it seemed to him that her expression
was one of sympathetic concern.

"Do you remember the events of November sixteenth"? she asked in a
kindly tone.

"Which November"? McMak asked vaguely, he was always vague about
dates at the best of times.

"The November in question, mister McMak", she responded, with care.

"Which November would that be"? McMak wanted to know.

"In the evening, on November sixteenth three thousand two hundred and
fifty", she clarified.

"I'm not very good with dates"?

"The evening that you killed your wife", the young woman seemed to be
losing her patience.

"I'm married"! McMak feigned surprised, "Who am I married to"?

The judge intervened, "Oh come now mister McMak, this charade will
not fool the court, you've heard the prosecution plainly tell you your wife was
found outside the airlock on that evening. Her head had suffered a blow from
a blunt object and she suffocated due to lack of oxygen".

"When was this your honour"?

A young man in an Edwardian frock coat of plush sable rose to his feet,
"It's as previously claimed your honour, my client has suffered serious mental

damage as a result of prolonged use of snufz. He does not know where he is, from one minute to the next".

"So it's claimed, your honour", the young woman added, "But a psych-eval proved mister McMak to be fully compos mentis".

"And that evaluation is challenged by the defence your honour".

"Yes, yes we have heard all about that", the judge snapped impatiently, "But as stated, the good doctor believed the accused to be feigning said, by reason of some bizarre sort of defence. Prosecution will proceed".

"That panelling, your honour", McMak suddenly asked, ""It's not real wood is it, I mean to say, real would on Callisto, it would have cost a fortune to bring it by freight".

"Mister McMak, this is a serious affair, you are charged with murder and this court will view frivolity in a very dim light, a very dim light indeed, do you understand"? The young female prosecutor tried vainly.

"Do you mind if I take some snufz your honour"? McMak asked then, "Only if I don't use it regularly the buzzing starts and then the transmissions from deep space"?

"I think we've heard quite enough", his honour said then, "I'll listen to closing arguments in the morning we are adjourned".

McMak was lead from the witness box and taken to the cells beneath the court, in short order Bluwalker came to visit him. The court constable let the solicitor in and then exited, locking the gate behind him.

"Dale, come in, sit, sorry but I have nothing to offer you, how are you keeping"?

"That fiasco didn't fool the judge for a second, McMak, I told you not to go for your unhinged mind ploy", Bluwalker scolded.

"Maybe not but it was fun", McMak smiled, "Come on Dale how much worse can it be, she was found knocked out and then tumbled out of the airlock to suffocate and freeze dry. I have no alibi for the night it happened, what was I supposed to do"?

"The psych-eval proved you fit to stand trial, the doctor saw through your little game, what am I supposed to say in your defence, in the morning"?

"Well, let's see", McMak leaned backward on the chair which groaned as it's rear legs were unaccustomed to such stress.

"You could point out that when I married Fedrie I had thirteen thousand in my account and I was happy. Then five years later, I'm harnessed to a scheming, lying, conniving, nagging harridan who's bled me dry of every sestersius and every scrap of self esteem. So, in my one moment of rebellion, I hit her over the head with her favourite resin ornament and dumped her out the nearest airlock; but I don't think it would help my case do you"?

Bluwalker put his head in his hands, "No, McMak that would not be a good idea".

"So", McMak reasoned, "I think you should put the onus back onto that rather attractive piece of skirt who tried to get some answers out of me today. One of proof, beyond reasonable doubt, Dale. One of proof".

"Go on".

"Although I have no alibi, neither does anyone else. Was my DNA on my dear departed wife's head, no, was my DNA on any part of the airlock or any part of my wife's clothing? No. What the prosecution has is a body, and that my dear Dale is all. The rest is supposition. I am the obvious suspect, but there is no real evidence to convict me".

"Just between you and I how did you manage that"? Bluwalker asked in a hushed tone. "You've admitted to me that you did it, but how is it that there is no DNA to prove you guilty"?

McMak smiled, "Maybe I didn't do it, maybe I've told you I did, because I'm a snufz head after all".

"There are no other suspects though, it couldn't have been aggravated burglary as nothing was missing from your quarters. Why would anyone simply randomly murder missus McMak for absolutely no reason at all"?

"No reason that you know of, Dale", McMak teased, "How well have you gone into Fedrie McMak's background, do you know everything there is to know about her? Her past associations, her past friends, her past enemies"?

"Now you're playing with me", Bluwalker reasoned, "We both know you're guilty as sin, but you just won't tell me how you did it so cleanly".

"I was in GroBtiefreich when she was murdered, Dale, smacked upside my brain on snufz".

"A long way from Pekko", Bluwalker reasoned, "How did you get there and who saw you while you were there"?

"The thing about snufz is it's a pretty solitary affair unless you want some sort of accident. I was on my own in a boarding house and I doubt my stay was noticed by anyone".

"Why didn't you tell her this, why the silly charade regarding your state of mind"?

"Which is the more believable? Do you believe I really am deranged, or do you think I 'was' in GroBtiefreich? Or; do you think I did it"?

"It's the judges opinion that matter's McMak, not mine", Bluwalker observed. "Now, which did you want me to tell him tomorrow"?

"Well not that I did it", McMak laughed.

"Look"! Bluwalker raised his voice in agitation, "Pekko has the death penalty for murder, you have to stop frinselling about now McMak, tell me what really happened that night"?

I was watching the tri-vid and not particularly unhappy, even though I had no money left to call my own (McMak began). Even now, try as I might, I cannot remember what the show was about, how bizarre is that? So there I was with my feet up, the tri-vid blaring merrily away and a bottle of lichen-beer in my fist and in came the object of all my misery.

"What are you doing", my dear sweet partner for life asked me in a piercing screech.

"I am seated my love and watching the tri-vid", I observed accurately if sardonically.

"You lazy good for nothing, why didn't you get your name down for overtime at the mine", she wished to know and has the audacity to lean over me, thus blocking my view of the tri-dimensional entertainment.

"Please move to the side my love", I beseeched, "The programme has yet to conclude".

"The show's finished for someone who doesn't want work", she nagged and seizing the remote from the couch killed the feed and put it to stand-by.

There were several things I could have done at this point. I could have turned the tri-vid back on, I could have asked my wife to do so, or I could have shown her the back of my hand. Or; I could had buried the bottle in my hand into her skull. I did none of those, for the bottle still had some beer in it anyway. No, what I did was think.

I wanted rid of dear sweet Fedrie, that was a no brainer. There was one stumbling block to that though, her inheritance. Though she had bankrupt me with her spending sprees, she was destined to gain vastly far more when her favourite Uncle finally shuffled off this mortal coil and left her his estate. So divorce was out of the question. Also if I killed her I would not get the money which was conservatively estimated to be in the region of three million, for uncle would surely not leave his niece's murderer his cash. I was therefore stuck

I left the apartment and went for a walk in the cramped bubble of the town, when a thought struck me, suppose I invented some commercial scheme and approached uncle for a loan, based on our future position as beneficiaries, would he look favourably upon me? The idea had merit, but first I had to think of the scheme.

Or rather somebody had to think of one? If I advertised myself, under an alias of course, as an investor looking for a project to fund, the scheme would fall into my lap, or laptop so to speak. The advertisement was the work of a few hours and then all I had to do was wait for someone to take the bait.

Sure enough I got a ping within an hour. When you offer money for anything, the response is always admirably velocitous. Some Polish miner from the pit at Orestheus had designed a new drill bit with a duridium head, that was said to last four times the duration of the current diamond tipped tools. I had my scheme. All I had to do was cut and paste and change a few details, create an e-mail and ping it off to dear Uncle.

The reply was a body blow I had to admit!

Fedrie had been lying to me for years, there was no inheritance, the reply told me that in no uncertain terms:-

> *Dear mister McMak* (it read),
>
> > *Thank you for the mirth and amusement your communication caused in this arm of the family, we read it several times through just to be certain of the exact nature of the content. It seems your dear wife has been misleading you by promising some sort of windfall when I pass over to the other side.*
> >
> > *Not only is this erroneous sir, but I would like to add that you are married to the most hated grimalkin in the entire family and she will get nothing from the Montpanlos estate, nor any other surviving member.*
> >
> > *I wish you sir, good luck with your future enterprise, married to Fedrie, you will need it - every gramme of good fortune that happens to come your way,*
>
> *Yours sincerely,*
> *Nedrostume Montpanlos.*

So there it was! My dear wife had spent all my money and there would not be any coming back, by way of compensation, not ever!

It was then that I realised she had to die. Divorce would be upsetting for sure, but it would not be final enough. She could marry again to some other poor sap and make his life a misery in turn. No, the solution to the problem of Fedrie McMak was quite simple and totally beyond doubt; she had to go!

I was then faced with the task of how to do it. Do it in such a way as a jury could not find me guilty of murder, due to lack of evidence. I knew all about forensic science and bashing her head in with the beer bottle, was totally and completely out. I had to do it in such a way as, even though I was the obvious suspect, there would not even be circumstantial evidence against me.

Now I can tell you Bluwalker, for under the privilege between us, you cannot tell anyone else and it came to me in a moment of inspiration and brilliance, which I am sure you will admire. For you see, I cannot bask in the simplistic audacity of it, unless I tell at least one other soul. So at least someone else will admire it's simple purity.

As you are aware all of us on Callisto have a space suit, incase the environmental controls fail and we need to don them until the atmosphere is replaced in the dome. Like everyone else I do not use mine from one month to another, but that night I put mine on, inside the apartment!

While dear Fedrie was in the bathroom enjoying a sonic shower. Taking up the resin eagle that she valued so highly I entered the bathroom and promptly rendered her unconscious, by way of bludgeoning her head with said.

Then I simply dragged her to the rear airlock and bundling her through, followed her and thence out through the outer lock. Once I re-entered the outer lock and was in the lock itself the biohazard purification began, before the inner lock could be safely opened. The eagle was in my fist all the while. Thus the biohazard of the facility cleansed all DNA from the suit, along with that collected onto the eagle.

The airlock had removed all possible evidence that I had just murdered my wife. Entering by way of the inner lock door, after safely replaced the eagle, I climbed out of the suit and hung it back in the wardrobe. Of course the Constabulary checked it, but what could they find except a clean suit, devoid of dust from the surface of Callisto? Any microbes that might be coming from the seas on this distant moon and any DNA belonging to either my wife or me were scientifically cleansed?

So there you have it Bluwalker, I have confessed to you, but you cannot use what you know, only in one way, as an argument to get me freed. There is no evidence against me, as far as the court is concerned I 'probably' killed Fedrie, but as far as the evidence is concerned, reasonable doubt exists, because of evidence; there is none. (McMak ended).

"You're a clever man, McMak", Dale Bluwalker noted when the defendant had finally fallen silent, "And tomorrow I think, you'll walk".

....

"And so I conclude your honour that, though there is an absence of any other suspect, in this case, there remains not a shred of real evidence that my client has committed murder and I ask for a verdict of unproven and for his immediate release".

The judge looked grave, he also looked sceptical, but the argument was powerful and he ordered a recess while he deliberated.

"You know in the past", McMak began in the cells beneath the court, "It wasn't a judge who decided cases like this"?

"Oh", Bluwalker sounded vaguely bored, "Is that so"?

"It is", McMak went on chirpily, "I don't know if you can believe this, but they used to take a dozen citizens off the street and press them into service, they called them jurors. Can you credit that? Amateurs, the general public trying to decide something this important. What's taking his lordship so long anyway, it's simple enough, there's no evidence to convict me"?

"Well", Bluwalker began, "As you say, it's a serious and professional business, it wouldn't do for him to make a mistake would it"?

"Ha ha ha, good enough for jam", McMak used the fashionable vernacular. "No as you say, he has to get it right".

A constable then appeared and said to his colleague just outside the gate, "Bring the two of them up Jerebeam, the verdict is going to be read".

The entire procedure was over in ten minutes and McMak and Bluwalker were standing facing one another just inside the portal to the bubble. McMak glanced at the constable who's name was Jerebeam and asked the solicitor,

"That's it then, I can't be put on trial again for the same thing"?

"That's it", Bluwalker agreed, "Because of the English system we use here on Callisto the term double-jeopardy refers to your case. You have been acquitted of an offence and cannot be re-tried; as a legal error or impropriety has not occurred".

With absolute delight McMak turned to the constable and said simply, "I did it, I killed her, I'm as guilty as sin".

"Well then, well done sir for getting away with it", Jerebeam congratulated, "Good luck for the future".

"Yes, thank you", McMak chuckled, "Well Bluwalker, I'm ready for off, open the lock will you and make way for this free man"?

The solicitor stood to one side and McMak's hand reached for the wheel himself in impatience. He heard the phut of the needle gun, felt the sting of it's barb in his back and then mercifully blackness engulfed him and he was dead before he hit the floor.

"I think this way is so much kinder don't you"? Jerebeam asked the solicitor, as he sided his weapon. "They always seem so elated, so idyllically happy just before I execute them".

"I agree", Bluwalker assented, "But in this case you'd have thought McMak would have done his homework a bit better on the workings of the court"?

"Well along with the method of execution, the tri-judge seat is secret isn't it"? Jerebeam the executioner asked.

Bluwalker nodded, "In every other detail he had us worked out though".

"So how did the vote go then, was it unanimous"?

"No", Bluwalker admitted ironically, "As defence I was forced to vote innocent, even though he had confessed to me. The judge and prosecution voted guilty though and that's why you had to pass ultimate judgement".

"He did look happy though", Jerebeam repeated, "They always do, just before they receive the judgement".